KU-615-947

# Death in Bordeaux

**ALLAN MASSIE**

Withdrawn from Stock

QUARTET BOOKS

First published in 2010 by
Quartet Books Limited
A member of the Namara Group
27 Goodge Street, London W1T 2LD

Reprinted 2010, 2011, 2012, 2013, 2014, 2017

Copyright © Allan Massie 2010

The right of Allan Massie to be identified
as the author of this work has been asserted
by him in accordance with the
Copyright, Designs and Patents Act, 1988

All rights reserved.
No part of this book may be reproduced in
any form or by any means without prior
written permission from the publisher

A catalogue record for this book
is available from the British Library

ISBN 978 0 7043 7190 3

Typeset by Antony Gray
Printed and bound in Great Britain by
T J International Ltd, Padstow, Cornwall

# I

*March, 1940*

His wife, Marguerite, said the Chambolley case was becoming an obsession with Lannes. This was unusual. Normally she took no interest in his work. In truth he preferred it that way. So she was right to this extent, that she had noticed it was getting on his nerves, no doubt about that. It had begun three weeks previously, with a telephone call at five in the morning. He had got up grumbling to himself but moving quietly so as not to wake the children, and had then to wait on his doorstep shivering in a clammy mist till the car from headquarters arrived, with young René Martin at the wheel, full of apologies because the bloody thing wouldn't start.

'So, it's a corpse, then.'

'All I know, chief. In the rue Cabanac between the station and the abattoirs.'

Not the first to have been discovered there.

'I'd have been as quick walking.'

He looked at his watch.

'Pull in to the station, there should be a bar open by now. We'll have a coffee.'

Coffee with a shot of Armagnac made him feel human, ashamed of snapping at the boy who wasn't reasonably to be blamed for a car that wouldn't start.

Two agents – uniforms – were waiting at the corner of the rue Cabanac, relieved to see the PJ arrive. That by itself told Lannes it was nasty.

'So?' he said.

Foghorns from a tug making its way up the Garonne drowned the reply. Then the shorter of the two said, 'There's no doubt it's murder, even though we haven't of course examined the body.

Never seen anything like it, superintendent. Jules here puked, and I don't blame him. Naturally when I say I haven't seen the like, I make an exception of what I saw in the trenches. But then, even there, well, war's natural, as you might say, you expect horrors, and this here, it's downright unnatural.'

He coughed, a spluttering choking kind of cough, as if he too might vomit, and then stood aside. Young Martin shone his torch and Lannes was able to see the body. There had been too many in his life, he often thought. All the same there was always a shiver of anticipation like that produced by the three hammer-blows before the curtain went up in the theatre. Now his first impression was of whiteness. The dead man's trousers had been pulled down round his ankles and the vast milkiness of flabby thighs held the attention. But the real horror came when René directed the light to the face and to the object held between the lips. He must have recognized it for what it was more quickly than Lannes, for, with a cry of disgust, he dropped the torch and turned away retching.

'That's right, it's the poor bugger's cock,' the shorter agent said. 'I told you it was downright unnatural. To cut it off and stuff it in his mouth – what kind of beast would do that?'

'Well, there's one less of them now, that's certain,' his colleague, recovered from his bout of nausea, but still sweating and mopping his brow with his handkerchief, said, with, to Lannes' mind, an unpleasant satisfaction in his voice.

'So that's what you think?'

'It's obvious, superintendent, isn't it? Clear as day. Filthy brutes.'

'You think he was asking for it then?'

'Not what I said, superintendent. But . . . '

Lannes sighed, knelt down, examined the body, touched the dead man's cheek lightly with his forefinger. He would have liked to remove but no . . . apart from the repugnance with which the thought of touching it filled him, that was something that had to be left to the specialists. Who were indeed soon with them, allowing routine to take over as they got to work. Lannes established that the agents had themselves discovered the body in the course of their patrol, told them he wanted their written report on his desk before they went off duty – 'and make it full, everything you saw, even if it doesn't seem important' – had a few words with the medical officer, Dr Paulhan, an old friend he could rely on, and told young René they might as well be off. There would be door-to-door inquiries to set up, soon as possible, before people left for work.

'But we'll keep these two clowns out of it,' he said.

'It's odd,' René said, starting the motor which this time sprang straight into life, 'nobody's opened a window or come on to their doorstep to see what was going on, and yet you'd think someone must have been woken up and curious, wouldn't you, chief?'

'He wasn't killed there. Just dumped. I'm sure of that.'

The light was turning to a pale grey. A baker pushed up the metal shutter of his shop, and a bar in the Cours du Marne was already open, as men dropped in for a coffee, brandy or pastis on their way to work. Lannes lit his first cigarette of the day.

'Wonder who the poor fellow was?'

'He's called Gaston Chambolley,' Lannes said. 'Was called.'

'Oh, you know him then, chief. A customer? That's not so bad.'

'No, not a customer.'

Though he might have been, or come to be, the way he'd come to live. He'd been lucky. Till now.

And then: 'At least I suppose it's Gaston, not Henri,' he said, to himself really, but speaking aloud.

'I don't understand.'

'Gaston and Henri . . . They're identical twins. But no, it must be Gaston.'

It was a few weeks after he came back, wounded, from his war that he met them. He had enrolled at the university, at his father's suggestion, even insistence. 'You've always had your nose in a book,' the old man had said, urging him to seek a career as a lawyer. 'There's always a need for them, God knows why. Least-ways they never starve.' That had been his opinion, admiring and envious, formed when he first came to Bordeaux from the farm, and worked in a bar near the law-courts. Actually, over the years, Lannes had come to know a good many lawyers, even here in litigious Bordeaux, who had never made it, whose careers had come unstuck – even if they didn't starve. Indeed Gaston Chambolley was one of these failures.

He had soon met the twins – they were on the same course, fat jolly boys, all the more jolly, he supposed with some resentment, because both had been judged unfit for military service. When he looked at them and thought of some of the poor runts who had been with him at Verdun, and were still many of them there buried forever in the mud or rubble, well, it gave him a nasty taste in the mouth. All the more so indeed when someone – was it sly little Bergotte? – had said, 'Of course, you know, their grandfather's a doctor, a very distinguished one, I'm told, a professor and consultant, and there's no doubt he found a convenient condition for the pair that would render them exempt.' Yes, it had been little Bergotte, a nasty type really, though, having got a bullet in his lungs at the first Marne gave him some cause to sneer at the twins. He had continued to do so, but Lannes himself had soon found his resentment fade. They were so full of life and jokes, so really and naturally blithe and cheerful, yet also both so intelligent, so interested in matters beyond the aridity of the law course, and yet so modest, gentle and eager to please, that he had very quickly accepted the friendship they offered. He owed them a lot. They had opened his eyes to many things, painting for instance, and novels he might never have found for himself.

Moreover, in snobbish Bordeaux, he was grateful that they had accepted him, the peasant's grandson, whose father kept a stationer's shop, as their equal and a friend. Soon he was saying to himself, 'If they managed to screw their way out of the war, good luck to them.' It wasn't till some time later that he realized that they were actually ashamed of having missed it, and that, contrary to little Bergotte's insinuations, the condition which had kept them out – something glandular affecting the heart, as he remembered – was absolutely genuine. Actually they were even a little in awe of him because of what he had been through – though this embarrassed him – and that they too were grateful for the friendship.

So much so that they continued to see each other after he met Marguerite, abandoned his law course to marry her, and, to his father's disappointment, became a policeman. Indeed Henri was godfather to Lannes's older boy, Dominique, himself now at the Front in this new war which nobody was yet fighting.

It was all miserable.

'Stop at that bar,' he said to René. 'We could both do with coffee and something stronger to go with it. It's a raw morning, and that was a horrible sight.'

There was worse to come: calling on Henri to break the news. He always hated his duty. 'By far the worst part of the job', he told Marguerite. And so much worse in this case. But he couldn't delegate it, was ashamed of wishing he could.

He found him still in his dressing-gown. The apartment above the bookshop in the rue des Remparts smelled of dust, tobacco, old books, leather, dog and coffee. Henri greeted him with a smile. They embraced as they had done for so long. Perhaps Henri felt some stiffness in Lannes, for he said: 'But it's not a social call, not at this hour since you know my habits, and from the look on your face you are not seeking information, for which, besides, you wouldn't have disturbed me so early. Therefore . . . it's Gaston, isn't it?'

'I'm afraid so. It couldn't be worse.'

They got through the formalities, the routine business, saying little to each other; then, at the morgue, the identification, for the necessity of which Lannes apologized; then went to his office.

He poured them both an Armagnac.

'Go on,' he said, 'drink it. It's no real help but it's a help nevertheless.'

'Poor boy,' Henri said. 'I've been afraid for so long it would come to this. He's been beaten up more than once, you know.'

At least Henri hadn't had to be confronted with the mutilation.

'No,' Lannes said, 'I didn't know. There's no record of a complaint that I'm aware of.'

'He'd have been ashamed. That can't surprise you.'

'I suppose not. He was still an advocate, a member of the Bordeaux bar, wasn't he?'

'Up to a point. He stuck to the law longer than I did, as you know, but he had scarcely practised for years now. Things haven't gone well with him. He was drinking too much, and also . . . '

He let the sentence die. Neither of them wanted to add to it. Lannes sought for words of comfort, could find none.

Henri said: 'It was disappointment, you know, the sense of failure, that drove him to it. To its expression that is, for he was always, I fear, inclined that way. But it was the emptiness of his life. He did once say that it was the excitement rather than the act itself that appealed. It was always better in anticipation than performance. But it became an addiction.'

A tear ran down his great moon face, and he began to sob. Lannes, still finding nothing to say, waited. Many people had cried, for various reasons, in that room, and he had never grown accustomed to it. It embarrassed him, even when, as sometimes, he also experienced disgust. At last Henri mopped his face with a white-spotted red handkerchief, and, to compose himself, gazed out of the window at the steel-grey of the sky. He picked up the photograph of Marguerite that stood on the desk.

'He wouldn't have wanted her to know what he was, what he had become. He never entirely lost his pride and he had a great respect for her, affection too. Now I suppose all the world will know.'

Lannes, touched by his friend's distress, searched for words of comfort, without success, then fell back on the necessary routine.

'When did you last see him? I'm sorry, Henri, but I have to ask these questions. The sooner the better. It's the way it is.'

'I understand. You've a job to do. Yesterday afternoon, as it happens. About four o'clock. The rain had just started and his hat was dripping when he came into the shop.'

'Were you expecting him?'

'Not really, but it happened two or three times a month that he would call on me at the shop. There was no need to give warning, you know. He was my best friend as well as my brother, and I'm sure he would have said the same of me. Twins have a special bond. But you'll know that, Jean, with Alain and Clothilde.'

'I suppose so, though it's not quite the same with them, boy and girl, not, obviously, identical like you and Gaston. How was he yesterday? Anything at all unusual?'

'Nothing at all. He was in good spirits. Despite everything, that was normal with him. He was resilient, you understand. He'd come for a good talk and also to borrow money.'

'Was that something that happened often?'

'Often enough. We called it a loan, but, well, I never looked for repayment. I have a good income and poor Gaston no longer has – had, I should say.'

'Did he say what it was for?'

'No, never. We were past that. And I didn't ask. What would have been the point? It wasn't necessary. Now I wish for the first time that I had refused him. Poor boy.'

'I hadn't seen him for a long time myself,' Lannes said.

'No, you were one of the old friends he preferred to avoid, and not only, or not at all really, on account of your job. He had an affection for you, and he respected you also, as he respected Marguerite, and he would have found it embarrassing. As a matter of fact, he saw very few people, and you could almost say he had become a solitary, a recluse. He spent most of his time at a small house in Bergerac he had inherited from one of our aunts, and, because he no longer practised at the bar, he occupied himself in writing a book, a history of Bordeaux and Gascony at the time of the English Occupation. How much of it got written I don't know, but the subject filled his days. That's to say, it featured in his talk and he had me set aside any relevant books that came my way. But really, you know, I have often thought it was an excuse, something that allowed him to pretend to himself that he wasn't a failure and what the world calls a degenerate. So he had very little social life, except what his compulsion drove him to, if you can call that social life. And now it's killed him, hasn't it?'

'Too early to say, but . . . Shall I walk you home?'

'No need.'

'He was such a happy boy,' Lannes said.

'That was a long time ago.'


Inevitably Lannes spoke to Inspector Troyat of the Vice Squad.

Troyat, lean, heavy-eyebrowed, lugubrious, sighed.

'Oh, I know who you mean. Course I do. He came my way a couple of times. Liked them young, you know, and there was a complaint, not from a parent but from a schoolmaster. I had my doubts about the man's motives, nevertheless had a word with Monsieur Chambolley. No more than that. Till lately he was discreet. Recently, I'm not so sure. It takes them like that as they get older. Time running out, you know. Like Judge Ballardin and that young girl, you remember. So I'm not surprised how it ended, but then I never am. Takes a lot to surprise me, after twenty years in Vice. Mind you, I liked him. Couldn't help doing so. He was always the gentleman. Rotten way to go. Hope it was quick.'

'Quick enough.'

Lannes was reluctant to speak of the mutilation which had, anyway, been performed when Gaston was already dead.

'Can you give me the name of that schoolmaster?'

'It was a couple of years back. I'll look it out for you. But you'd be wasting your time there. Nasty chap, but feeble, a pervert himself, that was my opinion. Meanwhile you might ask at Les Trois Roses in the rue de Saigon. Tell Jérome I sent you. He'll cooperate. He did of course, but it wasn't worth much. He knew Gaston, well naturally he did, but hadn't seen him that night, not for weeks really.'

'To be quite frank, superintendent, I was never happy having him here. It's not really his sort of place and I run a respectable house as Inspector Troyat will tell you. But when Monsieur Chambolley had had a few, which wasn't uncommon, he was inclined to become careless, demonstrative, you know. And I couldn't have that. Had to ask him to leave more than once. I wish I could help you because, despite everything, I liked the old boy, and it's always horrible to hear of one of my customers ending that way. But I'm sorry, I can't. Have a drop of red, will you? I've always been on good terms with the police, as Inspector Troyat will confirm.'

He smiled, displaying sharp canine teeth.

'Or a spot of Armagnac? Good.'


The investigation stalled. Nothing came of the house-to-house inquiries. That didn't surprise Lannes. Respectable Bordelais, he knew, may delight in keeping an eye on the activities of their neighbours, but prefer not to involve themselves in anything nasty. They expect the police to do their work without any help from them. Nor were inquiries made in the bars by the docks any more fruitful. Gaston was known there, but 'haven't seen him for weeks, not since last year, well before Christmas'. That was the stock response. It seemed likely that Gaston had picked up a sailor – a foreigner, of course, and that the man had taken exception to whatever had been asked of him. Or just indulged in a spot of robbery with violence. No telling. These things happen. The examining magistrate, Judge Rougerie, had his own explanation.

'One of these Spanish refugees. Many of them are degenerates, as well as being Reds. It's an unsavoury case. Keep at it a bit longer, superintendent, but if you don't get a lead within the next few days, then I think you can set it aside. It's something best forgotten. They're an old family, with a distinguished name, respected in Bordeaux for several generations. Their father used to be a guest in my parents' house. I examined Henri, quite informally, you understand, and his attitude – well, it's not so different from mine. Nothing, he admits, will bring his brother back, and we don't want a nasty scandal. That's the Mayor's opinion too, that only the Communists would benefit from a full disclosure. And we can't have that.'

Lannes wasn't happy, and not only because he had been fond of Gaston. Nobody should die like that and be unavenged. Murder was always vile, but murder that displayed contempt for the victim, that was abhorrent. And yet he got nowhere. He put Moncerre, the most experienced of his inspectors, a man with a nose for whatever was sordid and seamy, on the case. With no result. Gaston had certainly arrived from Bergerac that afternoon, called on Henri, and nobody could be found to admit to seeing him subsequently. So perhaps it wasn't a pick-up in a public place, but an assignation in a private house or apartment. There was no way of telling. Lannes himself went to Bergerac, found nothing there. Gaston hadn't apparently kept a diary, unless one had been removed by his murderer, and it seemed the only letters he received, or kept, were from scholars with whom he corresponded on matters concerning his research. He hadn't been killed where he was found. That at least was certain. He had been dumped there, as Lannes had suspected from the first. The body was already mutilated, which also argued against the theory of a casual pick-up being the murderer. There must have been blood. But where?

Lannes called again on Henri, ashamed to report no progress.

'Until we learn more about his life.'

'And he kept the dark part secret.'

Henri sighed, scratched himself under his left armpit. The little black French bulldog, Toto, pushed his head against his master's knees, demanding attention, offering comfort perhaps.

'No one should die like that,' Lannes spoke the thought that had been drumming in his head for days, 'die like that, unavenged.'

'Oh vengeance,' Henri said. 'It doesn't mean much to me. And now that we are at war there will be many still worse deaths, even more horrible ones, and rivers of blood crying out for vengeance. To me that's meaningless. You'll do what you can, Jean, I have every confidence in you, but even if you were to find the young man responsible – and I suppose it was a young man – what really would it signify? What good would it do? It's not only Gaston that's dead, it's part of my life that's been killed.'

'Part of my youth too,' Lannes said.

'You'll do what you can,' Henri said again. He ran his finger along the underside of the little dog's jaw. 'The times we live in. What word of Dominique?'

'He's bored. He says they none of them believe in the war.'

'Who does? But he's a good boy. You must be proud of him.'

'Yes,' Lannes said. 'And that makes it worse. Marguerite's miserable and afraid. He's her favourite, you know.'

'I used to envy you your children. Now, do you know, I'm happy that my own marriage wasn't blessed, as they say, with any.'

It had been a strange marriage. Lannes hadn't know Pilar well. A Spanish girl, at least fifteen years younger than Henri. An idealist. Caught up in the struggle in Spain. She'd gone, he thought, first to Paris, to work for a republican organization there, then to Spain itself. Missing. Dead? In one of Franco's prisons?

'It was on account of Pilar,' Henri said, 'that Gaston took up with the refugees. Those who came here first, early in the war, wounded, or perhaps for political reasons I am ignorant of, before the camps were opened for them when the trickle became a flood. Gaston and Pilar were close, you know. They thought alike about the war, about politics. As for me, my attitude was "a plague on the lot of them". Idealism and folly, they go together. Pilar couldn't understand me, disliked what she did understand. I tried to dissuade her from engagement. Pointless. She left me because of politics.'

Lannes looked at her photograph: a strong face, with the black hair pulled back tight, heavy jaws and lips that a novelist might call 'sensuous'. Picture of a zealot. He wondered what they had ever had in common, what they had talked about. Or had it been one of those silent marriages, such as his own was in danger of becoming?

'I didn't know that about Gaston,' he said. 'That side of him.'

'Does it help, do you think? Might it mean something? That he was serious about politics. To my mind, it was partly a means of retaining self-respect.'

Did it help? Who could tell?

Lannes said, 'I'm under some pressure to set the case aside. You've a right to know that. Judge Rougerie's embarrassed by it. So, according to him, is the mayor. That cunt.'

'You'll do what's right. I'm sure of that, Jean. And now it's time I took Toto for his walk.'

## II

*March 22, 1940*

Lannes turned up the collar of his coat against the chill rain drifting in from the Garonne. It was a blue-grey herringbone tweed from the English shop, a present from Marguerite on his last anniversary. The label, in English, told him it was "thorn-proof". He had looked the word up in his big Larousse dictionary, and found there was no precise French equivalent. But he liked what he took to be its meaning, and the sense of the word – "thorn-proof" – a good thing for a policeman to be, even if the coat itself, as he hadn't told Marguerite, wasn't at all suitable for a cop. It made him feel like an actor, a peasant boy aping the aristocracy. It was indeed the kind of coat one of the wine-barons from the Chartrons might wear – a minor baron anyway; the big ones, he assumed, went to London to have their coats and suits made to measure – in Savile Row, wasn't it? But Marguerite had been delighted with it. 'You look distinguished, my dear, for the first time in your life,' she said, and laughed happily. Rare that, these days, her laughter, and all the more welcome. So he couldn't not wear it. And it did keep out the cold and this rain too, more or less. In any case he had to admit that really he liked it, even its suggestion of swagger.

His hip was hurting. The piece of German shrapnel lodged there since November 1916 played up in this weather. Nothing to be done about that, others were worse off . . . Still . . . he turned into a bar for an Armagnac. The proprietor, a big fellow with a patch over a missing left eye, nodded, a touch sullen. Well, it was that sort of morning. Lannes was sour himself, and ashamed of being so. Nevertheless . . .

Actually he had reason, had been grumpy since leaving Rougerie's office. To be fair the little judge himself had been almost apologetic.

'It's not, superintendent, a matter of a crime, apparently not, so far, that is, as I understand it.'

He had paused there to take snuff, a habit Lannes thought affected in him, all the more so because, as the judge had once told him, it was 'English snuff, the very best, the finest quality, from Fribourg and Treyer in the Haymarket. Try some, will you?'

Lannes had refused, politely, he hoped. Not that he had anything against snuff. His mother's father, the tailor, had been addicted to it, spilling it all over his waistcoat as he snuffed and sniffed and sewed, and, as a boy, Lannes had been delighted to take a pinch. 'Protects against colds and the influenza,' the old man asserted. And perhaps it did. But the judge was speaking. Lannes had missed something; never mind.

'Not a crime then, and nor is it, I assure you, a matter of a favour for a friend. By no means. I scarcely know the gentleman. He is, however, a person of some standing in the city, yes indeed, of some considerable standing. An old family, not perhaps as distinguished as it was, but yet of some note in the annals of Bordeaux. Moreover he himself is elderly, and that demands our respect. So he has asked to speak of the matter to a policeman of suitably senior rank and of discretion – I repeat, discretion. I'm convinced' – pinch of snuff – 'that you fit, as they say, the bill. It may all be of some delicacy. Tact will be demanded of you.'

So now Lannes was crossing the public garden, leaning heavily on the blackthorn stick which he carried in breach doubtless of some regulation, sub-section this or that, but which made walking less painful for him with his damned hip in this filthy weather.

The rue d'Aviau was one of the most respectable streets in the city – one of 'the best addresses', as they would say – a fortress of the haute-bourgeoisie and people, as his father used to say, 'with handles to their name'. It was deserted now. The row of blank facades excluded passers-by. Each house was a citadel, shut-off, yielding nothing to the inquisitive, though inviting speculation about the life – or absence of life, he thought – within.

He mounted the step, rang the bell, and turned away to gaze on the silent street. He waited a long time, two or three minutes, till he heard a chain being loosed and the door was opened by an old woman with swollen arthritic fingers and a drip at the end of her nose. She sniffed loudly, retrieving it. Then without a word – doubtless Rougerie had telephoned to say he was on his way, though at the same time Lannes would not have been surprised to learn that there was no telephone in this house which gave the impression of having been asleep for the last fifty years – she ushered him in, across the dark shadowy hall, and into a high-ceilinged parlour or salon, the walls of which were hung with faded tapestries depicting mythological scenes, and portraits of what Lannes assumed to be ancestors stretching back to the time of Louis XIII.

An old man was seated in a high-backed armchair, Second Empire style, and winged as if to protect him from a draught which didn't exist in this stuffy overheated room. He wore a plum-coloured velvet jacket and a floppy bow-tie. A woollen rug was spread over his knees and tucked into the sides of the chair. The window shutters were closed, and in the dim light his complexion was the colour of damp ash. He sat very still as if waiting to join the portraits of his ancestors on the wall, but his eyes were alert and Lannes knew he was being judged. He was conscious of his coat, damp, steaming even, which the old maid or housekeeper hadn't offered to take from him. But he hesitated to remove it.

Monsieur le Comte de Grimaud took a thin black cheroot from a box on the little table at his side, and lit it, the match dancing in his quivering hand.

'Lannes. A Napoleonic name.'

'No connection,' Lannes said, as so often before.

'But you yourself are a Gascon like the Marshal.'

Lannes shrugged.

'A Gascon yes. Like the Marshal, that's something else.'

'A brave man,' the Count said. 'Foolhardy. But one of the glories of the Empire. As for us, we were royalists, missed all that.' He gestured with his cheroot towards the portraits in a manner that, thirty years previously, would have seemed arrogant. 'Not that we did anything. Even then, we lacked energy and enterprise. It was as much as my grandfather could do to join the emigration. He was a youth then, of no spirit. So we had no part in the glory of the Empire. Perhaps you don't think of it like that, as glory, I mean. No matter. I'm eighty-four. Nobody can expect anything of me now. A man of eighty-four is past everything. You must agree, I'm sure. Good for nothing but memories and trivia. Take your coat off, superintendent. You're sweating. My doctors insist that this room is kept at this intolerable temperature.'

Lannes, grateful, did as he was bid, saw nowhere to put the coat, let it fall to the floor. Waited.

'My wife, Madame la Comtesse, the fourth countess I have made, is thirty-five. Younger than you? Yes? I was sixty-seven when we married. Foolish of me, foolish of her. But that's no matter. You may think of it as my last spurt of virile energy. On her part it was what I now recognize as an atrocious adolescent impulse, a morbid desire to be the toy, the plaything, of a licentious old man. She has grown out of it of course. Naturally. But she has always treated me with respect. Even when my hands with their tobacco stains and the blemishes of old age were stroking her thighs, greedily, she never addressed me as other than "vous". Of course, apart from the difference in age, there was the difference of status. My eldest daughter, who is severe, reproached me for making a misalliance. Disgraceful, she said, for the Comte de Grimaud to marry the daughter of a tobacconist. I paid no heed. That's where I first saw her, behind the counter of her father's tabac off the Place

Gambetta. She was fifteen, ripe for plucking, and would have been content to be only my mistress. As indeed she was for two years. It was I who insisted on marriage. Odd of me, you think? Perhaps I was afraid of losing her? Perhaps I wanted to spite my children? I've forgotten.'

Lannes made no reply, waited, just as in boyhood, duck-shooting with his grandfather on the old man's little farm in Les Landes, he had learned patience crouching in the reeds by the edge of the pond till the birds came in a rush as darkness crept over the empty fields.

'There's brandy there, behind the books on the lower shelf. It's forbidden me, like so much else, but give yourself a glass. Give me one too. Forbidden pleasures are ever the sweetest, and all my life I've never denied myself them.'

Again he gestured with his cheroot and, putting it in his mouth, said, 'Push against that panel.'

It swivelled to reveal bottle and glasses. As Lannes restored the bottle to its hiding-place, he saw that a line of books bore the Count's name: a history of the Cathars, one entitled *Nuits Marocaines* and another, *Mémoires d'une Jeunesse Morte*; several novels.

'As you see, I once aspired to be a man of letters. But I lay no claim to these novels. They were my first wife's work. She was very cultured, very literary. When she died my ambitions in that direction withered. Perhaps I wrote only to impress her.'

Lannes poured the brandy. It was much better than what he had drunk in the bar.

'Another life,' the Count said. 'Poor woman. I made her unhappy. She was poisoned by a snake. In Morocco. It introduced itself into her bed one night when I was absent, pursuing another interest. Almost half a century ago. There are few left who remember her, and none who read her books, though they were praised in her day. I saw to that of course, for I loved her passionately, till she began to bore me. Are you married, superintendent?'

'Yes.'

'Happily? Forgive me, I am being impertinent, but a happy marriage is a rare thing. Rare and doubtless wonderful. However I am wasting your time which is, I suppose, the Republic's, and therefore to be valued.'

He sipped his brandy, taking no more than a sparrow might, or one of the canaries that flitted to and fro in the cage that stood on a pedestal behind his chair. Then he replaced his glass, applied another match to his cheroot, and, reaching into the inner breast-pocket of his jacket, withdrew some papers bound together by a green ribbon.

'I have read that it's our national vice, or one of our national vices, writing anonymous letters. You will, I'm sure know how common it is and have seen many. However these are the first I have ever received.'

'What is their theme? There's always a theme,' Lannes said. 'Often demented.'

'What would you expect? That my wife is unfaithful. That she has affairs. That she is a whore. The language is coarse, the tone vulgar and violent. And the information neither surprises nor pains me. How should it? At my age? What else should I look for?'

He held out the package.

'In that case,' Lannes said, weighing it in his hand, 'I am not clear as to what you want of me.'

The old man smiled. Maliciously? Perhaps.

'It's usually slow work,' Lannes said, 'identifying the writer of such letters. Slow work, disruptive and disagreeable for the family. I take it all are addressed to you? That your wife herself hasn't received any?'

'How should I know? Would you expect her to tell me? We are not on such terms. I believe there are bourgeois couples who claim to have no secrets from each other. Their lives must be very dull. The most recent of these letters declares that her current paramour is my grandson Maurice, a boy of twenty. I do not know if this is the case.'

'Would it disturb you if it was?'

'He's quite an attractive boy. Miriam is an attractive woman.'

'Miriam?'

'Yes, Miriam. My wife is Jewish. Ah, that does interest you?'

'Not particularly,' Lannes said. 'But with things as they are politically, the information may help me identify the writer. I take it, that's what you want?'

20

'I should like to know, yes.'

'Understandably. But it's not perhaps a criminal matter. Not yet. One is under no legal obligation to sign a letter. If the content is slanderous, that's another matter.'

'Oh, slander! The intention is clear. First, to disturb me, deprive me of such peace of mind as I enjoy. Second, to persuade me to rid myself of Miriam. I have five children, superintendent, legitimate children, by my previous wives, and they all dislike me and resent Miriam. They've resented her from the start. Resentment is a feeling which festers, as you know. The letters may be followed by something worse, I can't tell. As for Maurice, I am almost fond of him, he's quite an engaging youth. But, for the others, I am too close to the grave to indulge in false sentiment.'

'I can examine the letters,' Lannes said. 'I can, with your permission, question your children, your wife and grandson, though they will be under no obligation to answer my questions. And in the end, when I have stirred the pot, it's likely I will have discovered nothing. Moreover my interference may precipitate something, as you say, more unpleasant. Finally, unless you choose to lodge an official complaint, demanding a formal inquiry . . . '

'No. Talk to them, all of them, as you please, but informally. Now I'm tired. Marthe will see you out. My thanks, superintendent with a Marshal's name. I shall tell Judge Rougerie – I knew his father, a tiresome fellow – how grateful I am to him for granting me some of your valuable time.'

The rain had stopped. Lannes limped back across the public garden where drops still fell heavily from the branches of the chestnut trees, turned down the Cours Clemenceau and into the Allées de Tourny. Stendhal had written somewhere that he didn't know a more beautiful street anywhere in France, and Lannes, Bordelais by birth and long residence, was content to agree. But this morning he had a sour taste in his mouth: the conversation, not the Armagnac. The taste of corruption . . . he couldn't get the phrase out of his mind; it was as insistent as church bells.

He would go home for lunch, to the refuge of the family, without which, he often thought, he couldn't endure his life as a policeman, his exposure to cruelty, viciousness, resentment, fear, brutality. Why, he now wondered, wasn't the Count's grandson this 'quite engaging youth', Maurice, at the Front, crouched like his own Dominique in or behind the defences of the Maginot Line? They were the same age. What strings had been pulled to keep this Maurice out of the army?

The younger children, the twins, Alain and Clothilde, were already at table when he arrived in the apartment in the rue des Cordeliers, five minutes only from the Lycée Michel Montaigne which Alain attended and little more than that from Clothilde's convent school. He leaned over and kissed the top of his daughter's head. The onion-spiced smell of the 'taurin' rose from her plate and he realized that he was hungry. He took his place, poured himself a glass of Medoc and dipped his spoon in the soup.

Alain, resuming an argument that in one form or another had been going on for weeks now, said, 'But, no matter what you say, it was a mistake, wrong indeed, to ban it and absurd also because it was first shown two years ago. Wrong, because not only is it a masterpiece of French cinema, something we can all be proud of, but also because it speaks the truth: war solves nothing. It is what the title says: La Grande Illusion. I for one don't have any desire to die for Danzig.'

'Nobody's asking you to. You're only seventeen. And besides now it isn't a question of anyone dying for Danzig since the Boches have already taken it, it's a question of France now, not of Poland.'

'Clothilde, child,' her mother said.

'It's easy for you,' Alain said. 'You're a girl. But ask Papa. Did your war solve anything, Papa? Did being gassed and wounded at Verdun make for a better world?'

'That sort of question's dishonest,' Clothilde said.

'No, it's not. It's the whole point.'

Marguerite collected the soup-plates and took them through to the kitchen.

'That's enough of this argument,' Lannes said. 'Talking like this certainly solves nothing, and, more importantly, it distresses your mother.'

Who now brought in the main dish – blanquette de veau with

22

haricot beans – and said, 'Eat up now, or you won't have time for dessert. And it's your favourite flan, Clothilde.'

'I do wish they wouldn't argue like that,' she said, when they had collected their bags and departed, bickering again. 'It amazes me to reflect that they spent nine months together in my womb. Perhaps they quarrelled even then. Certainly I was never comfortable in that pregnancy, not like Dominique's.'

'Cat and dog. Yet they're close to each other,' Lannes said, as so often before. In any case, he thought, on this matter they're both right. War solves nothing, certainly mine didn't, and yet there are times when it becomes unavoidable. All the same, if it wasn't a question of dying for Danzig – certainly not now, as Clothilde had remarked – what precisely were the young men, Dominique foremost among them, being required to risk death for?

'There was a letter from him this morning,' Marguerite said, slipping her hand below the top of her dress and withdrawing a folded piece of thin paper.

Dear Papa, Darling Maman – Really we're doing nothing here. We huddle round the stove and are so numbed with apathy and till the last few days cold too that some of us don't trouble to wash or shave or even undress before going to bed (it's all right, Maman, I still do myself – and brush my teeth). Even our officers, who are mostly reservists and not regulars, think no differently from us. So we ask every day, 'Why not send us home since we are doing nothing to the point here, certainly nothing that's of any use?' Lots are hoping for an arrangement and some are quite sure there will be one. 'Just you wait and see,' a corporal said to me yesterday, 'it'll all be arranged. The English will get tired of it and climb down, and then we can all stop leading this life which is fit only for an imbecile, and forget all about little Adolf.' I don't exactly share this view, you'll understand, but I confess I have never been so bored in my life. If I didn't have a dozen Maigret novels to hand, I would cut my throat. (Don't worry, that's a joke, maman.) I think every day of you both and of Alain and Clothilde, and say prayers for you every night. And I wish – but what's the use? We have got ourselves into this fool of a war, and so we have to see it through. Maybe some good German – there must be some – will assassinate Hitler. That would be the best solution. I'm giving this to a friend who is just off on leave to post. So it won't have to pass the military censor. No word of leave for me yet, alas. I send you all my love, Dominique.

'He's a good boy, a really good boy,' Lannes said, and put his arm round Marguerite who was in tears, and hugged her and kissed her.

There was a pile of paperwork awaiting him in his office. He sighed and pushed it aside. Most was routine: a few notes, a tick here and there, a question-mark perhaps, and then his scrawled initials, would be enough to dispose of it. And yet he couldn't bring himself to attend to the task. Not for the first time, he thought: bureaucracy will one day smother police work.

He pushed his chair back, got to his feet, looked out of the window, across the Place de la République which was now almost deserted. The rain had started again, more heavily now than in the morning. There were yellow puddles in the roadway, and each time a car passed, it threw up big splashes of dirty water. Lannes stood there, a Gauloise stuck in the corner of his mouth, his right eye half-closed against the spiralling smoke.

It struck him as odd that in all his years in the city he had never heard of the Comte de Grimaud, and now the old man was so clearly fixed in his mind's eye, and he seemed to hear the chirping of the canaries in their cage behind his chair, though they had been silent throughout his visit and he had indeed been scarcely aware of them then. Yet it wasn't in fact so odd or remarkable, even if it was evident that the Count was, or had been, a figure of some reputation. Bordeaux was a city of innumerable self-contained compartments. No doubt Rougerie could tell him more, if he chose. But again he wondered if there was some other connection between the judge and the Count of which he was ignorant. His thoughts ran in circles.

He returned to his desk, lit another cigarette, and took out the letters. They were dated, which was unusual, till he realized it was the Count who had added the date on which he had received them.

The earliest went back several months. All were typed. It would no doubt be possible to identify the machine, something which he guessed the writer probably didn't know. The first ones were couched in general terms, mere unspecific abuse. The Countess was accused of immorality, but no lovers were named: she was a Jewish whore. It was only later that she became a corrupter of youth, and it was only in the last letter that the boy Maurice was named. There was no threat of public disclosure, no hint of blackmail. Was the intention only to disgust the old man, or to prompt him to discard, then divorce, his wife? Only the last letter was truly disgusting: Miriam was a piece of Jewish filth, sucking, sucking, sucking – the word was repeated three times and under-lined – the young Maurice into the Jewish cesspit and the stench of her ghetto-cunt.

Madness, Lannes thought. How could Grimaud bring himself to retain such filth, not consign it straightaway to the fire where it belonged? Had it excited the old man as much as it disgusted Lannes? Did he, deep down in the recesses of his being, indulge himself in picturing his wife enjoying congress with her lover, the boy of twenty who was his grandson and 'quite an attractive youth'?

There was a knock at the door. Lannes thrust the letters into the drawer of his desk, as if to be discovered reading them would be shameful.

It was Joseph, the old office messenger, fellow-veteran of that other war, which had cost him his left arm. He handed Lannes a note from Judge Rougerie suggesting that, if convenient, he would be pleased to see Lannes at five o'clock

'There's a lady to see you, won't give her name, but says it's in connection with the visit you made this morning. She's a bit of a Tartar if you ask me.'

'Won't do her any harm to wait then. Show her in, in ten minutes.'

When Lannes had followed the children out of the apartment, Marguerite cleared the table, did the washing-up, then settled herself to reply to Dominique's letter.

'It's so sad, darling, that you have no word of leave. We all miss you so much, my lamb, but perhaps, as you say, things will be arranged and then you can come home and resume your studies. If only . . . I try not to worry about you, but don't always succeed. These are bad times for everyone, though the way your brother and sister scrap in the same old style you might think that nothing had changed. They get on my nerves, I have to confess, and then I suddenly feel happy because they are going on as they have always done. You know what they're like, it's a joke we have always shared, isn't it? And then I feel a hollow pit in my stomach because you aren't here to give me that tender and understanding smile of yours. I worry about your father too. He has always been inclined to melancholia, as you know, but now it's as if he is weighed down by responsibility and a sense of oppression. Sometimes he wishes he was not a policeman. "We pursue the wrong people much of the time," he said the other day. Of course, as you know, I never inquire about his cases because he has always been determined to keep his horrid work apart from family life, and I approve of that. But now he has this dreadful one that has been hanging over him unsolved for a couple of weeks, and what makes it worse is that he knew the victim – we both knew him actually – when he was young. And he thinks of that time as his golden days before he was sucked into the morass of his work. Then, like me, he worries terribly about you, my lamb, and what you are experiencing, having been through it himself in his war . . . '

She stopped, laid her pen down and blotted the last line. It was impossible, a letter she couldn't send.

Folding the paper she put it away in the top right-hand drawer of her desk, along with other letters to Dominique she hadn't sent because they would make him unhappy, and wrote another, determinedly cheerful, full of little pieces of news, expressing nothing of what she felt, concealing her fears and longing for the boy.

The woman whom Joseph ushered in wore a black coat and a high broad-rimmed hat like an exaggerated version of a trilby. Her gloves were black too, and you only had to look at her pursed lips to judge that she lived in a chronic state of dissatisfaction.

'I've been waiting forty-five minutes,' she said.

'Did you have an appointment?'

'An appointment?'

It was as if she didn't know the word, or as if appointments were not for her.

'You are Superintendent Lannes? Very well, I must speak with you.'

'You have the advantage of me.'

Since he was already on his feet, he busied himself raking out the stove to get a better glow. Then he lit a cigarette and settled himself again behind his desk.

'Do you think it polite to smoke in the presence of a lady without so much as asking her permission?'

'In her house, no. Here, in my office, well, that's a different matter, especially since you have not troubled to make an appointment. In any case, you didn't come here to tell me not to smoke. So what is the purpose of your visit.'

The strong cloying scent in which she had drenched herself didn't altogether mask the sickly smell of unwashed flesh. He drew on his Gauloise.

'I have never been in a police station before,' she said. 'I wouldn't have thought I ever would be. It's quite foreign to me.'

'That's the experience of a great many people who nevertheless find themselves here. Would you care to tell me your name, Madame?'

Again she hesitated, then, the words coming in a rush, said, 'It's these letters, these abominable letters. You must know, my father wrote them himself. It's a game he's playing, a nasty game, not the first such, I must tell you, calling you in to investigate.'

'Your father is the Comte de Grimaud.'

'Of course.'

As if his question had been impertinent!

'And you are?'

'Madame Thibualt de Polmont. I am his eldest daughter. But that is not to the point. You must have realized, unless you are stupid, that he is senile. He indulges in fantasies, sick, disgusting fantasies. I have come to tell you to pay no attention to them.'

'Your father assured me that no one else knew of these letters –

except of course their author – and that he had shown them to nobody.'

'I tell you again, he is senile.'

'In that case, a sad and painful business,' Lannes said. 'You have my sympathy, Madame. But tell me, you have actually read these letters?'

'They're disgusting. There was no need to read them. I know my father.'

'I see. Do you live in his house, Madame?'

'But certainly, since I was widowed. I thought it my duty to return. To care for him.'

'Isn't that normally a wife's task?'

'I see very well you don't know my stepmother, though it's too ridiculous to call her that, seeing she is twenty years my junior. But that is immaterial. It's a large house as you will have seen for yourself, a family house. Where else, pray, should I have gone in my widowhood?'

Lannes shuffled the papers on his desk, then lit another cigarette. Really he didn't want to keep her there any longer, and not only on account of that disagreeable smell. Was she, he wondered, conscious of it herself? Perhaps he should thank her for coming and say that in view of what she had told him, the matter might be regarded as closed. Yet he was curious – the old man hadn't appeared senile. So, instead, 'It's helpful to have your opinion, Madame. Meanwhile however it would assist me to send in a report saying that in my view no further action or investigation is required, if you would be kind enough to answer a few questions. Would you say that your father's marriage, which is, I understand, his fourth, is unsatisfactory, even unhappy?'

'How could it be otherwise?'

'On account of the disparity in age?'

'On account of who she is and what she is.'

'And yet they are still together, they haven't separated?'

'She looks forward to being a widow, Madame la Comtesse. That's all I have to say about her.'

'And the allegations in the letters? Do they have any foundation? I value your opinion, Madame.'

'My father must think so, since he wrote them, which he didn't do only for his own amusement, you may be sure, but, if you mean, does she bring her lovers to the house, then certainly not. I would never permit it. Nor would my brother, the vicomte.'

'I see. There are six of you, I believe. Brothers and sisters.'

'Five, and one deceased. My youngest sister, Marie-France, was taken from us.' She made the sign of the Cross. 'It was the Lord's will. And my younger half-brother, Edmond, is rarely in Bordeaux. He lives chiefly in Paris, where he is a man of some influence, the editor of a review which is well-spoken of, and engages in politics. So there is Jean-Christophe, the vicomte, who is my full brother, and our two half-sisters, Juliette and Thérèse. They have never married and it's too late for them now.'

'And you are quite certain your father wrote the letters which he assured me he had shown to nobody till he gave them to me? You don't suspect your brother or your sisters of being the writer? I ask because, if you will forgive me for saying so, it has unfortunately been my experience that letters of this nature are very often written by spinster ladies. I don't wish to offend you by making this suggestion.'

'It's easy to see you don't know my half-sisters, superintendent. Juliette' – she sniffed loudly – 'aspires to be a saint and occupies herself with charitable works, while poor Thérèse lives in a world of her own, and has done for years, ever since. But that's not to the point. Which is indeed that my father is not only senile, but also bored. He wrote these letters to make trouble. That's his only amusement now. Which is also why he called you in. You may take my word for it. After all, I've known him all my life. I know what he's capable of.'

'Thank you,' Lannes said. 'You make it all very clear, and it seems probable the matter may be allowed to rest. There is one other member of the family living with you, I understand. Your nephew. Maurice, is it?'

'Edmond's boy. A mere child. A foolish adolescent who plays at being a poet. He counts for nothing, I assure you. And now, since, as you say, the matter may be forgotten, I must ask you to return the letters to me.'

'Return the letters?' Lannes sighed, theatrically. 'I wish I could. But it's impossible. They have now become official documents,' he said, confident that she would not understand they were no such thing. 'Were your father himself to request their return, that would be another question. But even he would be required to enter an official request, through the proper channels, you understand. I am sorry, Madame, but my hands are tied. I could no more do as you ask than I could fly out of that window.'

She wasn't pleased. She tried to argue the case, puffed up with indignation.

Lannes became more polite, still more apologetic, but remained adamant. He spread his hands – it was impossible. When at last she departed in a high temper, he smiled. Tiresome woman.

To Lannes' surprise Rougerie seemed uninterested in his report of his meeting with Grimaud, listening with ill-concealed impatience.

'Yes, yes,' he said, 'yes, I see,' and took snuff, sneezed, blew his nose into a dark-blue handkerchief, and treated himself to another pinch. 'It's not important, a foolishness, you've made that very clear, and in any case asking you to call on him was a mere matter of courtesy, courtesy, no more than that, towards a gentleman of good birth and some distinction, even if, for reasons we needn't elaborate, somewhat tarnished distinction. Least said about that the better. No, superintendent, it's that murder, that very distasteful murder, of Monsieur Chambolley. I've read your report, admirably lucid as ever, and it's evident you have arrived at a dead end, an impasse. As I expected, as indeed I warned you. Not necessarily to be deplored, indeed not at all, not at all. As the Mayor said to me yesterday, when it's a question of a man of good family who has, as you might say, fallen into degeneracy, then in these troubled times, with the Communists eager to stir up disaffection, there are things better kept from the public view. I agree entirely. So I think you can turn your attention elsewhere. Put the Chambolley case on ice, file it as "unsolved, no further action to be taken". Yes, that's it: gone to earth, as the huntsmen say.'

Lannes was furious, tried to argue his case, to no avail. The judge took snuff in what he no doubt thought of as a decisive manner, and said, 'This is no time to open a can of worms. That's official, superintendent, official and final.'

He didn't often swear. When he was a child his father had told him that swearing was unworthy of a man, showed a contempt for language. It had been different of course in the trenches. He had acquired a fine array of oaths there. Even so, he rarely employed them. Marguerite, like his father, deplored the habit. But now, leaving the judge, collecting his coat and stepping out of the building he felt savage and allowed his tongue free rein. He smacked his stick against a lamp-post and wished it was the judge's head. Then he stopped at a bar and drank a demi to wash the taste of dirt out of his mouth.

It was almost as an act of penance that he made his way to the rue des Remparts, splashing through the puddles like a small boy out of temper with the world.

'You've a face like thunder,' Henri said.

'How I feel. I'm ashamed, Henri, ashamed and angry. I've failed you, got nowhere, and have just been instructed to close the case down.'

'It's what I expected. I don't know why.'

He led the way upstairs, opened a bottle of St-Emilion and poured them each a glass, told Lannes to sit down, relax, take it easy.

'You're too much on edge.'

He put a record on the gramophone: Kirsten Flagstad singing the Liebestod from *Tristan*. They listened in silence.

'Wonderful,' Henri said. 'Such a beautiful voice. I play it every afternoon, about this time. Gaston adored Wagner too. It's comforting as if we were still sharing something. Does that sound silly?'

'Not at all.'

'Wagner,' Henri said, replacing the first record with the Prelude to the first act of the *Meistersinger*, 'sublime. It pains me to think that that little guttersnipe in Berlin pretends to love his music, when quite evidently he's incapable of love. Listen to this, Jean: it speaks of joy, love, reverence for life, not hatred, resentment and war.'

He sank back into his chair. The little dog Toto came and licked his hand, asking to be petted. For the moment, peace and contentment filled the room.

Then the music stopped. Only the sound of the needle going round and round.

'It's got to be finished. That's what people are saying, aren't they, about this war? Do you think we're up to it? I'm shy of asking because you are a veteran of the last war, and I'm not. People used to call us shirkers, Gaston and me. Worse than that too: cowards. It was painful. But what do you think?'

'I don't know what to think. I really don't, Henri.'

'In my opinion we're not the people we were in 1914. There's been too much suffering. I couldn't say this to anyone but you, Jean.'

Lannes thought: he may be right, but Dominique is every bit the man I was then, even though I still think of him as a boy, and for Marguerite he is still her baby. He's better than me in many ways, but those around him, I don't know. And the politicians and the High Command, well, that's another thing altogether. I've little faith in them.

He said: 'It's out of our hands, old man. We can only hope. Meanwhile I want you to know that, no matter my instructions, I'm not going to forget Gaston. Whatever they say, his case is still on my desk. Nobody should die like that unavenged.'

Henri got to his feet, moving like an old man now, and poured them both another glass of wine.

'You said that before, Jean, and I trust you to do whatever you can. But don't imperil yourself. Stay a little. I get drunk most evenings now and it's agreeable to have your company. But that's selfish of me. Marguerite will be expecting you.'

Nevertheless, as if to hold Lannes there, he put another record on the gramophone. More Wagner: the Pilgrims' Chorus from *Tannhauser*.

Lannes said, 'Do you happen to know the Comte de Grimaud?'

'Grimaud? Has he come your way? I don't like that.'

Henri occupied himself in filling his pipe, pressing the tobacco down with his thumb, then putting a match to it and emitting short rapid puffs to get it going. Then, frowning, said:

'He used to be a customer. In those days he had a passion for anything connected with mediaeval witchcraft, which he had theories about – how it was a survival of pre-Christian religion, as I recall. The cult of Diana, I think. But I haven't seen him in a long time. That doesn't distress me. I never cared for him. It's an old family, but not a good one. There was some story about the death of his first wife and he's had three at least, possibly four. I don't know how they live, he was always a poor payer, another reason I was happy when he stopped frequenting the shop. But how has he come to your notice? The elder son? Jean-Christophe? There was a scandal concerning him, some years ago. Under-age girls, was it? One of them was admitted to hospital, I seem to remember. Nasty anyway. But he's not up to much. His brother Edmond is more formidable. Gaston used to know him in the days when he wrote poetry. Edmond lives in Paris, edits a review, owns it perhaps. Clever but not to my taste, to the right of L'Action Francaise, inasmuchas that's possible. More modern anyway, Fascist rather than Royalist. Anathema to an old Radical like me.'

'Anti-Semitic then?'

'Unquestionably, but in a lofty intellectual fashion. Oh, I see, you're thinking of Miriam.'

'You know her too.'

'For years. Since she was a little girl. I get my tobacco from her father. What's all this about? I suppose you can't tell me. But be careful, Jean. That family is not good to know. But then I suppose that few of those you have dealings with are. I admire you, Jean. You know that, I hope, and I'm grateful for the way in which you are treating my poor Gaston's case.'

Lannes, embarrassed, said, 'There's a grandson too, I believe.'

'Edmond's boy. I know nothing of him. But there is bad blood in that family, much bad blood.'

33

# III

*April 1–2, 1940*

When Lannes was young, a senior policeman once told him: 'The trouble with you is that you get too involved with the people in a case, and let yourself be distracted from the facts. Facts, facts, my boy, that's all a policeman should busy himself with. Facts leave a trail. Follow it and you'll get there in the end.'

Good advice doubtless; advice he hadn't taken.

This Grimaud case, which wasn't a case, nagged at him, just like, on another scale, this war which wasn't a war, not yet anyway. He found himself waking in a state of anxiety before it was light, thinking of Dominique, picturing him waiting, waiting, waiting, for the German attack that would surely come. Lannes didn't believe those who said it would all be arranged, or the others who declared that the French Army was the strongest in Europe, that Hitler was a gigantic bluff and the German tanks were made of plasterboard. It didn't make sense. He knew how the Germans could fight. They were a great people, however perverted their leaders. So he would slip out of bed, pad through to the kitchen, make a pot of coffee and sit smoking till the light began to grow. Then he would look across the court and see other apartments coming to life as their occupants prepared to go to work behaving as if everything was normal.

He thought often of Gaston. How strong must have been that compulsion – to accept humiliation in the search for a few moments of pleasure which must surely afterwards inspire self-disgust.

Would they bomb Bordeaux? He remembered the newspaper photographs of Guernica. Or was Bordeaux still out of reach of their planes?

He couldn't read anything but newspapers. Even Dumas, his solace in so many black hours, failed him – how distant now seemed the gallantry of his beloved musketeers. No poison gas or hideous bombardments in their wars!

One morning Clothilde, rising for once before her mother,

found him there, gazing out of the window, turning his empty coffee cup round and round, an ashtray already full of stubs beside his saucer.

'What's wrong, Papa?'

'Nothing,' he lied. 'I couldn't sleep,' he added, reverting to truth. 'I couldn't sleep, that's all.'

'Me neither. Is it Dominique? It is, isn't it? I know you're afraid for him. We all are, Maman especially, though when I speak of him, she bites my head off and changes the subject. She'd be better to speak of it, wouldn't she?'

'Perhaps. It's not her way however.'

'It's not your way either, Papa. You're a pair of clams,' she said, and bent to kiss the back of his neck. 'But we're not children, Alain and I, you must understand that.'

'No,' he said. 'You're no longer children. You're not allowed to be children now. All over Europe childhood is being forbidden.'

She sat down opposite him, and stretched across the table to take hold of his hand.

'You don't think we're going to lose the war, do you?'

Her lips were trembling and her eyes damp as if she was about to cry. She was right. No longer a child, but denied what she was entitled to enjoy – her youth. He couldn't tell her he had no faith in their generals and less than none in the politicians who had stumbled into this war.

'I don't know,' he said, and felt ashamed.

Later that day – it was a Sunday – he went to watch Alain play rugby for the Bègles junior XV. The air was crisp, the sky a pale blue, there was no wind from the river, and it was possible to believe again in the promise of Spring. Alain, light but athletic, played with a zest and courage that filled Lannes with pride. The boy tackled bigger opponents as if his life depended on it, using his speed to cut them down. In the last minutes of the game, he swerved outside his marker in the centre to score a try under the posts, and came off the field flushed with happiness and triumph. Like a musketeer, Lannes thought. Like d'Artagnan himself. It was an old joke between them, one they had shared when Alain first played as a boy of eleven or twelve. But now it would only embarrass him. Lannes contented himself with clapping him on the back and saying, 'Good, well done.'

He had often thought rugby was the image of war without the guilt. But there was no getting away from the guilt of the real thing. Damn these politicians. Double-damn Hitler.

IV

*April 12, 1940*
There are slack times in the police force as in any other business. Crimes go on being committed of course, but only such as are easily dealt with by junior officers, or may at least be entrusted to them. It was in these periods, when his days were devoted to catching up with paperwork, that Lannes often questioned the value of his job. Pointless, naturally. At his age, forty-three, rising forty-four, what else could he do? When he shaved in the morning and observed the lines that now ran more deeply from the corners of his nose to his mouth, and saw that the mouth itself was now turned down at the left, he thought: anyone might say, it's the face of a cynic. But I don't think I'm that; not yet.

This slack period was all the more irksome because two days previously the war had come to life, the Germans marching through Denmark and invading Norway. Was it because he felt his deskwork to be a sort of self-reproach that he could not bring himself to drop the Grimaud case that wasn't a case? Or simply that he required the illusion of action to distract his thoughts from Dominique? No matter the reason; he made arrangements to interview the Count's wife, Miriam.

Not wishing to summon her to his office or to meet her in a public place, for that, Bordeaux being what it was, would give rise to talk and speculation, he suggested she come to Henri's book-shop. It wasn't the first time he had made use of it when the occasion called for delicacy. Henri was happy to let him have the sitting-room above the shop.

She was laughing when he came in, a deep full-throated laugh,

36

boisterous enough to set the dust flying. She was a big woman, running to fat, a woman from a saucy postcard. Her thick hair was dyed blonde and her tweed skirt hung squint. There was a ladder in her stocking and her crimson lipstick was smeared. It was impossible for Lannes to see her as the adolescent who had perversely desired to be the plaything of a lecherous old man.

'Henri tells me I can trust you,' she said. 'But I don't know as I have anything to trust you with.'

Upstairs, she said: 'So what's this about? I haven't a clue, you know, which is why I accepted your invitation. But is it usual for top policemen to make assignations of this sort? Not that I mind.'

She settled herself in a high-backed Louis Quinze chair, hitched up her skirt, crossed her legs – fat, but still well-shaped – and lit an American cigarette with a tiny mother-of-pearl lighter.

'So. Explain please. I hope you've a good story for me.'

'Are you on good terms with your husband?'

She laughed again.

'That's blunt. I could say, "What's it to do with you," but I don't mind telling you. The answer's "no". But then nobody is on good terms with him, except old Marthe, who's been his housekeeper for more than half a century, and he wouldn't have it otherwise. Does that satisfy you?'

Lannes said: 'This isn't a police matter, and so our conversation, which isn't an interrogation, is entirely unofficial, off the record, as they say. Your husband called me to see him because he had received a number of anonymous letters.'

'About me?'

'About you. Nasty letters, vile language.'

'That's usual, isn't it, the language, I mean.'

'Usual, yes, almost invariable, really.'

'I'm not so sure I like this,' she said. 'Perhaps we should have some coffee. Henri said to make ourselves at home. Or a drink.'

'Coffee for me. Like many policemen I'm an addict.'

She went through to the little kitchen in the room behind. She moved lightly for such a big woman; she would probably waltz beautifully, he thought. He heard the hiss of the gas stove as she prepared the coffee. It was the Neapolitan kind of pot that you turn upside down to let the coffee filter through when the water has boiled.

'None for you?' he said, when she placed pot and cup on the little table at his side.

'I think I'll have a whisky-and-soda. This sounds as if it's going to be unpleasant. I suppose they're anti-Semitic, Jewish whore, that sort of thing?'

'Yes,' Lannes said. 'I could show them to you, but really you don't want to read them. Madame Thibault de Polmont came to see me.'

'The old cow.'

'I was surprised because your husband told me he had shown the letters to nobody. But she knew about them.'

'She would. She's always snooping. It's impossible to keep a secret from her.'

'I can believe that.' Lannes sipped the coffee which was strong and good, and lit a cigarette. 'She gave it as her opinion that your husband had written the letters himself. To make mischief, she said. What do you think?'

This time she didn't answer at once. She drank some whisky, her lips leaving a red smudge on the rim of the glass. Toto who had been asleep on a Persian rug, woke, stretched himself and came to sniff at her ankles.

'I think she's a troublemaking old bitch herself. But I have to say it's not impossible. He's capable of anything, the old bastard.'

'I had wondered if she might be the author herself, since she not only knew about them but was anxious that I hand them over to her.'

'She's a cow, like I said. But I don't think so.'

Was it because she still spoke with the local accent, as he did, even if hers had been modified, the nasal vowels now less open, that he felt at ease with her?

'Or one of the Count's other children?'

'I wouldn't know. They're a rum lot, certainly. Have you met them?'

'Not yet.'

'You should, you really should. They're an education. I had no idea such people existed, though of course I've got used to them now.'

'Tell me about them.'

'Willingly, though I have to say that if they weren't so odd, so truly bizarre, they would bore me stiff. As it is, they're as good as a play. I make an exception for Edmond. He's clever and witty, which doesn't prevent him from being altogether horrible, but he's not boring. You would say he's a cynic except that he proclaims himself to be a man of convictions. If you've ever seen his review, you'll know what they are. I may add that despite his hatred of Jews, he has tried more than once to get me into his bed. Unsuccessfully. Then there's Jean-Christophe, the heir. I've had no trouble from him, I'm far too big. Little girls are his thing. You probably know about the scandal. That frightened him and he has to restrain himself. But he still looks. You can see him on the terrace of the Café Regent eyeing up the schoolgirls. All the same he's not your letter-writer. I simply don't exist for him. He looks right through me with his fishy eyes.'

'He doesn't resent you?'

'Of course he does. He resents everything that's happened since 1789. To give Edmond his due he once told him that in the days of the Ancien Régime his brother would have found himself in the Bastille, sharing a cell with de Sade.'

'Charming. And the daughters?'

'The girls, as my husband calls them, sarcastically since none of them will see forty-five again. Well, you've met the old cow, seen her, listened to her and smelled her too, I suppose, and that's enough to know her. I'm enjoying this. It's not often I have the opportunity to speak so frankly.'

'To an outsider, you mean? To someone who doesn't matter?'

'I wouldn't say you don't matter, superintendent. No, I mean to anyone. If I spoke like this to someone not in your position, it would fly round Bordeaux faster than a swallow. So I've learned to keep my thoughts to myself, which doesn't, as you may suppose, come easily to me. I can see you wondering why I endure it. I've often asked myself the same question and there's many a day I've regretted that I'm not behind the counter of my father's tabac.'

Lannes smiled. In truth it was easier to picture this big robust cheerful woman doling out chaff and cigarettes to customers in a tabac, and perhaps having a glass of red or pastis with them, than to imagine her in that gloomy house in the rue d'Aviau, like a mausoleum except for the Count's room which was as warm as one of the conservatories in the Jardin des Plantes.

'The girls,' she laughed. 'They're a pair, they really are. Juliette, you know, hasn't had a new gown since the year the old Pope died and I don't mean the one who went last year. She cuts her own hair with a pair of blunt scissors, chops it off really. But she's not a bad old thing, and I'm sure she didn't write these letters. Apart from anything else I presume they are full of words that a pious lady devoted to works of charity wouldn't know.'

'Indeed,' Lannes said, though he recalled the case of a nun who had starved herself to death, leaving a journal in which she had recorded her dreams – some of which were of a startling obscenity.

'Thérèse now,' Miriam said. 'She's a different one. There's some story about her, but I don't know what it is. She's simple, a bit touched in the head maybe, but I've seen an old photograph of her as a very pretty girl, and old Marthe has a rough tenderness for her. But I'm sure she isn't your letter-writer. For one thing I don't believe she actually dislikes me. She's afraid of her father, they all are, except Edmond, but I've seen her tremble when he speaks to her. As for Juliette, I should tell you that she prays every day for the conversion of the Jews, including me.'

Lannes poured himself the last of the coffee which was now lukewarm, and scratched Toto behind his ear. There was a wind getting up, smoke scurried from the chimney-pots across the street. The day he had watched Alain play rugby had belonged to a false Spring. Phoney Spring, Phoney War.

'Why are you pursuing this?' she said. 'Since, as you say, no crime has been committed.'

What could he say? That he didn't know? That it was like an itch he couldn't help scratching?

'What about the boy Maurice?'

'You can't suspect him surely. He's a sweet boy, unhappy but sweet. Misses his mother.'

'Writing anonymous letters is sometimes a sign of profound unhappiness. Is his mother dead?'

'Not dead, divorced. Her name's Nancy, she's English and I scarcely know her. She left Edmond and who could blame her? Anyway she returned to England but he kept the boy. To punish her in my opinion. And poor Maurice has suffered ever since.'

She spoke of him more like a fond and indulgent aunt than a lover. Nevertheless . . .

'You're accused of seducing him,' he said.

She started to laugh, then looked, abruptly, away.

'I don't like that. There's real malice there. It's not true of course.'

She looked him full in the face.

'I suppose anything I tell you can be in confidence, since this isn't official?'

'No reason why not, unless circumstances change.'

'That's a very cautious answer.'

'It's the best I can give.'

She poured herself another whisky, splashed in soda, took a big drink, and said:

'Maurice is a sweet boy who thinks he's a poet. But he's not interested in women. Not yet anyway. If I tell you he was a friend of Henri's brother, Gaston, well, that's enough, isn't it? Poor Gaston, is there any development in his case? Perhaps I shouldn't ask and you can't tell me.'

'I can tell you there's none. We've no leads.'

'I hope you don't think I've given you one.'

'I don't think anything.'

'Their friendship was literary, you understand. Maurice would show him his poems, that sort of thing. Beyond that, I know nothing. Poor Gaston! I've known him and Henri all my life. He used to make me laugh. As a girl I thought him a regular comic. It's wretched.'

Lannes said, 'I don't think I need take this further. You've been very helpful. One last thing. Do you find the existence of these letters distressing or alarming?'

She dabbed at her eyes with a handkerchief, then turned the full force of her personality on him.

41

'I'm Jewish. What is there in the world today that isn't distressing and alarming for my people?'

'I hope,' Lannes said, 'that if things get worse, you'll feel you can come and speak with me.'

'Thank you. You've been very kind, and they will get worse. I won't forget.'

As they descended the stairs, she said, 'Have you thought of old Marthe? She really detests me. She used to be Octave's mistress. Oh long before my time, and she still loves him, I'm sure of that, though she never addresses a civil word to him. Or to anyone, except Thérèse and perhaps young Maurice. All the same I can't see her writing these letters. Not really. For one thing she's never hesitated to abuse me to my face.'

## V

'Chief,' young René Martin said, blushing as he still often did when he addressed Lannes of his own accord, sometimes also indeed when he had to reply to a question. 'Can you spare a minute, let me have a word.'

'It had better be a quick one,' Lannes said.

Then, fearing he sounded abrupt and dismissive, added, 'Unless it's really important. I'm expected home in good time for dinner tonight. It's my wife's mother's anniversary and she's to be there along with my brother-in-law. The old lady can be difficult.'

'It'll keep till the morning,' Martin said, blushing more deeply, 'if that suits you better, chief.'

It did of course. Lannes wanted to be home. Visits from her mother upset Marguerite, especially now, and Alain was sure to say something to provoke his Uncle Albert. So Lannes liked to be there to steer the conversation, also to try to prevent Clothilde from shocking her grandmother with some remark that wasn't actually shocking in the least. But he read disappointment in his junior inspector's face. So he said, 'Come along then,' returned to his office and removed his thorn-proof coat.

'What is it, René? Don't hurry. Take your time. I can see that you've got hold of something that may be important.'

Martin was the only one of his inspectors whom he addressed as 'tu', which he did because the lad was almost young enough to be his son, and Lannes had known him since he joined the force when the boy had had to shave only a couple of times a week at most.

'Well, I think it's important, but I may be wrong. And I have to confess that I've stepped out of line because I know that the case of that poor Monsieur Chambolley has been officially filed, "no further action". But then I saw him dead, what was done to him, and you said yourself that no one should die like that, being insulted in that manner by his killers. Moreover Moncerre – he won't mind me telling you this – he hasn't been happy either. You know what he's like when he gets caught up in a case, he really hates letting go.'

'We don't call him "the bull-terrier" for nothing,' Lannes said, and smiled – he hoped encouragingly.

'So he kept digging, and a couple of days ago he asked me if I fancied doing some investigation – out of hours and unofficially, you see. It's these Spanish Reds, he said. Chambolley was seen with some of them – consorting, that was the word his informant used. So, he said, something makes me think that this may not be a sex-crime like we all thought, but political. Only, he said, I don't properly understand the buggers, their French is mostly lousy. So would I go to the bar where they meet, some of them anyway, and ask around.'

'Why you?'

Young René seemed surprised by the question.

'Because I'm from Perpignan. It's on my file. I speak Catalan because my grandmother came from Barcelona and she brought me up after my mother died, and we used to speak Catalan together. So it was natural he should ask me, and I think he's right, not a sex-crime at all, but political. It's only a hunch of course, but . . . Anyway it took some time but I brought the conversation round to Monsieur Chambolley, pretending I was a friend looking for him, and at first they clammed up, it was as if the subject made them nervous. But they weren't hostile as I think they would have been if the case had been what everyone assumed, that sort of disgusting thing. Just nervous and shy, it seemed. Of course they didn't twig that I was a flic, I'm sure of that because of what followed. One of them, a great big fellow with a beard and a limp – Javier, he's called – took me outside and said that at first they had all been suspicious of Monsieur Chambolley, him being a bourgeois and "maricon" – that was obvious to them – but then they accepted that he was sincerely trying to find out what had happened to his sister-in-law, a Spanish lady, who had worked for the Republican cause, and disappeared. So Javier concluded that in spite of appearances Monsieur Chambolley was OK, and neither a pervert on the look-out for a pick-up nor a spy, which they thought he might be at first. All the same he insisted that he didn't know anything himself and warned me it might be dangerous to ask questions. So, what do you think, chief? It does seem to me to make things look different. I know I've stepped out of line, but all the same.'

'It certainly casts a new light. You've done well, René. We'll discuss it in the morning – with Moncerre. Ten o'clock. Meanwhile you are to resist the temptation which I'm sure you feel to find this Javier again and try to learn more. That's an order, and this time one to be obeyed. Understood? Go and see your girl instead.'

This time René's blush covered his whole face.

So, Lannes thought, as he walked home, it wasn't just to avoid embarrassment that Rougerie had been so quick to clamp down on the investigation. Someone had leaned on him. Interesting.

He was late and there was awkwardness in the air. It was usually like that. His mother-in-law would have arrived in a good temper, declaring herself delighted to see her two darling grandchildren, who would however soon be reproached for neglecting her, As if their lives weren't sufficiently occupied, Lannes thought, without running after a selfish cantankerous old woman who was dissatisfied with everything. Then she would have started talking about Dominique, her favourite, always such a good boy, so attentive to his old grandma, and she would have distressed Marguerite by saying again, as she had ever since the war started, that she was sure she would never see him again, he would be killed in this cruel war like his grandfather, her Achilles, in the last one. Lannes, going through to the kitchen to greet his wife, found her in tears.

'You mustn't listen to her. It's just the way she talks.'

'I can't help it. She says aloud what I'm afraid to think.'

In the salon his brother-in-law Albert was now holding forth. He worked in the Mayor's cabinet. His every pronouncement echoed his master's voice, and he brought Marquet's name into his conversation with tedious frequency, tedious and irritating for Lannes who had no high opinion of the Mayor and indeed thought him an out-and-out Fascist.

'As Monsieur Marquet said to me only yesterday,' Albert now said, his long-nosed head dipping in emphasis, 'we have blundered into an unnecessary and stupid war. For Poland, I ask you. What's Poland to us? In any case, France and Germany should be friends, there's really no reasonable alternative. The Mayor is convinced that together we can build a New Europe. On sure foundations, sure foundations, his very words. Besides, if you ask me – and this is the Mayor's opinion also – France has two real enemies: the Communists at home and the English abroad, the English who are jealous of our empire and are also our commercial rivals. And both – Communists and the English alike – are abetted, if not actually controlled, by the Jews. So this war is folly, madness. But I am confident matters will arrange themselves, and you don't need to worry about little Dominique, Maman. Why should Hitler attack us? He knows the strength of the Maginot Line. He respects the French Army and has no quarrel with the real France, the authentic France. So, when we have a change of government – Monsieur Marquet is confident that Marshal Pétain must come to power, if only temporarily and perhaps, given his age, as a figurehead, a rallying point – then you will see how all will be arranged. Meanwhile, here in Bordeaux, these Spanish refugees, Reds one and all, are causing anxiety. I'm sure you find the same thing in your office, Jean,' he added, acknowledging Lannes' return to the room.

'I don't understand, Uncle Albert,' Alain said. 'Surely Hitler aims at the German domination of Europe, creating a new German Empire indeed, and that means that France would be subject to him. Moreover, as far as Communism being the enemy, how do you explain the Nazi-Soviet Pact and their military alliance which saw the Russians invade Poland from the east while the Germans marched in from the west.'

'That's no way to speak to your uncle, young man,' Madame Panard said. 'It's impertinent. Well-brought-up children should listen to their elders and learn from them.'

Lannes dug his nails into his palms, and gave Alain a smile willing him not to reply, to let it go. But at the same time he approved of his son's answer, even while remembering with some amusement that this was the boy who had insisted he had no intention of dying for Danzig.

'My poor child,' Albert said, 'you speak truth only when you say you don't understand. That Pact with the Soviet Union was a mere ruse on Hitler's part. Just you wait and see. When matters have arranged themselves in the west, as they must do, then Hitler will turn east and destroy the Soviet Union.'

'That might not be so easy,' Alain, obstinate, said.

'Not so easy? Not easy? When Stalin has liquidated the Russian officer class. I assure you, Hitler will go through Russia like a knife through butter. Take it from me. In any case the Fuehrer has always said that he has two enemies whom he is determined to destroy: Bolshevism and international Jewry. Not France, do you hear? Not France. We are his natural allies, for his enemies are ours too. This is another reason why matters must arrange themselves.'

Alain thrust out his lower lip, looked mutinous, but, catching his father's eye, gave a half-smile and kept silent.

'You see,' Madame Panard, massive and complacent, said, 'your uncle knows about these things. You are fortunate to have him to instruct you. But I dislike talk of war. I have suffered too much. It's sufficient to know that all will be arranged, as your uncle says, and that our dear Dominique will soon be home, safe, and normal life will be possible again. I must say I would like to get a night's sleep, or as near to one as I ever achieve, without lying awake tormented by anxiety.'

She smoothed her black bombazine dress with pudgy fingers.

'Clothilde,' she said, 'that dress you are wearing is quite unsuitable for a well-brought-up girl. It's immodest. Really, your poor mother . . . '

Who, fortunately, now appeared to summon them to dinner, and Madame Panard demanded Alain's arm to help her out of her chair. Then, clutching her ebony cane and leaning heavily on her grandson, she led the way to the table. The prospect of food always raised her spirits, and she was even able to praise the setting, though declaring that she detested to see flowers as a centrepiece, and expressing the hope that Clothilde had been at least of some help to her mother.

'Of course,' Marguerite said, 'she always is. But she has also a lot of schoolwork to do, Maman.'

'Schoolwork – that's not what is important for a young lady.'

The pâté de foie gras was approved, Madame Panard taking a second helping, and so was the magret de canard. Clothilde had lit candles on the table and sideboard, and they made the atmosphere warm and intimate. Conversation was steered on to safe topics: family history, relationships and so on, well away from public affairs and the war. Madame Panard launched into a long account of the difficulties she was having with some of her tenants. Albert mentioned the Mayor only some half a dozen times. Alain was polite and attentive to his grandmother. When they had eaten the cheese, which was Roquefort, and then the flan, Marguerite's speciality, Lannes opened a bottle of Veuve Clicquot that they might drink Grand-mère's health on this her happy anniversary; and after coffee the evening was at last over.

In bed Lannes drew Marguerite to him and kissed her.

'That went off all right. The children behaved well, I thought.'

'I hate it when Albert talks in that domineering way and expresses his opinions so brutally. It makes me ashamed to be his sister.'

'They're not his opinions, in the sense that he has formed them for himself. He just repeats what he has heard the Mayor and those around him say.'

'Does that make it better?'

'Not really.'

She sighed.

'What is it? What's wrong?'

'It's the first of Maman's anniversaries Dominique has ever missed.'

He drew her more closely to him, kissing her first on the cheek and then on the lips. They made love, gently and without passion. She fell asleep in his arms. Moonlight crept through a gap in the shutters, falling on the silver frames of the photographs of the children on their mother's dressing-table.

## VI

*April 14, 1940*
He was a great bear of a man, black-bearded and round-shouldered. A ruined bear, Lannes thought, with his limp, heavier than mine, his sagging flesh and bloodshot eyes. Formidable all the same. Dangerous? Perhaps. Hunters always say a wounded animal is the one to fear. He had had too much sense to resist the cops sent to bring him in, but made it clear that he was there, in Lannes' office, under protest. Still, he didn't break into complaints, which would have been futile, but sat in the chair, which he filled, and looked surly.

'Xavier Cortazar?'

'Javier, with a "J". I'm Catalan, not Spanish. I must be losing my mind to speak as I did to that kid. I should've spotted he was a cop.'

He spoke French slowly, carefully, with a heavy accent.

'You may smoke,' Lannes said, and called for coffee. 'This isn't an interrogation. You're not under suspicion. Indeed you're at liberty to leave whenever you wish. But I hope you won't. I hope you may be able – and willing – to help us.'

'Soft soap. Why the hell should I trust you? And what's this all about anyway?'

'You know what it's about,' Lannes said. 'I've had a look at your dossier. You've been here nearly three years, and we've no reason to think you have engaged in any activities that would cause the French Republic any anxiety. So as far as I'm concerned you're clean. You came here first for medical treatment, I see. Is that correct?'

'I got a bullet in my balls at the Guadaljera. Not an experience I would recommend.'

'You were in the CNT militia.'

'I won't deny it.'

He blew smoke across the desk.

'Yes, I'm an Anarchist. Hitler, Musso, Stalin, fat-arse Franco, the King of England and whoever is Prime Minister of France this month, they're all one to me and I've no time for any of them. Are you going to lock me up for speaking my mind?'

'I don't think so,' Lannes said, enjoying the theatrical performance. 'I might even go some way to agreeing with you. Now drink your coffee and stop playing games. You know why you're here. I'm investigating the murder of Gaston Chambolley, and, as you told my young inspector, you had some dealings with him.'

'I won't deny that. Actually, I liked the poor sod. He was a gentleman and there aren't many left. That surprises you, eh? That an old dyed-in-the-wool Anarchist should praise a man for being a gentleman? But to my mind that's not a matter of class and still less of money. At first, like I said to your inspector whom I won't insult by calling him a police spy – me being to my way of thinking a gentleman myself – at first then I thought, "This fellow needs a kick in the arse," for I don't care for men of a certain age who run after boys, though that's a matter of taste, I agree, and it takes all sorts, as they say. It's just that it revolts me. But I changed my mind.'

'Why? What made you?'

Javier Cortazar looked up at the ceiling and took a long time to answer. A bluebottle buzzed round the electrolier. Lannes waited, lit a cigarette, drank coffee. A policeman learns when to push the person he is questioning, when to give him time. Patience, Lannes had always told his subordinates, is an essential quality in a cop.

At last: 'He was after information about his sister-in-law of whom he appeared to be fond. She was Spanish herself and a good Republican. I knew of her by reputation, no more than that. But I was willing to ask questions on his behalf. That was as far as we got. I can't see as this has anything to do with him being bumped off, and it's that which you're investigating, not his politics. Right? Or mine either if it comes to that. He was an innocent, you know. That's what I trying to get across.'

'This isn't a good world in which to be an innocent,' Lannes said.

He questioned the Catalan for the best part of an hour and a second pot of coffee, inquiring specially, in more than one way, if Gaston had established intimacy with any of the other exiles, if he had quarrelled with any, or asked awkward questions. But he got nowhere. 'You've got it wrong,' Cortazar said, 'it's nowt to do with any of us. He was an innocent, I keep telling you that, he didn't know where he was going' – as if this settled the matter. Lannes was just about to call a halt when the Catalan said, 'There was one night he didn't come alone, or leave alone, I can't remember which. There was a Frenchman with him who said nothing but gave the impression of listening to everything. I wasn't comfortable with him.'

'Can you give a description?'

'Certainly, for I took good notice of him, thinking he might be a spy of some sort, which is probably the case. Short, stocky, mid-thirties perhaps, brown hair cut short, dark eyes. He smoked English cigarettes, don't know the brand, a yellow packet.'

'Have you seen him since?'

'Neither before nor since, and don't want to.'

'But you would recognize him?'

'Certainly, because you could see he thought we were trash, and I didn't like that.'

'Good. Then you'll please let me know if he comes your way again.'

When the Catalan had been shown out, Lannes called in Moncerre to join him and young René.

'We've made some progress,' he said. 'I think you're right, Moncerre, and this isn't a sex-crime but political. And that's why they're so keen to close it down. On the other hand we've got nothing to open it up, nothing that might persuade or force Rougerie to rescind his instruction.'

Moncerre, the bull-terrier, had been using a match as a toothpick. He now removed it from his mouth, broke it in half, and said, 'No chance of that with what we've got which is no more than fuck all.'

'Quite. So I can't authorize you to pursue investigations. Not officially, that is. Does the description of the Frenchman mean anything to you.'

'Sure: short, stocky, brown hair cut short, it describes several hundred of our worthy fellow citizens. You can see half a dozen that fit that description on every café terrace in Bordeaux. Very helpful. On the other hand, the English cigarette – not many people smoke them, even in Bordeaux. Paris may be different of course. I don't know.'

Like a true Bordelais, Moncerre thought Parisians stuck-up and not to be trusted.

'I spent a holiday in England last year,' René Martin said with a blush, 'and I think the brand is called Goldflake.'

'That takes us a long way,' Moncerre said.

'Not far, I agree,' Lannes said. 'Nevertheless we know more than we did.'

## VII

*April 16, 1940*

Judge Rougerie was very small, pot-bellied, pink-faced, with tufts of fleecy white hair that sprang out horizontally just above his ears. There was a certain charm to his manner when he was in a good temper, for then he always seemed on the point of telling a funny story, even if Lannes had never actually heard him do so. But he looked ridiculous when displeased, and this always awoke a curious sympathy in Lannes.

'I should have thought my instructions sufficiently clear,' he said.

'Indeed they were, and the case was set aside, the file closed. I conveyed as much to Henri Chambolley, who, though naturally disappointed, understood.'

'So you say, superintendent. But why do I now learn that you have been questioning a certain Spaniard by name of . . . ' he shuffled his papers . . . 'His name is immaterial – about a case which I have made it clear was to be regarded as dead? Answer me that, please.'

Lannes was more interested to find that the judge had learned of Cortazar's visit to his office than perturbed by his anger.

'And why wasn't it reported to me, as proper procedure requires?'

Really, the little man's indignation made him look more than ever like a character in a comic film!

Lannes scratched his right eyebrow.

'It sometimes happens,' he said, 'that we in the police judiciaire come to learn of things which may or may not have a bearing on a case in hand, or even, as in this instance, on one where it has been decided that it is vain to pursue inquiries. In such circumstances it is a routine matter to check the information in order to determine whether it makes any material difference to the position in which we find ourselves. Naturally, this is usually done in an informal, even, if I may say so, unofficial or scarcely official manner. As in the case of the Spaniard you mention. I did indeed question him, but he added nothing to what we already knew, which, as you are aware, is very little. Therefore I had no reason to approach you with the suggestion that it might be expedient to re-open the case. That is the long and short of the matter. Had my conversation with him – and it was a conversation, not an interrogation – which is why I have filed no record of it – altered my view of the matter, then I should have immediately acquainted you with what I had learned. But since it didn't and since I learned nothing, I saw no reason to burden you with it. Like so much police work, it yielded no useful result.'

Was he protesting too much? It seemed not. Rougerie nodded, twice, and took snuff.

'Your explanation is satisfactory. Naturally with all my respon-sibilities I have no wish to be burdened – as you perceptively put it – with the minutiae of police work. Nevertheless it was dis-pleasing to be informed by a third party that you were pursuing an investigation that we had agreed should be laid aside.'

And who was your third party? Lannes thought.

Back in his office Lannes summoned Moncerre and René, and suggested they cross the square to the Brasserie Fernand for lunch. As usual Fernand, grandson of the brasserie's original Fernand, greeted Lannes as a favoured client and showed them to a corner table in the back room where their conversation wouldn't be overheard.

'It's a cold day,' he said, 'cold for April certainly. So I recommend the cassoulet and a couple of bottles of good St Emilion. We shall all be glad of such comforts if the war turns against us, as I fear it will.'

Lannes at once pictured Dominique in his trench or wherever he found himself behind the Maginot Line, and felt a tremor of fear. But he didn't resent Fernand's pessimism – he had a son in the front line himself, and the scar on his right cheek was his legacy of the old war, in which indeed he had been decorated with the Médaille Militaire.

'And first,' Fernand said, 'some escargots.'

Lannes led the conversation away from the war, in his own interest and also to avoid embarrassing young René who had sought permission to transfer from the PJ to the army and been refused. Lannes knew that the boy had had to endure abuse from some who thought him a shirker.

The cassoulet was all Fernand had promised, the preserved goose full-flavoured and the sausage fine and spicy.

'Makes you proud to be French, a dish like this,' Moncerre said, mopping up the juices with a piece of bread. 'Good there's something that still does.'

Lannes reported his conversation with the judge.

'Interesting? Yes?'

'I don't like it,' Moncerre said.

'What do you mean?' René said.

Moncerre smiled. He was always pleased to find himself a step ahead of a colleague. It was, Lannes thought, one of his weaknesses as a policeman.

'It's obvious, kid,' Moncerre said. 'We're being watched. They're keeping tabs on us.'

'Who are?'

'That's asking. If we knew the answer we'd be half-way home.'

'The immediate question,' Lannes said, 'is how we rate on disobedience.'

'We rate high,' Moncerre said. 'You always have, chief.'

'I don't like being leaned on, or spied on. That's certain. But the truth is we really know almost nothing. Our only lead is that man the Catalan described, who smokes English cigarettes. What did you say they're called, René?'

'Goldflake.'

'Goldflake. Whoever he is, Monsieur Goldflake has protection. I think we can assume that. But I don't like to see murder going unsolved and unpunished. It's a prejudice of mine. It offends me.'

'Offends me too,' Moncerre said. 'So we ask around.'

'That's right. We start to make nuisances of ourselves and maybe we'll stir something up. Get Monsieur Goldflake to break cover. René, now that we've talked with your friend Javier, it would be quite safe for you to look him up again, stand him a couple of drinks, see if you can loosen his tongue, and use your Catalan to talk with some of his comrades. If they see that Cortazar has accepted you, they may be ready to talk, and it's possible that one of them may know more than he does. All right?'

'Absolutely,' René said, delighted to have been trusted with this responsibility.

Moncerre said, 'I've a couple of snouts I'll sound out. They may know something. No harm in trying.'

Fernand brought them coffee and a bottle of Armagnac with four glasses.

'I'll join you if I may. The way things are, it's perhaps a patriotic duty to drink as much of my good Armagnac as we can – before the Boches get here and requisition it.'

'You don't think that's likely, do you?' René said.

'Don't I? Who knows? Let's just say it's not a possibility I'm inclined to discount. The news is not exactly encouraging. Sounds as if the English are on the run from Norway.'

'Oh well, the English, they've never been the best of allies,' Moncerre said.

He picked up his glass, 'Vive la France, all the same.'

## VIII

*April 16, 1940. Afternoon.*

Lannes limped across the public garden towards the rue d'Aviau. The breeze was still cool, but the sun had come out and the young leaves of the chestnut trees, damp after early morning rain, sparkled. To his surprise he found himself almost happy, effect of Fernand's bracing pessimism perhaps. Or, more likely, the Armagnac.

Or the combination. Also the eagerness to step out of line that both Moncerre and young René had shown. He stopped a moment, leaning on his stick, to watch the puppet show which had drawn a crowd of perhaps twenty small children, with mothers, grand-mothers or nursemaids, and hummed a tune – 'La vie qui va' – which the young singer Charles Trenet had made popular a year or two back. He would speak briefly to the Count, tell him he had got nowhere, that he didn't think the matter worth pursuing, ask him if he wanted these loathsome letters back, and then go home, enjoy a family evening, and the shoulder of lamb with which Marguerite had promised to make his favourite navarin with lots of spring vegetables. For a moment, in the growing sunshine, even his anxiety for Dominique was stilled. The English might indeed be pulling out of Norway, but Norway was far distant. Bordeaux was tranquil and the promise of Spring at last real this afternoon.

The old woman, Marthe, opened the door after keeping him waiting even longer than on his first visit.

'So it's you again. I don't know as the Count can see you. He certainly shouldn't. He's poorly.'

Nevertheless she stepped aside to let him enter the hall which, in contrast to the sun lighting up the street, appeared even more gloomy and sepulchral.

'People bother him. There's Monsieur Edmond down from Paris and that aye puts him in a state. Not but what it's his own fault, the stubborn old fool.'

'You've known him longer than anyone, I suppose?'

'And what if I have? What's that to you? Nothing to my mind.

But I'll tell him you're here. You'll be no worse for him, I daresay, than the rest of them.'

She shuffled away in her carpet slippers which made no noise on the parquet floor. He rather took to this crabbit old woman who so evidently had no time for him, or apparently for anyone except the Count whom she no doubt bullied and bossed even while she cosseted him. He heard a door close overhead and knew that someone was watching him. He turned away, giving his attention to a large still-life, dark and too heavily varnished, which dominated one wall: a painting featuring, as far as he could make out, more dead animals and birds than seemed credible. Extraordinary to think that someone had chosen to buy it. But it had doubtless appealed to the taste of 1860 or thereabouts.

'He says you're to go in, but I'll ask you not to stay long and not to upset him. It's me that will have to sit up half the night if he has one of his turns.'

'I'll be careful and as quick as I can.'

She sniffed noisily, in disapproval or disbelief.

'Police in the house. We could do without that again.'

The Count wasn't alone. The chair Lannes had sat in on his previous visit was now occupied by a lean dark-complexioned man, with thinning hair that glistened with oil. He had a pencil moustache, and, without rising from his seat, extended a well-manicured hand in Lannes' direction. It was offered as an acknowledgement that stopped short of a handshake, and was quickly withdrawn.

'Marthe has announced you as a policeman,' he said, 'which makes me curious. I trust my dear brother has not been up to his old games?'

'Your brother?' Lannes said, pretending not to understand. 'Games?'

There came a dry chuckle from the Count who seemed to Lannes even older and frailer than on his previous visit.

'It's natural that you should think so, Edmond, and it's mere politeness on the superintendent's part to pretend to ignorance. Superintendent Lannes, forgive me. I haven't introduced my younger son to you. He edits a review in Paris. They say it's well thought of, in certain quarters. It has even been described as "significant" – whatever that implies. So, to our business. Have you discovered anything? No? You may speak freely, for Edmond will certainly regard this little affair as of the utmost . . . insignificance.'

'In effect,' Lannes said, 'nothing.'

The Count laid aside his thin black cheroot and closed his eyes.

'And yet,' he said, 'there has been one consequence of your willingness to interest yourself in my concerns. There have been no more letters.'

'There was however one matter I would like to raise.'

'You refer to my eldest daughter's visit to your office?'

'It surprised me because you gave me to understand that nobody but yourself – and of course their author – knew of the letters. But Madame Thibault de Polmont was evidently well-informed.'

'So you suspect her? That would be amusing.'

'The possibility occurred to me,' Lannes said. 'No more than that.'

'Perhaps,' Edmond said, 'I might be permitted to see these letters? I might be able to throw some light on the question, speaking as a literary man, indeed a critic. There may be nuances that would, with all due respect, superintendent, escape the eye of a policeman.'

'That seems unlikely,' Lannes said. 'Nuances are not what their author deals in.'

'And my wife?' the Count said. 'She could suggest nothing?'

'Nothing at all. Naturally she found the idea of the letters, which I did not however show her, distressing.'

'So you advise I let the matter drop?'

'Unless you now wish to make an official complaint. In which case . . . '

'No,' the Count said, 'I'm too tired,' and closed his eyes.

Lannes made to leave, but to his surprise found Edmond rising and accompanying him to the door. He took Lannes by the elbow and held him there in the hall.

'I'm very pleased to have made your acquaintance, superintendent. If you have a moment I should like a word with you. You have? Good.'

He led Lannes into a dark little room off the further recesses of the hall. It was over-furnished with armchairs and a sofa in a dull velvet, perhaps plum-coloured, though in the half-light it was difficult to be sure; two cages of stuffed birds stood on a mahogany table.

'You haven't had occasion to speak to my son Maurice about this stupid affair.'

'I've seen no need to.'

'I'm glad to hear it. He's very young – young for his age, I would say – and impressionable. He thinks he's a poet, though I doubt if he is. Many young men make verses – and inflict them on me as an editor – but very few of them are poets. I'm inclined to think more verses are written than read, which is perhaps as it should be. But that's not the point. Do you have sons yourself, superintendent?'

'Yes,' Lannes said, disinclined to say more than that.

'Then you will understand my anxiety, and it is this which has brought me from Paris at a time that is, to speak truly, decidedly inconvenient.'

He waited as if expecting a reply or question, then took out a leather cigar-case.

'Have one of these, superintendent. Genuine Havanas, I assure you, not these Italian abominations my father smokes. No? You prefer a cigarette? Very well.'

He clipped the head off his cigar and lit it with a long match. When satisfied it was drawing well, he shifted his position in the armchair, crossed his legs, and said, 'I understand you're in charge of the investigation into the murder of Gaston Chambolley. May I ask how it is going?'

Lannes smiled.

'You can't really expect an answer to that question. But in turn I might ask why my investigation should interest you.'

'I used to know him. We were even friends once. It's natural that I should be curious.'

'Curious enough to take me aside and question me? I find that a little strange if you'll allow me to say so.'

Edmond rolled the cigar round between his lips, removed it, blew out a cloud of dark-grey smoke, looked hard at Lannes, then said, 'I'm concerned that my son isn't involved in the matter of subject to investigation.'

Lannes made no reply, waited.

'Maurice had made the acquaintance of Gaston Chambolley. As I've said, he fancies himself as a poet, and Gaston, as you may not know, once enjoyed a certain reputation as a critic. Indeed he wrote for my review in its early days when he was still a serious person, before his life became disreputable. How they became acquainted, I don't know, but you will not be surprised to learn that I was displeased to learn of it. Any father would be. You have sons yourself, and will appreciate my concern. I wrote to Maurice ordering him to break off this quite unsuitable association. But I have been occupied in Paris, and I don't know if he obeyed me. Now, given the manner of Gaston's death and the suspicions it must give rise to – suspicions and rumours sadly likely to taint anyone of his acquaintance – you will understand why I wish to be assured that nothing in your investigation touches Maurice. I have, as you may know, political connections, interests and ambitions, which might be damaged by any scandal concerning my son.'

No doubt he was indeed seeking reassurance, but Lannes was also aware of the threat implicit in this last sentence: your investigation may damage me, but I'm a man of influence, so be careful yourself.

'I can assure you, monsieur, that you need not disturb yourself.'

Lannes paused. He thought of his conversation with Rougerie. Was Edmond perhaps one of those who had leaned on the examining magistrate? If so . . .

'I think I can tell you that this investigation has been closed, case filed, not to be pursued. Such are my instructions. You'll understand that I can't enter into more detail – which, dammit, I don't know – But I can assure you of this. Your son has not been questioned, and I cannot envisage the circumstances which would alter that.'

'The investigation has been closed? That is surely unusual. Closed so quickly, filed away?'

'Unusual, certainly, in a murder case. I'm not, you will appreciate, at liberty to say more.'

He got to his feet. Then, before he reached the door, turned, and, speaking as if it was an afterthought, said, 'I'm a little puzzled.

59

You evidently knew of these anonymous letters, and yet you asked if my visit was in connection with your brother and any possible misdemeanours.'

'Oh that? I was teasing my father. He despises my poor brother whose grubby little history is one of the few things still capable of disturbing him. As to my knowledge of the letters, you've met my eldest sister, Amélie-Marie. Well then, you must realize that she thrives on indignation and must share it with others. Naturally she wrote to me at length – in green ink with many underlinings – about these notorious letters.'

'I see. Thank you. And, a last question, have you any idea who might have written them?'

'None at all. How should I have? The matter is of no interest to me.'

The light was fading and the yellow sandstone of which Bordeaux is chiefly built was taking on a leprous look as Lannes, stick in hand, limped away in the direction of the Cours de Verdun and the Monument to the Girondins. He didn't share his fellow-Bordelais' admiration for these high-minded liberals who had so enthusiastically engaged France in war. They had died well, that was the best to be said for them, but dying well was often easier than living well. Many a scoundrel went bravely to the guillotine.

He heard running footsteps behind him and a voice calling. Momentarily he tightened the grip on his stick. Then a young man was beside him, breathing heavily in short abrupt spasms from his exertions. His blond hair, worn too long, flopped over his left eye. He wore a high-necked woollen jersey, like a Breton fisherman, and loose-fitting corduroy trousers.

'I have to speak to you.'

'So it seems.'

'I was watching you from the landing at the turning of the stair, but then I had to wait till my father rejoined Grandpa in his study before I could slip out of the house, and I was afraid for a moment I had lost you.'

'Well, we can't speak in the street,' Lannes said and taking hold of the boy's arm – in case he should suddenly change his mind? –

led him into a café. He ordered a beer for himself and a lemonade for the boy who had first protested that he wanted nothing. The boy was agitated and there were pink spots on his cheeks, which were probably usually pale.

'So?'

'It's difficult, and now that I've found you I don't know where to begin.'

'Take your time.'

Lannes lit a cigarette and pushed the packet across the table.

'So you're Maurice.'

'Yes of course,' the boy said and took a cigarette. His hands were shaking as he lit it, and he held it awkwardly, as if he wasn't accustomed to smoking. 'But, first, I wonder what news you have of Dominique.'

'You mean my Dominique?'

'Yes, of course,' he said again. 'Not that I can claim to know him well, we've not met more than half-a-dozen times, but on two of these occasions we talked at length, about everything really, and discovered an affinity. Then the army took him and I'm ashamed not to be in uniform myself, but I suffer from asthma, you see. So I would like to write to him, very much like to, only I don't have an address.'

Lannes, not for the first time of course, was brought up against a truth of parenthood so easily forgotten: that your children have lives of their own in which, often, there is no part for you, and that, in the company of their friends, their mates, *les copains*, they are different people.

'All the same,' he said, scribbling Dominique's army number and direction on the back of an envelope, 'it wasn't only to get Dominique's address that you came running after me. If that had been all you wanted, you could have asked me on my way out, couldn't you?'

The boy twisted the lock of hair that flopped over his eye and took a quick – anxious or just inexperienced? – puff of his cigarette.

'What did my father want?'

'Reassurance.'

'About me?'

'Who else?'

'I don't understand it. It's not as if he cares about me. Indeed he's always despised me, I think, and resented me too because of my mother who left him. She was English, you know, and he hates the English, and is always on the look-out for the Englishman in me. I'm afraid of him really. That's a terrible thing to have to say about your father, but it's true, even if he has never so much as laid a hand on me or anything like that. I'm talking too much but I think it's because you're Dominique's father and because Miriam said you were all right. So it's almost in spite of you being a policeman, as it were.'

Lannes thought: this is an unhappy boy and near breaking-point. His barriers are collapsing and he needs to confess whatever it is that's troubling him. He'd seen it so often as he approached the end of a long interrogation: that moment when it becomes a relief to speak the truth which you have so long denied or hidden from.

'But this too isn't why you ran after me,' he said.

The boy hesitated, then the words came in a rush.

'No, it wasn't, and I have to speak because I think I'm going mad keeping it to myself. Miriam told me that the investigation into Gaston's murder has been abandoned, called off, and I thought, how can that be, surely the police don't give up on a murder. And I was the more surprised because of how she had spoken of you. Of course I don't know about these things, why a case may be abandoned or shelved. But you see it shouldn't be, not this one, and then I thought, it's my fault.'

Lannes pushed the cigarette packet towards the boy again, but this time he shook his head. He wasn't far from tears.

'It's because I've been withholding evidence. That's the phrase, isn't it? You see, I was there that night. Oh, it's so hard to explain.'

'There's no hurry.'

'He had a room in the rue Belle Etoile, quite near the station, off the Cours du Marne. Did you know that? It was his secret place. That's what he called it. We used to meet there. No, it's not what you think. I mean, I knew he was a pederast, well, it was obvious, and he was maybe a little in love with me, but he never made what they call advances, I'm glad to say, for the idea revolts me. So all we did was talk. I would read my poems to him and he would criticize them, advising me, he was really helpful, and we discussed literature in general and certain books in particular. He was really interesting, and it pleased him to regard me as his pupil. He was a natural teacher, far more so than any of my profs, and I learned a lot from him. I'm not naïve, whatever you may think, and I knew why he kept that room and guessed what use he put it to, though of course we didn't talk about that. He did say once that in Bergerac where he lived most of the time, he had to be respectable because of his housekeeper whom he didn't want to offend. He made a joke of it, and perhaps he hoped I would react in a certain way, but that's all there was to it. Despite everything – I mean, his vice, as I suppose it was – he was a good man, kind. Miriam says the same and she had known him all her life. But this isn't to the point.'

He took a quick swig of his lemonade, and touched his lower lip with his tongue. Two men came into the café, and Lannes saw through the briefly opened door that the light was dying in the street. One of the men called for two big glasses of red. They stood at the bar, and when Lannes looked at them, stared back, asserting themselves. Snatches of their talk came to him. The taller, taking off his hat and laying it on the bar, mopped his brow with a blue handkerchief. 'If you ask me,' he said, 'the real danger doesn't come from the Boches. We can handle them, but from the Reds and the Jews. We should round them up and put them in camps. You have to admit that in this respect at least Hitler has the right idea.'

Maurice, no doubt also aware of their presence and conversation, lowered his voice and began to speak very quickly.

'I left him before seven o'clock, probably nearer half-past six. My aunt makes a fuss if I'm late for dinner, you see, and I was expected. Gaston was alive then, naturally, and not at all drunk, which was less usual. But I had been drinking tea and he had had only a single glass of white wine, a Graves. He always made a joke about that – an English joke. I read English of course on account of my mother and there's a line of the poet Byron – "only sextons drink Graves" – it's a pun, sextons are grave-diggers, you see. Gaston loved the English Romantic poets and so he would lift his glass and say – in

63

English too – "This wine puts me in funeral mood." It's not very funny, is it, not really. Do you speak English, monsieur Lannes?'

'A little. Enough to get the meaning.'

'It's terrible to remember how he made his usual joke that night . . . I'm sorry, it upsets me to think of it, and I'm sorry to be so long in getting to the point.'

'That's all right. Take your time. Compose yourself. Believe me, these details are useful to me. Knowing the victim helps you to understand a crime, even solve it sometimes.'

'Fact is,' the smaller of the men at the bar, middle-aged, wearing a striped suit, said in a booming voice, 'we need someone like Hitler in France. Not exactly like him, I grant you, because he's a guttersnipe, but still a strong man to clean up this disgusting Republic of ours.'

Maurice looked up, sharply, at the speaker, then quickly lowered his eyes, and keeping them fixed on the table, said in a voice that was now little more than a whisper, 'It's difficult partly because I'm ashamed not to have come forward. I was afraid. That's something Dominique and I discussed – fear and the nature of fear. But he had more reason, going to the Front, while I . . . have never had to fear anything worse than disapproval.'

Perhaps, Lannes thought, his relations with Gaston weren't quite as innocent as he says, not that it matters, poor boy.

'It's as I was leaving. Two men were on the doorstep and pushed past me to enter the building. There's no concierge there, and it strikes me now that they were waiting for someone to come out, though I may be wrong. They went upstairs to Gaston's room.'

'Can you be sure of that?'

'Yes indeed, because . . . '

Colour flooded into the boy's face and he spoke in a rapid mumble.

'Because I heard one of them say, "That'll be one of his bumboys, a good time to catch him." And his companion laughed and made some reply, but he spoke in Spanish which I don't really understand. Now of course I wish I hadn't continued on my way home.'

Lannes said nothing and Maurice, probably afraid that he was angry, apologised again for not speaking sooner.

'Would it have helped if I had? Can the investigation be re-opened now that you have my evidence?'

There was no point answering the first question. No point making this boy feel more guilty than he already knew himself to be. And, in any case, the speed with which Rougerie had moved to close down the case suggested other pressure would have been put on Lannes if he had seemed to be making progress.

So, now, he only asked Maurice if he could describe the men.

'It's difficult. I saw them only a moment as they brushed past me, and then I was embarrassed by what was said. And it was weeks ago now. The one who spoke Spanish was tall and thin, and the other, well, short, stocky, like a little bull, certainly French. He was smoking a cigarette – an English cigarette. I recognized the smell of Virginia tobacco because it's what my other grandfather – my mother's father – always smokes. It's a smell I associate with him and it pleases me. Is this any help?'

'It may be. You haven't spoken of this to anyone else.'

'No, certainly not.'

'Not even to Miriam?'

'No, nobody. As for the cigarette, I'd forgotten it till you asked me for a description. It's not much of one, I'm afraid. Of course ever since I keep thinking that if only I had gone back upstairs Gaston might still be alive. But then all I was thinking of was getting home and not being late at table and being spared my aunt's reproaches.'

'Understandable,' Lannes said. 'As for what you've told me, continue to keep it to yourself. This isn't a simple crime, that's about all I know. And if it's any comfort to you, though the case is officially closed, to my mind it remains open. You've helped a lot. And with regard to the other thing, please do write to Dominique. He'll be glad of your letter. The poor boy is bored. There's a lot of boredom in war, more boredom than anything else. Now you'd better get home before awkward questions are asked about your absence.'

'I'll say I went for a walk, and lost count of time. I often do that.'

Lannes watched him out of the door, found coins to pay for their drinks, heard the man in the striped-suit say, 'And then there are the pederasts. Paris is full of them, you know, and not only in the theatre. In politics too, I'm told, on good authority. If I had my way I'd string the lot of them up.'

His companion laughed. Lannes got up, said good-bye to the barman, and left for home.

## IX

*April 18, 1940*

'I'm new,' the concierge said, sniffing deeply. 'I know nothing about it. I moved in only last week, and the lodge has been unoccupied for months. The state it's in, you'd think it had been years.'

'Indeed,' Lannes said, 'our information is that there was no concierge.'

'And neither there was. My predecessor was in hospital since before Christmas last, her gall-bladder, they say. More like her liver, judging by the empties I've had to clear out. And now she's dead. So I can't help you, except to say that you seem to have made a mistake, for there's no one of that name among my tenants. Here's the list, see for yourself.'

Lannes put his finger on a name.

'Monsieur Biron, third floor, left, number 7, what can you tell me about him?'

The woman sniffed again, and leaned on the handle of the broom with which she had been sweeping the floor.

'Nothing, nothing at all, for the very good reason that I've seen neither hide nor hair of him. I assume he's away, certainly he hasn't made himself known to me, as he should, if he has any manners. Perhaps he's on the run from you gentlemen.'

'And the apartment opposite, Madame Robertet?'

'Her! She's at home, certainly. Thinks very well of herself, that one. A widow. Not one to give you more than the time of day, which she does as if conferring a favour.'

'I'll have a word with her. Meanwhile you will please give me the spare keys for number 7.'

'There's not going to be trouble, I hope. I was assured this was a respectable house. Not that I can be held responsible for anything, having just moved in.'

Maurice had spoken of Gaston having a room, but the little apartment consisted of a sitting-room, bedroom with double-bed, wardrobe and washstand, a tiny kitchen with a single gas-ring for cooking, and a WC. All was in a state of disorder, books pulled off the shelves and thrown to the floor, and the desk ransacked. The atmosphere was cold, dank and stuffy. The apartment smelled of stale tobacco smoke, unwashed clothes and dirty air. An empty wine bottle lay on its side on the table and the ashtrays were full. In the middle of the room there was a wooden chair with bits of rope tied round the legs and arms. The rope had been cut and hung loose. René drew Lanne's attention to a reddish-brown stain on the pale-coloured rug below the chair, and knelt down to sniff it.

'There's no doubt he was killed here,' Lannes said.

He picked up a scarf lying by the chair.

'They gagged him.'

'So they were searching for something. Maybe he was killed because he wouldn't talk,' René said. 'Or do you think they found it, whatever it was?'

'May have. The house in Bergerac hasn't been ransacked like this. But what on earth could Gaston have had sufficiently important to provoke all this? Nothing makes sense yet.'

A waste of time to speculate. In any case what he pictured was horrible. One moment talking about poetry with a nice-looking boy and making his little joke about graves, then minutes late, tied to a chair, terrified, tortured, murdered, and mutilated.

He would call in the technical boys to make a thorough examination – their boss, Argoud, was an old friend, wouldn't ask awkward questions about the propriety of working on a case that had been officially closed. A nod and a wink would be enough for Argoud, no great respecter of authority himself.

'We'll have a word with the lady opposite,' he said, 'before we're once again forbidden to pursue the investigation.'

'Why should we be, after what we've discovered.'

'Because there's a lot besides the murder itself I don't like.'

Madame Robertet was very small, very old, and very neat. She wore a black dress with a little nosegay of Parma violets pinned to its lapel. Her face was yellowish, wrinkled and looked soft as taffeta. In the room beyond a wireless was on.

'I was listening to the news,' she said. 'I don't know why because it speaks of things I'd rather not know. If it's Monsieur Biron you want he's across the landing. But he's not there, I haven't seen him for weeks now. He comes and goes, always very polite when we meet, and so kind when my cat strayed, spending hours hunting for him, and then the wicked fellow just trotted up the stairs and cried to be let in. Of course cats never show any sign of feeling guilty, do they?'

Lannes showed her a photograph of Gaston.

'This is Monsieur Biron?'

'Why certainly. He isn't a handsome fellow as you can see, but always the gentleman. I hope nothing has befallen him?'

'He seems to have disappeared.'

'But I expect he's in Paris.'

'In Paris? Why do you say that?'

'Because that's where his main residence is. Or so I have always understood.'

'Does he have many visitors?'

'Really, I wouldn't know. I'm not one to keep an eye on my neighbours. His students of course.'

'His students?'

'He's a historian, though without a post, as I understand. Did he say he had retired from the university? You must excuse me, my memory isn't what it used to be. But he does take a few students, I know that. Privately, that is, poor boys who haven't had the education they deserve. It's so kind of him. But that's his nature. When I was ill last year, he saw to the feeding of Abanazar. That's my cat. I call him Abanazar because he's a Persian, a Red Self, very beautiful but so naughty. And with a will of his own. Monsieur Biron is the only person besides myself whom he allows to pick him up. He's very particular. For instance, he doesn't at all approve of the new concierge. No, I'm sure you'll find Monsieur Biron is in Paris. I haven't been there myself since before the war, that's the last war, you understand.'

She sighed. In the background the news gave way to music, a military band.

'The students are all boys?'

'But certainly. It wouldn't be proper for Monsieur Biron to receive girls in his apartment, now, would it?'

Lannes said, 'We're interested in the evening of February 26 and in two men who called on Monsieur Biron then. Do you remember hearing anything unusual on that date.'

'I'm afraid that at my age one day is much like another. But why don't you ask Monsieur Biron himself?'

'Unfortunately that's proving difficult. Do you happen to have his address in Paris, Madame?'

'Good heavens, no. His address in Paris? What would I need that for? I haven't been in Paris since 1914 and that's a long time ago, even if at my age it sometimes seems like yesterday. How my dear mother used to love the Bon Marché, and what a thrill it was when their Christmas catalogue arrived. Do you know, I still have sheets of the Bon Marché linen, untouched in their original wrappings. I sometimes take them out of the cupboard, just to look at them and remember.'

As they left, René Martin said, 'Why didn't you tell her he's dead, chief.'

'Couldn't bring myself to do so, hadn't the heart. It's obvious the old lady knows nothing. Why distress her? It might have been interesting if she had had a Paris address for him, though I doubt if it exists.'

## X

*April 18, 1940*

'Today,' Fernand said, 'I recommend the hare, mountain hare, marinaded in red wine and juniper berries, very good, my grand-father's favourite dish, cooked according to his recipe. I have a good robust St Emilion, *cru bourgeois* to go with it. The hare demands a vigorous wine, none of your delicate creatures. Good? Eat well then. Who know what privations we shall suffer as the war advances?'

Outside Spring had retreated again. It was neither good nor bad, the sky grey, clouds unbroken, a chill wind. But the back room of the brasserie with its gilt and mirrors, its marble-topped tables and plush banquettes, was as ever reassuring, a safe place.

Moncerre's mood was sour as the wind. He had spent the morning questioning a young lout who had held up a jeweller's shop in the rue du Temple Beaubadat, and then lost his nerve when the shop assistant, returning from making a delivery, had shouted in alarm.

'The young idiot struck out, and it's lucky that the old man will survive. What a cretin – for three hours he protested his innocence and said he was the victim of a misidentification. He hadn't even been within a kilometre of the shop, didn't even know where it was, had been playing billiards with his mates, and so on. I kept at him and of course he cracked eventually and burst into tears. I'd send him to the army rather than prison, for we all know what he'll learn there. It depresses me. What's the use? I hope your morning has been more profitable, chief.'

Lannes forked a piece of the pickled herring that Fernand had brought for their first course, with a warm potato salad.

'Well,' he said, 'we've made progress. We know where Gaston was killed. We can even guess why – they wanted information from him. And it's probable they didn't get it. But I don't think I can get Rougerie to agree to re-opening the case.'

'You'll tell him you were acting on information received?'

'Certainly, but for the moment at least I want to keep the boy Maurice out of it.'

'You think he's reliable?'

'He'd no need to approach me and involve himself in the case.'

'He wasn't put up to it?'

'I don't think so. On the contrary I think he had to brace himself to speak to me. He's the nervous type.'

'A pity he took so long to brace himself, as you call it. And even now we know very little.'

'That's so. Argoud's technical boys may give us something, though I wouldn't bet on it. There won't be fingerprints, I'm sure – they were professionals. Nevertheless, it's moving. René, I'd like you to look up your Catalan friend again. See if he remembers anything more. One of his mates may be able to offer a better description of the man who smokes English cigarettes.'

The hare had been as fine as Fernand promised, the wine too, but Lannes was in low spirits as he left the brasserie. The murder had been nasty, and now that he was convinced the motive was political, that was nastier still. Every policeman knows that when politics enter a case, things are never straight. People lean on you, facts are concealed or twisted, and Lannes resented this. Moreover that morning Marguerite had been in tears after Alain and Clothilde left for school. When he put his arm round her, she shook her head, and, freeing herself from his embrace, said, 'I do so hate this war.' Which hasn't started, Lannes thought, not properly.

He couldn't face the office yet. So he turned around and made his way to the rue des Remparts, telling himself he should bring Henri up to date.

The bookshop was closed. Lannes rang the bell for the apartment. No answer. He had turned away when he heard his name called and saw Henri approaching with Toto on a lead. They shook hands. Henri unlocked the door.

'You've had lunch? Then we'll have some coffee and perhaps the merest spot of Johnnie. Miriam liked you. But I don't suppose it's business that you've come about.

'You had another session with Rougerie, I gather.'

'Oh yes, I've known him for years of course, since the days when I was a young aspiring advocate myself. A silly fellow I thought him then, like a cushion, you know, bears the imprint of the last person who's sat on him. And he hasn't improved. I didn't like what he had to say, but then, I don't know, do I really want the wretch, whoever he is, some silly young fellow who probably panicked and lost his head . . . I mean, what good will it do? Then I think of all the decent young men who are going to be killed in this war, and I ask myself whether a murder, even my brother's murder, is of any significance set against that. I'm sorry, Jean, I shouldn't speak to you of all people like this, when you are so anxious about Dominique. But the truth is I'm in a bad way. I can't sleep unless I stupefy myself with whisky. I wake up crying. It's grief of course, but also guilt, because I keep thinking of how we

71

were both unfit for the last war, your war, and were called cowards by some. I'm not making much sense, am I?'

He poured coffee and sank into a chair. Toto came and licked his dangling hand.

Lannes said, 'You were surprised when Rougerie said the case was being set aside?'

'Yes, naturally, and angry at first, but then . . . I've tried to explain to myself.'

Lannes felt a surge of pity for his old friend. He had lost weight in the last weeks. His flesh seemed to hang loose, and when he lifted his coffee-cup his hand trembled as if he had been overtaken by old age or had become the sort of drunkard who needs a couple of morning nips to cure him of 'the shakes'. And Lannes found himself thinking, 'After all I'm fortunate perhaps to have the sort of fear that my anxiety for the children provokes, whereas this poor Henri now has nothing but his little dog.'

He said, 'This visit is unofficial. Indeed I may be inviting a reprimand.'

'What do you mean? I never think of your visits as official, seeing we are such old friends.'

'Simply that, despite all instructions, I haven't abandoned the case, and I've come to tell you that I'm not all but certain Gaston wasn't killed for the reason we supposed.'

It's what had always disturbed him. He couldn't believe that a young man who had objected to demands Gaston might have been making would have mutilated him and moved the body. Hit him on the head, like the young idiot Moncerre had locked up that morning – that would have been more likely. But there was no need to say any of this to Henri.'

'I'm going to hurt you more,' he said. 'I'd like to ask you about what you know of the circumstances of Pilar's death.'

'But why? What has this to do with Gaston?'

Henri passed his soft white hands over his face as if to wipe away memory.

'I know nothing really,' he said. 'Beyond that she was determined to go to Madrid to serve the Republic and did not return. But why do you ask, why now?'

'Because Gaston was making inquiries about her, among the Spanish refugees and probably elsewhere. And I believe this was why he was murdered. Perhaps in seeking to find out what happened to Pilar, he was trying to repay you to some extent for all that you had done for him.'

'But that's terrible. It makes me in some manner responsible.'

'You mustn't think that,' Lannes said. 'We're none of us responsible for what others choose to do.'

'So you say, Jean, but you yourself assume responsibility for others.'

'If I do, it's on account of my job. It's my metier. Now, please, tell me more about Pilar. I hardly ever had a real conversation with her myself.'

This was because on each of their meetings, which hadn't been numerous, he had been aware of a reserve, even hostility, on her part, no doubt quite simply because she distrusted the French police. But there was no need to say that.

Henri said, 'I know now that I never really knew her. I loved her, but my love was ignorant.'

A nerve jumped in his cheek. He took a big red handkerchief from his pocket and dabbed his eyes. Lannes got up and crossed to the window to give his friend time to compose himself. It had started to rain and the dark sky seemed infinitely sad to him. The few pedestrians hurried by hidden under umbrellas. A large car of German manufacture nosed its way along the middle of the road. Henri blew his nose, loudly, and began to talk, his words tumbling over themselves and interrupted by long pauses.

Was it a mistake from the start? He had often asked himself that question in recent months. A mistake for her, he meant, not for him. She had brought light and movement into his life. He had never imagined that he could win such a woman, so beautiful, so vital.

'Look at me,' he said. 'I'm not made to be a great lover.'

Why had she accepted him, a fat man who passed his life among dusty old volumes and whose only previous experience of sex was with prostitutes?

'Perhaps she was looking for security?' Lannes said.

Henri shook his head. She wasn't made for security. She was a rebel by nature. Her father was an impoverished Castilian nobleman of the old school, the oldest school, proud and pious in the manner of the sixteenth century. Pilar's mother died young. The little girl was sent to be reared in a convent where the nuns totally neglected her education. Contempt for her father and hatred of the nuns were the result.

'Nevertheless that hatred was mingled with pity because these women were themselves victims of the backwardness and bigotry of Spain.'

She was a fierce anticlerical. She was modern. That was what she knew herself to be, and as soon as she could, she broke free. She came to France, to Bordeaux, to lead a modern life.

'Yes, even our reserved, secret, self-regarding Bordeaux seemed modern to her.'

She had a little money – Henri never knew the source. From her dead mother perhaps? They met when she came to his shop in search of Marxist literature. What he loved in her first was her Castilian pride which was perhaps more like her father's (whom he had never met) than she would have acknowledged. The pride which had led him to retreat from the world and regard it with disdain was transformed in Pilar into a conviction that it was her duty to change the world. As to how she had lived in her first months in France, Henri had never inquired. It was none of his business. And as to why she had married him . . . He shook his head in puzzlement.

To Lannes' mind it wasn't so mysterious. He could imagine this ardent young woman recognizing goodness and honesty in Henri and surrendering to these qualities.

1936: the year of the Popular Front in France and of Franco's war against the Republic. For Pilar one was light, the other darkness. Her world was a battlefield between good and evil. But she had been shocked and disgusted by the refusal of France to come to the aid of the Republic. She couldn't understand it.

Henri got heavily to his feet, stood as if bemused a moment, then padded through to his little kitchen and returned with a bottle of whisky, a soda siphon and two glasses.

'I know you prefer Armagnac, Jean, but Pilar drank whisky, and Johnnie Walker is the only one of her friends left to me.'

Naturally she couldn't stand aside from the conflict in Spain. Henri himself, sceptic in what he considered the true spirit of Aquitaine, which was Montaigne's, would have said 'a plague on both your houses'. But he had kept that thought to himself. Should he have tried to dissuade her from engaging in the struggle? As well command the Atlantic waves to stop rolling!

Lannes left Henri in tears and a little drunk. He didn't doubt that his friend would seek further consolation in the bottle, and find none. He couldn't blame him. What had most appalled Henri was discovering how little he had known the woman he loved, and that she appeared to have confided in Gaston and not in him.

'We can't be sure of that,' Lannes said; but really he was.


## XI


*April 23, 1940*

He had been half-expecting a summons from Rougerie, for days now, really . . . The language was polite – the little judge would never fail in formal courtesy. Nevertheless the underlining of the words 'as soon as is convenient for you' spoke of his impatience and, perhaps, anxiety. Lannes sent old Joseph through to the other wing of the Palais de Justice with the message that he would be with him in half an hour if this was, in its turn, convenient.

Meanwhile he rocked his chair back, balancing it on its hind legs, and smoked and tried to sort out what he knew.

It didn't amount to much. Gaston was as ignorant as Henri of Pilar's fate, he suspected, but his inquiries among the Spanish refugees suggested he knew more than his brother of her activities on behalf of the Republic. That was only supposition, reasonable nevertheless. On one occasion he had been accompanied by the Frenchman who smoked English cigarettes. But had they gone there together or had this fellow been spying on Gaston and following him? He was almost certainly one of the men who had brushed past Maurice in the doorway of the house in the rue Belle Etoile, and it was probable – though Lannes even in the privacy of

75

his mind shied away from the word 'certain' – that the two men had tied Gaston to the chair, interrogated him, tortured him, and murdered him before searching the place for something – a document presumably. As to its importance he could only guess: did it compromise them or whoever was employing them? Then they had mutilated the body to make it look like a sex-crime, and dumped it. What next? The murderers or, more probably, their employers – Lannes was sure they were agents acting on instructions – had leaned on Rougerie. So whoever they were working for was in a position of some influence, even authority. And if Rougerie was eager to see him now, then they were keeping tabs on him, knew of his visit to the rue Belle Etoile.

Lannes stubbed out his fifth cigarette and went to keep his appointment. The little judge was agitated. He had spilled snuff all over his waistcoat.

'I'm amazed,' he said, 'amazed and disappointed.' His voice had risen an octave on the second 'amazed'. 'I have always considered you reliable, which was why I selected you to deal with the delicate matter of the Comte de Grimaud's request. And now I find that you have been harassing his grandson, and, secondly, that you have been guilty of disobedience in continuing to pursue an investigation which I had commanded you to abandon.'

Lannes was surprised to find himself feeling sorry for the judge. Whoever had leaned had leaned hard.

'Harrassing the Count's grandson?'

'Indeed yes, I have received a complaint from the boy's father, Edmond de Grimaud, who is not only a political figure of some importance but the publisher and editor of an influential review. Moreover he tells me that he had specifically asked you not to question the young man. And what reason could you properly have had for doing so?'

'None at all,' Lannes said.

'In that case . . . '

Lannes was tempted to say nothing, to let the judge make the running. But the little man seemed so at a loss, taking more snuff and spilling it and spluttering, that he continued: 'I was asked if I had questioned the boy Maurice in connection with the anonymous letters sent to the Count, and said that I saw no need to do so. Then, leaving the house, I found myself pursued by the boy who wished to speak to me. We went to a café and talked for a little. I can't think why his father should suppose I had been interrogating him. It sounds to me as if the interrogation, if there was one, came from Monsieur de Grimaud himself.'

'And what was the subject of this conversation?'

Lannes said, 'He's an emotional young man, a poet they tell me, and apparently fond of his grandfather's wife. He wanted to know more about these letters. Their existence had aroused what I can only call his sense of chivalry. I tried to set his mind at rest.'

Would that serve? Lannes waited, his gaze fixed on a photograph of a former President of the Republic. Rougerie took a fountain-pen from his pocket and made a note. Then, still holding it poised above the paper, said, 'But why should the young man's father conclude that you had interrogated the boy?'

'Who knows? Perhaps it suited the boy to give his father that impression, for reasons I can't guess at.'

Again the judge made a note, hesitated, took snuff, and said, 'But to the more important matter. I am given to understand that, in defiance of my instructions, you continue to investigate the Chambolley case. Would you please explain this.'

Lannes pressed his head back so that his gaze was fixed on the ceiling and he could feel the muscles of his neck tighten. His silence irritated the little judge, he could sense that. Nevertheless he took his time.

'Please answer.'

The question was: how much did Rougerie have to know? What indeed was it wise to let him know? And how little could Lannes get away with saying?

'Police work,' he said, 'is messy, often a matter of scraps of information that lead nowhere. Informers are necessary, necessary evils, if you like, and certainly often of a type that a gentleman like yourself would scorn to have dealings with. You might call them scum, often with good reason. Nevertheless one can't, simply on account of their dubious character, safely ignore, set aside, the information they offer. Which is not however always reliable, is sometimes prompted by malice. One can't tell . . . '

He let his voice drift away and for a moment it must have seemed to the judge that this was all he was going to say in reply to his demand. Lannes was conscious of the little man's impatience. It went beyond the norm.

'Please come to the point.'

'The point?'

'I suppose there is a point to these remarks, that you are not simply being evasive.'

'Evasive?' Lannes made as if to consider the word. 'Evasive?' he said again.

'No, I wouldn't say that. As to the point, yes indeed, one of our informers – "snouts" we call them – laid information that led me to believe there might be a development in the case. It was by no means certain – as I say, such information is often worthless, no matter how inviting it may seem. Which is how it was in this instance.'

'What do you mean?'

'Simply that one was led to follow a false trail, a diversion, that led nowhere. In short, information was received which suggested that Gaston Chambolley had a lodging here in Bordeaux, rented a small apartment, no doubt for purposes of vice – that's to say, for what you naturally found disagreeable, unsavoury was your word, as I recall.'

The judge coughed. Lannes, conscious of how Rougerie had been embarrassed by what he had learned of Gaston's sexual proclivities, stretched out the silence again. Then he shifted his gaze to look the judge in the eye.

'One was obliged to follow this up. But it was, as I say, a false trail. The apartment in question was rented by quite another man. I spoke with the tenant of the apartment on the same floor, a most respectable old lady, a widow. She assured me that her neighbour lived in Paris and made only occasional visits to Bordeaux. He was a Monsieur – no, for the moment, the name escapes me, though I can of course supply it from my notes if you wish. The old lady spoke feelingly of his kindness and gentility, and affection for her cat. So there we were. It was nothing to trouble you with. Naturally, had it been otherwise, had we any firm evidence that the apartment had indeed been rented by Monsieur Chambolley, it would have been my duty to apprise you of this and perhaps to ask if you would consider re-opening the investigation. But as it is . . . as it is, we are no further forward. The case remains closed.'

Rougerie sniffed.

'It's clear that you have run up against a dead-end.'


'A dead-end name of Rougerie,' Moncerre said.

He took a big swig of beer and licked the foam from his lips.

'Yes,' he said, 'someone is buggering us about.'

'It's not the judge himself,' Lannes said.

'That old woman. Maybe young René will get something from his Catalan, but I wouldn't bank on it. We're stuck.'

'Maybe we're looking at this case from the wrong end,' Lannes said. 'Maybe we should be trying to find out what happened to Henri's wife – if she's dead – how she was killed and why. That was Gaston's question, wasn't it, and – an assumption – he may have been killed because someone thought he was getting close to an answer. Does that make sense?'

'It makes sense all right, but I don't see as it gets us any further forward.'

'Maybe not, but it's at least a new point of departure. We'll talk about it tomorrow. Meanwhile we have wives of our own to return to.'

Moncerre picked up his glass and drained it.

'I'll have another beer first. Till tomorrow.'

It wouldn't be only one beer. Moncerre was unhappily married. His wife resented and disliked police work. She would have preferred he had a job with regular hours, so that he had no excuse for not being home within half an hour of his office closing. Lannes sometimes thought that the difficult marriage made Moncerre a better policeman, and not only because he was prepared to work all hours rather than go home.

'I shouldn't have made that crack about wives to return to,' he thought.

He stopped at a flower-stall and bought a large bunch of mimosa for Marguerite. As he climbed the stairs he thought how terrible it must be to come unwillingly home. Marguerite opened the door for him as if she had been listening for his step. They kissed. She thrust her face into the mimosa.

'Lovely,' she said. 'There's a young man to see you, he says he's a friend of Dominique, and Alain and he have been chattering away as if each has discovered a twin soul. Clothilde's jealous.'

'No, I'm not, but they are rather rude to ignore me.'

'What are they talking about, poppet?'

'Oh, Literature, with a big "L". It's boring. They even like the same authors.'

Maurice got quickly to his feet when Lannes came in to the sitting-room. His face was flushed and he pushed away the lock of blond hair falling over his left eye.

'I hope you don't think it rude of me to have called on you without warning or invitation, but Madame Lannes has been so kind and it is a great pleasure to meet her and Alain and Clothilde.'

'Not at all,' Lannes said, aware that Clothilde had started to giggle, no doubt on account of Maurice's excessively formal manner. Though he spoke of course in French, Lannes was reminded by something in the way he held himself, both resolute and shy, that he had an English mother. Indeed he seemed like a young actor in one of these dreadful English comedies which leave you wondering if the young lovers have the faintest notion what to say or do when they are at last alone together . . . and as for bed . . .

'The truth is that I owe you an apology, superintendent, and I have also something to add to our previous conversation.'

'In that case, perhaps we should talk privately for a moment. Alain?'

The boy took the hint and went to join his mother and sister in the kitchen.

'An apology? For what?'

'Because I have been telling lies,' Maurice said. 'About that conversation. My father questioned me closely when I returned home, and I allowed him to understand that I had been asking you about these anonymous letters.'

'It seems as if it is your father to whom you should be apologising.'

'No, you see, it's because I allowed him to think that you had been grilling me. I didn't, you understand, want him to know that we had been talking about Gaston. And only partly because he disapproved of that friendship. You do understand, don't you.'

'Yes, I understand and of course I accept your apology.'

An apology that would have amused Lannes if the boy hadn't so evidently been nervous and anxious.

He lit a cigarette and pushed the packet towards Maurice who, as on the previous occasion, hesitated a moment before accepting it and lighting up himself.

And the information?'

Maurice hesitated, drew on the cigarette, and said, 'It may not amount to much, for really it's only my impression, and then too it's only come to me since I started thinking about that evening after we talked together. You understand?'

Lannes nodded. The boy resumed, speaking fast and in an undertone as if ashamed, or afraid, of his own words.

'That night Gaston was eager for me to go. Usually it wasn't like that. Quite the reverse. I've confessed to you that I knew he was in love with me, a bit in love anyway, though he never said so in so many words. So often when I was ready to leave him he would try to detain me, inventing reasons. For instance he would, suddenly as it were, think of some book he wanted to show me or some poem to read to me. Anything to prolong the conversation, keep me with him. But that night was different. He didn't try to stop me. It was almost as if he was eager for me to be gone, hurrying me out. And so, now, I think he was expecting these men to arrive and wanted to be rid of me before they did so. I don't know if this is of any significance, but I thought I should tell you, even if it's only, as I say, my impression, and one I wasn't obviously aware of at the time.'

An appointment, Lannes thought, it made sense. The man who smoked English cigarettes had perhaps promised to come with information about Pilar. That way he could be sure of finding Gaston at home. Yes, it made sense, but it didn't lead anywhere.

'Thank you for telling me,' he said, and added, 'it may indeed be useful,' principally to put Maurice at ease.

He stubbed out his cigarette.

'Is your father still in Bordeaux?'

'No, he's returned to Paris. He says he wants to be there when the Germans arrive. That's his idea of a joke, I think.'

'And have you eaten?'

'No, it's not important.'

'Then you must stay and have supper with us.'

'Will that not incommode Madame Lannes?'

'Not at all, since you're a friend of Dominique. And it's a casserole of some sort, so one more will make no difference.'

It was a sort of pity for the boy that had prompted his invitation. How did he pass the time in that dreary house in the rue d'Aviau?

Maurice had good manners. He spoke to Marguerite of Dominique with warmth and admiration. He paid attention to Clothilde, even though he blushed whenever he addressed her or she offered a reply. Over coffee Alain asked him if he had read a novel published the previous year – *La Nausée*. He answered enthusiastically. It was wonderful. They fell to discussing it. Clothilde joined in, speaking animatedly and with authority, though Lannes remembered that she had cast the book side saying it was boring and therefore stupid. Now she was full of admiration for it. This amused Lannes. He recalled picking up the book himself and quickly deciding it wasn't his sort of thing. As for Marguerite, she smiled and busied herself darning Alain's socks. She felt no need to engage in the conversation. It was enough for her to see the young people happy. 'As if there was no war, this evening at least,' Lannes thought. The black cat, originally a stray which Alain had found half-starved under a bridge, came and jumped up on the boy's knee. He stroked it, running his hand the length of its body which was now plump and well-fed, the coat glossy. It was a handsome cat with a very short neck. That was how Clothilde addressed it: 'No Neck'. But Alain called it Sylvestre, and at nights it slept on his pillow, sometimes across his chest. Lannes opened the window and leaned out. The evening smelled of rain. A tram-bell sounded from the Cours Victor-Hugo. He smoked contentedly and listened or half-listened to the young people. It didn't matter what they said. There was comfort in the soft music of their talk. Then the telephone rang.

## XII

*April 23, 1940. Late evening.*
It was young René Martin.

'Sorry to disturb you, chief, but it's not good.'

'Bad?

'Bad as could be. Can you come here?'

There was no need to say more. René gave him the address, in Meriadeck, a poor quarter, part Jewish, the rue Xantrailles, near the barracks. Lannes knew the district and liked it. An aunt had lived there when he was a boy.

He called a taxi, explained he had to go out, urgent. Sorry. No one asked why. Policemen's families know when not to. He kissed Marguerite and the twins, told them not to wait up, Lord knew how long he'd be, shook hands with Maurice, thanked him for coming, told him to keep in touch, hoped he would eat with them again. As he left to wait in the street for the taxi, he heard Alain say, 'But, seriously, it's impossible to believe in this war, and yet you can't deny its reality. We exist in freedom, but necessity holds us prisoner. Isn't that so, Maurice?'

Lannes didn't wait for the reply. Descending the stairs, he thought, 'Alain's right, we know we're free – that's what our consciousness tells us; yet we are caught up in a web of circumstances that deprives us of the freedom to act.'

The rue Xantrailles was a street of small two-storey and three-storey houses, dirty yellow in colour, the soft stone covered with a blanket of grime. He stopped the taxi at number 35, under a line of washing stretched out on a pole. The door was open and he went upstairs. There was the sound of dance music from a radio in the apartment to his left. He knocked on the door across the narrow landing, and heard a bolt being withdrawn.

René said, 'I haven't called anyone else. I thought you'd want to see it for yourself first. It's not pretty.'

He led the way through to the back room. The Catalan, Javier Cortazar, was stretched out on the bed. He lay on his back. There was a stink of vomit. His eyes were open but he saw nothing, would never see anything again.

'There's no sign of a wound, chief, but . . . look at his hands.'

He turned away as if he couldn't bring himself to look at them again. Lannes saw why. The nails of all ten fingers had been pulled out.

'He must have screamed. Surely. Anyone would,' René said, 'but I asked across the way and they didn't hear anything. They're French, a couple, middle-aged, respectable. But how do you think he died? Could that have killed him? It doesn't make sense.'

The boy's distress was evident. Not for the first time Lannes wondered if young René wasn't too sensitive to be a cop. He leaned over and closed Cortazar's eyes. Was it imagination or did they look as if they couldn't believe the horror? He found himself remembering the man's solidity, self-assurance, obstinacy and humour; he'd liked him.

'There's something else,' René said, and pointed to a high-backed wooden chair between the bed and the window. 'Ropes, just like in Gaston's apartment, which connects the two cases even more closely than they were already connected. They don't care much about leaving evidence, do they?'

'No, they don't.'

'It's as if they were laughing at us.'

Perhaps they were

'Go and call Paulhan, will you?

'There's no telephone here. I had to go out to a café on the corner to ring you.'

'Right. You know the doctor's number?'

Left alone, Lannes took stock of the apartment. It was his habit to try to fix everything in his mind, a mental photograph. But here it was too easy. There was little to note. The place was almost as bare as a monk's cell. A pair of socks drying on a rail below the window looked pathetic. The stink was vile; not only vomit but shit. He stretched up and opened the window.

'Poor bugger,' he muttered and thought again how much he had liked him.

There was a shelf of books, political mostly, in Spanish and Catalan. A copy of *Don Quixote*, a few French crime novels and also, he saw with a pang, that book of Sartre's which Alain and Maurice had been enthusing over. Alain had quoted something as 'a marvellous sentence'; 'as if there could be true stories; things happen one way and we tell them in the opposite sense'. It wasn't absurd, that observation. Every policeman knew the truth of it.

He opened the drawers of the chest that stood against the wall to the right of the bed. Shirts, socks, pants, a couple of shirts and jerseys, handkerchiefs. No papers. He went back to the other room: a half-eaten loaf of bread on the table and a sausage from which several slices had been cut, a litre of vin ordinaire, half-drunk, and a box of cheap Brazilian cigars. Beside it, a wireless. He turned it on and got a burst of static.

The drawer of the little desk to the left of the window had been pulled open and hung loose, empty. Any evidence of the Catalan's history and concerns was gone. And how much living in any case had he done in this apartment?

From across the street came a burst of music. Piaf, singing her song of love: 'Heaven and earth may crumble, but nothing matters if you love me.'

If only that was true.

René returned to say Dr Paulhan was on his way.

'Right,' Lannes said, 'when you got here . . . no, tell it from the start.'

'It's not difficult. I went first to the bar, as before. It's only a couple of streets away, in the rue de Madrid. Indeed it's called the Café de Madrid, no doubt why they chose to frequent it. But they said they hadn't seen him for a couple of days. That wasn't unusual. "He's a serious man," one said, "who spends his evenings reading and writing, not really one of your boozers." "And fucking, don't forget that," another said.'

René blushed because it wasn't a word he would have used himself and it even embarrassed him to repeat it.

'I think they didn't want to say more because they know now I'm a cop. But of course I had his address and so I came straight round here. The outer door was open and so to my surprise was the door of this apartment. It's as if whoever killed him didn't care how soon he was discovered, which is unusual, surely. I called out but got no answer, so came in and found, well, you know what I found. I didn't touch anything, just established that he was dead. Then I went to call you, shutting the door behind me of course. When I returned I spoke to the people across the way. As I said, they seem respectable, he's a clerk in the municipality, not the kind that ever gets promoted, I should say. Anyway it was his wife who did all the talking. She insisted they had heard nothing, which I find hard to believe. She kept saying "we keep ourselves to ourselves". My impression is that she disliked the Catalan simply because he was a foreigner.'

'I'll have a word with them myself, though I'll be surprised if I get anything more from them than you did. Call me when the doctor arrives. You've done well.'


The door was opened on a chain. Lannes showed his identification and was admitted by a scrawny woman, with her hair pulled back tightly into a bun. She wiped her hands on her skirt and led him into a small stuffy sitting-room. She turned down the wireless that stood on a table beside the chair where her husband sat. He had removed his collar and wore carpet slippers.

'We've made more complaints than I can number,' he said. 'As we told your young colleague we prefer to know nothing of our neighbours. It's better that way in our opinion. Nevertheless there are things you can't ignore.'

'That's enough of that, Benoit,' his wife said. 'It's up to this gentleman to ask questions and for us to answer them if we can. Which is unlikely, monsieur, for, as my husband says, we keep ourselves to ourselves. There's no law says you have to take notice of your neighbours, especially when they are foreigners.'

'Quite so,' Lannes said. 'How long has Senor Cortazar occupied the apartment across the way?'

'Too long, at least eighteen months too long, it's a scandal. There are decent French folk, my own sister's niece and her husband, for example, who would be happy to find such an apartment, but a foreigner gets it and my husband here, though he works in the town hall, can't do anything about it. It's a scandal and I don't care who hears me say so.'

'A Red too, not only a foreigner but a Red.'

'Don't interrupt, Benoit, though my husband is right all the same, superintendent – or is it commissaire – in drawing your attention to the man's politics. Why do we let such people into the country, that's what I'd like to know, Reds and Jews and other foreigners – the country's overrun with them. Why can't they stay where they belong, that's what I'd like to know. And if they're here we should shut them up in a camp. There: that's what I think.'

'Does your neighbour have many visitors?'

'Too many and, from the looks of them, people I would cross the street to avoid.'

'Women too,' her husband said.

'Sluts, that's what I would call them, sluts and prostitutes.'

'And this evening, did you see any visitors he might have had?'

'Certainly not! It's not as if I look out for them. Quite the contrary. We keep ourselves to ourselves. It's the best policy in the world today.'

'And did you hear any noise from his apartment this evening?'

'Nothing at all, not even a door banging, no shouting on the stairs as there often is. Besides we've been listening to the wireless. It's a cheap pleasure and one we can afford. But even if we'd heard anything, which we didn't, we would have paid no heed. There are things one doesn't choose to get mixed up in.'

'What do you mean by that? What sort of things?'

'Just what I say. I believe in minding my own business and so does my husband. Your young colleague tells us the Spaniard has been murdered. Good riddance, I say. We've been troubled by him and his likes long enough. Perhaps the apartment will now be let to a decent French person, my sister's niece, for instance, though I have to say her husband isn't all he might be.'

Lannes was happy to be interrupted by young René coming to say Dr Paulhan had arrived. He had no doubt that this disagreeable couple knew more than they were ready to admit, but was equally certain that they would insist they knew nothing even if he made it clear he was sure they were lying. He knew the type only too well.

Paulhan shook hands, muttered a greeting, without removing his Boyar cigarette from his mouth. It would dangle from the right corner of his lips while he examined the corpse. Indeed he chain-smoked even when performing an autopsy; it was a protection against infection he used to say.

'You've spoiled my evening's Bridge,' he said, 'but fortunately I was dummy when young Martin called. A contract of four hearts, doubled. I don't think my partner will have made it.'

He passed through to the bedroom and Lannes saw him lean over the body, blowing smoke from his nostrils. Then he told René to go and ask the tenants of the ground-floor apartments if they had seen or heard anything. He picked up the bottle of wine and found a couple of clean glasses. The wine was rough. His hip hurt. He felt immensely weary and it was hard to believe that only a couple of hours ago he had been happy as they sat at the dinner-table and he listened to the enthusiasm in the young people's voices. He drank the wine and poured himself another glass.

Paulhan came through from the bedroom.

'Give me a glass of that too, old man,' he said, and lit another cigarette from the tip of the one he had been smoking. 'Nasty business, but I may be about to disappoint you. I can't be sure till I've done my autopsy, but my impression is a heart-attack.'

'Brought on by torture?'

'Can't say, but it's a reasonable hypothesis. Does that count as murder? Not for me to decide. Get him round to me and I'll deal with him first thing in the morning.'

'Time of death? Any idea?'

'This evening, certainly. Four hours ago, maybe five, maybe six. Can't tell.'

'The couple across the landing claim to have heard nothing. Is that likely?'

'Shouldn't think so. I'd have screamed if they done that to me. He may not have. He looks as if he might have been a tough customer.'

'I think he was. He was probably gagged of course. Nevertheless I'm sure they are lying.'

'Can't surprise you, surely. This is rough stuff. Still . . . ' he picked up the bottle and poured himself another glass and one for Lannes. 'What we need, I'd say. Not a pretty sight through there. What word of your boy?'

'Dominique? He says he's bored.'

'That won't last, I'm afraid. Word is the English are pulling out of Narvik. It was on the wireless. That's Norway gone then. Won't be long before Hitler turns his attentions to us.'

'You think so?'

'Don't you?'

Lannes nodded and drank.

'We had worse pinard than this in the trenches,' he said.

'We'll win because we are stronger,' the doctor quoted the popular slogan. 'Wish I could believe that.'

'Quite.'

'Well, I'll be on my way. My partner needed a risky finesse to make that contract. I'm afraid I'll be out of pocket. Make sure chummy's ready for me first thing. As I say, I think it's a heart attack, but, all the same, poor sod. Does it ever strike you, Jean, as trivial that we fuss over a single death when the whole balloon is about to go up?'

'Often, but what else can we do? It's our duty, after all.'

'So it is. Here's your young man. We'll speak tomorrow. Don't take it to heart, Jean. It's one death and there are going to be tens of thousands, hundreds of thousands. Sorry, shouldn't have said that to you, in the circumstances.'

They listened to his steps descending the stairs. Lannes fingered the stubby glass. They heard the car door shut and the doctor drive away. A dog barked from across the street.

René said: 'On the ground floor left, there's only a young mother and her baby, her husband's at the Front. I'm afraid I woke her, she came to the door with a dressing-gown over her nightdress, very pale and tired. It seems that the baby's teething and she got no sleep last night. So now, because the baby – a little girl called Véronique – was quiet and indeed sleeping, she had gone to bed early. Well, actually, she said, she fell asleep in a chair, woke an hour ago and got ready for bed then. She thinks it was steps on the stair or the banging of the outer door that woke her, but didn't look out, and it was perhaps me that she heard. At any rate she's sure that if there had been any loud cries from above the baby would have woken up, and I must say that seems likely to me, not that I know anything about babies. On the right there's a couple, in their thirties, nice enough. He's not in the army because he's a cripple since falling off his motor-bike. He works in an office as an accounts clerk and she is a shop assistant in a draper's. I've got their work addresses, but I doubt if we need to check on them. They'd been out to the cinema and returned only half an hour ago. At the Olympia which he said "is a cut above our usual style – and our purse – but it's our wedding anniversary". They had something to eat on their way home in that big brasserie in the Place Toulouse-Lautrec. One of the waiters there is the woman's uncle. I've got his name too. So I don't think there can be any doubt about that. In any case I don't suppose we're regarding them as suspects. They say the Catalan was always polite, and the young woman with the baby, Madame Dourthe, says he always had a kind word for her and even gave the baby a soft toy, a blue cat apparently. "Poor man," she said, "his own family is destroyed." Incidentally the other couple – the Patinets – say that our friends across the landing are "a pair of bitches and she wears the trousers". But I haven't found out anything useful, I'm afraid, chief.'

'Patience,' Lannes said, as so often before, 'patience and time.'

He left René to arrange for the collection of the body and for sealing the apartment. Then he set off for home. There were no taxis and he had to walk. A mist had closed in and it began to rain.

## XIII

*April 24, 1940*
It often happens that a slack period is brought to an end by a day when everything seems to happen, events pile up on you, demands come from every side, and you scarcely know which way to turn. It was like that now and it didn't help that the rain had cleared away and it was a beautiful morning of Spring in full flower, with the candles aflame on the chestnut trees, a lightness in the air which

invited you to pass the hours idly, sitting outside a café in the Place des Victoires or Place Gambetta. That was impossible, and, worse, Lannes had a sour taste in his mouth which he blamed on that rough vin ordinaire; moreover his damned hip was aching, though it usually behaved itself in warm weather. Then, to cap it all, the *Sud-Ouest* made depressing reading. There could be no doubt about it; the English were on the run from Norway, a humiliating defeat threatening others to follow. He stopped off at the Rugby Bar in the rue de Cursol, adding a nip of armagnac to settle his stomach and, he hoped, dull the pain in his hip.

Moncerre was already in the inspectors' room. Lannes called him into his office and brought him up to date.

'I'll wait till I get Paulhan's report before I alert the Parquet,' he said. 'It looks as if it may be hard to prove murder. Meanwhile I'd like you to go over there and find out whatever you can. We haven't yet questioned anyone across the street. Then the couple I spoke to – what's their name? – Brune – you have a word with the woman. You may get more out of her than I did, which wouldn't be difficult.'

He didn't add: she's the same sort of woman as your wife, so you may know how to speak to her.

When Moncerre had left, Lannes thought: actually I'm by no means certain that Moncerre and his wife speak to each other at all now. Or rather, from what he says, she speaks plenty, nagging him from the minute he sets his foot over the door; but does he reply?

Young René came in looking eager. He might be the most junior of the inspectors, but clearly he thought of this new case as being peculiarly his preserve. Which to some extent it was. His face clouded when Lannes told him of the assignment he had given Moncerre, but brightened when Lannes went on to say, 'You're the only one who speaks Catalan. So I want you to go among them, find out as much about poor Cortazar as you can, see if he said anything which might give us a clue. If he's been worried. Anything, really.'

As René was about to leave, Lannes called him back.

'And be sure to inquire if there has been any further sign of our friend who smokes these English cigarettes. What did you say they're called?'

'Goldflake.'

'I'm sure he's our man. Somebody must have seen him.'

The telephone rang.

'Jean? Henri here. Something very strange has happened. I've just received a document, a disturbing one. Can you come round? Or would you rather I came to you?'

Certainly not; he didn't want Henri coming to the office.

'I'll come to you. I'm waiting for a report but it may not be in for some time.'

'So I can spare you half-an-hour.'

In any case he'd be glad to be out of the office. He looked up and was surprised to see René still hovering by the door.

'Yes?'

'I don't know if I've done right chief, or stepped out of line, but I've a mate who works in the municipality and I thought I'd ask him about that fellow Brune. As it happens, he works in the same office which is the department responsible for public works, and he says Brune is a real creep, he wouldn't believe a word he says. Of course it's only my friend's opinion, but I have to say he's a good mate.'

'I daresay he's right.'

'But he added that he's the sort that's careful never to step out of line, always covers his back, sucks up to the bosses, a toady or, as my mate put it more coarsely, an arse licker. I'll be off then.'

Lannes lit a cigarette and made ready to follow him. Then there was a knock at the door and old Joseph came in with a letter.

'This has just come by hand. I didn't see who delivered it, for I was out of my box for a moment, answering a call of nature, but it's marked urgent. What's urgent to one isn't necessarily urgent to another, we all know that. And what do you think of the news? Great, isn't it? If you ask me the English will rat on us as they've ratted on the Norwegians. That's always been their style.'

He hobbled away, grumbling under his breath, as was his habit. Lannes slit open the envelope. There was a single sheet of paper, which read:

Supperintendent Lannes, The Count told me to call you. It's important. Come to the rue d'Aviau at once. Marthe Descamps.

It was written with a scratchy nib so that the ink had flowed irregularly and it was the hand of someone unaccustomed to writing, though 'Supperintendent' was the only word spelled wrong. Should he go there before he called on Henri? The laconic message intrigued him. And Henri had spoken for a document which could surely wait. On the other hand he had sounded agitated. Finally the rue des Remparts was on his way to the Count's house. If you had asked him, he would have said that the old woman, Marthe, was probably illiterate.

The shop was shut. He rang the bell for the apartment. Henri let him in. As Lannes followed him upstairs he saw that his trousers now sagged behind.

'It's extraordinary,' Henri said, 'and disturbing. I've had a letter, a long letter, from Gaston. No, I haven't gone mad, Jean. I should have had it weeks ago, immediately after his death. That's what's marked on the envelope: "For my brother Henri, in the event of my death." '

'So why the delay.'

'It seems that he lodged it with a notary in Bergerac, who's been ill, away in the mountains convalescing, didn't learn of Gaston's death till he returned the day before yesterday. Shocked and full of apologies. So in this way I get a letter from beyond the grave. Horrible. I hope it may help you, but I have to say it makes me feel worse. Not about Gaston, but Pilar, how I let her down. Take it away, Jean, I don't want to watch you reading it.'

There was whisky on Henri's breath: ten 'clock in the morning. He's been weeping too, his cheeks were tear-stained.

'Will you be all right?'

Henri shrugged: 'Does it matter?'

'I'll call when I can, perhaps in the evening.'

But what condition would Henri be in by then?

He slipped the letter into his pocket. Temptation to stop off in a bar and read it was strong. But he held off. Yet his fingers itched for it as he crossed the Cours del'Intendance and made his way up the

Cours de Clemenceau and the Cours de Verdun towards the rue d'Aviau. It was hot now and women were wearing summer dresses for the first time that year.

The door was opened for him before he could ring the bell.

'You've taken your time,' Marthe said. 'He was dying when I sent for you. And now he's dead. I wanted to call the doctor, but he told me not to. I should have disobeyed him. I don't know why I didn't. It's not as if I haven't, often enough. But something held me back.'

He was sure she wasn't accustomed to speak like this.

'He just repeated, over and over again, "call that policeman" and now that you're here, I don't see what use you can be. He died in my arms, that's something.'

What had happened? The Count had fallen down the stairs; that was all. She'd found him lying there when she got up, no, not then, of course not, she'd been up for hours, there was always so much to do and no one to help her, not that she wanted the help of a lazy slut such as young girls were now, you understand, but when she went to bring him his chocolate, and there he was.

As she spoke she led him upstairs, along a corridor and opened the door of a bedroom. Lannes was surprised to see the Count laid out on the big Louis Quinze bed.

'I wasn't going to leave him lying there on the floor.'

It was no use to reprove her for interfering with what might be a crime scene. This was her idea of respect, what she owed to the man with whom for so many years she had snapped and argued, whom she had nagged but yet, he suspected, had loved in her own savage way more than any of his wives had.

The body looked very small, pitiably small, stretched out on the big bed. The Count wore a dressing-gown in faded red brocade silk, and under it a nightgown. His feet were bare and he looked like a very old little boy, corrupt and wizened but still a child. There was a bruise on his left temple where he had hit his head in falling.

Why had he insisted on Lannes being called?

'That's for you to find out.'

'Did he say anything else? Messages for his wife and any of the family?'

'As if he would!'

'What do you mean by that?'

'Work it out for yourself. You're the policeman.'

She was taking pleasure in witholding any information she might have, and yet she had summoned him as the Count demanded before even calling the doctor.

He had her assemble the family in the big salon that ran the whole width of the house on the first floor. It was furnished and decorated in Second Empire style, no doubt by the Count's grandmother. The high-ceilinged room with its floor-length mirrors in dark-gilded frames and its pseudo-historical paintings made Lannes uncomfortable. The two daughters he hadn't met sat side by side on a chaise-longue. Both wore black and one of them fingered a rosary. Madame Thibault de Polmont occupied a high-backed winged chair while the vicomte, Jean-Christophe, lolled on a sofa and busied himself with a gold toothpick. Maurice stood by the window, uncertain where to sit; he coloured when Lannes addressed him by name.

'This is impertinence. I don't understand it,' Madame Thibault de Polmont said, 'I'm not accustomed to being ordered about in this fashion.'

'Be quiet,' Marthe said, taking to their evident surprise a seat in the middle of the room. 'It's as your father instructed. Maurice, sit down, child, stop fidgeting, and listen to what has to be said. Get on with it, Mr Policeman.'

There was no doubt but that the old woman was in charge of proceedings, no doubt either than in a strange way she was enjoying herself. And yet Lannes would have wagered that she was the only one there feeling any real sorrow. As for what he had to say himself . . . well . . .

'Let me explain why I am here. It's by the Count's request, as Marthe has told you. He ordered her to call me, even as he lay dying.'

The two women on the chaise-longue – which was which? – simultaneously made the sign of the cross. The vicomte removed his toothpick and said, 'But it's ridiculous. There can be no question but that my poor father met with an accident. He's been unsteady on his feet for years, it's only a wonder, even a miracle, that it hasn't happened before now. So why should a policeman intrude into a house of mourning?'

Lannes repeated, 'I am here only at your father's request.'

'We have only Marthe's word for that.'

'And isn't my word good enough for you?' the old woman said.

'Perhaps you would tell me, monsieur,' Lannes said, 'when you last saw your father?'

'At dinner of course. When else? Nobody sees my father in the morning, except for Marthe. And, I suppose, his wife when she is here. On the rare occasions when she is here. So you see it couldn't have been anything but an accident unless you are going to accuse Marthe of pushing him downstairs. In which case she would hardly have summoned you, would she?'

'Where is Madame la Comtesse?'

'Who can tell? I assure you I have no interest in her movements.'

And with that he restored the toothpick to his mouth and closed his eyes.

'With her lover, I assume,' said Madame Thibault de Polmont.

'And he is?'

'How should I know?'

Lannes changed tack.

'As I think you all know, I came here first at the Count's invitation because he was disturbed by a series of anonymous letters he had received.'

'He wrote them himself. I told you that.'

'Indeed you did, madame, and you may be right. But if you are, then that suggests a new question. If his expressed reason for summoning me was spurious, what was his ulterior motive? Why was he so eager to draw my attention to this house and this family?'

Nobody answered. The vicomte continued to pick his teeth. Madame Thibault de Polmont emitted a little snort. Maurice shuffled his feet. The two spinsters looked blank, as if they hadn't understood a word Lannes had spoken. Then came a cackle from the old woman, Marthe.

'Oh he was a sly one. He knew there was something rotten about this lot.'

'Be quiet, Marthe,' Madame Thibault de Polmont snapped. 'How dare you speak like that? It's outrageous.'

'I speak as I please. Outrageous, am I? But I've worked for my living. I haven't sponged off an old man and robbed him blind.'

'That's enough, do you hear. More than enough. If you can't keep a civil tongue in your head and remember your place, you must leave the room.'

'I'll leave when I please, Amélie-Marie, and not a moment sooner.'

Lannes said, 'The police doctor will come to examine the body. I can't yet say whether an autopsy will be necessary. It's possible. And I'll send one of my inspectors round this afternoon to take statements from you, all of you. I would like to know your movements this morning. Please don't prevaricate with him. It simply wastes time, apart from arousing suspicion. He'll ask you questions about these letters too. I'm not satisfied with what I have been told about them.'

It was all something he could have done himself, there and then. But the truth was he couldn't wait to get out of the house. The two old girls on the chaise-longue might be all right, even if perhaps touched in the head, not really all there. But the other two disgusted him. He couldn't say precisely why, but that's how it was.

Out in the street, in the sunshine again, he wasn't surprised to hear footsteps behind him, and then to find Maurice at his elbow.

'You don't think much of us, do you?'

'What I think of your family is no great matter.'

'But you think it wasn't an accident, that someone pushed Grandpa down the stairs.'

'It's possible, but I have no opinion, one way or the other.'

'Because he told Marthe to fetch you? That's why, isn't it?'

'Again, I have no opinion.'

'But he might have wanted to say something about the letters, even if he knew he was dying, to confess that he had written them himself.'

'It's possible, again. Maurice, do you know where Miriam is?'

'You can't suspect her.'

'I haven't said I do.'

'Well, I don't know but I can tell you this. She's not with a lover. She doesn't have one. My aunt Amélie-Marie has always hated her. That's why she says such beastly things. She's an awful liar.'

'Yes,' Lannes said. 'That doesn't surprise me.'


## XIV

*April 24, 1940 (continued)*
Instead of returning to his office, Lannes settled himself at a table on the terrace of a café in the Place de la Comédie. The sunlight sparkled on the Corinthian columns of the theatre, and the atmosphere was animated, as if with the arrival of Spring it was possible to set aside all thoughts of the war. He ordered a beer to wash away the sour taste of that house in the rue d'Aviau, drank half the glass in one long welcome swallow, and took Henri's letter from his pocket and began to read.

Dear Henri, I've had too many secrets from you, my dear twin, and it has seemed better that way. Everyone who knows himself to be a failure has secrets, unless he has arrived at that miserable point where pride and self-respect have withered and died. There are friends whom I would be ashamed to introduce to you, and yet they are friends and some have been more than friends.

But there is one secret I have kept from you for a respectable reason.

It concerns Pilar.

There, that's broken the ice, and I can move forward.

I loved her, you know, with the strange sort of love that a man formed as I am may sometimes feel for a woman whom he recognizes as a dear sister.

She truly loved you, though you were never quite able to believe that, and thought you were the one who kissed while she only extended her cheek.

Yet I always sensed a timidity between you, perhaps because neither believed the other could fully understand.

Am I making sense? It's curious how you can ponder a letter or any piece of writing for a long time and then find yourself unable to say just what you mean. But then it seems to me that it was a comparable inability to speak frankly and freely which led Pilar to deceive you.

There. It is out.

I don't mean that she deceived you with another man, nor of course with a woman. She was virtuous, you can't doubt that. No it was with an idea that she cheated you.

You know that her sympathies were of the Left, and I think you approved that. Where indeed but on the Left can anyone of sensibility be today? But, to cause you less anxiety, she let you believe that when she planned to return to Spain her purposes were purely humanitarian.

In reality she was engaged in the desperate attempt to get arms to the Republic. Her own association was with the Anarchists. As you know, the Republicans have been a house divided. There has been a civil war within the civil war, and at the command of Moscow, the Communists have sought to destroy the Anarchists – and indeed the social democrats. Pilar was caught up in this internecine struggle and was betrayed. That was how she died: shot by the Fascists. But where she was taken and who precisely betrayed her, these are the questions to which I have been seeking answers.

My quest has taken me along strange paths. One of the Spanish refugees here, a Catalan, Anarchist, by name of Javier Cortazar, has been a great help. He lives in the rue Xantrailles, number 35, in Meriadeck. Seek him out if anything befalls me, which it will have done if you are reading this letter.

I learned from him that Pilar, at great risk to herself and with great courage had infiltrated, under orders, certain Right-wing circles in Paris. I don't know why she was required to do this.

But I have contacts there myself, if the connection is frayed. You will remember that I used to be friendly with the two sons of the Comte de Grimaud. I know that you disapprove of poor Jean-Christophe, doubtless with good reason. If I have remained in sympathy with him, it is because I understand what it is to be in the grip of a shameful obsession. As for Edmond, I used to write – long ago – for his review, though I haven't seen him for years because I find his political views detestable. But I approached Jean-Christophe and asked him to act as an inter-mediary, which, if reluctantly, for he is also on poor terms with Edmond, he consented to do.

I have as yet had no direct contact with Edmond.

However one evening when I was talking with Cortazar in a café frequented by the refugees (all of whom arrived in France before the trickle fleeing the Fascists became a flood and our authorities started to incarcerate the poor creatures in camps), I noticed a Frenchman on the fringe of our group. He accosted me as I left, introducing himself only by his Christian name, Marcel, and told me he was an associate of Edmond recently returned from Spain. He was in a position, he said, to be of some help.

I have seen him twice subsequently. And he has not as yet divulged any useful information. Instead he has questioned me closely about Pilar. But he assures me the secret lies not in Spain or in Bordeaux but in Paris, and promises that he will produce the evidence I am looking for.

He has gone to Paris and I have an appointment with him for when he returns in two days time. But I am suspicious and afraid. My fear is that he seeks such information as I have, rather than providing me with what I need. It is on account of my uncertainty that I am writing this letter – my uncertainty and the fear that is gripping me. G.

The writing deteriorated, straggling unevenly, in the last para-graphs.

Back in the office Lannes handed it to Moncerre, who read it, and said, 'I would guess he was drinking when he wrote it and drunk by the time he finished it. It doesn't tell us much, does it? If the poor sod knew anything, he didn't know its significance. So I don't see that it tells us anything.'

'I'm not so sure,' Lannes said. 'It connects this Marcel with Edmond de Grimaud. That's interesting. And it makes it clear that Cortazar knew a lot more than he was willing to share with us. Idiot.'

'Idiot, like you say. Have we had Paulhan's report on the Catalan?'

'Heart attack. Paulhan's certain. As to whether it was brought on by what he suffered, he can't say more than that it's probable. The heart was diseased, blood vessels blocked. He might have gone any time. Oh, and there's evidence, bruising round the mouth, that he was gagged, like Gaston. So it's just plausible that our friends across the way, the Brunes, really did hear nothing, because there was nothing terrible to hear.'

'Maybe not, but they're a right pair. I could cheerfully have throttled them both. They might be the three monkeys, except that when either of them speaks, something nasty dribbles out of the mouth. The minute I tried to put on pressure, he said, "I'll remind you that I work in the City Hall and am respected there, and have protection." He had the cheek to tell me not to overstep the mark or I'd be sorry. I'm certain one or other of them saw the Catalan's killers and could identify them. For one thing she's as inquisitive as a mongoose, for all her talk about keeping themselves to themselves. And they hated Cortazar and would certainly keep an eye open to see who visited him, if only in the hope that they could make something of it. But they're saying nothing and he's not the sort you can throw into a cell and thump till he speaks. Indeed I don't doubt but that he will already have complained about my way of questioning him. Makes me sick.'

Lannes himself disliked bullying witnesses, saw this as a weakness. It was sometimes necessary, the only way to get results. So he experienced self-reproach, even shame, when he left it to the likes of Moncerre. There's nothing honourable in relying on others to do the dirty work you dislike. He often wondered if, deep-down, Moncerre despised him for this weakness.

He set another inspector, Fattorini, a Niçois of Italian extraction, to take statements from the Grimaud family, choosing him because he had soft spaniel eyes, an inviting smile and gentle ingratiating manners. His reports were always reliable and well-written. He missed little. In this instance it seemed there was nothing to miss. All affirmed that they had not seen the Count since he retired to bed the previous evening. All were sure he had fallen. The two spinsters agreed with their brother that he had been unsteady on his legs for months now.

'What of Madame la Comtesse?'

'There's no mystery, it seems. She went yesterday afternoon to visit her father who keeps a bar and tabac off the Place Gambetta, as you know. It appears that he hasn't been well and yesterday took a turn for the worse. So she spent the night there – her mother's dead and there's only a woman who comes in to clean during the day. She returned to the rue d'Aviau towards noon to learn that her husband was dead. When I asked why she hadn't let anyone know she was staying at her father's, she smiled and said there was nobody who would care where she was, though, she added, "I've no doubt you were supplied with scandalous explanations of my absence." She doesn't care for them any more than they care for her, I'd say.'

'Did you have any difficulty?'

'Not a lot really. The two old girls were in tears and not making much sense. The boy Maurice looked as if he had been weeping too, for his eyes were red. He's a charmer, isn't he, which always makes one suspicious, but I think he really was distressed. He said it was partly because he had been afraid of his grandfather and never able to love him, and now felt guilty. That struck me as true, probably. Madame Thibault de Polmont made it clear she regarded my questions as impertinent, but she did say one thing that may be of interest: that her father had summoned you only to make mischief. "He couldn't even die like a respectable person," she said. As for the vicomte, who is now, I suppose, the Count, he made two complaints which contradicted each other: first, that I was intruding into a house of mourning – though I saw little sign of that – and second, that he would now be obliged to miss the race meeting at Le Bouscat on Sunday.'

'And the old woman, Marthe?'

'There's a one.' Fattorini smiled. 'She took me up to the third floor where all the rooms are bare. No furniture, no paintings, no carpets, no hangings, nothing. It seems that the Count has been keeping afloat for years now only by selling things. "There's no money left," she said, not without satisfaction. "They'll have to shift for themselves now. Monsieur Edmond won't cough up, whatever they think. If you ask me, he's broke himself. We'll have the bailiffs in, mark my words." She hates them, except for the boy and the two spinsters who are poor things in her opinion. "Fit only for a convent," she said, "and that's where they'll end up." I suppose it really was an accident, chief?'

'There's no good reason to think otherwise.'

But why did he send for me? Lannes was sure the Count had been devious; that was why he had called his attention to the family in the first place. The question occupied his mind, distracted him. That evening, over supper, he was scarcely aware of the conversation.

Later, when they were alone, Marguerite started crying.

'I do so hate this war and I'm afraid for Dominique and for what it will do to us.'

He kissed her, held her in his arms. There were no words of comfort that weren't lies. Later she fell asleep, restlessly. I'm sure he was pushed, he thought, but I doubt if it can be proved. And in any case, does it matter? Set against Marguerite's misery and the suffering that is to come, how can it matter? That fellow, 'Marcel' whoever he is, wherever he is, a killer, no doubt in my mind, but one who has protection. Unable to sleep, he eased himself out of bed and went to the kitchen to make coffee and wait for the dawn.

## XV

For three months the PJ had been without a commissaire, and Lannes had been doing what should be his boss's work as well as his own. Now came word of a new appointment, and it was necessary to have everything up-to-scratch before he arrived. Meanwhile Moncerre and young René had nothing worthwhile to report. Nobody would admit to having seen anyone entering the building where Cortazar had lived and been killed. 'We're banging our heads against a brick wall'; that was Moncerre's opinion.

It had turned hot. The pavement cafés were crowded and at lunchtime the public garden was full of young people eating their sandwiches stuffed with cheese or jambon de Bayonne, talking and flirting. For them the war was still far away.

In the gloomy mansion in the rue d'Aviau it was as if it didn't exist. Lannes apologised again for intruding on a house of mourning, and the old woman Marthe smiled sardonically. 'They're not mourning,' she said, 'they're afraid of what lies ahead of them.' Lannes explained that he would like to speak to the vicomte or rather, as he supposed, the new count. 'It's nothing related to his father's death, you may tell him, another matter altogether.' He would be glad if the Count would spare him a few minutes.

'I'll see that he does. He's got naught else to do,' she said, and showed Lannes into the study where he had twice met the old count and which still seemed redolent of his presence.

Naturally Jean-Christophe kept him waiting. He had his new dignity to think of. Lannes put his finger into the bird-cage and one of the canaries permitted him to scratch the back of its neck. He felt intolerably weary.

At last the door opened and Jean-Christophe appeared. He wore a black velvet smoking-jacket, a white ruffled shirt open at the neck, black and white checked trousers, and brown carpet slippers. His face was puffed and purple and he was sweating. Lannes again apologised for his intrusion and added that there was no indication his father's death had been anything but accidental.

'Well, I told you that,' Jean-Christophe said, and settled himself in the old man's chair.

How long had he looked forward to the day when he would be able to do that?

'It's another matter altogether.'

'Another matter? I can think of none that concerns you that may concern me.'

'You were a friend, I believe, of Gaston Chambolley?'

Jean-Christophe pursed his lips, but made no reply.

'You will know of course of his murder.'

'It was in the papers. I read what was there. A nasty business of course, but . . . yes, we were acquainted, "friends" is too strong, and it was not an acquaintance I had any interest in maintaining.'

'But you had dealings with him recently.'

'Not at all. Certainly not.'

'So I am misinformed?'

'Absolutely. Why should I have wished to renew our acquaintance. He had become disreputable, was received nowhere. He was known to be a degenerate, you see.'

Lannes took a copy of Gaston's letter from his pocket, and slowly unfolded it.

'I'm puzzled,' he said. 'You see, monsieur, I have here a letter which Gaston wrote to his brother in which he says that you promised to act as an intermediary between him and your brother Edmond in relation to investigations he was pursuing into the disappearance and probable death of his sister-in-law, Henri's wife; and yet you now tell me you have had no dealings with him recently. How do you explain this?'

Jean-Christophe shifted from one buttock to another.

'It's obvious. He was lying.'

'Someone is lying, certainly. But who? Policemen are accustomed to being told lies and so we develop a nose for what is true and for what isn't. Now I can see no reason why Gaston should have lied to his brother.'

'This is intolerable. It's persecution. And impertinence. May I remind you of who I am; a person not without influence in this city.'

Lannes smiled.

'Naturally, monsieur, you are at liberty to exert such influence as you may possess. But your own reputation is, apparently, not unblemished. Such things are taken into account. Did you in fact speak to Edmond?'

The sweat was now flowing on Jean-Christophe's face. He shifted again in his chair, as if he might be suffering from piles.

'You've no right to speak to me like this. In my own house too.'

'If you prefer, we could conduct this conversation in my office.'

'No, no. You're bullying me. I can't stand being bullied. I've got a weak heart.'

He began to snivel.

'They do things to you in police stations, horrible things.'

Lannes waited.

'All right then, I did speak to Edmond, which I don't often because . . . it's not my fault I am as I am. I suppose you despise me too.'

'I despise nobody. But there's been another death, you know. A friend of Gaston's, a Spaniard in whom he had confided. He was tortured before he died. What did your brother say?'

The vicomte, now the Count, moaned and placed his hand on his heart. Tears ran down his fat cheeks. Lannes crossed to the book-case, pressed the panel, took out the bottle of brandy and poured two glasses. He gave one to Jean-Christophe.

'Drink this and tell me. You'll feel better when you do.'

He swallowed the brandy in one gulp, and shivered.

'Edmond said to leave it to him and say nothing to anybody. How could I when I know nothing?'

'Tell me about Marcel.'

'I don't know who you mean. It's a common name.'

'Common enough,' Lannes said. 'Not so common to smoke English cigarettes as this Marcel does.'

'I don't know who you mean or what you're talking about.'

'Think about it,' Lannes said. 'I'm not surprised you're afraid. He's a dangerous man, a killer. But I think you know that already.'

'I don't know anything, I tell you. You're bullying me again. I'll make a complaint, report you.'

'Do that then. But speak to Edmond first. Speak to him about Marcel. Say I'm interested in him. At the moment, monsieur, you know too much and too little. You'll be safer when you have told me everything.'

'I can't. I mean, I don't know anything. Now please leave. You're upsetting me and I have a weak heart. Any strain is bad for me. Please go away and leave me in peace.'

'Speak to Edmond,' Lannes said again.

## XVI

*April 28, 1940*

Lannes accompanied Marguerite and Clothilde to morning Mass. He wasn't a believer himself, had indeed been reared as an anti-clerical, nevertheless now found himself grateful for his wife's faith. The Church of St Michel in the Place Canteloupe was packed. Prayers were said for 'our men at the Front', our gallant poilus. The priest made sacrifice the theme of his homily. Lannes thought of his war, of priests and ministers of religion on either side of the struggle invoking the blessing of God. But the Nazis didn't pray, did they – not to the Christian God? Lannes bowed his head and thought of Dominique who would himself perhaps at this very moment be kneeling in prayer. He took after his mother; Alain, the free-thinker who, when Marguerite wasn't present, would call the clergy 'croaking crows', after him. The war news was bad. There was no doubt now that the British had been well beaten in Norway. 'It'll be our turn next,' the refrain on so many lips.

Afterwards they went to a brasserie in the Place des Victoires – 'victories!' he thought. Alain joined them. They ate the last oysters of the season and fried sole, which Marguerite rarely cooked because, she said, the smell hung around the apartment. Clothilde had her first ice-cream of the year. They didn't talk about the war.

*April 29, 1940*

Lannes rose before six, sat drinking coffee in the kitchen, listened to the radio, found it intolerable, nevertheless felt Monday as a relief. He could bury himself in work, even if much that had piled up on his desk was of no real importance.

Before going to the office he made a detour to the café-tabac off the Place Gambetta. Miriam was behind the counter. She gave him his coffee, then a small glass of marc.

'On the house,' she said. 'Or does that count as a bribe? Did you come to speak to me? If so . . . '

She called on a slim dark girl of about sixteen, busy preparing sandwiches, to take charge of the bar, and she and Lannes retired to a table at the back of the little room.

'My niece, Esther,' she said, 'my younger sister's child, a good girl. But what a time to be a girl of that age!'

Lannes asked how her father was.

'Poorly, very weak, I think he's on his way out, though he may last for a bit. He's tough, you know, has had to be.'

'I'm sorry. You haven't been back to the rue d'Aviau?'

'No. Why should I? That part of my life's over. There's nothing for me there. I'll have to attend the funeral of course, but, after that, I'm finished with the lot of them. Good riddance, they'll say.'

She dropped two lumps of sugar into her milky coffee and said, 'It really was an accident, I suppose?'

'I've no reason to think otherwise. The old woman says there's no money left.'

'I wouldn't know, but she probably does. You may think me callous, but the fact is that I couldn't care less what becomes of them.'

She smiled. Lannes, again, felt her attraction.

'I've come home,' she said. 'Probably I should never have left. Almost twenty years of my life a sad mistake. Amusing, isn't it? What do you want of me?'

'I don't know,' Lannes said, 'not exactly. When you were a child, did you ever play a game called "Blind Man's Bluff"? Police work is like that, often. You grope about in the dark, touching things and trying to make sense of them. Why is Jean-Christophe afraid of his brother?'

'Because he is what he is and Edmond is what he is. Isn't that reason enough? Edmond has a tongue like a whip.'

'There's more to it than that, I think. Do you know a man called Marcel?'

'Lots of them, it's a common name.'

'This one smokes English cigarettes.'

'I'm sorry, I can't help you. We don't sell many of them here, you know. A dozen packets a week perhaps. You look tired and anxious.'

Lannes shook his head, sipped the marc which was fiery and invigorating.

'This Marcel?' she said. 'What about him?'

'He killed Gaston and another man, I'm sure of that. Him and a confederate who may be Spanish. That's all I know. There's no trace of him anywhere, but he's guilty, I've no doubt. I had hoped you might know who he is. Something else. Why did your husband want to draw our attention to the rue d'Aviau? Have you any idea?'

'None at all, but I'll tell you this. He was a wicked old thing, but in a strange way, he had a sense of honour. So, if there was something that made even him ashamed, well . . . I don't know if that's of any help.'

'I don't know. There are days when it seems nothing is.'

As for Marcel, Moncerre was probably right in thinking he was no longer in Bordeaux.

Back at the office René greeted him with the news that over the week-end the Spanish refugees had been rounded up and taken off to a camp.

'I talked to a couple of the gendarmes, but they weren't at all forthcoming. "Orders," they said. "Question of national security. Should have been done months ago." I don't myself know that it matters – to us, I mean – for I did manage to speak to some of them on Friday evening and got nothing useful. Another dead end, I'm afraid.'

There was a knock at the door. Old Joseph shuffled in.

'It's the new commissaire. He's arrived a day early. Very keen, you might say. It's not right, is it. He wants to see you, superintendent. "If it's convenient to you," he said. Don't know what he'd say if you replied it wasn't.'

'Right, Joseph, tell him I'll be with him in five minutes.'

'Have you anything for me?' René asked.

'You'd better write me a report of your conversations on Friday. Then we can file it and forget there ever was a dead man called Javier Cortazar.'

The new commissaire was behind a bare desk in the office that had been untenanted for months now. It had been suggested that Lannes, as acting head of the PJ, should move in there, but he had declined. He was glad of his refusal now. It might have looked as if he was expecting promotion to the job himself. Never likely; there were too many black marks against him for him to be promoted here in Bordeaux.

The new man got to his feet, came towards Lannes, and held out his hand.

'Gustave Schnyder,' he said, 'I've heard a lot about you, superintendent Lannes. So I have the advantage of you. You're a bit of a maverick, they say, which is presumably why you haven't got this job which you might think yours by rights.'

'I don't think anything,' Lannes said, 'and besides I knew they'd bring in someone from outside.'

Schnyder gestured to him to sit, himself crossed to the window and looked out.

'Smoke,' he said, 'by all means. I'm a cigar man myself.'

Lannes watched him. The new commissaire was solid, blond, fair-skinned, big-bottomed.

'It's always the same,' Schnyder said. 'Bring in someone who knows nothing about the place. I see from your file you were sounded out about promotion, as commissaire, to – where was it? – Nantes? Tours? But you weren't interested. Why was that? Because you thought you'd inherit here?'

Lannes drew on his cigarette and smiled, 'As you said, they always bring in an outsider. I would have been that outsider in Nantes. But I'm a Girondin. So is my wife. We have children in school.'

'So you're a contented man? Not ambitious?'

'Have you ever met a contented policeman?'

'Can't say I have. We're all fucked-up, one way or another. Come, we'll go to lunch. You can tell me what fucks you up and bring me up to date on your cases and the sort of crime we have to deal with here. Remember: I'm the outsider. I know nothing.'

'We'll go to Fernand's.'

In the back room, at the corner table, as usual, under the mural – bad mural of d'Artagnan defying the Cardinal, painted by Fernand's younger brother twenty years ago, now mercifully faded. Introductions made. Fernand suggested the carré d'agneau, with pâté de foie gras first.

'It's as good as you'll get in Strasbourg,' he said to Schnyder. 'A special occasion, your first lunch in Bordeaux? Then a bottle of Cheval Blanc '28. That'll be on the house, to honour your arrival. Besides, I'm eager to have my best wine drunk up, things being what they are like to be. What can't be drunk must be buried.'

'Pessimistic cove,' Schnyder said, 'but he's got me with that crack about Strasbourg. I'm an Alsatian which, as you will understand, puts me in an anomalous position just now. I was born a subject of the Kaiser. My elder brother was killed at Verdun – his name's on the wrong memorial. So what does that make me? A Frenchman, certainly, since I was sixteen. But before then? A German, unwilling one if you like.'

'A Rhinelander?' Lannes suggested.

'Undoubtedly.'

'A European?'

'Whatever that means. I have German cousins, you know. On the other hand my mother's father left Alsace and moved to Paris when the Germans annexed the province in 1871. Opened a brasserie across the square from the Gare de l'Est – another cousin runs it now. So this war makes no sense to me, or would make no sense if it was just against Germany. But that's not how it is this time. The Nazis are scum, crazy scum. I hope you agree.'

He cut himself a piece of the pâté.

'Good, very good. The boss – what d'you call him? – Fernand, is it? – was right, just as good as in Strasbourg. So?'

'I'm a Radical,' Lannes said.

'Which means you don't like the rich, don't like the Reds, and apart from that, have no politics. Right? I'm told you've a son at the Front.'

'My elder. And you?'

'No children, which has been a sorrow and is now a relief. A couple of years ago I'd have envied you. Not now. Tell me about Bordeaux because really I know nothing. I've never before now spent as much as a week south of the Loire. Are you Gascons all fire-eaters, as they say?'

What to reply? That the Bordelais, at least those belonging to the well-to-do classes, are no longer Gascons, on account of centuries of gentility and 'good breeding'? That Bordeaux is anti-Paris, complacent, pleased with itself, conscious of its moral superiority, yet jealous of the capital? That it was the first outpost or colony of the English empire, that it looks away from France, that . . . all these notions he had so often pondered suddenly seemed ridiculous, not capable anyway of being articulated.

So, instead, he said: 'You know about our Mayor, don't you, Marquet? He used to be a Socialist, now calls himself a National Socialist. He's a man who gets things done, pushes himself forward which is not the Bordelais way. Here, power has always preferred to operate behind the curtain. But we keep electing him, he's got the city sewn up. He built that monstrosity, the Union Hall, very Mussolini-style. He's a chum of Laval and if the war goes wrong, he'll have his snout deep in the trough, you can be sure of that.'

It was a relief to speak his mind about the Mayor, rash of course considering Schnyder's position and his ignorance of his views. He broke off. The commissaire was no longer listening. His gaze had slid away and was fixed on the woman sitting on a banquette on the other side of the room.

Ah, Lannes thought, I've got you now: womaniser.

'That's Adrienne Jauzion,' he said. 'She's the star of the Bordeaux theatre, and, yes I agree, she's very beautiful. She was a failure in Paris, too much the lady, they say, but she's adored here.'

'You know her then?'

'Me? A poor policeman? Certainly not, though a couple of years ago when she had some jewels stolen I was in charge of the case. So I could introduce you, except that the gentleman now joining her, the Comte de St-Hilaire, owns one of our finest vineyards and is reputed her lover, or perhaps protector.'

'Some other time then.' Schnyder clipped the end off a Havana cigar and lit it. 'Brandy, do you think? I've been doing my homework. You've had no success with this Chambolley case, I see.'

'I'm surprised the file was on your desk. The case has been closed. Officially.'

'And unofficially?'

'To my mind no murder case is ever closed until the murderer has been arrested.'

Schnyder nodded.

'I think we'll be able to work together,' he said. He glanced across the room to where Adrienne Jauzion was straightening the Comte de St-Hilaire's tie. 'I hadn't realized this was a fashionable restaurant.'

'It isn't. But it's an old one. Fernand's grandfather started his working-life as a footman in the St-Hilaire household. More than a footman, it's said, which is how he came to be set up with this place.'

'Interesting. My wife won't be joining me here by the way. We've separated. Have you a suspect in the Chambolley case which you are not investigating?'

'I know who did it. I don't know who he is or where he is to be found.'


## XVIII

*May 1, 1940*

The funeral was over. Lannes had not attended the service in the Cathedral, but waited for the cortège at the Cimitière de la Chartreuse, where the old count was to be interred in the family vault. It was a beautiful day of early summer. There had been a shower of rain around dawn and the new leaves on the trees still glistened in their bright green while shadows lay like freckles on the young grass. Only a couple of dozen men had accompanied the hearse drawn by black horses, their heads decorated with plumes. Maurice, very pale and looking absurdly young in a morning coat that was too small for him – the Count's perhaps? – it was certainly shabby enough – held his uncle Jean-Christophe by the arm, as if he might fall down if unsupported. Jean-Christophe's face was bloated and he stumbled as he made an uneasy way up the path to the vault. Drunk, Lannes thought, a couple of drinks short of being dead drunk. The ceremony was brief, even perfunctory, as if the dead man was an embarrassment to be shuffled off. When it was over Edmond detached himself from the group of mourners and approached Lannes.

'I'm surprised to see you here, superintendent.'

'A mark of respect, courtesy.'

'Only that?'

'What other reason could I have for being here?'

'What indeed? My father's death was an accident, not something to concern you. Isn't that so?'

'I've no cause to think otherwise.'

'Since you are here however, and since I must return to Paris this evening, I wonder if we might have a word before I go.'

'As you wish.'

'Good. I must attend to family matters first, but perhaps we might meet at, say, five o'clock at the Hotel Splendide. Would that suit? My train leaves at 8.30. The American Bar?'

Despite its name, the bar of the Splendide was a place of red plush, gilt mirrors in the style of the Belle Epoque. Lannes settled himself in a corner, ordered, as if in defiance of the ambience of the bar, a pastis, lit a cigarette. The chasseur said, 'I trust you are not intending to make an arrest, superintendent? As you know, we dislike awkwardness.'

He smiled to show that he understood Lannes, and was making, he hoped, a joke.

'Nothing of the sort, Pierre, I assure you.'

'Good. If there's anything else you want.'

'I'm quite content.'

Which was a lie, or at best a polite fiction.

Edmond was late. Lannes had smoked four cigarettes and ordered a second pastis before he arrived. He had changed into a double-breasted grey suit, but retained his black tie. He shook hands without apologies and ordered a bottle of champagne.

'Two glasses. You'll split it with me of course,' he said.

Lannes touched his own drink.

'I'm happy with this.'

Edmond said nothing more till the champagne was brought and, despite Lannes' refusal, two glasses had been poured. Then he clipped the end off a cigar, held the flame to it, drew on it, and said, 'I understand that, despite everything, you are still pursuing your investigation into the death of that wretched Monsieur Chambolley.'

'Certainly the murderer has not been identified, let alone arrested.'

Edmond blew out a big cloud of smoke, toyed a moment with his glass. Around them a babble of conversation as the bar approached its busiest hour.

'And yet you gave me to understand that the investigation had been abandoned, might be considered closed. Isn't that so?'

'At that time we had no leads.'

'And now you have?'

'As you like.'

'Is that why you subjected my unfortunate brother to your questioning? About a certain Marcel, he tells me.'

'Do you know the man?'

'I? How should I? I am as ignorant as my poor brother. But more curious, more inquisitive.'

Lannes was all at once weary of the fencing-bout. He thought of Gaston, so fat and jolly as a young man, so disreputable in middle age, now so dead; of Cortazar, for whom he had felt respect, even liking, also dead. He thought of the torture to which both had been subjected, and of the insult to Gaston in death. And he heard the tinny laughter of society ladies and their companions around him, and resented the air of superiority of this Edmond who had commanded his presence there.

He said: 'Monsieur, since you have discussed this matter with your brother, you know very well why I questioned him, which I did informally, out of respect for his recent bereavement, which of course is yours also. I know that Gaston sought your help in his search for his sister-in-law, or rather in his attempt to find out where and how she had been killed, and I would like to know what help you gave, and, more importantly, what interest you have in this affair.'

'But I gave no help, no help at all. This is what I wanted to say to you. Why should I, since I have neither knowledge of the affair nor any interest in it? It is true that I received a letter from Gaston Chambolley, an incoherent letter, but I'm afraid it went straight into that useful repository, the waste-paper basket. I had never heard of his sister-in-law and had no idea why he should have supposed I might know something concerning her. Subsequently – that is, since I learned that you had spoken to my son, which, if you recall, I had asked you not to do – I have indeed made some inquiries, which have yielded nothing. Except perhaps this: are you so sure that the woman is dead?'

'The evidence points that way. Is it to suggest that she may be alive that you asked me to meet you here?'

Edmond smiled, and poured himself another glass of wine.

'Not at all. The idea came to me only this instant.'

'Gaston is certainly dead,' Lannes said. 'So too is a Spaniard who was assisting him.'

'Of a heart-attack, I understand.'

'You are well-informed.'

'I make it my business to be. It's necessary for a man in my position. I do wish you would drink your wine, superintendent. It's really quite good. No, I asked you to meet me in the hope that I might persuade you to leave my family alone, to stop pestering them. They know nothing of the business you are investigating, and certainly nothing of this mysterious Marcel.'

'I note what you say: that none of you knows anything.'

Lannes downed his pastis, put his cigarettes in his pocket and got up.

'I've learned by the way that your son Maurice is a friend of my older boy, Dominique. He is now in the army, as you may also know, but Maurice and my other boy Alain seem to have hit it off too. He's a charming boy. I congratulate you. We hope to see much of him. And now I must be off.'

Edmond also got to his feet.

'My dear fellow, with a son at the Front, you have much to be anxious about. As for Maurice, it's my misfortune that, for a variety of reasons, I scarcely know him. I'll accompany you to the door.'

They stepped out into the late afternoon sunshine, shook hands.

Edmond said, 'How strange on a perfect evening like this to think that we are at war.'

He turned away.

Lannes didn't hear the shot. Once as a boy he had been kicked on the shoulder by a horse when he was picking out its hoof. That was just what it felt like now. He was thrown a yard back across the steps. There were people all round him, faces flickering before his eyes. Then he lost consciousness.

## XIX

*May 13, 1940*
Lannes had spent eight days in hospital, five recovering at home. He had been lucky, everyone was sure of that. It seemed that he had turned away just before the shot was fired. So it had hit him in the shoulder, not the heart. But he had developed a fever, which delayed recovery, his temperature one day touching 103 degrees.

Schnyder called on him in the ward. It was a murder attempt, no question, he said. The shot had been fired from a car, a little grey Renault. That was established.

It had driven off immediately. Maybe it had been driven off too soon, disturbing the gunman's aim. They couldn't tell. One witness said it was moving before Lannes hit the ground. The car had later been found abandoned on the Quai du Palutade, near the station. So it was presumed that the gunman and the driver had left Bordeaux straight away. Perhaps on the 8.30 Paris train. The car had been reported stolen, two hours after the shooting. That might mean nothing. Its owner claimed to have been at the cinema with his wife. There was no reason not to believe him; in any case he'd produced the stubs of the cinema tickets. He was a respectable man, name of Cortin, an official in the City Hall. 'A colleague of your brother-in-law actually, who vouches for his integrity. Shocked to find his car had been put to such a use, shocked and indignant.'

'And Edmond de Grimaud?'

'Acted efficiently. Gave orders for the ambulance. Made a statement to the first policemen on the scene. Apologised for being unable to remain – apparently on account of an urgent appointment at the Ministry of the Interior at 10 o'clock the following morning. But very correct. Telephoned me the next day to inquire about your condition. Repeated the call in the afternoon. Then suggested to me that the shot might have been intended for him. "We were standing side by side," he said, "having just shaken hands, and I won't conceal from you that I have political enemies who might be happy to see me dead, or at least out of the way for a time." That sound likely?'

'It's possible,' Lannes said. 'I don't know if he is as important as he thinks he is. On the other hand he was the only person who knew I was going to be at the Splendide.'

'I'd wondered about that.'

'Of course you had. And the Chambolley case touches him, even if it's not clear in what manner.'

'I'd thought of that too.'

Now today Lannes was on his feet for the first time, though still weak as a kitten, unable to do more than totter to an armchair in the sitting-room where he managed to take some of Marguerite's onion soup and drink Vichy water. Alain's cat, Sylvestre, sat on his lap and purred as Lannes stroked it, and listened to the wireless. Melancholy dance music alternated with grim news. It was three days since the Germans had launched their attack in the west, invading the Netherlands, Belgium, and Luxembourg. There were reports of heavy fighting in the Ardennes, but all was confusion. Then this morning a bulletin announced air attacks on French positions south of the Meuse. It was impossible to know just what was happening. Lannes studied a map, tried to make sense of the information coming through. It was all too incomplete.

In the afternoon, towards six o'clock, Moncerre telephoned to ask if the chief was well enough to receive a visitor. Marguerite would have liked to say no. Though she probably didn't admit it to herself, Lannes knew that it pleased her to have him convalescent and dependent. She liked the role of nurse. Even in ordinary times, it satisfied her to have him at home for a few days with flu or a stinking cold. Needing her care, away from his job which she accepted as necessity, the way of life she had joined herself to, but which in her heart she feared and found distasteful. It was absurd, he thought – as if he wasn't in reality always dependent on her! Without Marguerite, and the children too, he would surely have succumbed to the depression, the sense of hopelessness, the fear that all he did was ultimately pointless, which recurrently assailed him. But he had never found words to tell her this, and in truth the admission would have embarrassed them both.

And of course these weren't ordinary times; far from it. At least while he was confined to their apartment, she didn't have to bear her anxiety about Dominique in solitude. Even so, they hadn't dared to speak of their fears for him since the real war broke out. Only when he laid his hand on hers and pressed it as she put the bowl of soup on the tray across his knees did they come close to expressing their dread and their need for each other.

Now, perhaps because she saw a spark of light in his eye when he realised it was Moncerre on the telephone, she said, 'Well, it's the first day he has felt like smoking, so I think he would like a visit from you.'

Which was generous, even a sacrifice, on her part.

Moncerre himself was ill-at-ease, seeing his chief in this role, as a family man. No doubt it brought home to him how barren his own domestic life had become. But in any case he was a creature of cafés, bars and restaurants, most himself in public places where the only obligation was to pay your way.

'We've missed you, chief. To your speedy return,' he said, lifting the glass of pastis Marguerite had brought to him. 'I can see you're on the mend. Old Joseph sends his regards. So, naturally, does young René.'

René, like Moncerre, had visited him in hospital and seemed evidently distressed.

'Not that I've any good news for you. Schnyder has kept your case in his own hands. He seems keen, but I can tell he hasn't got anywhere. He intended to go to Paris to interview that Edmond de Grimaud, but it seems that's off, now that the balloon has gone up, and ordinary crime, even the shooting of a policeman, has to take a back seat. There were no useful fingerprints in the car, I can tell you that, and inquiries at the station have got us nowhere. It seems that the Paris train was packed and, if they left by it, well, who's to say who they were. We've no description. One witness says she saw the gunman leaning out of the car window, but his hat was pulled down over his eyes and he had a scarf tied over the lower part of his face. Perhaps. If you ask me, she may well have been watching too many gangster movies. Still, she's the only witness we have, even if, in my opinion, her evidence isn't worth a Jew's fart.'

Realizing what he had said, Moncerre looked embarrassed, in case Marguerite was within hearing, then quickly added, 'There's one thing though. We found half-a-dozen fag-ends in the car, and its owner doesn't smoke. What's more, they were Virginian tobacco, English we think, but we can't tell the brand because they were smoked from the other end. That speaks of a professional.'

'Not so professional to leave the stubs as evidence,' Lannes said.

'Careless, yes. Maybe they panicked.'

'Maybe. At least you've given me something to think about.'

Which was a relief, or a distraction from his more pressing anxiety.

'As to other matters,' Moncerre said, 'there's no progress. Since it's certain that Cortazar died of a heart attack, we're supposed to shrug our shoulders and forget it. In any case what does the death of one Spanish Red matter. Schnyder says he's not pleased, but I don't know. I can't work him out. He seems keen and was certainly cut up and angry when he learned of the attempt on your life. But you know me, chief, I don't take anything at face value. And of course your Grimaud case is judged to be no case at all. Actually I took it on myself to annul your order to have the telephone in the rue d'Aviau tapped, since it had produced nothing of interest. I can tell you however that the Countess hasn't returned there. She's moved out for good. I called on her yesterday. Some woman, I have to say! She asked after you, shocked to hear of the shooting, hoped it wasn't connected with what you had talked to her about.'

'Which it must be,' Lannes said.

'To sum up, chief, we're stuck, in the dark, properly fucked.'

Lannes looked beyond him out of the window at the sky which was still deep-blue, not yet flecked with gold. Swifts and swallows flashed across it, then came the drone of an aeroplane. What sort of planes were flying over Dominique? In his last letter, which Lannes had read in hospital, the boy had spoken of lying in a field and listening to the larks high above him. 'It's strange how birdsong makes me happy, yet I'm filled with foreboding at the same time. It's the fear that I will be proved lacking in courage.'

'Tell him,' Lannes had said to Marguerite, 'that every soldier shares that fear. I certainly did.'

He turned his attention back to Moncerre.

'In the dark, sure. But properly fucked? I don't know. That someone chose to take a pot at me is surely an encouraging sign.'

That same evening Alain and Maurice were in the Café des Arts, Cours Victor Hugo, drinking lemonade. The elderly waiter with the flat feet that are evidence of long years in that employment, said, 'So it's started. No more Phoney War. It won't be long before they come for you lads. No, it won't.'

'He likes that idea,' Alain said. 'You've no need to be embarrassed, it's not your fault you have asthma.'

'Sometimes I think it is. A moral weakness. Psychosomatic, developed to keep me out of the war.'

'That's bosh.'

'Is it? It makes awfully good sense to me. How's your father?'

'Recovering. He says he's had worse wounds, and more painful ones. I think that's showing-off, gasconading. He looks ten years older.'

'It was terrible,' Maurice said, 'and he was with my father, which seems strange to me, and then my father hurried off to Paris without even waiting to see if yours would survive.'

'Oh there was no question of him dying. It takes more than a single shot from a toy gun to kill a Gascon. Do you know, Maurice, I was against this war, called myself a pacifist, said I certainly wasn't going to die for Danzig. But now I don't know. Everything's different. What does your father think? He must hear things in Paris. Since we met I've read two back-numbers of his review in the library, and he's clearly well-informed.'

'Oh he never speaks to me about public affairs. He still regards me as a child. I think he despises me.'

'But that's ridiculous. In any case it's our fathers' generation has let us in for this war. So he has no right to despise you.'

'So you say, but, if he doesn't despise me, he dislikes me. I think he sees my mother in me.'

Alain didn't immediately know what to reply. Maurice was the first person he had known whose parents were divorced. Then he said, 'Is that so bad?'

'Terrible, from his point of view.'

At which they both laughed. Maurice laid his hand on Alain's.

'I'm so glad we've met. I feel we can talk about anything, that I can say whatever I think, and you'll understand.'

'Me too.'

Alain freed his hand, lit a Gauloise and pushed the packet over to Maurice. It was true. They could speak about anything and everything: philosophy, poetry, novels, films, politics, even their own feelings. They were at that stage in life when the perfect friend seems as necessary as desirable. They laughed at the same things, the sillier the better, and now, when Maurice frowned and said, 'No, really, it's because of my resemblance to my mother that he dislikes me,' both were seized with a fit of the giggles.

Then Maurice stopped, abruptly, bit his lip so hard that the blood seemed to flee from it.

'But how can we laugh like this, after today's news, and when you must all be so worried about Dominique.'

'Of course we are, but the news doesn't forbid us from laughing. In any case it's only the first phase of a battle, and surely we shall counter-attack.'

## XX

*May 20, 1940*

Paulhan had passed him fit for duty, reluctantly. 'You really should take at least another week off,' he said, 'but I can see you're fretting.' Marguerite realized this too, therefore, self-denying, acquiesced. Lannes kissed her good-bye, wondering if he should tell her about the dream he had struggled to recapture when he woke. The setting was unclear, a field somewhere, under a fine blue sky. Dominique appeared, walking out of a beech wood. He said, 'You've got the wound that was intended for me.' He sat beside him a long time in silence. It had been strangely comforting, and Lannes woke feeling good. But Marguerite might interpret it differently. So he said nothing.

Mounds of paperwork awaited him. He buried himself in it. The administration must be carried on, sacred tenet of the Republic. So he sat and smoked and read, annotated and initialed: futile activity like that of the bluebottle buzzing infuriatingly round the lampshade. It could not occupy his whole mind, distract him from the war news which was terrible and alarming. The Germans had turned away from Paris, marching along the line of the Somme to encircle the French and their British allies to the north; these were now trapped between the Wehrmacht and the sea. There were reports of refugees streaming south. It's a debacle, he thought, it has the makings of a debacle. It's not 1914, but 1870. Still, the hardest fighting seemed well to the west of Alsace where Dominique was stationed.

There was a knock at the door. Young René Martin entered.

'It's good to see you back, chief. But are you sure you're sufficiently recovered?'

René, like Moncerre, had visited him at home, in his case simply out of courtesy or concern, with nothing to report. When he left, Marguerite said, 'That's a very nice boy,' and Lannes saw Clothilde flush.

'Commissaire Schnyder told me to inform you he has gone to Paris, by the overnight train. He has managed to make an appointment to see Edmond de Grimaud, though he added, "That's if he keeps it." It must be strange to be in Paris now, but they say we're about to counter-attack. That's what everyone says and the word is that it's to launch the counter-attack that General Weygand has taken over.'

Weygand, disciple of Marshal Foch, organizer of victory in 1918 and apostle of attack, had been recalled from commanding the French Army in the Levant, and appointed yesterday as commander-in-chief in place of General Gamelin who was so fat he had to be helped in and out of his staff-car.

Lannes got up from his desk, and, opening the door, asked Joseph to have them send up two coffees from the bar below.

'There's nothing we can do about the war, we can only wait,' he said.

'It's difficult to get on with our normal work all the same,' René said. 'However I've had a word with Cortin – that's the name of the chap who owns the grey Renault, you remember. He's a little man, fiftyish, bald as a coot, and jumpy in manner, with very bright eyes. He was certainly on edge and indignant too. He kept saying, "It's not my fault if my car is stolen. If the police were doing their job properly that wouldn't happen." I pointed out that preventing that sort of crime wasn't the responsibility of the PJ, which made him even more indignant, so much so that I almost laughed. He insists he hadn't left his keys in the car, would never do a thing like that. Which is of course beside the point – it's not difficult to start a car without keys if you know how. But the thing is, the more I questioned him, the more I began to suspect that he knows more than he will admit, that indeed his car may not have been stolen at all. I think you should have a word with him yourself, chief, if you're up to it.'

The waiter from the Bar des Mousquetaires brought in the coffees. Lannes took a bottle of Armagnac from his desk drawer and added a shot to each cup.

'Interesting,' he said. 'I trust your judgement in such matters.'

René might be inexperienced, but he was sensitive and alert to what might lie behind the responses of those he was questioning.

'You've done well, Lannes said. 'Arrange for him to be brought here. Not today. Call him now and make the appointment for tomorrow morning, Make it sound a formality, but leave him in just a little doubt if you can. Let him sweat on it overnight. 9 o'clock tomorrow and make it clear, if he demurs, that's while it's only a request, I'm very eager to speak to him and suppose he would prefer that I don't call on him at the City Hall.'

'Sure, chief, I've got it. Softly, softly, but . . . '

Late in the afternoon he left the office and made for the rue des Remparts. Henri had visited him in hospital, and also at home; but on the first occasion Lannes had not been up to conversation, and then in the rue des Cordeliers with Marguerite present they had spoken first of Dominique and then of the past.

Crossing the Place Rohan he encountered his brother-in-law. Albert was agitated. 'The news is awful, we're done for, betrayed. It's the fault of the Jews and the Communists, no one can doubt it . . . Still at least the Marshal has now been brought into the Government . . . to stabilise things, to secure an honourable peace, it's our last hope. I've heard the Mayor say so. It's a disaster but he believes we can recover.'

Was there a note of unholy satisfaction behind the excited, disjointed speech? Lannes had no reply to offer. Others, he knew, were muttering 'remember the Marne', recalling how in 1914 the Germans had been driven back by General Joffre when almost within sight of Paris, troops ferried to the Front in the city's taxis. A miracle, they had said then, a veritable miracle. But one to be repeated? We're not the people we were then, he thought. That war exhausted us for generations. He said something about an appointment, and left Albert. It was a long time since he had stopped pretending that his brother-in-law didn't disgust him.

It was a golden afternoon. A soft breeze from the river scarcely ruffled the leaves. The café terraces were thronged. Little children rolled hoops in the square. Jackdaws chattered and squabbled around the cathedral.

Henri was busy with a customer. Lannes browsed the shelves till he had completed his transaction and left.

'So people are buying books even now?'

'We have to pretend that life remains normal, and after all the war is hundreds of miles away to the north. Come upstairs and have a drink.

Henri left his assistant, a retired schoolmaster called Bloch to mind the shop.

'Close when it suits you.'

He poured whiskies, added a splash of soda to each, handed Lannes a glass.

'Bloch speaks of making plans to leave. I can't blame him. He has a cousin, other relatives too, I think, in Oran. I suppose it may be safer there for Jews if . . . if it comes to the worst. How are you, Jean? You still look pale and a bit fragile.'

'I'm all right, as right as anyone is these days.'

'Indeed yes. War disturbs the natural course of life. Revolution destroys it.'

'Revolution?'

'There must be one surely. Of the Left or of the Right. Who can tell which? The Communards or Napoleon? Not that I see a possible Napoleon.'

'Is that what you think?'

'Some of the time. But, in reality, like everyone else, I don't know what to think.'

Lannes stretched out in his chair. He had, over the years, spent many hours at this time of day here in companionship with Henri, almost his oldest friend, and he had come this afternoon in the hope of lightening the load of apprehension that weighed him down. But it was no good and his brief conversation with Albert had depressed him further. He repeated it in answer to Henri's speculations, adding, 'He's a fool of course, with no mind of his own. So I suppose he's only repeating what those about Marquet are saying.'

'Pétain? He's eighty-four, must be that. Who ever heard of an octogenarian saviour? I speak of a Napoleon and you offer me Pétain. It's ridiculous.'

'I served under him at Verdun. He did well there, pulled us through.'

Henri picked up the bottle, as if to wish away memories of his generation's war in which he had not served.

'Have a drop more Johnnie for comfort's sake. You remember what Napoleon said? "After thirty-five a man is no good for war." Any news of Dominique?'

'Nothing for days. I suppose all mail deliveries from the Front have been suspended.'

'I feel for you both, I really do. If prayers were any good.'

'Marguerite prays. I can't.'

For a little they sat in silence, smoking and sipping their drinks as if it was an ordinary evening of an ordinary early summer.

Henri said, 'I had a visit from your new boss, the Alsatian. It came as a surprise. He said he wanted to assure me that no matter what orders came from above, Gaston wouldn't be forgotten. "There's no time-limit on murder," he said. I know of course, Jean, that you look at it like that, partly out of friendship, but this chap. What do you make of him? Or shouldn't I ask?'

'I think he sees himself as a man who goes his own way. At the same time my shooting has stirred him up. He disapproves of guns being fired at policemen.'

'Naturally enough.'

'Oh yes.'

Henri said, 'Well, I was pleased to hear him say so, even if I fear he may be prevented from acting on his words. But there's something I didn't mention to him, chose not to indeed. I'd a visit last week from a young man who said he was a friend of Gaston. I wasn't welcoming at first – you can guess why. But he was persistent, he wanted to know who was in charge of the case. When I told him it has been abandoned, or suspended, he said, "That's awful, I should have come forward sooner, but you can understand why I didn't." He's actually quite a respectable young man, a clerk in the Banque des Pyrenees, it seems. But whether he knows anything useful, that's another matter.'

'He gave you no indication?'

'None, and I didn't ask. But I said I would see what I could do. He lives with his mother – as I say, all quite respectable despite . . . '

'Then I imagine he'd rather I didn't call on him at home or at the bank. I suppose you can get a message to him? So tell him to be in the Buffet de la Gare at seven o'clock tomorrow evening. That's anonymous enough. I'm interested because as you will understand, I'm ready to catch at any straw.'

As he made his way home, he thought, I should have mentioned the possibility Edmond aired: that Pilar may not be dead. But I didn't dare, I'm a moral coward.

## XXI

*May 21, 1940*

Cortin was early, already seated on the wooden bench in the corridor outside the inspectors' office when Lannes arrived. Nevertheless he let him wait a bit longer. He had woken with a blinding headache which three aspirin hadn't yet dispelled. Also he felt stiff and old. It had been an impulse to have René call Cortin in, and he didn't expect to get anything useful from him. Was it in fact because Cortin was a colleague of his brother-in-law that he had chosen to question him?

When at last he admitted him, the little man's indignation had reached a high pitch. It was intolerable that he had been kept waiting. Didn't the superintendent realize that he was himself of some importance, an official with essential work to do. In case the superintendent didn't know, he must tell him that he was not the least valued member of the Mayor's cabinet.

'Stop it,' Lannes said. 'It doesn't impress me in the least. We are both public officials, servants of the Republic, and it's your duty to assist me in my inquiries. Do you know a man called Brune?'

'Brune?'

'Employed in the department of public works, I understand.'

'Oh, that Brune, certainly. But what is this all about? I understood that you asked to see me on account of my car, which was stolen. I don't understand what Brune has to do with it. You can't suspect him of being the thief. He's a most respectable man and a diligent official.'

'We'll come to your car later. I wanted your opinion of Brune. He's a witness to a crime, you see. Only he's proving difficult, what we call a reluctant witness. That's to say, he refuses to tell us what he knows. Which is an offence, withholding relevant information from the police. I'm close to requesting that he be arrested and held as a material witness. That's within my powers, you understand, whether he's a diligent official or not.'

Lannes got up from his desk, crossed to the window and lit a cigarette. He stood there smoking, his back to Cortin, for some minutes, and was aware of uneasiness behind him.

'You understand what I'm saying. It's the duty of the citizen to co-operate with the police in the investigation of a crime.'

He resumed his seat.

'You reported your car stolen. What time was that?'

'When we returned from the cinema. We live in the suburbs, in Chiquet, and, because we have no garage, I park my car in a little cul-de-sac round the corner from our house. We travelled by bus, because I don't like leaving the car unattended in the city centre. It's our first car, you see, and naturally I am careful of it. Well, on our return, I recalled that I had left some papers in the car. So I went to retrieve them, only to discover it wasn't there. I was alarmed of course, and telephoned at once to report it stolen. I telephoned from the café in the Place de la Rotonde because we have no telephone at home. There will be a record of the precise time of the call, I assume.'

'No doubt, no doubt, Monsieur Cortin, but it's very odd.'

'Odd?' Cortin said, 'it's outrageous, that's what it is, outrageous that the police can't protect private property.'

'You misunderstand me. What I find odd is the nature or circumstances of the crime which I am investigating, which is not the temporary theft of a car, but the attempted assassination of a policeman. Odd that the criminals should have gone to the trouble of stealing a car in Chiquet rather than in the city centre. You see my point? Your version of events is unsatisfactory. It makes me wonder if your car was indeed stolen, if perhaps it was borrowed with your knowledge. In which case of course you will be able to supply me with the name of the man or men to whom you lent it. Which is why I spoke to you first of your colleague Brune, and the possible consequences of a refusal to assist the police in their inquiries. Do I make myself clear?'

The little man pushed his chair back and stood up.

'This is intolerable,' he said, squeaking in his indignation. 'Are you accusing me – a public official, an important member of the Mayor's cabinet – of being an accessory to an attempted murder – if that's what it was? I don't have to listen to you. On the contrary, I have every intention of lodging a complaint. Yes, that's what I'll do, lodge a complaint. You have no right to speak to me as you have, superintendent. Be assured, you haven't heard the last of this.'

He paused, as if waiting for an apology. Lannes however merely smiled and said, 'As you wish. I look forward to receiving official notification of your complaint. It will give my colleagues the opportunity, and the authority, to investigate you thoroughly.'

This time Cortin made no reply, but turned and left the room.

Lannes lit another cigarette and called for young René.

'You're right. There's something fishy about that one. Find out what you can about him, family, acquaintances and so on. I don't believe his car was stolen at all. We may at last be on the point of a breakthrough.'

Lannes turned on the wireless. There was a report that the British had re-taken Arras, then another that this was the beginning of the promised counter-attack. Meanwhile General Weygand was meeting the King of the Belgians, to stiffen his army's resistance, and form plans to take the Germans in the flank. 'Morale is high,' the announcer declared. 'General Weygand's assumption of command has instilled a spirit of optimism.' But other reports spoke of refugees still streaming south. Lannes wondered how Schnyder was faring with Edmond de Grimaud. He wished he could remember clearly whether Edmond had indeed detained him outside the hotel. He couldn't believe the suggestion that the shot had been aimed at Edmond rather than himself. That made no sense.

The Buffet de la Gare was crowded. A number of rail-employees in blue overalls were at the bar drinking beer or pastis. A couple of whores, both approaching middle-age, sat at a table, with glasses of white wine before them, while they waited, no doubt, for the train from Paris. Lannes knew them both by sight; he had come on them often in the waiting-room at headquarters. Half a dozen men were playing cards, and at another table two businessmen were talking, rapidly, earnestly, with gestures.

He recognized one of them as a Jew called Simon, proprietor of a tannery. He looked anxious – well, he had reason enough, Lannes supposed. Then he spotted what must be the boy, at a table in the corner. He was reading a book and twisting a lock of dark hair round and round the index finger of his left hand. Lannes approached, pulled out a chair, and sat down.

'You're expecting me, I think.'

'I am?'

'Superintendent Lannes, and you're Gaston's young friend, yes?'

'If you say so.'

The boy placed his book face-down on the table – it was a volume of Balzac, and he was half-way through. He was a pretty boy, slightly built, with a soft unformed face, olive complexion and dark-brown eyes.

'I was surprised to get the message. Monsieur Chambolley told me the case had been abandoned.'

'Set aside, let's say. But I gather you have something to tell me.'

'Have I? I don't know. I'm not the sort that has much reason to trust the police.'

'I understand that, but what I take you to mean doesn't concern me. You're not a minor, are you?'

'No, I'm eighteen, I'm waiting my call-up. The way things are it looks like that may never happen. What do you think?'

Lannes spread his hands as if to say that the answer to the question was beyond him. He was struck by the boy's air of self-possession.

'My name's Léon. Do you want me to tell you about me and Gaston?'

'Only in so far as it might be relevant. You work in a bank. That's correct?'

'Certainly, and that's where I first met him. He came to my counter to ask about getting foreign currency, which is not something I deal with as it happens. He said he was planning to go to Spain.'

'When was this?'

'I can't say exactly. Sometime last autumn, October perhaps, after war broke out anyway. I remember that because my first impression was that he was intending to get out, escape the war. But I could see he was interested in me, liked the look of me. You can always tell. So it wasn't exactly a surprise that, when I went out for lunch, there he was in the street. He pretended to be surprised to see me, which I knew he wasn't, and invited me to accompany him to a brasserie. That's how it started. I liked him, you know. He was interesting and he made me laugh. It wasn't just, you know what, though there was that too. I'm not ashamed to admit it. Perhaps you think I should be?'

For the first time he looked Lannes in the face, and smiled. Defiantly? Mockingly? Lannes wasn't sure.

'That's no business of mine,' he said, 'I've no opinion on the matter,' though in truth the idea of Gaston in bed with the boy disgusted him.

The waiter came over and Lannes ordered two beers – 'If that's all right with you?'

'Fine,' Léon said. 'Are you sure you really are a policeman. You don't seem like one.'

'We come in different shapes. Go on.'

'He was lonely, you know, and not very happy. I found him sympathetic. He was really interested in me, not just for you know what. For example, he got me reading. Balzac' – he tapped the book – 'I'd never read anything like that before. Now I can't stop, it's wonderful. Then I discovered that he knew my aunt.'

'That didn't embarrass you?'

'Well, it did at first, but I was sure he wouldn't make anything of it. Though I'm equally sure it wouldn't have mattered. She's a countess by the way, though she's my mother's sister, and we're not rich, my mother works as an assistant in a dress shop in the rue Château d'Eau, which is convenient because my grandfather keeps a tabac in the rue Toulouse-Lautrec, just behind the Place Gambetta.'

'So you're Jewish.'

'I'm not ashamed of that either.'

'Why should you be?'

'You know my grandfather then?'

'Your aunt Miriam anyway.'

'He doesn't know about me, what I am. In any case he's ill, very ill, dying I think. As for my mother, nor does she and she'd be shocked, I think. But Aunt Miriam does, or at least suspects, though of course we've never talked about it. I just know she does. This isn't what I expected to talk to you about. As for being Jewish, yes, certainly, seeing that my mother is, but we don't practise, don't attend the synagogue, and besides, my father, who died six years ago, was a Gascon of the Gascons, as he used to say, and also, as it happens, a Protestant. There: now you know my family history.'

The waiter brought two glasses of beer. The boy took a swig and licked the foam off his upper lip.

'It's quite fun, you know, leading a double life, being one thing at home and in the bank, and another elsewhere. Besides, I was good for Gaston. I stopped him cruising the bars and picking up sailors. I think he really loved me, a bit anyway.'

It was probably true, Lannes thought, and, as for the boy himself, he gave the impression of having at least had a liking for Gaston, couldn't be more than that, surely.

'Is it true he was mutilated?'

'Who told you that?'

'One of my mates. Only the other night. It made me shiver all over and then I was sick. That's really why I went to speak to his brother. But is it true? It wasn't in the papers.'

Lannes hesitated. There were tears in the boy's eyes and a tremble in his voice. He deserved the truth.

'That's horrible, that's really vile.'

'Yes,' Lannes said, 'horrible. I wonder how your mate heard of it.'

Something that should be followed up, though it was probably scarcely worthwhile to do so. These things always get out and are noised abroad. It was surprising, really, that this boy, this Léon, hadn't got to hear of it sooner – and his reaction to Lannes' confirmation of the report suggested that he wasn't lying when he said he had learned of it only recently from his friend.

The train from Paris was announced. The two prostitutes got up, smoothed their dresses and went out towards the platform. The businessman Lannes didn't recognize shook hands with the pro- prietor of the tannery, tucked his briefcase under his arm, and left the buffet. Lannes wondered if Schnyder was on the train; no, too soon surely, unless, arriving in Paris, he had found that Edmond has skipped their meeting. Even if he had, would Schnyder have turned round straightaway?

He said, 'I'm sorry I couldn't say it wasn't like that. Now, do you feel you can tell me just why you wanted to see me?'

Léon took a cigarette from the packet of maize-paper Gitanes that lay on the table by his book, tapped it on his thumb-nail before lighting it with a wax match.

'I don't know that I know anything of value,' he said. 'I may be wasting your time. But thinking about it, well, it seemed strange to me. Do you have any suspects?'

'I can't answer that,' Lannes said.

The boy rolled his cigarette round between his thumb and first two fingers.

'All right then,' he said. 'It didn't seem significant at the time. It's only since that I've wondered. It was one night we were in a café in the Cours du Marne – it's called La Chope aux Capucines – I'm sure you know it. Gaston liked it because it was quiet and dark in the evenings, if you sat at the back which was what he preferred. He'd been in Bordeaux for a couple of days and he was leaving later by the last train to Bergerac. We'd spent the evening together – I don't need to tell you about that – and we were both relaxed and at ease. You could say we were happy. We'd come to eat something and drink a glass of wine. As I remember, not that it's important, he had only an omelette, a cheese omelette, I think, and I had andouillettes and frites – you can see I'm not a good Jew, I don't mind eating pork products. Then it sounds silly, melodramatic, but he went as white as a sheet and started sweating. Then he said we must change places so that he was sitting with his back to the door. Obviously there was someone he didn't want to be seen by, in company with me, I thought at first, which rather annoyed me, but then I saw that he was scared, not embarrassed. He lost his appetite, just picked at his omelette when it arrived, and ordered a large brandy. I resumed our conversation about Balzac, but he wasn't listening. Instead he said, "That couple at the table in the window, they're still there, are they?" Well, then I looked at them for the first time and I recognized one of them.'

Lannes had curbed his impatience while the boy spoke. He knew how it was often necessary to let a witness tell the story in his own way, however rambling that might be; and, besides, the details contributed to his picture of Gaston in the last weeks or days of his life, out of his depth, alarmed by the darkness into which his search for the truth about Pilar was leading him.

'Yes?' he said again.

'I've never met him,' Léon said, 'but he's a vicomte and, what's more, he's my aunt's stepson, which is absurd because he's at least fifteen years older than she is. She's got no time for him, and, from what she says, he couldn't frighten anyone. Nasty but feeble and as much spirit as a wet dishcloth, that's her opinion. So it must have been the other man, his companion who gave Gaston the shivers.'

'Can you describe him?'

'Well, you'll understand that I didn't care to look too closely at him in case this attracted his attention and he recognized Gaston who obviously wanted to avoid him. So all I can say is that he was short and stocky and his hair was light-coloured, not blond, but sort of fairish, cut short, I think. What did strike me is that he was wearing a heavy overcoat, even though, as you may know, la Chope aux Capucins is kept very warm.'

'You'd never seen him before?'

'No, certainly not. Nor since of course.'

'But you'd recognize him if you saw him again?'

'I'm pretty sure I would, because Gaston asked me more than once if they were looking at us. So I had to check to see. We sat on till it seemed as if Gaston would miss his train, but then they left and in fact there was plenty of time for us to walk to the station, which is after all only ten minutes away. Nevertheless Gaston got the barman to call a taxi – in case the men were out in the street still, and, when it arrived, he pretended to be lame, so that the driver wouldn't make a fuss about being called for such a short journey. And he insisted I accompany him to the station and see him safely on to the train, which of course I was quite happy to do. He was still agitated. He didn't even embrace me before getting on to the train. And that was the last time I saw him. I don't know if this is of any use to you. It's not much, I realize. Only I thought you should know that Gaston really did seem to be frightened by the sight of this man, though all he said when I asked him was that he'd had an embarrassing encounter with him years ago. I knew that was a lie.'

'You were right to tell me,' Lannes said, 'and please get in touch with me if you ever see him again. But be careful. Don't approach him. You see, I rather think you are one of the few people who can identify your friend's killer.'

Should he add that one of the others who might have done so was now dead himself, after being tortured? No, he'd surely said enough. Meanwhile he promised himself the pleasure of another word with Jean-Christophe who had denied all knowledge of the man Lannes knew as Marcel.


## XXII

*May 22–29, 1940*
Schnyder was still in Paris. He wired to say he might be detained there several days by matters too complicated to explain except in person. He did not say whether Edmond de Grimaud had kept his appointment.

The mood everywhere was edgy. Even Moncerre, the bull-terrier, relaxed his grip.

'Frankly, chief,' he said, 'finding out who killed that poor sod doesn't seem of much importance compared to the war news. Of course we'll keep at it because that's our job, but, all the same, nobody just now gives a fuck whether we catch murderers or not.'

Lannes received a summons from the Prefect, who was, ultimately, in charge of the PJ in Bordeaux. He had had few dealings with him in the three years he had been in place, but believed him to be a good man as well as a conscientious official. Moreover he was a man of the moderate Left which seemed to Lannes now the only honourable place to be.

The Prefect managed a smile as Lannes entered his office, but it was a nervous half-hearted one, and began filling his pipe. Then he had difficulty in lighting it. His desk was in disorder, files scattered over it, and some of them spilled on to the floor.

'I've had a complaint from the Mayor's office,' he said. 'That you've been harassing one of his staff, a fellow called . . . ' He searched among the papers for the one that would give him the name he had forgotten.

'Cortin,' Lannes said.

'Apparently he's engaged in work of national importance.'

Quotation marks were audible round the last words.

'He's concealing information about a crime,' Lannes said.

'Nevertheless you're to lay off.'

'Is that an order, sir?'

'Let's say it's a request with only one possible answer. I don't like it myself. But that's how things are today. Besides, and I say this, you understand, with some reluctance, because I respect you and your work as an officer, but if things turn out as I fear they are likely to, then I must advise you to consider your position. Do you understand me?'

'Only too well. You mean that pursuing this inquiry will do me some damage if the war turns out worse than it is even now, and there's a change of government, even perhaps of regime.'

'Precisely. It's not something I look forward to either,' the Prefect said, 'and I have to add that in that eventuality I'm not likely to be here myself. You would then be in a very exposed position.'

Lannes left the Prefecture ashamed. He accepted the logic of what had been said, and resented, even despised, himself for doing so. He had intended to go home for lunch, but telephoned Marguerite to say he was detained at the office. In fact there was nothing but paperwork that seemed more meaningless every day to keep him there, and lying to his wife intensified his feeling of shame and general worthlessness. He would have liked to get drunk, but instead walked across the city in the direction of the docks and, when he entered a brasserie with which he wasn't familiar, restricted himself to a single beer and ate a badly overcooked steak.

It was a beautiful afternoon, the sun high in an intensely blue sky, and, if you were ignorant of the news, nothing in the streets and squares would have suggested that the war was going badly. The café tables were thronged and waiters were busy bringing ices and citron pressés, tea and cream cakes to women showing off their summer frocks and wearing, many of them, extravagant straw hats to shield their delicate complexions from the sun.

For three days his morose mood prevailed. He spoke little even at home where however he exerted himself to try to maintain a pretence of normality and to support Marguerite whose nervous depression expressed itself in long silences and bouts of weeping. At the office he buried himself in paperwork, and told young René there was nothing else to do, he might as well go and have a couple of beers with his mates.

On the 26th came news that the British were withdrawing to the Channel ports, preparatory to evacuation.

'The buggers are on the run,' Moncerre said. 'They've let us down. Well, it's not the first time the goddam English have betrayed their allies.'

Schnyder at last returned from Paris on the 28th. His face was grey, there were bags under his eyes and his suit was crumpled.

'I've come straight from the train,' he said, 'it was packed, like sardines in a tin, and I got no sleep. They're nervous as kittens up there. Everything's going wrong, they're preparing for the worst, and yet, you know, people are still drinking cocktails and champagne in the bars on the Champs Elysées. It's unreal. At the Quai des Orfèvres half of them are busy destroying dossiers.'

The Quai des Orfèvres was the headquarters of the PJ in Paris.

'Did you manage to see Edmond de Grimaud?'

'More than once. That was what detained me, apart from arranging for my almost ex-wife to go to her parents in Dijon.'

'And?'

Schnyder sighed, sat down heavily, felt for his cigar case, and holding an unlit cigar between his fingers, said, 'Well he still insists that the shot must have been intended for him and that you got in the way. He asked why anyone should wish to shoot a conscientious officer like yourself. More than once by the way he told me how impressed he was by your "integrity" – his word.'

'He's a liar,' Lannes said.

'No doubt, no doubt. "In my position," he said, "it's natural I have enemies – the Reds, the Jews" and so on ad nauseam. Do you think he exaggerates his importance?'

'I've no idea,' Lannes said.

'However, he arranged a meeting for me at the Deuxième Bureau. Well, like most of us in the PJ, I distrust the spooks, but naturally I went along. Naturally too the officer I saw went by the name of Dupont – it would be less insulting to give no name at all. But he obligingly gave me a look at a dossier on Madame Pilar Chambolley, according to which she had been identified as an agent of the Comintern. "We don't know," Monsieur so-called Dupont said, "what has become of her. She crossed into Spain for the last time we know of in the summer of last year and there has been no trace of her since. She may be dead shot by the Anarchists with whom she associated in order to betray them. She may be in one of Franco's prisons. She may have been spirited away by her masters in the Soviet Union. We only know France is well rid of her." How does that sound?'

'If she worked for the Comintern,' Lannes said, 'then everything she told her husband Henri, and Gaston, was a lie. I find that hard to believe.'

'But possible?'

'What isn't possible these days? And of course if she was a Comintern agent, her whole life would be a lie, I grant that. I just find it hard to believe.'

Schnyder drew on his cigar, his brow furrowed. The fingers of his left hand beat a little tattoo on the desk. He got up and began to walk about the room. He stopped behind Lannes and put his hands on the superintendent's shoulders, pressing down hard. Then he relaxed his grip and crossed over to the window.

'The spooks are all liars,' he said. 'Nevertheless, according to friend Dupont, she was a known associate of two men, Andre Labarthe, an engineer in the Air Ministry and Communist sympathiser, and Louis Dolivet, reputedly the most important Comintern agent in France. She frequented a club, the Cercle des Nations, in the rue Casimir-Perrier, which had been established by Dolivet. Part of their business was smuggling planes and guns to the Reds in Spain, the guns passing through Bordeaux in a manner facilitated by a customs official and trade union activist called Cusin. Do you know of him?'

'Cusin? Yes, he was a figure here in Bordeaux for some years, a labour organizer in the docks, said to be honest. But he's no longer about.'

Schnyder sat down again.

'Does this put a different complexion on the case? Assuming for a moment I wasn't being lied to – big assumption – does it merely complicate matters further? For, if Madame Pilar was indeed a Soviet agent, who is interested in preventing this from being disclosed, and who could have a reason to murder Chambolley? Would these indeed be the same people?'

Lannes made no reply.

Schnyder said, 'I don't mind telling you my head's spinning.'

Lannes said, 'In any case, since I've now been instructed by the Prefect to take things no further, it's not going to be possible to find an answer to these questions. He said it was for my own good that he gave the order. I'd still like to know of course.'

At six that evening came the news that Belgium had surrendered to the Germans. Prime Minister Reynaud told the French people in a radio broadcast that history had never seen such a betrayal. 'It's only the first,' Lannes thought.

For almost a week now he had hesitated uncertain of how best to act on the information the boy Léon had given him. Each time he thought of following it up, he pictured Javier Cortazar lying dead with his nails torn out. But it nagged at him and the Prefect's warning-off order provoked his obstinacy. If d'Artagnan could defy and outwit the all-powerful Cardinals, he thought, what kind of Gascon am I to give up? The thought made him smile; it was so ridiculous. Nevertheless, ridiculous or not, action might serve as an antidote to the war news. So he picked up his blackthorn stick and limped off towards the rue d'Aviau.

It was still warm in the street, but when old Marthe admitted him to the house, the hall was dark and chilly. Some of the furniture had gone, also paintings from the walls.

'Yes,' she said, 'it's over here. Everything will have to go in time, the debts are enormous. If it's the Count you want, I doubt if you'll get any sense from him.'

Jean-Christophe sat, as on Lannes' last visit, in his father's chair with the canaries hopping and chirruping in their cage behind him. He had a bottle of brandy and a glass by his side, and his eyes were glazed.

'He's been drinking for days, and he won't eat,' the old woman said, 'and, what's more, he didn't go to bed last night, but sat there in a stupor. Here's that policeman to see you,' she said, shaking Jean-Christophe by the shoulder.

Then she settled herself on a stool by the door, and said to Lannes, 'Carry on, don't mind me. You may find you've some need of me however.'

Lannes pulled up a chair and sat silent for some minutes looking at the wreck of a man opposite him. Jean-Christophe's gaze focused on him a moment, blearily, then moved away.

'You're afraid, aren't you?' Lannes said. 'Afraid of what you know and what the consequences may be. Isn't that so?'

A tear trickled down the Count's fat cheek.

'I know nothing, nothing at all. Don't hit me,' he whimpered. 'Don't beat me. I can't stand being beaten.'

His hand stretched out, tremblingly, for the brandy glass, but Lannes was too quick for him, removing both glass and bottle.

'You're a liar,' he said, 'but nobody's going to beat you, certainly not me.'

He topped up the glass and held it out, just beyond Jean-Christophe's reach.

'Tell me the truth, and I'll give you a drink. Who is Marcel? Where can I find him?'

'I don't know who you mean. I've told you before. Don't beat me, I can't stand being beaten.'

'Nobody's going to beat you,' Lannes said again. 'Come on now. You were seen with Marcel, La Chope des Capucins, Cours du Marne. So there's no use pretending you don't know who he is. Tell me where I can find him and I'll give you your drink. Or would you rather I made this a formal examination, in my office, after you've spent a night in the cells and had time to consider your position – without a drink. You're in trouble. I've enough evidence to hold you as an accessory to murder. Do you understand what I'm saying?'

The fat man was now blubbering freely, but when he at last found himself able to speak, it was the same refrain: 'I know nothing, I tell you I know nothing, don't beat me, I can't stand being beaten, I've done nothing to be beaten for.'

Lannes hesitated. It was a disgusting spectacle and his own part in it revolted him. He passed the glass to the wretched man and watched him take a big gulp, shudder, and sit there holding it between his hands.

Then the moaning started again.

'You've no right to treat me like this, no right. I've a bad heart. I can't stand being beaten.'

The old woman said, 'He's afraid of you but he's more afraid of another.'

'Who?'

'Come downstairs and I'll tell you what you need to know.'

Lannes followed her. As he closed the door he heard the Count whining, 'I can't stand being beaten. Don't hit me, I can't stand it, I've a bad heart, don't beat me, please, please.'

The old woman led him to the back of the hall and down a steep stair to her kitchen in the basement. It was a long cavernous room with a stone-arched ceiling and stone flags on the floor. A couple of hams hung from hooks attached to a beam that ran across the room, their skins darkened by smoke from a black range in which there was a glow of embers. She directed him to a high-backed winged wickerwork chair by the range, while she disappeared into a cupboard or pantry, from which she returned with a bottle of marc and two stubby tumblers. She poured a couple of inches into one of them which she passed to Lannes, and a smaller drop into the other. Then she settled herself opposite him in the chair that flanked the other side of the range.

'That it should come to this,' she said. 'I've lived in this house for sixty years and it's always been a place of wickedness. As you sow, so shall you reap.'

Lannes waited, now without impatience. She would come to what she wanted to tell him, in her own time and in her own way.

'The old count was wicked, but he was a man. That poor creature upstairs, he's never been that. He wrote the letters his father gave you, but perhaps you know that already.'

'Why? What was his motive?'

'I know nothing of motives, but I tell you this. He wrote what he didn't have the courage to say. He's always been a coward, and then he's eaten up with jealousy and the knowledge that he isn't a man. Isn't that reason enough?'

She paused, and chewed her lower lip. A wall-clock ticked loudly in the silence of the vast kitchen. Lannes relaxed and sipped his marc. He recognized the moment, he had experienced it so often, that moment when someone who has never spoken his thoughts arrives at the breaking of the dam, when the need to communicate becomes irresistible. You could never be certain what would bring a person to it. Sometimes it was fear, sometimes grief, sometimes anger, most often an immense weariness.

'Sixty years,' she said again, 'and much wickedness.'

'Were you the Count's mistress?'

'Of course I was. Not a month after I came to the house and he took me from behind. Oh, he was a man. His first wife, poor creature, was asleep in their bed and he had me on the couch. So it continued. Wives came and went but he always returned to me. Until the last one. She was like me, you know. Of the people. I didn't hate her, though she thinks I did. To tell the truth I was relieved. It had got wearing at the age I was. But not him, he came back to me, insisting, always. Even in the last years he would have his hand up my skirt if I let him.'

'You loved him?'

'Whatever that means. It's not a word I ever think about. He was my life, that's all. Naturally he used to tell me I was the only one he had truly loved, but that was just blethers. He couldn't love anyone, and sometimes he hated me because I understood him.'

She knocked back her marc and cackled.

'Oh yes, he was a man. And now it's all finished. He was disappointed in you, I have to say. He thought you would discover it was that poor sot upstairs who wrote these letters.'

'He wasn't interested in them, though, was he?' Lannes said. 'He had some other reason for directing my attention to this house. What was it? Tell me about this Marcel. You heard me ask Jean-Christophe about him. When I asked you before, you denied all knowledge of him. But that was a lie, wasn't it. You know who I mean, and if I tell you that Jean-Christophe has been seen with him and I'm sure Edmond also knows who he is, what do you say?'

She sniffed loudly, picked up the bottle with fingers twisted by arthritis, poured herself a glass, drank it, and passed the bottle to Lannes.

'It's natural to know your own family, even those who are born the wrong side of the blanket. I wouldn't speak of him before because he used to run barefoot about this kitchen when I had the nursing of him, but now it's different, since he killed his father. I didn't know that before, you see. It was that sot upstairs who let it slip, that the man you call Marcel was in the house the morning the Count was killed.

'Marcel is the Count's son.'

'As I say, and worse than that.'

'What do you mean?'

'There's much wickedness here, I told you that. Thérèse wasn't always the half-wit she is now, spending half her days on her knees in prayer. She was ever a bit simple, that's true, but a cheerful girl and as pretty as could be. She was a woman at sixteen, in body but not in mind, and he couldn't keep his hands off of her. Then one day it was more than hands, and nine months later . . . So, you see, Sigi, which is what we called him, is the Count's son and also his grandson. No wonder the poor girl took to religion.'

A year younger than Clothilde – it didn't bear thinking on.

'So . . . ' the old woman was deep in her story now, this story she had guarded for so long. 'So it couldn't be thought of that the poor girl should rear the baby herself. It was sent to a wet-nurse in Les Landes. But later nothing would serve but that the Count should bring him back here, and hand him over to my care. And an engaging scamp he was, full of merriment and laughter and tricks.

The Count doted on him and would come down to my kitchen and sit playing with him for hours. Aye and reading books to him later, though they weren't what I who have no book-learning thought suitable for a bairn. But then Thérèse fell into hysterical fits at the thought of her shame here in the house and maybe the Count was afraid of exposure – though, if so, it's the only fear I ever knew him act upon. Be that as it may, the lad was sent away to be cared for by a tenant's wife in the mountains. He was fifteen when he learned the secret of his birth, who his father was and his mother too.'

'How did that happen?'

'Monsieur Edmond of course. Who else would dare to? I boxed his ears for him, but he only laughed and called it an interesting experiment. That's his way.'

The old woman folded her hands on her lap. It seemed to Lannes that, though she knew the enormity of the story she had told, she had lived with it so long that she no longer felt its horror. But of course that's how it is. You can get used to anything. A pathologist goes serenely about a task that makes the novice onlooker retch and spew.

'What happened to Marcel then, or Sigi as you call him?'

'He ran away, disappeared, vanished for years, as if he had never been, to Algeria, as we later earned, then to Lyon and eventually to Paris where he ended up in prison. It was Monsieur Edmond got him out, how I don't know, perhaps he had completed his sentence, it doesn't matter. Then two years ago he turned up on the doorstep. I knew him at once and he had the impudence to embrace me before insisting he must see his father. He's had money from him ever since – what do you police call that? Blackmail, is it? But it wasn't the money that interested him, it was the knowledge that he had power over the Count. And then he killed him. He always meant to. It was what he said to me before he ran away. "One day I'll have my revenge, don't you doubt that." That's what he said. I should never have let him into the house.'

'Where is he now?'

'How should I know? Monsieur Edmond takes care of him, you can be sure of that.'

## XXIII

*June 4–19, 1940*
'If the English are running away,' Alain said.

'Sailing away, you mean, ass,' said his sister.

Alain waved the interruption aside.

'No, but I'm serious,' he said. 'Can we continue to fight the war? Without Allies? Can we, papa?'

They were at table, the wireless turned off as soon as Marguerite came through from the kitchen with a dish of pipérade and Bayonne ham. It had become an unwritten rule of the house: that she should not be subjected to news bulletins. But the subject was inescapable; how to find anything else to talk about?

Lannes said, 'We've no means of knowing. It seems that we're still holding the line between the Somme and the Aisne. But really we know nothing certainly.'

He felt inadequate. A father should, even in the worst of times, find a means of encouraging his children.

The day after his conversation with Marthe he had called on Miriam in the tabac. But it was closed. A notice on the door gave the explanation: on account of a bereavement, the death of the respected proprietor, M Saul Boniche.

Impossible to intrude with his questions on a house of mourning.

Instead he went to the Banque des Pyrenées, Cours de l'Intendance, where the boy Léon was employed. Reluctant to make his presence known in the bank, he waited at a café from which he could watch its door and intercept the boy when he left. Was it, he wondered, at this same café that poor Gaston had lurked eager to make his pick-up? Léon at last emerged. Lannes followed him as if casually, waited till he had turned into the little rue de la Vieille Tour before calling out his name.

'Don't be alarmed,' he said. 'It's merely that I would like you to give your aunt Miriam a message. I'm sorry to learn of your grandfather's death.'

'Is that the message. You don't need me for that surely? Besides it may be for the best.'

'No death is for the best,' Lannes said, 'though it may often seem so. But, apart from asking you to offer her my sympathy and condolences, I need to ask her some questions, and this isn't a suitable time. So will you please ask her to get in touch with me as soon as she feels able to do so. That's all. It won't embarrass you to be the bearer of a message from me, will it?'

Léon smiled: 'If it does, then I've brought it on myself, haven't I?'

That was two days ago, and she hadn't yet responded.

In the evening Alain and Clothilde went out to meet Maurice and go to the cinema. The previous year Marguerite would have said, 'It's such a lovely evening, how can you go and waste it sitting in the dark?' Now she summoned up a smile, told them to enjoy themselves, but not to be late home.

Lannes stretched out on the sofa and tried to read. Impossible: he couldn't concentrate. The words flickered before his eyes.

He said, 'Come, let's go for a walk and perhaps eat an ice somewhere.'

Anything that would serve as distraction.

But, as they strolled hand-in-hand along the quay in the gold and blue of the soft evening, the war never left them, and when they turned down the rue du Chapeau Rouge to a café in the Place de la Comédie, it hovered like a vulture over them; and sitting at a table with strawberry ices, coffee and a glass of marc for Lannes, they found no words to speak. Others round them chattered like birds in springtime and Lannes didn't know whether to admire their insouciance or condemn their indifference to the reality that oppressed him. But then the war was still several hundred miles to the north, and perhaps they had none of them a son, like Dominique, at the Front.

Maurice returned to the apartment with the twins. They talked about the film and then Alain said: 'It's disgusting. When we went for a lemonade afterwards, I heard someone in the café say, "Have you noticed? The town's filling up with Jews," and his companion replied, "Well they're always the first to run, they're not really French, you know." I almost hit them both.'

'I'm very glad you didn't,' Lannes said.

Clothilde took her mother aside, and whispered something to her, and then they both left the room. Maurice looked embarrassed. In a little Clothilde came back and said, 'That's all right then, Maman's perfectly happy about it, she's making up another bed in Alain's room. Maurice is going to stay with us a few days, Papa.'

'I hope you don't mind, sir,' he said. 'It's intolerable now at home.'

Schnyder called Lannes into his office, first thing in the morning. The Alsatian was buoyant, smart in a double-breasted grey suit, blue shirt and tie decorated with white horses. His hair shone with brilliantine, and he looked like a man on top of the world. Lannes felt himself shabby in comparison. His hip was hurting and he had slept badly.

'Strange times,' Schnyder said. 'I've come from the Hôtel de Saige. The Prefect says, quite simply, run-of-the-mill crime doesn't really matter at the moment. Things are falling apart, no use our occupying ourselves with little matters like murder, burglary and so on. He's convinced the war's already lost, now the English have deserted us. The Government's about to abandon Paris. It'll transfer itself here, as it did in 1870 and 1914. The city will be flooded with refugees. Maintaining order's going to be the issue of the day. What do you think?'

'Not our job,' Lannes said. 'Our business is detection.'

'I'm so glad you agree. That's what I told him myself. So, any progress on the crimes we've been forbidden to investigate?'

'Yes,' Lannes said, 'our man's got a record.'

He gave Schnyder an edited version of Marthe's story.

'Trouble is, we've no idea what name he was convicted under, not his own, I'm sure of that. He'll have had false papers most likely. And we don't actually know what he's calling himself now, nor where he is. I took it on myself to wire Paris, asking them to run a check. But there's been no reply.'

'You won't get one. Not with things as they are.'

'You're probably right. Edmond de Grimaud's the key.'

'Well, if things turn out as they look like doing, I've no doubt he'll be here before long. What about his brother? Should we haul him in for further questioning? Even if we've been forbidden to?'

'He's very near collapse, total disintegration. Putting him in a cell might tip him right over the edge.'

Alain skipped school to wander the city with Maurice. The sun shone, enlivening even the narrow streets of the Old Town. Then the light was swallowed up in the grime which covered the soft yellow stone of the buildings. For a long time they strolled without aim, talking little, yet contented with each other's company. Then Alain had an idea. They caught a bus for the beach on the lake. They swam, and stretched out in the sun.

'You're well-muscled,' Maurice said.

'It's rugby. I'm smaller and lighter than most who play, so I have to be stronger for my size.'

Maurice put his shirt on, went to the café and came back with two orangeades.

'The war's lost, isn't it?' he said.

'Oh, I don't know.'

'What will we do?'

'Go on, I suppose. What else can we do?'

He sipped the orangeade, lit a cigarette and passed the packet to his friend.

'Why did you really leave home and come to us? Not that I'm not delighted that you did. So's Clothilde by the way.'

Maurice drew on his cigarette, blew out smoke, failing to make the ring he attempted.

'It was old Marthe,' he said.

'Who's she?'

'I suppose you might call her the housekeeper, but I rather think she used to be my grandfather's mistress too. A long time ago, she's ancient. Anyway she said, "You must get out, this is no place for you now." '

'And so you did, obeyed her just like that?'

'Oh yes, I always have, you see. I can't explain it, but she's formidable. Besides it was what I wanted myself, though I didn't know it was till she told me. Does that sound feeble? Or crazy?'

'Not to me, might to others. In any case, the whole world's crazy now.'

Maurice turned over and lay on his back looking up at the deep blue of the sky. Two storks flew overhead, towards the hills in the direction of Spain.

He said, 'Maybe I shall go to England. That would make sense. Why not come with me, Alain? If the war's lost, why don't we get out? What do you think?'

A boat crossed the lake, coming within twenty metres of them. A dark-haired man with a thin moustache pulled at the oars and a pretty girl sat in the bow eating cherries from a brown paper bag.

I've seen him before, Maurice thought. But where?

'I couldn't do that,' Alain said. 'Not with the uncertainty about Dominique. It would distress Maman, even though it's Dominique that's her favourite. Besides, what would I do in England? They'd probably put me on the next boat back to France. What would you do?'

'My mother's there, remember? I'm sure she'd make you welcome. And what will there be for us here if the Nazis occupy the country. Have you thought of that?'

'Yes, of course I have. It would be an experience, I suppose. In any case I can't run away.'


There was a message for Lannes from Miriam. Could he come, please, to see her, earliest convenience?

Good. It would get him out of the office where he felt stifled. As he was about to leave. Joseph brought him a note from Rougerie, marked urgent. Lannes passed it back.

'You haven't found me, Joseph. Let me have it when I return.'

Miriam was dressed in black and wore no make-up. She looked ten years older. Lannes, awkwardly, repeated the condolences he had sent by way of Léon. The words were meaningless, yet had to be spoken.

She said, 'He wasn't unhappy to go. In his last moments of lucidity he urged me to leave France.'

'And will you?'

'Why should I? I'm French. I have no other nationality.'

'That's not what "they" think – and by "they" I don't mean only the Boches.'

'No,' she said, 'I know you don't. But I'm damned if I'll be driven out of my own country. However it wasn't to speak of these matters that you wanted to see me.'

'I've been talking to old Marthe. Listening to her, rather, for I had no need to ask questions. She told me a strange story.'

'Wait a minute,' she said. 'I'll make some coffee. You like it strong, don't you?'

The silk of her dress rustled as she edged past him sitting in the chair that, he feared all of a sudden, might have been her father's favourite. But surely not? She had directed him to it. He watched the swing of her hips as she left the room, and thought, if I wasn't a married man and faithful husband . . . He had cheated on Marguerite only once, and the memory of that betrayal, a dozen years ago, still tasted sour. But sweet too, of course, that was the truly painful thing.

Miriam returned with the coffee and a plate of little almond biscuits.

'I made them myself, to a recipe of my grandmother who's been dead for more than twenty years. So, tell: what had old Marthe to say?'

Lannes recounted her story.

'What do you think?'

'That my husband was murdered? It's not something you are likely to be able to prove, is it?'

'You said before that you had no knowledge of this man we were calling Marcel. But what of Sigi? You must have heard him spoken of?'

'Never, I assure you. To think of poor Thérèse . . . It's too wretched. But, yes, I believe it all. He was perverse, you know, or do I mean perverted? I'm ashamed to say that was part of his attraction for me. In the beginning. Later there was – and this may surprise you – a sort of companionship. And finally only pity. He was a man who took what he desired and was never satisfied. But, no, I never had a hint of this awful story or heard mention of any Sigi. What ignorance I lived in! Do you know, in a strange way, I have the feeling that my real life is only now beginning.'

Lannes envied her that feeling, delusory as it might be. For him the daily problem was how to go on, how to find a reason for doing so.

He said, 'It's clear that Edmond and this Sigi are close. In some way. If you hear anything, or remember anything, or anything occurs to you, please get in touch. Meanwhile, take care of yourself. There are bad times ahead, but you know that. And tell your nephew Léon, who seems a nice boy, but silly if also intelligent, to watch how he goes. I think you understand what I mean.'

The judge was agitated, scattering snuff all over his waistcoat. There were little pink spots on his cheeks and when he spoke, his words tumbled over each other.

'I've had a high regard for you, superintendent,' he said. 'I thought you prudent, trustworthy, reliable. But I've received complaints, complaints which I can't ignore and indeed don't choose to, about your conduct. Which has been intolerable, intolerable and in-subordinate. The new Comte de Grimaud whom, it seems you've been harassing, in defiance of my instructions, has, it appears, tried to kill himself and is even now in hospital. His sister, Madame Thibault de Polmont, a lady of considerable standing, as you must be aware, holds you responsible. It was all I could do to dissuade her from lodging a formal complaint such as must lead to your suspension. What have you got to say for yourself?'

Lannes had had enough. He was tired of it all, tired of the obfuscation, tired of cover-ups, tired of this assumption that there were people of 'good birth' whose position in society meant that they had to be handled tenderly, meant that they were to be excused from being subjected to the ordinary routine of investigation. Something snapped.

He said, 'If Jean-Christophe de Grimaud has indeed tried to kill himself, it's not on account of me, it's because he is guilty and afraid, and his nerve and judgement are destroyed by brandy. As for Madame Thibault de Polmont, if she was not who she is, and protected by those in high places, I would have had her in my office subjected to interrogation and in all probability charged with withholding information relevant to the investigation of a crime. More than one crime indeed. One man has been murdered, mutilated repulsively after death, another has been tortured so brutally that he suffered a heart-attack and died, and I myself, a police officer, have been the victim of attempted assassination. The same man is responsible for all these crimes, and he has a close connection with the Grimaud family and that house in the rue d'Aviau. And you require me to desist? To neglect my duty as an officer of the police judiciaire, which duty, I take it on myself to remind you, is to investigate serious crime and lay evidence before you in your capacity as examining magistrate? Now either you apply for my suspension, which is a matter for my superiors in the PJ and ultimately for the Prefect, or you leave me to get on with my job.'

He got up and left the room before Rougerie could reply. He closed the door firmly behind him, and felt better.


## XXIV

*June 11–17, 1940*
Lannes' satisfaction at having spoken his mind was short-lived; his loss of control emphasised his impotence. Waking before dawn, in dark silence, his persistence seemed futile. What did it matter who had killed Gaston and tortured the Catalan, even who had fired at him? As for the old count's death, absurd. They were tiny incidents unremarkable in the chaos of a war that was being lost, a catalogue of the fallen that might at any moment include his own son. 'We've entered a world in which private life is overwhelmed by public disaster, is indeed all but abolished.' The words – his own or someone else's – rang in his head, participants in an endurance dance.

He got up and made a pot of coffee. Last night the news service had admitted that the Government had left Paris. All France was on the run. Bordeaux was filling up with refugees, would soon be swamped by them. They flocked south as if in flight from the plague.

Who was responsible? The question brought him up, hard, against his policeman's creed. There was always someone responsible for a crime, whatever mitigating circumstances might be found; there was always one finger on the trigger, even though the gun might have been supplied, and the gunman primed, by another. If you dug long enough, you came up with an answer, what they liked to call a solution. You could then tie a red ribbon round the dossier and hand it over to the examining magistrate. Your job was done, case solved, what happened next no concern of yours. But responsibility for a national disaster? Could that ever be determined?

He went outside. At the end of the street there was a black Citröen, one of the new ones with 'traction avant', and it was full of people, asleep: father, mother, three children and a wire-haired fox-terrier, an English breed lately fashionable among the rich. The car had Paris plates. They must have arrived during the night, too late, or unable, to find a hotel or other lodging. The man's mouth was open; the sound of his snores would be unbearable in the confined space, but, apparently, all were too exhausted to be disturbed.

They were erecting stalls at the Marché des Capucins, and the little cafés were opening, their windows steamed up. There was a smell of coffee, and blue-overalled market porters and some of the stall-keepers were having their morning wake-up 'invigorator' – a black coffee with a shot of rum or marc. It might have been any morning in peace-time, people going about their work without anxiety. The sun was beginning to dispel the mist that had crept in from the river and Lannes was touched by the normality of the scene. He entered a bar, ordered a coffee and marc, lit a cigarette, and listened to the conversation swirling around him. That too was normal, concerned with everyday matters, and he even heard a couple of jokes cracked. Nobody spoke of the war. Yet every one must be conscious of it, and some would have sons or brothers in the army. Was it tact or fear? – surely not indifference – that held them from speaking of the catastrophe engulfing France?

He looked at his watch. It wasn't too early to call the house in the rue d'Aviau. Marthe would surely be up, padding about in her carpet slippers. There was a public telephone in the corner of the bar. He got a token from the woman behind the counter and asked the operator to put him through. The bell rang a long time, and then the old woman answered.

'Oh it's you,' she said. 'There's nothing amiss with young Maurice, is there?'

'Nothing at all, he's fine and we're happy to have him with us. I'm told that Jean-Christophe has tried to kill himself.'

'Stuff and nonsense. He's had his stomach pumped, that's all, and now he's at home again, in the study with his bottle.'

'Is he making sense?'

'What do you think?'

'Listen, Marthe, you'll have heard the news.'

'Much heed I pay to that.'

'Nevertheless you must know that people are fleeing Paris, and it's likely that Edmond will soon be in Bordeaux. Will you find a means of letting me know when he comes to the house, and also, which is more important, if there is any sign of Sigi. Will you do that?'

The receiver was replaced without a word. All the same he thought she would do as he asked. He had come to trust the old woman.

Moncerre was already in the office. He lay back in a chair and explored his teeth with a matchstick. There was a cup of coffee on the table by his side. When he saw Lannes, he removed the matchstick and said, 'It's my opinion, chief, that the world is badly arranged. It's the women who should be sent to war, not men. Sorry, forgot about Dominique, but my wife's three sisters all landed on us yesterday with their brats – that makes eight altogether. Running away from the Boches, though if they'd stood their ground it's the Boches would have turned tail. I was told I'd to sleep on the couch, and then they all went on yattering, yattering until eventually I gave up and came here to try to sleep on the bench in the waiting-room. I'm thinking of heading north myself and finding a German to surrender to.'

Lannes smiled. Moncerre's bursts of bad-tempered gloom usually cheered him up.'

'You look terrible,' he said.

'I feel worse.'

'Well I've something for you. That precious pair, the Brunes . . . '

'Hey, are we on the case again?'

'Officially no. Otherwise yes. I had a row with Rougerie yesterday. He put my back up.'

'Bloody lawyers.'

'Exactly.'

He handed Moncerre one of the photographs of Sigi old Marthe had looked out for him.

'See if they recognize him. Be as tough as you like.'

'This is our man then?'

'I'm sure of it. But we need identification from a witness and we've never believed, have we, that they didn't see anyone that night.'

'It'll be a pleasure,' Moncerre said. 'I'll put them through the wringer. I'll treat them like they were my wife's sisters.'

He began to whistle, then turned at the door and said, 'Hey, know what? Who do you think I saw the Alsatian with last night? You'll never guess. That actress, you know the one who's the Comte de St-Hilaire's fancy piece. What do you make of that? Quick worker, our Alsatian. Nice to find someone whose mind isn't on this bloody war.'


## XXV

*June 17, 1940. Noon.*

Lannes had come home for lunch, early. It was bizarre. Bordeaux was bursting at the seams, packed with more refugees than you could number, more perhaps than the total of its usual population, but at the PJ all was tranquil. The department seemed in a state of suspended animation. Moncerre said, 'I don't know about you, chief, but I'd like to get stinking rotten drunk. What else is there to do?'

At twelve o'clock it was announced that Marshal Pétain would speak to the nation.

'Why Petain?' Maurice said. 'Why not Reynaud?'

'There must have been a change of government,' Alain said. 'What do you think it means, Papa?'

'We'll soon know.'

The Marshal's voice was firm, the tone mournful.

'At the request of the President of the Republic I am from today assuming the leadership of the Government of France. Certain of the affection of our admirable army, which has fought with a heroism worthy of its long military traditions against an enemy superior in numbers and arms; certain that it has through its magnificent resistance fulfilled our duties towards our allies; certain of the support of the war veterans whom I had the honour to command; certain of the confidence of the entire French people, it is yet with a heavy heart that I say to you today that it is necessary to cease fighting. I have this last evening approached the enemy to see if he is ready to try to find, between soldiers, with the struggle over and in honour, the means to put an end to hostilities.'

The old man's voice died away.

'This talk of honour . . . ' Alain said.

'It's a word,' Lannes said, 'a mere word, nothing more, to put our conscience at ease.'

'Does this mean it's over, Papa?' Clothilde said.

'Very nearly. For now anyway.'

'Thank God,' Marguerite said, 'so Dominique is safe.'

She made the sign of the Cross. Seeing Alain about to speak, sure that he was going to point out that the Germans might not agree to the Marshal's proposal or might – this was Lannes' own thought – impose terms that would be found intolerable – Lannes said, 'We must hope so,' and gestured to Alain to keep quiet.

'What will happen now?' Clothilde said.

'We'll have to wait and see. It depends on the Germans.'

Marguerite got to her feet. 'He spoke very well, didn't he? You wouldn't think he was eighty-four. Come, Clothilde darling, help me prepare lunch. You can make the salad. It's only charcuterie, I'm afraid.'

When they had left the room, Alain said, 'It's humiliation.'

'Certainly not an occasion to open a bottle of champagne. But, if your brother's safe, then we've something to be thankful for, as a family.'

'What sort of terms do you think they will demand?' Maurice said.

'Heavy ones. No doubt about that. Even Hitler can't have thought it would be so easy.'

1870, he thought again, only worse, because this time there's no Gambetta to inspire and organize resistance, and the Nazis are worse than Bismarck's Prussians. Alain is right: humiliation, and this is only the beginning.

But in the streets that afternoon there was no sense of that. The sun still shone, the cafés were busier than ever. He overheard a well-dressed woman say to her husband, 'Well, I suppose we can return to Paris now. I always said there was no need to run away, but you insisted. Don't you feel rather stupid now? We must hope that the Reds haven't plundered our apartment.'

Schnyder arrived in the office and found Lannes at his desk smoking, the ashtray already half-full of stubs.

'What'll you do if there's a shortage of tobacco?'

Lannes smiled, 'I hope it won't come to that. If it does, then I hope there's a flourishing black market.'

'I was at the bar of the Splendide. It was crowded. You'd have thought the old man had announced a victory.'

'Cracking open the champagne, were they?'

'That sort of thing.'

'No surprise,' Lannes said. 'Whoever suffers, it won't be the rich.'

'Edmond de Grimaud was there. He asked after you, hoped you were fully recovered.'

'Kind of him. Perhaps. I suppose he's one of the winners.'

'Are there any French winners?'

'Must be.'

'I'm afraid you're right. Fuck them all.'

'Good,' Lannes said. 'We think alike. What of us now?'

Schnyder crossed to the window, looked out on the square.

'Everything's so normal, so damned normal. What of us? We've no choice, have we? We're servants of the Republic. Besides, how things turn out will depend on what sort of terms the Boches impose.'

Lannes thought, he speaks of them as the Boches, but he was born and reared a subject of the Kaiser. Odd position he finds himself in.

As if reading his mind, Schnyder said: 'One thing's certain. They'll annex Alsace again, and Lorraine of course, and thousands of young men there will be drafted into the Wehrmacht, poor buggers.'

'Have you still family there?'

'Cousins. Not close. At least your boy should be all right now. That's one thing to be thankful for.'

He sat down, heavily, in the chair where Lannes usually placed those summoned for questioning. He hunched his shoulders, lowered his chin, and frowned.

'One thing though, and it gives me no pleasure to say it. If my judgement as to what's to come is right – and I rather think it's the same as yours – then we might as well wrap up these investigations. Cases closed. I hate to say it, but there's no use pretending things will go on as before, even as far as the PJ's work is concerned. You understand me, don't you?'

'Yes,' Lannes said. 'It's not only the war we've lost.'

'By the way, Edmond de Grimaud said he would like a word with you.'

'Not just about my health, I assume. Well, it's up to him, but I'd have thought he might be fully occupied. I shan't seek him out.'

'Of course not,' Schnyder paused. 'But don't antagonize him. We may need his good will, whether we want it or not. And remember: what's now unfinished business may one day be re-open.'

# XXVI

*June 22–28, 1940*

It was four days before the Armistice terms were made known. In that time, believing the war to be already over, almost a million French soldiers allowed themselves to be taken prisoner. One of them was Dominique, though there was nothing voluntary about his surrender. He was wounded, a bullet in the knee, on June 18, and taken a few days later from a field hospital to a POW camp in Germany. It would be another month before his parents learned of this. In that time hopes of his early return flared up, and died away.

'So,' Henri said when Lannes called on him in the rue des Remparts, 'we're to be occupied.'

'So it appears.'

Bordeaux, like the whole Atlantic coast of France was included in the Occupied Zone, the department of the Gironde being cut in half by the demarcation line which separated that part of France which was to receive German garrisons from Unoccupied France where there were to be no German troops.

'Where does that leave you, Jean?'

'Strangely enough my position is unaffected, technically anyway. The police, like the rest of the administration, remain under the authority of the Republic, in our case, that is, of the Ministry of the Interior. But we are requested – or, I should say, required – to co-operate with the Occupying Power. We have, it seems, no choice but to obey. At least I can't see what would be gained by refusing. How it will work out, well, who can say? Things may be different later. Meanwhile, I've come to apologize.'

'For what? I can't suppose, my dear Jean, that you have anything to apologize to me for.'

'I'm afraid I do. I spoke to Edmond de Grimaud this morning.' He paused. 'I think I will take that whisky you offered.'

De Grimaud had come to the office which surprised Lannes who had expected a summons. He looked relaxed, confident, at ease with himself and the world. He wore a dark blue suit, double-breasted, a pale blue shirt, red tie, dark red carnation in his button-hole, and smelled of an expensive scent.

'I'm so glad to have caught you,' he said. 'Everything's confusion. The Government's on the move – you know I'm a minister now, admittedly only a junior one at present. We don't even know where we're headed for. Some say Clermont-Ferrand, but that won't do, it's a ridiculous idea. So I don't have long. You've been listening to old Marthe, I understand, and speaking to my poor brother – I do wish you would leave him alone, he's a sick man as you must realize. But Marthe's been talking, I gather, talking wildly. The old thing's obsessed. I hope you didn't take her ramblings seriously. The idea that my poor father was murdered, you must see that's sheer fantasy.'

'Really?' Lannes said, 'and your half-brother Sigi, whom your brother denies all knowledge of, is he fantasy too?'

Edmond smiled.

'Poor Sigi, part of the old woman's obsession. She adored him once, and then – I don't know why – turned violently against the poor boy. He's been unfortunate, gone wrong, I admit, more than once, but the suggestion that he murdered my father, it's absurd, utterly absurd. Moreover you are mistaken – another of Marthe's delusions, I'm afraid. Sigi is my nephew – illegitimate, certainly, it's a sad story – but not my half-brother. You must realize, my dear chap, that old Marthe . . . '

He broke off, tapped the side of his head, and smiled again.

Lannes waited. The temptation to tell de Grimaud that his unfortunate Sigi was in the frame for two other murders was powerful, but, mindful of what Schnyder had said, he held off. In any case he was sure that Edmond hadn't come merely to tell him to leave his family alone and forget what old Marthe had said. He must know that the collapse of France had altered everything.

'I'm grateful to you, superintendent, for having taken Maurice into your home. The boy's a puzzle to me, I don't know what to do with him, and now that I'm a minister, I have even less time than before to be the father to him that I suppose I should be. You don't find him troublesome, I hope, not a burden?'

'Not at all. My wife also is pleased to have him and my younger son and daughter seem to have struck up a warm friendship with him. He's an intelligent boy, and well-mannered.'

'And your other son? In the army. Any word?'

'None.'

'With luck you will soon have him back with you. This defeat has that compensation at least. But if there are difficulties, be sure to let me know. I am not going to be without influence in the new regime.'

A promise? Or a warning? Or both?

'That's good of you,' Lannes said.

'There are times,' Edmond said, 'when even a conscientious and punctilious officer may find it useful to have a friend at court. I've developed a respect for you, superintendent. That's why I should be sorry to see you go astray. This Chambolley case you have been pursuing so doggedly, despite official requests, even, as I understand it, orders, to the contrary – well, I admire a man of spirit and independent mind. But now, you must see that it's finished. Everything has changed. Chambolley was an innocent, a blunderer, quite out of his depth. That was his misfortune – and his folly. The woman, his sister-in-law, was engaged, I can tell you now, in activities prejudicial to the interests, indeed the security, of the French State. So it may be that she was eliminated, or her elimination was arranged. I don't know. Unfortunate, sad, but that's the way things are.'

He paused, crooked his hand, and examined his well-manicured nails.

'It's water under the bridge,' he said. 'The past is being swept away. We must look to the future, to our part in the great task of regenerating the Republic. It's to be a National Revolution. I should wish you to be involved. You understand me?'

Lannes had made no reply. The temptation had been there, of course it had, the temptation to say he wanted nothing to do with it, that he was a policeman responsible for the investigation of serious crime, nothing more; national revolutions were none of his business; he would just get on with his job to the best of his ability. In which connection, monsieur de Grimaud, would you now please explain to me why you denied all knowledge of this man Marcel or Sigi, since he is, as you admit, your nephew, and also, despite your denial, your half-brother? Tell me that, sir. Explain why you chose to conceal information relevant to the commission of a crime from the police, which is itself, as I surely need not remind you, a criminal act. But he had said none of this. Perhaps he had even smiled some sort of acknowledgement. Because of course de Grimaud had won. They both knew that. Schnyder was right. There was nothing they could do. Not now, perhaps not for a long time to come, perhaps never.

Moncerre had reported that the precious couple, the Brunes, had refused to make any identification when he showed them the photograph of Sigi/Marcel.

'Never seen the man. They almost laughed in my face. I couldn't make them the least bit nervous. Someone's got to them, I've no doubt about that.'

So, now, Lannes looked Henri in the face, and said, 'I'm ashamed.'

'Perhaps we should all be ashamed. Bloch has gone. He took my advice and left for Oran. As for me, I shall continue to sell books which is, I suppose, my way of keeping my head down and cultivating my garden. Who knows? Perhaps the Germans will turn out to be good customers, and that will intensify my shame.'

He gave Lannes the whisky-and-soda.

'It won't be long before I can get no more Johnnie. Any news of Dominique?'

'None.'

'I'm sorry. Tell Marguerite, will you, Jean? Not that my sorrow or sympathy can be of any comfort. Still, they say "no news is good news", don't they?'

'Only because it's not bad news.'

'When do we expect the Germans?'

'Very soon. Three or four days at most. A grand reception is being prepared. According to my brother-in-law, Marquet says there's a New Order in Europe and France must play a leading role.'

'A New Order? I don't like the sound of that.'

'Nor do I. But it's what we can't escape.'

He walked home in an evening of soft yellow light. Roses were in bloom and the city was quiet.

## PART TWO

### I

He wasn't the poster-boy Aryan. On the contrary, the officer of the GFP (Geheime Feld-Polizei) who presented himself in Lannes' office only a few days after the German troops had rolled over the Pont de Pierre and up the Cours Victor Hugo, watched by a sullen, silent crowd, was short, thin, dark-complexioned, his face wrinkled like an apple left too long on the tree. He had arrived without warning, and now when he held out his hand in a gesture intended perhaps to suggest that they were really comrades with interests in common, Lannes detected irony in his eyes and in the twist of his lips as, without bowing or heel-clicking, he introduced himself:

'Lieutenant Schussmann.' Was it on account of his recognition of this irony that he accepted the offered hand? Could be, for there was something in the lieutenant's manner which seemed to acknowledge that theirs was, and indeed must be, a relationship false from the start. Or was it simply because he looked ill-at-ease in his uniform?

Lannes glanced at the note he had found on his desk when he arrived that morning: the Mayor's instructions to all officials who were enjoined 'to collaborate in a loyal and courteous fashion with the German authorities, and acquiesce in all their demands'.

And Marquet, author of this humiliating order, had been appointed Minister of the Interior in the Marshal's government, with the brief, as he put it, 'to reconcile the German and French points of view, for on this collaboration depends the return to normal life'. Normal life? With your city occupied by the army of a foreign power? It was the height of absurdity.

'I am so pleased to make your acquaintance,' Schussmann said. He spoke as if repeating a sentence learned by heart from a phrasebook. But in fact his French, though slow, measured and stilted, would prove to be adequate, if without any idiomatic fluency.

Should Lannes apologize for having no German? Damned if he would. He contented himself with inviting the lieutenant to take a seat and resumed his place behind his desk, just as if he was about to interrogate a suspect.

Schussmann said: 'You understand that we wish to be correct. Indeed that is required of us, though I am happy to say it is also my personal inclination. We have no intention, still less any desire, to interfere with the administration of the French State. In so far as I understand the function of the police judiciaire, I see no reason why we should find ourselves at cross-purposes. We have a common interest, do we not? The maintenance of order, the suppression of criminal activities. Your role is to investigate crime. Yes? And this concerns my department only on such occasions as any crime may touch the interests of the Reich, that is to say, if it appears to have any political connection. Apart from that we should only to see good order maintained.'

'Public order,' Lannes said, 'is the responsibility of the gendarmerie and the municipal police. The PJ, as you say, occupies itself only with the investigation of serious crime, under the direction of an examining magistrate and, ultimately, of the Prefect and the Ministry of the Interior.'

That sod Marquet, he thought.

'Good,' Schussmann said, 'excellent. We have, I think, a basis of understanding. May I add, superintendent, that you have been recommended to me as a man of integrity. You are well-spoken of. Therefore I am confident that you are a realist, and that we can work together. It is in a spirit of co-operation that I invite you to approach me, freely, whenever you seek information or have information to impart which in your opinion impinges on the interest of the Reich.'

'Schussmann?' Schnyder said, rolling a cigar between his fingers, sniffing it, clipping the end, and holding a match to it before putting it between his lips and drawing deeply. 'We had a word too. What did you make of him?'

'Very "correct".'

Lannes put audible quotation-marks round the word.

'You thought so?'

'He may even be a decent fellow, but I don't trust him. He flattered me, you see.'

He left the office early in the afternoon. There were German soldiers everywhere, many with cameras, as if they were tourists. And, while they gaped at the sights and snapped them, ordinary Bordelais, going about their business and now for the most part rid of the refugees who had flocked back to Paris and the north, stared at them. This too was a sort of tourism, Lannes thought, or a visit to the zoo. But which were the caged beasts and which the onlookers?

Miriam was behind the counter of the tabac. Seeing him enter, she called on her niece to take over and directed Lannes to the parlour behind the shop. Then she fetched coffee and a bottle of marc. She looked as tired as Lannes felt.

'Yes,' she said, 'I'm not sleeping well. I don't know whether it's on account of grief or anxiety. Curiously, I do feel grief for him, as well as for my father. We did have a sort of companionship, he could make me laugh, you know, and I keep remembering too how willingly, even avidly, I gave myself to him when I was seventeen. And anxiety, we all feel that, I suppose. What's going to become of us? Have you any word of your boy?'

'None as yet.'

'I'm sorry.'

He couldn't tell her why he had come. That too was shameful. It wasn't that he wanted to make love to her, or, rather, he had no intention of doing so. He was in search of comfort. Marguerite's unhappiness, her fear for Dominique, oppressed him. There was nothing he could do or say to help her. Neither could find the words they needed to speak, and so they spent hours in a silent desert. In her misery she snapped at Alain and Clothilde, and, though he assured them that her anger was not directed at them but at the world, he couldn't blame Alain when he said, 'It's not my fault that I'm not of an age to be in the army and Dominique is.'

Strangely it was with Maurice alone that she seemed at ease, her old and true self; it was as if she saw him as someone as much at a loss as she was.

Miriam said: 'And so Edmond is now a great man! Enjoying the spoils of defeat and national humiliation! Well, he's welcome to them, that's what I say.'

She didn't ask the reason for his visit, but, when she said, 'You've nothing to tell me, have you?' he felt she understood that he regarded this back room behind the tabac as a sort of refuge where he would have liked to sit in companionable silence or to exchange merely the banalities of small talk. There were many, he sensed, in Bordeaux, and indeed all over occupied humiliated France, who could not allow their conversation to go beyond that. Talk of what really mattered was to venture into a dark forbidding forest. Yet on the other hand reality irritated him like an itch he could not refrain from scratching. So he found himself telling her of his meeting with Schussmann and of how the assurance that he had been recommended to the German as 'a man of integrity' grated.

It was an insult, or at least something which diminished him. Yes, that was it: diminishing like the Marshal's insistence that the honour of the defeated army was not tarnished but still shone bright.

'It's as if he was trying to recruit me.'

'Do you know what I saw yesterday?' she said. 'The old cow with a German officer on either side coming out of the Chapon Fin where they had evidently been lunching.'

The Chapon Fin was a Michelin-starred restaurant patronised by 'le tout Bordeaux'. Lannes had no need to ask whom she meant by 'the old cow'.

'Marquet would approve,' he said. 'He has decreed that the return to normal life depends on a sincere collaboration with the Boches. Not that he calls them that of course. Lunch must qualify as sincere collaboration.'

'Normal life? I assure you that the old cow hasn't been able to afford to eat there for years, and has certainly found nobody to treat her. Mind you, to be fair, I remember that her late husband had German cousins. I met one of them once. He was in the wine business, manufacturing a horrid sweet ersatz champagne. No market for that in Bordeaux! So perhaps one of these officers was family. Who else – who but family, I mean, would feel obliged to stand the old cow lunch?'

She refilled their glasses.

'Liquor helps, I find,' she said, and lit one of her American cigarettes. 'I must tell you I've been selfish. Not knowing how long these will be available, I've removed several cartons from the shelves and put them aside for my own use. If there's going to be a general tobacco shortage, I'll do the same for you. But at the moment your Gauloises are in good supply.'

She crossed her legs and smoothed her skirt. In normal times, Lannes thought, she would soon find another husband, she has too much vitality to remain a widow. But now?

'Actually,' she said, 'I'm very glad you've come, apart from the normal pleasure of seeing you. Speaking of family. I'm worried about Léon. Of course I hesitate to speak of it when you have your own anxieties and fears for your son, but there's no one else I can trust.'

'Léon?'

'It's not what you might suppose, though naturally that worries me too. It's more serious, dangerous, I think. He was here yesterday, talking wildly. First, about poor Gaston, saying he was murdered by Fascists – is that right, or can't you say?'

'It's not impossible. There are indications – I can say this much – that the motive was political.'

What had he told her about the man who went by the name of Marcel, but was really Sigi, and, it seemed, her late husband's bastard, fruit of incest? He couldn't remember.

'Go on,' he said. 'Gaston was only part of it and not what's really worrying you?'

'That's right. It seems Léon heard the broadcast by that General who's gone to London – I forget his name – the one who insists that the war isn't lost, isn't over – and the boy has been enthused by it. "We can't just accept this Occupation," he said, "we can't knuckle under." He kept coming back to that, like a refrain. It's as if he has changed altogether in these last weeks and I don't understand it. For instance, he also said, "We're Jewish, aunt, and we're not going to be allowed to forget it." He's never spoken as a Jew before. It has meant nothing to him, for his father was a Protestant, you know. I'm afraid, dreadfully afraid, that he'll do something stupid. Will you speak to him? Is that too much to ask?'

'Of course I will. Get him here. Tomorrow evening when he leaves the Bank, and I'll have a word with him.'

The boy who had immersed himself in Balzac . . . did he see himself now in the role of a Balzacian hero struggling for his place in the world? And what of Alain, of Maurice too? Could any young man of spirit not find this talk of collaboration contemptible, intolerable? He was ashamed not to have been aware of the danger.

## II

'I'm ashamed that my father is a minister in this government.'

Maurice pushed back the lock of hair falling over his eye as he delivered himself of this verdict.

Alain, without removing the cigarette which dangled, tough guy, Jean Gabin style, from the corner of his mouth, said: 'It's not your fault. So why be ashamed? We're responsible for ourselves and our own actions, nobody else's. That's my philosophy.'

'I don't know. I daresay you're right, Alain, nevertheless . . . '

He stopped in mid-sentence. They were crossing the Place Pey-Borland behind the cathedral, and he took hold of Alain's arm.

'Look. That man there, the one with the thin moustache. Do you see him? Remember that day by the lake, he was rowing a boat, and I said afterwards I had seen him before, but couldn't place him. Well, it's just come to me, and we must tell your father. But first we must follow him.'

'What sort of game is this?'

'No sort of game. It's deadly serious.'

At that moment the man disengaged himself from his companions, kissing the lady's hand. He crossed the square with long elegant assured stride, and rounding the cathedral, entered its darkness.

'You follow him, Alain. I'll keep watch here. It's you must go in, he might recognize me.'

'You're mad, do you know that? Crazy. All right then, if you insist. Hold this for me.'

He handed Maurice his half-smoked cigarette, and, with a shrug of his shoulders, did as he was bid.

Maurice waited, on edge. He had been a fool not to recognize the man in the boat, but now he was certain. It was the taller of the two he had passed that night as he left Gaston's apartment, the one who had laughed when his companion identified him as 'one of his bum-boys'.

Alain came out first.

'Have you lost him?'

'Not at all. He's in the confessional. I could hardly follow him into the box. What's all this about?'

'Murder. Don't laugh. I mean it. He's a wanted man. He may even be the chap who shot your father too. So we've got to track him.'

'Oh charming. I can just imagine what he's saying to the crow: "Listen hard, Father, I don't just have ordinary sins like fornication to confess, I've done someone in and taken a pot-shot at a cop also." Great. So, what now?'

'Like I say, we can't risk losing him. Or should we telephone to your father? I don't know. Follow him, find out where he lives and then call your dad? What do you think?'

'What do I think except that you're crazy?' Alain lit another cigarette, looked his friend in the face. 'You really mean it, don't you? So, not a game, or rather a game played for high stakes. Fine. I'm with you. One for all and all for one. D'you suppose he's armed?'

'I've no idea. Only . . . '

'I expect he is. Just in case. You know. In case he has to shoot his way out.'

'Look, here he is.'

'A quick confession. Routine one, don't you think? Confessing to murder might take a bit longer.'

The man stood on the cathedral steps. Maurice turned half-away.

'What's he doing?'

'Nothing, really. Smiling. Waiting. Ah, the crow's joined him.'

The pair set off side by side up the rue de Ruat. The priest, who was short and fat, had to break into what was almost a trot to keep up with his long-striding companion. The boys followed, thirty metres behind.

'If he did confess to murder, it doesn't seem to have worried the crow.'

'You still think it's a joke, don't you?'

'Not at all. But it is sport.'

The tall man and the little priest turned right, then left past the Prefecture. They crossed the Cours de l'Intendance, and paused in the Place des Grands Hommes. They stood chatting for a moment. The tall man laid his hand on the priest's shoulder and laughed. They shook hands and the priest turned away to enter a café, while the other continued up the rue Jean-Jacques Rousseau towards the Place de Tourny.

'Would you recognize the priest again?'

'I've an eye for crows.'

Without glancing behind him, the man proceeded up the Cours de Verdun. It was a long straight street and almost deserted. He was sauntering now, like one who is early for an appointment. The boys held back. There was a gate leading into the public garden and for a moment he stood there as if perhaps searching for a pretty woman. He had that air, Alain thought. Then a car approached, a big open Mercedes with a chauffeur and two German officers in the back seat. One of them raised a gloved hand to the tall man who half-turned to watch the car till it was out of sight, then resumed his walk. He turned left at the end of the garden. Maurice seized Alain's arm as they rounded the corner after him. He had stopped at the door of one of the big handsome houses.

'I don't believe it.'

'Believe what?'

'Of course you've never been here, have you, but that's our house.'

As he spoke, the door was opened and the man entered.

'It doesn't make sense.'

'What now? We know where he is at least.'

'Yes, but . . . this way.'

He turned and slipped into a narrow street, no more than a lane, which ran behind the houses. He opened a garden gate and descended a flight of six or seven steps which took them to a basement door. It wasn't locked and they went in. Maurice opened the door which led off the stone-flagged passage and they were in a kitchen. An old woman stood bent over the range on which a pot simmered.

'Marthe.'

'What in the name of the saints are you doing here, child? This is no place for you. I've told you that, and still less now.'

All the same she allowed Maurice to give her a hug before she pushed him away.

'What's happening?' he said.

'What should be happening? We've got German officers lodged here, that's what, and your uncle's still at the brandy.'

'Who was that tall man with a moustache who's just entered by the street door?'

'And what's that to you, little one?'

'Marthe, I'm not a child. I have to know.'

'Have to know, you say? And I say there are things better not known. In any case I don't know who you're talking about. People come and go here, and nowadays it's none of my business. That's been made clear to me and I'm glad of it. I cook and clean and ask no questions. Now, be off with you, child.'

Maurice hesitated as if he was about to obey this old woman whose authority seemed to Alain so strangely compelling. But, instead, he repeated, 'I have to know, Marthe. It's important, it really is.'

'Important, is it? Well, I'm no judge of that. I don't set myself up to decide such matters. We've four German officers landed on us, which has at least meant that the rest of the furniture hasn't had to be sold, and that's all I know. I don't ask questions about them, none of my business. Then there's your uncle and your aunt, Amélie-Marie, who's having the time of her life, the old bitch. And that's enough, more than. Your other aunts have retired to a convent, I'm glad to say. There's nothing for them here anymore than there is for you, my lad. As for "having to know", take it from old Marthe who nursed you when you were a little boy, the less you know about anything here, the better. So, you and your friend, whoever he is, be off with you, and let me get on with my work.'

'Marthe absolutely refused to tell me anything more,' Maurice said. 'She just clammed up like an oyster. All the same, sir, I'm absolutely certain that he was one of the two men I met going up to Gaston's apartment. Should we have waited in the street to see if he came out and followed him again, since I don't think he's actually living there?'

'I'm very glad you didn't,' Lannes said.

Especially, he thought, if he is indeed the man who shot me, as seems likely.

'So: do we act on this information?'

Schnyder leafed through the papers on his desk.

'Vichy is proving even worse than Paris,' he said. 'All this bumpf. Depresses me. You've only one witness, you say, and though you're sure he's reliable, you also tell me he can't be produced, and you'd rather not even tell me who he is. It's not satisfactory. You must see that. In any event it relates to a case we've been ordered to file away.'

'Gaston's murder, yes. The attempt on me, that might be a different matter, don't you think?'

'It should be. It bloody well should be. On the other hand you admit that you have nothing but supposition to connect your man with that.'

'Sufficient to justify questioning, however.'

'So you say, so you say.'

Schnyder shuffled his papers again and didn't look at Lannes who, watching his boss, thought, he's a weak man after all.

'I've got responsibilities,' Schnyder said. 'We all have, naturally, goes without saying, but mine are peculiar. The first of them is to secure our independence, to safeguard our ability to keep functioning as we should. But in the circumstances this comes with strings attached. It's conditional, has to be.'

At last he looked up, then put a match to his cigar which had been lying forgotten in the ashtray.

'It may be a long war and, certainly, however long it lasts, and maybe for some time after, so will the Occupation. That's how it is. I want to keep us as free as possible from interference by the Boches. You can't disagree with that. Now this type you want to question obviously has relations with them. So straightaway they are involved. He's in a special category. Straightaway you yourself become an object of suspicion. That's bad, and no good to me either. "Not reliable" – that'll be the note on your dossier. On mine too. We can't have that. So the answer to your request for the time being – note, I say, for the time being – must be no. Your man will keep. We won't forget him, Jean. Be sure of that. As I've said, I don't approve of people shooting at my men, and you're the chief of them. Nor of murder. You understand?'

'I understand. Naturally I understand. But, if I may say so, sir, I don't approve. In fact, to be honest and blunt, I deplore your decision.'

'Which you will nevertheless obey. For Christ's sake, man, do you think I don't deplore the position we're in. It stinks, stinks like rotten fish, but we have to live with the stench. And in it. For now. For God knows how long. Clear?'

Lannes felt dirty, humiliated, nevertheless reported the conversation more or less word for word to Moncerre and young René Martin.

'So it's still hands off,' Moncerre said. 'Fuck them. And this time the order isn't coming from an old woman like Rougerie but from our own boss. It makes me sick.'

'I see his point of course,' Lannes said.

'You do?'

'Reluctantly.'

'He's running scared, that's what I see,' Moncerre said. 'He's shitting himself.'

'What about the priest?' René said. 'We've a description, don't we? He could be questioned, unofficially if you like, just in the way of gathering information.'

'Leave him to me,' Moncerre said. 'I've a way with priests.'

The boy Léon was already in the back room of the tabac when Lannes arrived. He had come straight from his work at the bank and wore a thin black suit. He had loosened his tie and undone the collar button of his shirt, as a mark perhaps of release from bondage. His hair was now cut short, lying close to his scalp, and in profile he looked Jewish as he hadn't at their first meeting when his hair was long. Lannes wasn't pleased to find himself thinking this.

'My aunt says you want to speak to me.'

'She tells me you've been talking wildly, foolishly even.'

'That's as may be. What's foolishness to one is good sense to another. It's a matter of opinion.'

'It's a matter of fact,' Lannes said. 'There's talk now which is foolish that would have made good sense a few months ago. That's not an opinion, Léon. As I say, it's fact. How it is, how things are. Harsh fact certainly, just as the German Occupation is a matter of harsh reality, something we have to live with. Here, read this.'

He took a paper from the inside breast-pocket of his coat and handed it to the boy.

'It's a copy of a notice which will be published tomorrow. Read it.'

He watched the boy as he read the words which he himself already knew by bitter heart.

'Two days ago, when the Guard of Honour was about to raise the flag, near the Gare St-Jean, the Jew Israel Karp, of Polish extraction, threw himself forward brandishing a stick at the drum-major and musicians of the German band. By decree of the military tribunal, he was condemned to death for an act of violence against members of the German Army. In accordance with this judgment, the condemned man was executed this morning.'

'What do you make of that, Léon?'

The boy's face was in shadow, but it seemed to Lannes that the colour drained from it, and his voice was unsteady when he looked up and said, 'It's monstrous, horrible, beyond belief.'

'Agreed. It's also how it is.'

'For brandishing a stick . . . Only that. It doesn't even say he struck anyone.'

'He didn't. He was prevented. Overpowered before he could do so. Now do you understand why your aunt is worried. Keep your sentiments – and your opinions – to yourself, Léon. And forget you are Jewish, for as long as you can.'

'You think that's easy. It's not even possible, superintendent. I've just been given notice by the bank, not because of anything I've done wrong, but because of what I am. And by that I mean because I'm a Jew, not the other thing. It's to be a good Jew-free bank. What do you make of that? So I'm out of work, as from next week. What should I do? Go on the streets, offer myself for rent? That too'll be easy, won't it, once they make us wear the yellow star, like in Germany.'


### III


Lassitude, indifference, depression: Lannes knew them all these next weeks, as the glorious summer collapsed into autumn rains and in the morning a chill wind blew up from the Garonne. Alain and Clothilde had returned, reluctantly, to school. Maurice received an imperative summons from his father: he was to go to Vichy where plans had been made for his future. He left unwillingly; there were tears in his eyes as he looked out of the train and waved to Lannes. Marguerite spent more hours on her knees in the Church of Sainte Eulalie than in the kitchen.

In October the Marshal met Hitler at Montoire-sur-le-Loir and affirmed the intention of France to pursue 'the path of collaboration'. 'It is with honour,' he said, 'and in order to maintain French unity, a unity ten centuries old, in the framework of a constructive activity of the new European order that I have today entered the way of collaboration.' Schussmann, calling on Lannes the following morning, expressed warm approval. 'It's a decisive step, a decisive step, I assure you,' he said. 'Believe me, the Fuehrer has a great respect for the Marshal. Together, the Reich and the

État Français will create that New Order of which the Marshal spoke so warmly. It's a historic day in the long and often unhappy saga of Franco-German relations. We are at last in a position to put these divisions and that long miserable conflict behind us. A new dawn is breaking over Europe.'

'We'll see,' Lannes said.

Schnyder reproached him for making his lack of enthusiasm evident.

'It serves no purpose. You might at least put on a show. For the moment all we can do is keep our seat in the saddle.'

Lannes called on Miriam in the tabac a couple of afternoons a week, ostensibly just to reassure himself that all was well with her. In reality? He preferred not to dwell on that. How would she respond if he expressed a desire to make love? He couldn't tell. In any case, he held off, said nothing. It was better that way.

In one spark of activity he arranged for Léon to take over Bloch's job as Henri's assistant in the bookshop.

'So long as his presence doesn't embarrass you,' he said. 'I'll be grateful. It may help to keep the boy out of trouble.'

'I suppose it's a small act of resistance,' Henri said, 'replacing one Jew with another. And he'll be a link with poor Gaston, even if also one that saddens me.'

Miriam was also grateful.

'But I wish I could get him out of the country,' she said. 'I'm so afraid he will do something rash. He's become so bitter, even savage, in his talk.'

As for the boy himself, he blamed Lannes for the failure to bring Gaston's murderers to justice, 'Since I've no doubt you know who they are.'

'Justice?' Lannes said. 'My poor boy, Justice is asleep.'

There were days when he thought of handing in his resignation from the force. But if he did so, what would they live on? And wouldn't the very act of resigning immediately render him politically suspect, mark him down as a subversive?

At last came good news: a letter from Dominique, itself delayed for weeks, in which he reported that he was a prisoner of war, held at Stalag IXA. The letter was short, lacking detail, presumably also censored. He assured them he was well and had recovered from his wound – of which they had of course been ignorant. That evening Marguerite sang as she prepared a stew of river fish; her prayers had been answered.

'He'll soon be home, won't he? That'll be arranged, won't it, now that the war is over? There's no call for them not to send all the prisoners home. Surely that's so.'

'We must hope it is,' Lannes said, unwilling to disillusion her when for the first time in months there was a smile on her face and she looked like the girl he had fallen in love with.

But he knew better. The war wasn't over while England still resisted Hitler and the POWs would be put to work in Germany, as was permitted, except in the case of officers, by the Geneva Convention.

Nevertheless the boy was alive and their worst fears allayed.

His mother-in-law and Albert were invited to supper to share the good news. Albert was in expansive mood; he had just been promoted. He assured his sister that he would do all in his power to secure Dominique's speedy repatriation.

'There are strings that a man in my position can pull,' he said.

Madame Panard nodded in agreement.

'You can rely on your brother,' she told Marguerite. 'You see now he was quite right when he said this war was a mistake. But it's all over now and things will soon return to normal.'

Lannes gestured to Alain, who was on the point of saying this was all nonsense. He took the message, obeyed, but looked mutinous.

Later, alone, he said to his father: 'It's all lies, isn't it?'

'You're right of course. But there's nothing to be gained by saying so.'

'Talking of that, I don't see what's to be gained by my remaining at school. We none of us do, none of my mates, that is. I mean, what's it for?'

'The war isn't over. I agree with you there. But it won't last forever, and, when it does end, then you will need to have passed your exams, if you are to have the career you're capable of. In any case, for the time being, it's the best place for you. You're safe there and kept busy,' he said, avoiding the word 'occupied' which had first come to mind. 'As long as you don't do anything foolish. And you won't, will you?'

'As to that – being foolish – only this afternoon I saw the man Maurice and I followed – which you said we were foolish to do. He was with a German officer and another man, French, I think, in civilian clothes anyway. It's all right, I only looked, from a distance. They were sitting outside a café in the Place de l'Ancienne Comédie, drinking champagne. Then they were joined by the priest, the same one, you remember we told you about him too?'

'I remember.'

Lannes had prevented Moncerre from questioning the priest as he had proposed. Hearing what Alain said, he was surer than ever that he had been right.

Nevertheless . . .

'Can you describe the other man?'

'Oh yes. I watched them for some time, you know, from across the square. I'm sure they didn't take any notice of me, if that's what's worrying you. I mean, why should they? He was short, solid, like a front-row forward, his hair which was thick and fair cut en brosse. He wore a double-breasted grey suit and looked smart and well-fed. Prosperous. He smiled a lot. Of course I couldn't hear him speak, but I'm sure he was French, though I don't know why, just something about him. I had the impression he was formidable.'

Marcel – Sigi – whatever. Lannes had no doubt. Formidable indeed, the boy was right.

'Does my description help?'

'Help? I don't know. Perhaps.'

'But do you recognize him from it?'

'I think so. Probably. If you see him another time, keep well clear. If he's the man I think he is, he's dangerous. Bear that in mind, Alain.'

It infuriated him to think that Sigi was back in Bordeaux, if indeed he had ever left – and that he was happy to be seen taking his ease in public, confident that he was protected. He hoped that they hadn't indeed taken note of Alain. But he couldn't be sure and felt a stab of fear.

'Are you playing rugby this week-end?' he said, to divert them both.

'Yes, if I'm picked as I'm confident I will be. "The image of war, without the guilt," didn't you once say?'

## IV

It was his birthday. Forty-five. An age by which a man should know himself, know his qualities and defects, how far he can go, his ability to persevere, know what he is and accept that, for better or worse. Know too when to wear a mask, and not forget that it is only that, something that denies and can be denied.

Lannes pushed the papers on his desk aside; nothing there to demand his attention. He stretched himself, lay back and lit a cigarette. There was no sound from the world beyond. Little traffic except the transport of German troops moved in Bordeaux now.

That morning Marguerite had said: 'Do you think my brother can really arrange to get Dominique home?'

'He says he can.'

Did she hear the scepticism, distrust, even malice, in his voice?

'It would have been a wonderful birthday present for you.'

'The best. Perhaps by Christmas.'

There was a knock on his door. He called out and young René came in, light-footed, eager, his face flushed.

'Chief, I don't know, can't be certain, but we may have a break-through.'

'Yes?'

'You remember Cortin, the little clerk whose car was stolen, the one you were shot from. Well, they've just fished him out from the Garonne. Just under the Pont de Saint-Jean. They were able to identify him so quickly because he had a pass from the Mayor's office excusing him the curfew, carried his papers in a sealed packet, it seems, which is unusual in itself. But that's not all. It seems that though he was found in the river – early this morning by a fisherman – he wasn't drowned. He was strangled or, to be more precise, garrotted. What do you make of that? It opens the case up. There must be some connection, surely?'

'There may be,' Lannes said; then, seeing a shadow of disappointment darken the boy's face, relented and said, 'There probably is, as you say. Only I don't want to jump to conclusions. To begin with, has anyone identified him formally?'

'I don't know about that, but there doesn't seem to be any doubt, according to the report I've had.'

'He's in the morgue, I take it. Then let's go there.'

'His lungs would be full of water if he'd drowned,' the attendant said. 'I know that, though I'm no doctor. I've seen drowned men enough, suicides mostly. Besides, look at his neck.'

He drew back the sheet and pointed to a thin livid line across the throat.'

'That's wire made that, take it from me. No question. You don't have to be a doctor to tell. Besides, I've seen the like before. One of those murdering Spaniards, you'll find.'

'It's Cortin all right,' René said. 'I recognize him, even as he looks now.'

Lannes had disliked the little clerk, nevertheless felt indignation on his behalf.

'We still need a formal identification. Has his wife been told? He did have one, didn't he? All right, we'd better have her sent for.'

'I knew he'd bitten off more than he could chew.'

Madame Cortin sat very upright in the chair in Lannes' office. He'd given her the one with arm-rests, in case she needed support, though she had shown no emotion when she looked at the body and agreed that, yes, it was indeed her husband's. Now she twisted her handkerchief in and around her fingers and occasionally dabbed at her eyes.

'What do you mean?'

'Mean? What should I mean? How would I know? He kept things from me, but I always knew when he was doing so and told him straight. "Out with it," I said. We're respectable folk, always have been, naturally, Jules being in the administration.'

She paused and dabbed her eyes again.

'Has your husband been anxious about anything lately?'

'Anxious? Who isn't anxious these days? Tell me that. Jules has always been anxious, he's conscientious, the nervous type, I have to say that. He didn't like it when you had him in here for questioning – it was you, wasn't it? – though he kept that to himself for three days, till I got it out from him. He did well for himself, you know, a position in the Mayor's cabinet, and he deserved it because he was clever and hard-working. But I had to push him, he could never quite believe in himself. He wasn't at home in the city, not really, not like me. I'm a true Bordelaise. But Jules was a country boy – even if he was happy to leave the mountains where his old brute of a father used to beat him and say his foster-brother was twice the man he would ever be. That's because Jules liked to read books, which is harmless enough, you see, when he should have been doing . . . whatever peasants do. Because that's all his father is when you come down to it, a peasant, even if he boasts of how he could buy up all his neighbours. And I daresay he could, for he's clever, even if he can't do more than sign his name. Jules wouldn't have made it as he has but for me. I've prodded and pushed him all the way. I've had to. It's not been easy, I'll tell you, though I'm not the sort that complains. And what's to become of me now, after all I've done? Will they even pay me the pension I'm entitled to, with things as they are? Can you tell me that?'

Lannes didn't try to interrupt the flow. It was a maxim of his: let them talk and they'll usually reveal more than they want to.

She took a sip from the glass of water René had placed on the table by her side.

'Did your husband have any enemies that you know of?'

'Enemies? Why should he have enemies? People like us don't. We're respectable, I tell you. Jules was respected. The Mayor always addressed him as Monsieur Cortin. If he had had enemies, I'd have known, and, since I don't, then he hadn't any. You can be sure of that.'

'So, no enemies that you know of, and yet someone killed him.'

'No enemies at all. As I say, he couldn't have kept that from me. That's why his death must have been an accident. Or a case of mistaken identity. Or someone attacked him in order to rob him. These days, you can't rule that out, even here in Bordeaux. The streets aren't safe these days. It's as bad almost as Paris or Marseilles. And you say his body was found by the Pont de Saint-Jean. That's near the railway station. Which is where they hang out, these types, criminal types and foreigners.'

'Were you worried when your husband didn't come home last night?'

'Of course I was worried. It wasn't like him. And then we've this curfew, even though as one of the Mayor's cabinet he had a special pass that allowed him to breach it. He was very proud of that pass. But it wasn't like him all the same. I didn't have a wink of sleep, lying awake worrying that some accident had befallen him. That's what I thought: an accident. What else could have kept him out?'

'But you didn't report him missing?'

'Certainly not. We're not people who like to draw attention to ourselves.'

'Why in fact was he out?'

'He had a meeting, a late meeting. It was public business, he said, and that was enough for me. I'm not one to pry. He was excited about it, not anxious as you suggested, excited. He said it was going to make a big difference to us.'

'But you didn't enquire further?'

'He'd have told me in good time. I'd have seen to that. He told me everything, eventually.'

Lannes had been here too often, heard too many wives – also, though more rarely, husbands – assert their complete knowledge of their spouse. It was never true. Everyone had secrets, a part of themselves they kept to themselves. It was usually innocent, a day-dream of escape into another life, which they would be ashamed to confess and which they would very seldom put into action. But he had known that happen; known men who had walked out of a marriage without warning and with as little apparent fuss or drama as they might display stepping out of a train on to a platform. Perhaps Cortin had been like that, in his dreams.

'I questioned your husband about the car he reported stolen, the car from which a shot was fired. I didn't altogether believe him.'

'Of course it was stolen,' she said. 'What other possible explanation could there be. My husband was truthful. Besides he had no imagination. He was incapable of making up stories.'

'You said he had bitten off more than he could chew. What did you mean by that?'

'Did I? I don't remember.' She dabbed at her eyes again and sniffed. 'You must excuse me. I'm confused and distressed. Seeing him lying there, it's not natural. I never thought he would be the one to go, not with the palpitations I suffer from. I should like to go home now.'

'Just one other thing. You spoke of your husband having a foster-brother. Can you tell me something about him?'

'Him!' She sniffed again, twice and deeply. 'I want nothing to do with him. He's trouble. That's what I told Jules when he turned up again. The bad penny, I said. Trouble. A good-for-nothing, a jailbird even, for all his smart suits and hand-made shoes. You'll have nothing to do with anything that one proposes. That's what I said.'

'And did he take your advice?'

'Advice? It wasn't advice. It was an order. And of course he obeyed. Why wouldn't he? I've always been the one as has to take the decisions. He knew I knew best.'

'And do you know,' René said, 'when I saw her home and asked if there was anything else I could do for her, she didn't even reply, not a single word, and no "thank you" of course, but shut the door in my face.'

'So, kid, for once your charms failed,' Moncerre said. 'There's no need to blush. But think how much worse for you if she'd said "come right in, little one, and give me what my old man could never manage".'

He drank up his beer and gestured to the boy behind the bar.

'How long will the Boches allow us beer? What do you think? Or will we just run out of it? So: make the best of it while we can. That's the way to live now. Enough beer and I can even forget that there are still three women in our apartment.'

'No sign of your wife's sisters going home?' Lannes said.

'They've forgotten they have any home except mine.'

The boy brought their drinks, beer for Moncerre and René, an Armagnac for Lannes.

'So the foster-brother's our Marcel, is he?' Moncerre said. 'I like it.'

'It's possible, even probable. I'll have to see old Marthe again, find out if she knows the name of the family the child was sent to.'

'I like it. I like it a lot. How about this? Cortin lends his car to his foster-brother, unsuspecting – and why not? But he doesn't tell the wife because she disapproves of Marcel and he's scared of her. Then he finds out what it was used for and when Marcel appears in Bordeaux again, threatens to shop him like a good little paper-shuffler. So Marcel tops the silly bastard. Yes, I like it a lot.'

They were alone in the little bar in the rue de la Vieille Tour. It was four o'clock in the afternoon and through the bead curtain they could see the rain falling steadily, dancing in the yellow puddles. The boy put a record on the gramophone: Marlene Dietrich singing 'The Boys in the Back-Room'. 'And when I die, don't pay the preacher/ For speaking of my glory and my fame/ But see what the boys in the back-room will have/ And tell them I'm having the same.' The film it came from, *Destry Rides Again* had been shown in Bordeaux the summer before the war. Lannes remembered Alain singing the song over and over again on the way home, till Dominique begged him to stop. He crooked his finger to summon the boy.

'It's fine by us, but I wouldn't advise you to play English-language songs these days. You might be misunderstood.'

'But it's American and nobody's at war with America.'

'And she's German but Hitler doesn't like her. Put it away, son, till the war's over.'

'I thought it was over. Didn't we sign an Armistice?'

'So we did. I'd forgotten. All the same it's good advice I'm giving you. The way things are, you can't be too careful.'

'What about blackmail?' René said. 'That seems to me Cortin's style, and he told his wife his meeting was going to make a big difference to them.'

'Certainly made a big difference to him,' Moncerre said. 'Silly bugger.'

'Could be,' Lannes said. 'But if you're right, René, then I'll wager that Madame Cortin knew all about it. Hence her unguarded remark about her husband having bitten off more than he could chew.'

'But if she knew,' René said, 'why pretend she didn't? Doesn't she want her husband's killer caught?'

'That remains to be seen. Anyhow before we leap to conclusions I'd better have that word with old Marthe, and, I suppose, bring Schnyder up to date.'

'If he can spare time from his lady-friend,' Moncerre said. 'Did you see the photo of them in the *Sud-Ouest* at the races on Sunday? He looked like a cat that had got at the cream. Cream she is, of course, that one.'

## V

Schnyder stretched, arching his back and thrusting his arms upwards.

'Do you know what the trouble is with our new masters?' he said. 'They're bores. I've just endured two hours with Schussmann. He's not stupid, you know, but he still requires you to explain everything twice. "I like to make sure that every 'i' is dotted and every 't' crossed," he says, and, by God, he does. Actually, though, he's a fundamentally decent sort and as such is terrified of his masters. Can't blame him for that. So, what's this you have for me, Jean?'

Lannes recounted his interview with Madame Cortin and the ideas it had given rise to. Schnyder sighed and tapped his fingers on his desk.

'This foster-brother . . . It's your obsession again, isn't it?'

'Obsession? Not the word I would use.'

'That's what it is nevertheless. Oh I don't say you may not be right. You probably are. But you don't, or rather won't, acknowledge the reality of our position. It's no good, Jean. We used in the PJ to have a category of people who we said were "above suspicion", which was often not the case. Still we handled them, if we had to, with kid gloves. We've got a new category now, a new class whom I call the "Untouchables". If this foster-brother is the chap you think he is, well then, I'm sorry, but that's the class he belongs to. He's untouchable. You know that in your heart. You just won't admit it.'

What infuriated Lannes, depressed him also, was that he couldn't deny the cogency of what Schnyder said.

'What about justice?' he said, momentarily forgetting his reply to Léon when he had used that word.

'You know very well, Jean, that we in the police are not concerned with justice. That's the responsibility of the judges and the courts. We supply the material, that's all, tie it up with a red ribbon and hand it over. In any case the angel of justice now has her wings folded over her eyes and wears a gag in her mouth. As for this fellow Cortin, believe me, there will be worse deaths in Bordeaux in the months and years ahead. My job – and yours, Jean – is to ensure that we are still in place when the war ends, one way or another.'

If the tabac off the Place Gambetta was a sort of refuge or sanctuary for Lannes in these weeks, it was one to which he felt obliged to restrict his visits. Even spending time in easy conversation with Miriam felt like a small betrayal of Marguerite. All the more so when his anger made him distrust himself; he couldn't be sure that he might not say what he shouldn't. So it was to the bookshop in the rue des Remparts that he turned.

Léon was dusting an old calf-bound volume when he entered. Without removing the cigarette from the corner of his mouth, he said, 'So, you see, superintendent, I'm being a good boy. Don't think I'm not grateful to you. Henri's in the apartment. He'll be glad to see you.'

'Yes,' Henri said, pouring Lannes a whisky-and-soda, 'he is a good boy, and to my surprise I find I'm happy to have him here. Yet I ask myself how much longer this can go on. But for my old friend Johnnie' – he waved the whisky bottle – ' I'd find it hard to get through the days.'

Lannes, seeing how ill and miserable his old friend looked, was all at once ashamed of his own black mood.

'I never had much time for Sainte-Beuve,' Henri said, 'but I was reading one of his essays when I heard your voice below and I'd just come on this passage: "There is a moment in this meal we call life when saturation is reached; it needs only one drop more for the cup of disgust to overflow." Good, isn't it?'

'The cup of disgust,' Lannes said. 'I don't think it can overflow because we are all compelled to drink so deeply of it.'

'My poor Jean, here I am sunk in self-pity while you live with death and its consequences every day.'

'We all do that now. Death and dishonour. I'm a policeman forbidden to do my duty. What do you make of that, Henri?'

But you don't give up, he said to himself. Because if you do that once, then it's easier to do it a second time and a third, and then it becomes habit. You stop caring. So, leaving Henri, he made his way past the rails of the public garden, once again leaning heavily on his stick, and cursing the pain in his hip, towards the rue d'Aviau. This time however he went to the kitchen door.

'Oh it's you again,' Marthe said, wiping her hands on her greasy apron.

For a moment it seemed she would bar the door, but then she stepped aside to let him enter.

'I won't keep you. I've only a couple of questions.'

'Which I may answer, but then again I may not.'

Nevertheless she directed him to one of the basketwork chairs which stood either side of the black range on which a pot of soup was simmering.

'And then again,' she said, 'I don't know why I stay here, except it's been my home for more than fifty years and I've nowhere else to go. But I have to tell you I take no notice now of what they do upstairs, for I've no time for the lot of them. So you've allowed young Maurice to go to his father in Vichy where he'll no doubt be corrupted. I had a postcard from the boy. You should have sent him to his mother in England, that's what you should have done.'

She turned away and began scouring a pan in the sink, presenting Lannes with a view of the backside which the old count had fondled even in his last years.

'Is Sigi still in Bordeaux?'

'It's not for me to keep track of his comings and goings,' she said, still busy with the pan which she now scrubbed as if she had an ill-will at it. 'He knows I'll have nothing to do with him or say to him since he murdered his father.'

'You told me he was sent as a child to be reared by a peasant family in the mountains. Do you happen to recall their name?'

'It would be strange if I didn't seeing as it's mine and Jules Cortin is my cousin, being the son of my mother's brother.'

'So you have another cousin, one generation down, also called Jules, who has been employed here in the Mayor's office.'

'And what if I have?'

'Then I've bad news for you, I'm afraid. He's dead. Murdered too.'

She turned round and began to dry the pan.

'That's nothing to me. He was always a feeble fellow, a long drink of water, as they say, and married to a woman who wouldn't give me the time of day. So, much I care what may have happened to him.'

The old woman hung the pan on a hook and, without looking at Lannes, said, 'And if that's all you have to tell me, you'd best be off, for it's of no interest to me at all.'

'Very well,' Lannes said. 'Is there anything I can do for you, Marthe.'

'How could there be? There's nowt I need from anyone.'

He took a card from his note-case, and scribbled on it.

'Will you give this to Sigi? Please.'


## VI

Lannes was in the Café des Arts, Cours Victor Hugo; waiting. He ordered a coffee improved with a dash of marc and lit a Gauloise. He had no doubt that Sigi/Marcel would accept his invitation. He had never known a serious criminal who wasn't conceited, believing himself smarter than the police as well as ordinary people, his victims. Domestic murderers were different, often weaklings provoked beyond endurance, but professional killers assumed the freedom of the gods. Moreover Sigi knew himself to be protected – one of Schnyder's class of 'Untouchables'. The invitation was a challenge his vanity couldn't permit him to refuse, an opportunity also to flaunt his power.

What did Lannes himself hope to get from the encounter? A difficult question. Perhaps no more than a sighting of his white whale?

Who was now before him, in a high-collared, double-breasted, belted trench-coat, dripping with the rain that had started since Lannes settled himself in the café. He'd been waiting longer than he thought; there were half-a-dozen stubs in the ash-tray. Sigi removed his grey trilby hat and held out a hand which Lannes declined. He smiled as if mocking or gently rebuking this refusal, gave hat and coat to the waiter, and settled himself opposite Lannes. He wore a dove-grey suit, also double-breasted and with padded shoulders, a cream-coloured silk shirt and a black, neatly knotted tie with a gold pin. His sandy hair was cut short. He was clean-shaven and square-jawed. It was, at first glance, a hard face – self-consciously hard? – but the dark-brown eyes gave it an unexpected suggestion of delicacy, even sensitivity.

'The black tie – for your father or foster-brother?' Lannes said.

Sigi smiled again.

'Poor Jules,' he said. 'Who would have thought he would go like that? Such a careful man, always correct, with a gorgon of a wife who bullied him and kept him on the straight and narrow. But when you say "my father", you mean, surely, grandfather. Edmond tells me you've been listening to old Marthe. You really shouldn't, you know. She's half-crazed, poor darling. Still, you're right. I have too many reasons to be in mourning. But so do we all these sad days! Poor France, full of widows, orphans, bereaved parents and desolate lovers!'

'This isn't an official interview.'

'Naturally not, or we would be in your office. What shall we drink? Waiter, a whisky-soda for me and whatever my friend is having.'

He took a silver cigarette-case from his inside breast-pocket and offered it to Lannes.

'English cigarettes,' he said, 'best Virginian. You see, I'm not afraid to display my tastes, though who knows how much longer these will be available. "Goldflake" they are called. In my opinion the best cigarettes in the world. Ah, you prefer to be a patriot and stick to your Gauloises. Very well. For my part I am a citizen of the world. I'm happy to proclaim myself that. Perhaps the English will soon realize that it is stupid to pursue this war. What do you think? I am told Churchill is a drunkard, which may explain his foolish obstinacy. But surely the City of London knows that we all have a common enemy, which is Communism, the Bolsheviks, and that Germany and the Fuehrer are the true defenders of Europe, which is to say of civilization. Believe me, my friend, I fought in Spain and I know what atrocities the Communists are capable of. If you had seen what I saw . . . with my own eyes, I tell you. It doesn't disturb you that I address you as "my friend".'

'Address me as you please,' Lannes said. 'It means nothing.'

'In any case I'm delighted to meet you, superintendent.'

He raised his glass and held it out towards Lannes as if about to propose a toast or drink his health.

'Edmond de Grimaud who, I'm happy to say, does not disdain to acknowledge me as his nephew, despite my illegitimacy – see, I conceal nothing – has spoken admiringly of you. Which, given his present position in the Ministry, can do you no harm, super-intendent. I find that interesting.'

'You fought in Spain? I didn't know that.'

'Why should you have? But, yes, I did, till I was wounded. In a noble cause, if I may say so. And fought not ingloriously, my friend.'

'Your foster-brother, Jules Cortin, was murdered.'

'Poor Jules! He wasn't much of a man, even as a boy. He was afraid of his father, who adored me, which he resented. I pitied him, you know. He had ambitions he was incapable of realizing. Is it of Jules that you want to speak? Believe me, my friend, I know nothing of the circumstances of his death. Surely it was a robbery gone wrong or something of that sort. I can't imagine anyone having a good reason to kill poor Jules. He was always insignificant.'

'When did you last see him?'

'Oh, months ago. I had no cause to seek his company and his gorgon of a wife had the ill taste to dislike me. Which gave me some amusement, I admit.'

He gestured to the waiter to bring him another whisky-and-soda.

'For you, my friend?'

Lannes shook his head.

'It's strange,' he said. 'You know, don't you, that I was shot on the day of the old count's funeral, shot from your foster-brother's car.'

'My dear superintendent, you can't suspect poor Jules of trying to kill you. That would be too ridiculous. Besides, even if he had – and the fact that you weren't killed, only, happily, wounded – might, I admit, suggest that your assailant was an incompetent – like that poor Jules – I am quite certain that the Gorgon would have supplied him with an alibi. She did? Then there you are.'

'There were cigarette-butts in the car. Virginian tobacco.'

'And for this reason you suspect me? You must do better than that, superintendent. If I tell you that poor Jules was always cadging cigarettes from me, whenever we met, which was seldom, what would you say? Come, let's be frank. You're fishing, superintendent. I know – and you know that I know – that you have been warned off, forbidden to interrogate me, which is why we are having this charming conversation here in this café and not in your office. Now I'm not going to report you for exceeding your powers or disobeying your superiors, because, well, that's not my way, and I admire a man with a talent for insubordination, but don't push me, my friend. It's in your interest not to.'

'There have been too many deaths,' Lannes said. 'Do you want me to list them?'

'As you please.'

'I have a witness saw you enter the apartment block where Gaston Chambolley was murdered, you and your companion who is, I think, Spanish.'

'And will this witness testify? No, of course he won't. So his evidence is worthless. Besides, entering an apartment block is no more evidence of murder than calling on the Jewish woman who is my grandfather's widow is evidence of adultery. I really think we are, as the Americans say, quits there.'

'Five deaths,' Lannes said.

'So many? You must take me for a monster, a veritable Landru. Don't you find your position peculiar, my friend? With the world as it is, I mean. To be so concerned with a handful of individual deaths. Five, you say. I admit to nothing, but I won't insult you by pretending not to know which deaths you are referring to. My grandfather, a wicked old man who fell down the stairs. What of that? Gaston Chambolley, a pervert and degenerate, hovering on the verge of public disgrace. That Spaniard, whose name I forget. A Communist or perhaps an Anarchist. And my poor foster-brother who lived in terror of stepping out of line. Do any of them matter? In a few months, believe me, when spring comes, Germany will be at war with the Soviet Union and France will engage itself in alliance with Germany in this battle for Europe. Deaths will be numbered in hundreds of thousands, even millions, and you concern yourself with the removal of a handful of men of no significance whatsoever. It's grotesque. As I say, I admit nothing, but do you suppose that if I was guilty as you imagine, I should lose a night's sleep over these deaths? Five, you say. I've counted four. Who is your fifth man?'

'No man. A woman. Pilar was her name.'

'It means nothing to me. Spanish, I suppose. Another Red? Or do you think me guilty of a crime of passion? I assure you that is something I have never experienced.'

'That I can believe,' Lannes said.

Sigi smiled, held his glass of whisky up against the night, and said, 'Edmond admires you. That interests me. Perhaps we are more alike than you think, my friend. In inviting me to this meeting you show your contempt for your superiors who have undoubtedly forbidden you to question me. I like that. It shows you are a man. Not like poor Jules. When his father beat him, he whined and howled and hid his face. When the old man took the birch to me, I refused to submit. He never mastered me and he came to respect me for my defiance. It made me strong. I learned as a poor outcast child, the shame of my mother, that only one thing counts in this world, and that is Will, the strength of your Will. Do you read Nietzsche, superintendent? "Der Mensch ist etwas, das uberwunden werden soll." You don't speak German? Very well, I translate: "Man is something that has to be overcome." Good, yes? There are two moralities: "Herren-Moral und Sklaven-Moral" – the morality of the Masters and the morality of the Slaves. I chose mine when I was twelve, before I had read a line of Nietzsche. I think perhaps it is your philosophy too, even if you won't confess to it, for I feel you are no slave, which is why Edmond admires you. I tell you, my friend, there are glittering prizes for those bold enough to accept the world as it is, which is a jungle, a place where there is one Law – the survival of the fittest – and one form of Justice – the justice which is to be found in the strength of the Individual. Believe me, everything else is false, lies concocted by priests and so-called democrats to force humility on us. But humility is only a few letters away from humiliation, and that I refuse. You begin to understand me? Good. It has been a pleasure meeting you. Finally, you will not be offended if I give you a word of advice. There are opportunities for a man like you who does not fear those set in authority over him, rich opportunities in the New Order of Europe which is unfolding. I shall pay for our drinks. No, I insist.'

## VII

Lannes walked home through the dark streets, deserted on account of the curfew the Germans had imposed. The street lights were turned off, for fear of English air raids, though there had been none in Bordeaux for weeks now. A brisk wind sent clouds careering over the half-moon and rattled the shutters of the houses. They were all closed and gave no hint of the life being dragged out behind them. Why did that word come to mind? Dragged-out? Families were doubtless sitting round the table at their evening meal or talking together or playing cards, listening to the wireless, reading books in companionable silence. Yet it felt to him like a dead city, or at least one in which all life was suspended.

Sigi's final words had disturbed him: the assumption that they had much in common, the offer which he had held out. For hadn't he in fact said, 'Join the winning side, superintendent, admit that you belong to the tribe of those of us to whom all is permitted? There is only one Law and that is the Law of the Jungle.' If Lannes had a philosophy, it was Scepticism, distrust of certainties and big words. How to maintain that in this New World of boastful rhetoric? In this New Order where the Will was supreme? It was his task to defend decency, to protect the Village against the Jungle.

Was this still possible when the Elders of the Village – Rougerie, Schnyder and their superiors too – had withdrawn their support and given at least tacit acquiescence to the New Order. 'Keep your head down till the gale has blown itself out.' That, in essence, was Schnyder's advice, instruction even. But the gale was blowing stronger than ever. A sentence from a book read in childhood ran in his mind: 'The Jungle and the Village Gate are closed to me.' To me? Against me? Same thing, really.

He had killed Germans in his war, or supposed he had; you could never be sure. But, apart from that, he had killed only once, an armed robber who had fired at him, missing, and whom he had shot in self-defence. That was ten years ago at least, and yet the look on his victim's face – astonished, even indignant – was something he had never forgotten. It was the only time he had fired a gun in his twenty years of police work, and now this Sigi, for whom murder was a matter of perfect indifference, presumed to call him 'friend' and to treat him as a brother.

'You look terrible,' Marguerite said. 'Bad day?'

'Very bad.'

'Tell.'

'It's not worth it.'

Not worth it? Impossible, even if Sigi hadn't stirred his sense of guilt by speaking of his visits to Miriam, words which hinted – did more than hint – at blackmail. Call your dogs off, or I'll set mine on you!

It was a relief to sit at table with Marguerite and the twins, to ask them about their day at school, though he scarcely listened to their replies. Marguerite apologised for the meal – a tortilla made with too few eggs and too many leftovers. 'There was no meat in the market today,' she said. Food shortages were becoming acute.

'Doesn't matter. I'm not hungry,' he said. It was more important that the children got enough.

'We had a discussion in the Phil class today,' Alain said. 'Is it permissible to tell a lie? If so, when and in what circumstances? I said, that you have to sometimes, either so as not to hurt someone or simply because it's good manners, as when I pretend to agree with Uncle Albert. Not that I mentioned his name, you understand. What do you think, Papa?'

Before he could answer, Clothilde said, 'That's hypocrisy.'

'Well, hypocrisy's another name for good manners,' Alain said.

'Since when were you so keen on them? You know you only pretend to agree with Uncle Albert because Papa will give you a row if you openly contradict him. I don't call that good manners. I call it cowardice.'

'No, it's not, and anyway Papa wouldn't give me a row, or not a real one, because chances are he would agree with me. He doesn't like what Uncle Albert says, or respect his opinions, any more than I do.'

'You mustn't speak of your Uncle Albert like that,' Marguerite said. 'He's older than you and you should treat him with respect. His opinions may not be yours, but you should remember that he has far more experience and knowledge of the world than you do.'

'Sorry, maman, but all I'm saying is that you often have to lie, for the best of reasons. Suppose, Clothilde, that you have a friend who engages in an act of Resistance – for example, sticking up posters denouncing the Occupation or listening to the BBC – and you were questioned about him, you would lie then, wouldn't you, say you knew nothing at all about it.'

'I hope you won't do anything so stupid, Alain,' Marguerite said. 'The Occupation is something we have to live with. I'm sure nobody likes it, but there's nothing we can do about it.'

Later, in bed, she said, 'I'm worried about Alain, the way he talks so wildly. I know he's clever, but I'm afraid that simply because he is clever and sure of his own mind and high-spirited, he will do something foolish. Before you came home this evening, he was saying these anti-Jewish laws are wicked. Well, I see that they are, even though I've never cared for Jews myself, and I don't see why the country has to be flooded with foreign ones, but it's no good speaking about such matters, is it? And if he talks so rashly at home, then I'm afraid he will do so at school as well, and then someone may denounce him. There are sure to be others there who approve of the measures. Of course, I don't know anything about these things, as you know I've never taken an interest in politics, but I'm afraid. Speak to him about it, will you? He respects your opinion.'

'All right,' Lannes said, and took her in his arms and kissed her. Her face was wet with tears. Then she fell asleep, her head against his shoulder. He thought of Miriam and wondered if she was lying awake, afraid for herself and Léon and her sister. Sigi's words came back to him: Herren-Moral und Sklaven-Moral. Was there any morality between the two, as he had always believed? Or were they all now condemned to make the choice between being Masters and Slaves?

In the morning he rose, as usual, while it was still dark. The melancholy sound of fog-horns came from the river and when the day dawned mist clung to the chimney-pots. He drank coffee, smoked cigarettes, and read the previous day's newspaper. There were letters approving the Vichy decree of 4 October which authorised the internment of foreign-born Jews in 'special camps'. One writer declared it was a fitting punishment for their role in dragging France into an unnecessary war. 'This demonstration of our solidarity with the German Reich is necessary if collaboration is to be a reality and the hardships of the Occupation are to be alleviated.' He recognized the writer's name, Labiche, a member of the Bordeaux Bar who two years ago had successfully defended a man arrested by Lannes and charged with the attempted murder of his wife's Jewish lover.

'All alone, Papa?'

He looked up to see Clothilde, barefoot and still in her night-gown.

'Your mother's still asleep. We won't wake her. She needs her sleep. Put something on your feet, child, or you'll catch cold.'

'That's all right. Don't fuss. I'm not a baby.'

She compromised however by settling herself on a chair and tucking her legs up.

'There's something I want to ask you,' she said. 'It's about the Germans. I know they're our enemies of course, but are they all?'

'Probably not, personally and as individuals. Nevertheless . . . Why do you ask?'

'You know the Romiers upstairs have had a German officer billeted on them? Marie says he's ever so nice. Well, I met him yesterday as I was coming home, and . . . yes, indeed he was nice, very friendly. He's young, not much older than Dominique. We chatted for maybe ten minutes, not more, but I could tell he wanted to be friends. I think he's lonely. He said it was difficult being away from home. His home's in Wurttemberg, he said, I didn't catch the name of the town, but he'd been at university there when he was called up. It's the first time he's been away from home, really away, from home, he said. I liked him, Papa. Is that wrong?'

'No, it's natural to like people. Being German doesn't mean he's not a human being. He may well be nice, as you say, but . . . '

'But what, Papa? That's what I wonder. What should I do?'

What indeed?

'Be polite yourself, and friendly, but, darling, no more than that. No more than that, please.'

'But it's not wrong?'

'No, it's not wrong, but some people might think it is.'

Others, he thought, would approve, and more than approve, applaud, as an exercise in collaboration, but this was not somewhere he wanted to go with his daughter.

## VIII

There was a newspaper on his desk, folded back to draw his attention to a photograph. Crosses had been penciled at each corner of the picture, just to make sure he didn't miss it. It showed Schnyder and his actress friend at the races. He remembered how Moncerre had laughed about it. So presumably he had laid it out for Lannes to see. The 'bull terrier' was right: Schnyder did indeed look like a cat that had got at the cream. Well, good luck to him, Lannes thought; we all need diversion or consolation these days, and in any case Schnyder and his wife were separated. Not that it would have been any of his business if they were still together. He was about to toss it aside when his attention was caught by the man visible behind the actress: a tall man – a head higher than her – with a thin pencil moustache and black, or at least dark, hair which even in the photograph seemed to shine with the lotion that kept it so neatly in place. He wore a ribbon on his lapel. The nose was high and arched and the eyes sunken.

Lannes knew he had never seen him, and yet . . . it would be a ridiculous coincidence . . . but it fitted the picture of Sigi's Spanish companion which he had formed from the descriptions given by Alain and Maurice. He could show it to Alain, but, no, keep the boy out of it, he thought, remembering what Marguerite had said last night. Or Schnyder? Ask him if he happened to have been introduced to the man who, he now saw, had laid a hand in familiar fashion on the actress's shoulder. Again, no: Schnyder had warned him off too many times. Admittedly he had done so in a friendly manner, but his patience probably wasn't inexhaustible. Lannes hesitated. He might have sent young René to question the Spaniards again, but they had been rounded up and were interned in a camp somewhere. And yet he had to know.

He had a friend who worked on the *Sud-Ouest*. He picked up the telephone to call him and ask him to make inquiries, then replaced the receiver before asking for an outside line. It was absurd, but he couldn't be certain that a tap hadn't been put on his phone. Ridiculous, but . . . Better to call him from a bar. He stuffed the newspaper into the inside pocket of his thorn-proof English coat and went out.

Jacques Maso was with him in less than twenty minutes, a short balding man with weary eyes. They shook hands, asked after each other's families, agreed it had been too long. Then Jacques said, 'You've got something for me? That pen-pusher in the morgue?'

'Afraid not, old man. That's well and truly under wraps.'

'Like everything nowadays. Pity. I could do with a good story.'

'The times we're in, the best stories can't be told.'

He hesitated. Jacques was an old friend. He'd always found him reliable, trustworthy. So why not?

'Some of them can't even be investigated.'

'Like that, is it?'

'Just like that.'

'Same with me. I know more than I can write. Any word of your boy?'

'We've heard he's a prisoner.'

'Could be worse. I was glad mine were too young to be called up. Now I don't know. There's talk – only talk as yet – of youngsters being sent to Germany as labourers and factory-workers. So, if there's no story, what is it, Jean?'

Lannes placed the paper on the table between them and put his finger on the corner of the photograph.

'Your boss, isn't it? And the fair Adrienne. That's going it.'

'No, not them, Jacques. That's no business of mine. It's this chap behind her who interests me. Do you know who is he by any chance? Or, if you don't, can you find out? Tactfully.'

'Like that, is it? Tact's certainly in demand these days. I'll do what I can. Chances are the photographer didn't know or bother to get his name. It's the fair Adrienne he'll have been interested in. and her new escort, of course. Quick worker, your boss, isn't he? Helps to be an Alsatian with a German name these days, don't it?'

Back at the office Lannes found a message from Rougerie. The little judge would like to see him 'as soon as convenient'.

He opened the door that led into the inspectors' room and called to Moncerre and young René.

'What's up, boss?'

'Rougerie wants to see me, but it's not that. Thanks for the photograph, Moncerre – I take it, it was you laid it out for me. Did you happen to look at the man behind Adrienne? No? I think it may be our Spaniard, Marcel's chum.'

'Have you asked Schnyder?' René said.

'And be told to keep his nose out if it,' Moncerre said. 'Be your age, kid.'

'No. I've asked Jacques Maso – you know him, don't you – to see if he can get a name.'

'Me and Jacques go back a long way,' Moncerre said. 'In fact we were in the same class at school. He's all right, Jacques.'

'Fine. Now I want you, Moncerre, to go and have another word with Madame Cortin. Press her about the meeting her husband went to. I'm sure she knows more than she let on. If she's difficult, then go over the story about the stolen car again. Don't hesitate to come down hard. I doubt if she's the grief-stricken widow. Ask her if she ever met the foster-brother's Spanish friend. Show her the photograph. Oh, and remember she knows Marcel as Sigi. As for you, young René, I want you to interview that young mother who lives on the ground-floor of the Catalan's apartment. I know you've spoken to her several times, but I'd like you to try again. She may just have remembered something else. We'll meet for lunch chez Fernand.'

'So the case isn't dead,' Moncerre said.

'Officially it's dead as mutton, but to my mind it's still breathing. One other thing. Because it's dead, nothing concerning it is to be discussed on the telephone. You understand?'

Moncerre laid his forefinger along the side of his nose.

'Like that, is it?'

'Like that. I should warn you to go carefully.'

'No need, chief. I know. If we're not careful, we're all deep in shit. So what? It's all shit nowadays.'


The little judge was agitated, hands flapping, snuff scattered all over his waistcoat.

'I've always stood by you, superintendent,' he said. 'You're what is called a maverick, even a loose cannon, and you're said to have flair, though I distrust that. Nevertheless I've always defended you against your critics, told them that you get results. That is why this is upsetting, so very upsetting.'

Lannes said nothing, waited.

'I don't want to think ill of you, you understand. You're a man I value. But I can't overlook complaints coming from the Mayor's office, now can I?'

'They've been complaining?'

'Yes, that's the first thing I have to say. It seems that this dead man – what's his name? Cerdan?'

'Cortin, sir.'

'Whatever,' the judge took another pinch of snuff and sneezed. 'It seems he was well thought of there, and they want his killer found. Naturally. But there's been no action. They complain that you're dragging your heels.'

'It's only forty-eight hours since he was fished out of the river.'

'Well then, and what progress have you made? Why have I, the examining magistrate, been kept in the dark?'

Best place for you, Lannes thought, but said only, 'In the dark, sir? The investigation's at a very early stage, or would be, were it not for the fact that it appears to be connected with other cases I've been forbidden to pursue. It seems that it raises political questions, very sensitive ones.'

'Political questions?'

'So I'm told, sir. Perhaps you should speak with Commissaire Schnyder. He knows more about the political aspects than I do.'

'If there are political considerations, that puts a different complexion on it,' the judge said.

'However – and speaking tentatively – I think I can say that, despite these potentially embarrassing political connections, there is every indication that the unfortunate Monsieur Cortin may have been the victim of a purely criminal act, a street robbery that went wrong. This seems the most likely explanation and is the line we are currently pursuing, cautiously of course in view of the possible relation of this murder with these other delicate cases. Perhaps this will reassure the mayor's office.'

Would he swallow that? Ignore the about-turn Lannes had made in a couple of sentences?

It seemed he would, for he merely nodded and muttered something inaudible.

'Was there anything else, sir.'

'I'm afraid there is and it's most distasteful. Without precedent in my long experience. I'm embarrassed, superintendent, but it's my duty to bring it to your attention. I've received this. It's anonymous of course, and dirty, very unpleasant.'

He handed Lannes a sheet of note-paper such as any café might supply. Words cut from a newspaper were pasted to it, reading: 'Ask jew-lover Lannes why he is protecting a jewish rent-boy.'

'Can you explain that?'

'It means nothing to me, sir.'

'Is that all you have to say?'

'It's malicious of course. And quite without basis in fact.'

'So what do you suggest I should do with this . . . this piece of ordure?'

'That must be your decision, sir. You must see I can't advise you – whether to put it in the waste-paper basket or to file it.'

Alain was right: there are times when lying is not only permissible, but necessary.


## IX


'Partridge with red cabbage,' Fernand said. 'Don't ask me where I got the birds. And a nice St-Emilion? Good?'

'Sounds all right,' Moncerre said. 'After a session with that cow I'm in need of a good meal.'

There were more German officers than French people in the restaurant, but Fernand had kept the table in the back-room for them. Labiche, the advocate who had written the letter to the newspaper which Lannes had read with disgust that morning, was across the room at a table by himself. He was reading what looked like a brief and smoking a cigarette through a long tortoiseshell holder.

'Did you get anything from her?'

'Did I, hell. Nothing concrete, that's to say, but I'll swear she knows who her husband had gone to meet. Thing is, her mood was different. She was still disagreeable – she'll always be that, in my opinion – accused us of incompetence, the bitch. But I got the impression that she's afraid too, as if someone has put the wind up her. Well, we don't need to guess who that is likely to have been. What did Rougerie want, chief?'

'He's had a complaint from the Mayor's office. They think we're dragging our heels on the Cortin case. They want it solved.'

'And nobody else does,' Moncerre said. 'Fuck them all.'

'René?'

'Nothing either, I'm afraid, chief. She's a nice woman and I'm sure she would help us if she could. She liked Javier Cortazar and is horrified by what happened to him, but I really think she knows nothing. She's heard by the way that her husband's a prisoner of war, just like your Dominique. Worrying about him and caring for the baby – that's really all that's on her mind. Do you want me to have another go at the Brunes – the couple upstairs?'

'I doubt if it's worth it,' Lannes said.

'Is anything?' Moncerre said. 'Since we're evidently not going to be allowed to arrest anyone. We're being given the run-around and it's my opinion that we're wasting our time. Mind you, things being as they are, what else are we to do with ourselves?'

'Do you feel like that too, chief?'

'I'm tempted to agree. All the same we keep digging. In fact I'm more determined than ever.'

He paused. Should he mention the anonymous letter Rougerie had received?

No, not even to colleagues he trusted. It was too shameful. Disturbing nevertheless.

Fernand brought them the wine and put a basket of bread and a platter of charcuterie on the table. Lannes indicated Labiche.

'Is that one a regular?'

'I'm glad to say not. In fact the table was booked by the new Comte de Grimaud who's already half an hour late. They're two of a kind, both swine if you ask me. But these days I can't afford to be choosey about my customers.' He gestured towards the other room where the Germans were eating. 'If I was, I'd soon be out of business.'

'Never mind,' Lannes said. 'Our revered Mayor would approve. So would the Marshal. They'd call it an exercise in positive collaboration.'

'Shit – is my answer to that. Enjoy your meal, gentlemen.'

They were eating the partridge and red cabbage, every bit as good as Fernand had promised, and drinking their second bottle of claret when Jean-Christophe joined Labiche. His face was flushed and his gait unsteady, as if he had stopped at a couple of bars on his way to the restaurant. He shook hands with the lawyer who put his papers away in his briefcase and called out to Fernand. Jean-Christophe had sat down before he noticed Lannes. He gave no sign of recognition but began talking to Labiche in a manner that suggested urgency. The advocate looked over at Lannes and nodded.

Moncerre said, 'That's the cunt that likes little girls, isn't it? They say it takes all sorts to make a world but in my opinion we'd be better off without types of that sort.'

'He's not up to much,' Lannes said. 'He's a poor wretch but there are worse. Speaking of which, I broke bounds yesterday and had a word with Marcel. Sigi's his real name, as you know, and he's that fellow's nephew, perhaps even his half-brother too. I've known that for some time,' he added, and recounted what old Marthe had told him.

'And she really believes he killed the old man?' René said.

'She has no doubt about it, but it's not something that's ever likely to be proved. An old man – a fall down stairs – simple way to get rid of anyone – and unless there's a witness . . . '

'So,' Moncerre said, 'so you talked with him, and . . . '

'He's like a cock crowing on a dunghill. Happy to think he's one of the Untouchables, just as Schnyder told me.'

'Do you mean he admitted?' René said.

'He admitted nothing, and denied nothing.'

'And there's nothing we can do,' Moncerre said. 'Crazy world. Makes you sick.'

'He'll overreach himself. One day, he'll overreach himself. He's eaten up with conceit and vanity and so he'll do something stupid.'

'And we still won't be able to do anything about it.'

'We'll see about that. Meanwhile, let's hope Jacques Maso comes up with an identification of the man in the photograph and that he is indeed our Spaniard. If so, we concentrate our fire on him. I have a notion he may not be untouchable. He may prove to be Sigi's weak spot. In any case, nobody's warned us off him, because Schnyder doesn't even know of his existence. All he knows is that there were two men in the car from which the shot was fired at me.'

Leaving the restaurant Lannes headed for the rue des Remparts. It was raining softly and there were few people in the streets. Again he had the sensation of life being suspended, of Bordeaux drawing in on itself in apprehension and shame. For so many of the citizens there was now no security except within the family, and at home they were spared the sight of the occupying army. You could pretend that life was still as it had been before the war – so long as the shutters were closed and the outer world excluded.

He found Léon alone, sitting reading a book with his feet up on the desk. He looked up and, without taking the cigarette from his mouth, said, 'Oh, it's you. I thought for a moment it might be a customer. There hasn't been a single one all day, except for two German officers.'

'What did they want?'

'Something to read. What else?'

'And what did you sell them?'

'Nothing. They said our prices were too high. Don't worry. I was polite, respectful. Henri's upstairs, drinking whisky, I'm afraid. He doesn't do much else now. Sometimes when he's had a few, he comes down and talks at length about Gaston. I don't know if it does him any good, but it makes me feel guilty, though I don't know why. I gave Gaston what he wanted, didn't I? But I wish I had known him better, even in a different way actually. It's how Henri speaks of him, with admiration as well as affection. He recalls him as he was when he was young and eager and happy, before he became what he did. Then he's embarrassed because that's the side of Gaston's life I belonged to or was part of.'

'You don't have to blame yourself. What are you reading?'

Léon held up the book, so that Lannes could read the title: *Le Grand Meaulnes*.

'I've read it before,' the boy said. 'Twice actually. It was wonderful then and it seems even better now. It lets you forget how things are.'

'I suppose it may. I was in the trenches when I read it. The man who gave it to me caught it the next day, shot in the head. The author himself had already gone. Well, we all have our "lost domain" now. It's called Peace.'

He found himself liking the boy, even though the reminder of what he had done with Gaston, or permitted Gaston to do to him, was disgusting. Still, given his situation, he was bearing up well, bravely, showing some grace under pressure. In any case, no matter what disgust he felt, Lannes knew very well that the barricades of Reason and Decency are weak defences against sexual desire. Hadn't some Greek philosopher said that when Eros, the boy-god of love and servant of Aphrodite, lets loose his dart, his victim is wounded, poisoned, incapable of resistance, no longer responsible for his actions – a concept after all which the Code recognized, holding that the perpetrator of a 'crime of passion' was beyond rational restraint.

'I'll go up to see Henri in a minute,' he said, 'but I want a word with you first.'

'Me? I'm being good, I told you that, and nothing's changed. Not that I have much chance to be anything else just now.'

'I'm glad to hear it. Who knows I got you your job here?'

'Why do you ask?'

'Just answer, please.'

'Well, Henri, obviously, and Aunt Miriam, seeing as you spoke about it to her yourself. But I haven't told anyone else, not even Maman. As for my friends, well I scarcely see any of them since you advised me to lie low – what did you say? – keep a low profile, keep out of sight, and don't get into mischief. And anyway, even if I was chatting to any of them about my new job, I'm not likely to boast that a cop found it for me. Most of my old mates don't have much time for the "flics", sorry.'

'You're sure?'

'Naturally I'm sure. Why do you ask?'

Lannes was reluctant to tell him. To speak of the anonymous letter was humiliating – humiliating for the boy also. Still he was entitled to know, and to deny him that knowledge was to treat him as a child or inferior. Nevertheless the version he gave him was watered down; he steered clear of the word 'rent-boy'. He had no reason to think the accusation just, no evidence that Léon had ever prostituted himself. Gaston had picked him up. That was the boy's story and he had found no difficulty in believing him.

Léon swung his feet off the desk and looked away. When he spoke, his voice was shaky.

'I've got you into trouble, but I swear I haven't told anyone. Honest.'

He sounded close to tears.

'That's all right,' Lannes said. 'There's no reason from your point of view why you shouldn't have mentioned it, and I wouldn't blame you if you had. But I had to know if I'm to find out who wrote the letter.'

'It won't do you any good to be suspected of protecting a Jew, will it?'

'As to that, I don't give a damn.'

'They're rounding up the foreign Jews. How long before they come for us French ones?'

'A long time, I hope. Perhaps never.'

'You don't really believe that, do you?'

'I would like to. I'll go up to see Henri now.'

Henri might have blabbed, he thought. It's quite likely that he did if he really is in his cups much of the time, as I'm afraid he is. But I can't ask him. He already feels guilty about Gaston, which is probably why he agreed to take the boy on, even if I think he has nothing with which to reproach himself as far as his twin was concerned. He always behaved well to him, and in any case his natural kindness would probably have led him to give Léon a job when I asked him to, even if there had been no connection with Gaston. But I can't pile more guilt on him. So, after they had embraced and exchanged pleasantries, all he said was: 'Has anyone been asking questions about young Léon?'

'No. Nobody. Why?'

'Just checking, that's all. If anyone does come round asking questions, just say he came and asked you if there was a job going.'

'You think he's in some danger, Jean?'

'Probably not. Not yet anyway.'

Leaving Henri, he cut through the Place Gambetta to Miriam's tabac. He couldn't speak of Léon and the anonymous letter to

209

Marguerite or indeed to any of his colleagues, but he felt the need to unburden himself. So, when they were settled in the back room, with what was now the usual coffee and marc, he came out with it straight, verbatim.

' "Jew-lover", "Jewish rent-boy", I don't like it, Jean. It's malicious. Someone wants to destroy you.'

'I don't think it goes that far, not necessarily. Keep me in line, warn me off, more like.'

'Warn you off what?'

'I can't say exactly. There are always things people don't want investigated.'

'Is Léon in danger himself?'

'No more, I think, than he was. Than you all are. I've told him to keep his head down.'

'It's wicked,' she said, 'when all you've tried to do is help us.'

For some time they sat in silence. The little room was lit by only a single lamp with a low-wattage bulb. The silence was comfortable, companionable. Lannes relaxed. He searched in his pockets for a cigarette, found only an empty packet. Miriam went through to the tabac and returned with a carton of Gauloises.

'On the house,' she said. 'Don't argue, it's the least I can do.'

She lit one of her own Chesterfields.

'It's all getting you down, isn't it,' she said.

'Do you know an advocate called Labiche?'

'That bastard. He's a customer. Turkish cigarettes, expensive ones. Did you see his letter in the *Sud-Ouest*? I've a good mind to refuse to serve him any longer.'

'Please don't do that. It would be . . . rash.'

'Why do you want to know? If I know him, I mean.'

'I saw him today with Jean-Christophe. That's all.'

'They're two of a kind,' she said. 'No, that's not true. Jean-Christophe's only pathetic, while Labiche is really evil. I'm sure of that for he used to do business for my husband, and he, as you know, was a connoisseur of evil. Oh, it's all too horrible.'

He got up to go. She rose also and they embraced. He screwed his head round to kiss her on the lips. For an instant she responded, then drew away.

'No,' she said. 'No. Perhaps we both want to, but no. Let's not complicate things more. Besides you owe it to your wife for there to be nothing more than friendship between us. I don't want to lose you as a friend, Jean, which would be the result if . . . '

As he walked home, with his hip throbbing, he felt ashamed at having come so close to infidelity. He remembered the hint of blackmail Sigi had dropped.


## X


Dinner was over. Marguerite was sewing. The children were washing-up. Lannes stretched himself on the couch and read *Le Vicomte de Bragelonne*. He knew it so well that he skipped certain passages to arrive at his favourite ones. Nowadays he preferred the ageing d'Artagnan, face wrinkled, anxious about his future, to the dashing young musketeer of the earlier novels. But still capable of the most audacious strokes – the transporting of General Monk across the Channel in a box – marvellous. And the distrust of authority, of Cardinal and King – well, he was at one with him there.

'I don't know why it is that Alain always has a hole in the heel of his sock. Dominique never did.'

Alain, coming through from the kitchen, said, 'It's because, Maman, half my socks used to be his. Also I run more than he used to.'

'Didn't you say you'd an essay to write?' Lannes said.

'I'm brooding on it. Cogitating. Then when I come to attack it, it will flow quick as lightning.'

'Lightning doesn't flow,' Clothilde said.

'All right then, it'll dart like lightning. Does that satisfy your literal mind?'

'Don't bicker, children,' Marguerite said.

'What a bore this curfew is,' Clothilde said. 'This time last year we could have gone to the cinema. It's as if we were in a cage.'

'All Europe's a cage,' Alain said, 'and Herr Hitler's the keeper. "Heil the Fuehrer", I don't think.'

The telephone rang. Clothilde jumped up to answer it. The

instrument was in the hall and they couldn't hear what she said, but Lannes thought there was disappointment in her voice. Then she laughed.

'It's for you, papa. Someone called Jacques something, I didn't catch it. He took me for Maman, then said I sounded very grown-up. Well, I am nearly, I said.'

'Jacques? Any luck?'

'I think so. Do you want me to tell you now?'

'Are you speaking from your office?'

'Yes, I'm still at my desk, slaving away.'

'Can anyone hear you?'

'Well, the place isn't exactly deserted.'

'In that case, if you don't mind, let's meet in the morning.'

'Fine by me. Same place? Nine o'clock do you?'

'I'll be there. Thanks, Jacques.'

He had escaped the embarrassment of explaining he was afraid his telephone – here too – might be tapped. Was the suspicion – which he had after all no evidence to support – becoming an obsession?

Marguerite didn't ask the caller's name, though she must have been curious after what Clothilde had said. It was work, none of her business, part of his life she wanted nothing of.

'Jacques Maso,' he said, 'you remember him, don't you?'

'I haven't thought of him for years. He used to be such a good dancer. We used to meet at the "bals musettes" – oh long before you two were born.'

'Your mother and Jacques used to make a very distinguished couple. They were the best by far on the dance-floor whereas I was always told I had two left feet.'

'So you did.'

'I think he was what we used to call sweet on your mother. I'm not surprised he mistook you for her, Clothilde. He's a journalist now, on the *Sud-Ouest*.'

'Is he?'

Lannes thought: I treasure old friends because memories matter to me. Marguerite discards them happily. Family's all that counts for her now. Even Henri . . . I doubt if she has been to the bookshop more than a couple of times in the last five years, though he would love it if she dropped in, whereas I . . . I keep hold of the past like a drowning man clutching a rope that some passer-by has thrown him.

Alain said: 'You know that the Romiers upstairs have had a German officer billeted on them. He stopped me today as I came in. No, it wasn't anything to worry about, Maman. It was just because he noticed I was carrying a German book – *The Sorrows of Werther*, which is one of our set texts. He asked me if I was enjoying it. Actually I'm not – it seems dated and a bit silly – but I thought it polite to say it was all right. Then we chatted for a bit, his French is quite good. He seemed a nice enough chap – he's not much older than Dominique – but I didn't like it. I felt it was wrong somehow to be having a friendly conversation with him. What do you think, Papa?'

'They're going to be here for a long time. It's not always going to be possible to avoid them. So be civil, nothing more. That's my advice.'

He was careful not to look at his daughter in case she was blushing.

'Poor boy,' Marguerite said. 'He's probably lonely, and home-sick.'

## XI

The rain, still streaking the windows when Lannes sat with his morning pot of coffee in the kitchen, had stopped, and a pale sun was dispelling the mist that crept over the city from the river. He found Jacques already in the bar, scribbling in a notebook.'

'I don't know why I bother,' he said, stuffing the book into the pocket of his raincoat. 'I make notes for articles that will never be published.'

'And I pursue cases that can't be brought to a conclusion.'

They exchanged smiles, like conspirators. The waiter brought coffee and two small glasses of marc.

Jacques said, 'So be it,' and raised his glass in acknowledgement.

'I thought your daughter was Marguerite. She sounded so like her. Did she tell you?'

'Yes, and I recalled what a fine couple you used to make at our bals musettes. So long ago.'

'So long ago.'

They smiled again. This time, Lannes thought, it was as if each was hearing the accordion music of their youth.

'I've got your identification,' Jacques said. 'He's a Spaniard, Don Jaime Sombra, which may or may not be his true name. Who can tell nowadays? He's what they call a socialite, but, according to my informant, five years ago he was living in Paris and cadging drinks, meals whatever, in the cafés of Montparnasse. Or he was kept by a succession of rich women, in other words he was a gigolo, though he didn't last long with any of them. Do you want to know the name of my informant? I have to say he would rather you didn't.'

'Fine by me. Anything else?'

'Only that his money troubles seem to have evaporated, and my informant believes he may be one of Franco's agents, employed here to spy on Republicans and their sympathizers. Incidentally, he also has a French passport, though I don't know how he comes by it. Perhaps his mother was French? Perhaps he was born here?'

'You've done wonderfully, Jacques. I'm very grateful.'

'Is it impertinent of me to ask why you are so interested in this type?'

'Not at all, so long as you understand there's no story for your paper. It's because I'm pretty sure he tried to kill me.'

Back at the office, Joseph told him there was a gentleman asking to see him.

'A gentleman?'

'That's what I said. We don't get many of them here, but I can recognize one when I see him. He reminds me of a colonel I served under, stiff as a ramrod, but nevertheless cared for his men and saw that we were decently treated – as far as was within his power, that is.'

'Fine. Give me ten minutes and then bring him in.'

Moncerre was in the inspectors' room, shuffling a pack of cards.

'It's bad news when I'm reduced to playing patience,' he said. 'I hope you've got something for me, because I don't mind confessing I'm bored out of my mind.'

'Your old schoolfellow Jacques has come up trumps,' Lannes said. 'Listen.'

'Not bad,' Moncerre said, 'he sounds like the sort that needs his arse kicked. I don't mind obliging if that's what you want.'

'It may come to that. Meanwhile the only address we have for him is the house in the rue d'Aviau, which he visits even if he isn't living there, as I don't think he is. So I want you to stake it out, and, if he turns up, bring him in. A question of papers, or something like that, I don't need to explain the drill to you. Don't approach the house. There are German officers billeted there. Take young René with you. The boy needs to be kept busy.'

Joseph's 'gentleman' did indeed look like a colonel, a retired one certainly. He held himself upright, had a moustache like the Marshal's, a full head of snowy hair, neatly brushed, and highly polished shoes. He was wearing a charcoal grey suit, with a waist-coat and gold watch-chain, though the suit was shiny at the knees and had been sponged and pressed too often. His nose was like an eagle's beak and the yellowish skin of his face was leathery. There were liver spots on the back of his hands.

'Do you know,' he said, 'I'm over seventy and I've never before had dealings with the police.'

'That's not so unusual, I'm glad to say. How can I help you?'

'It was Henri Chambolley suggested I approach you, personally and informally. He said he was a friend of yours.'

'Since we were students.'

'So you also knew poor Gaston, a talented fellow, even if his talent rather flickered out. A wretched end. I scarcely dare to ask whether . . . '

'I can't answer that, I'm afraid.'

'No, of course not, I apologize for inquiring. To come to the point, the purpose of my visit, which is difficult and embarrassing, and which is not, I trust, properly speaking, police business. That's to say no crime has been committed, so far as I know, though then again I may be mistaken. But if I am, this is not something I should wish to see brought before the courts. I'm afraid I don't make myself plain, but that is because the matter of which I wish to speak is painful to me. Let me give you my card. You see, I'm a Professor of Literature, retired naturally, seeing as I'm seventy-five. I'm also a widower and have been for more years than I care to think. My only son – our only son – was an army officer, a major in the colonial infantry. He was killed the day the Germans crossed the Meuse.'

'I'm sorry.'

'He too was a widower. His wife died giving birth to their daughter whose guardian I now am, also of their son, a boy of seventeen. He's difficult, has been ever since he went to the lycée. I have no control over him whatsoever. He's not a bad boy, I'm sure of that, indeed he is charming and affectionate, but he is wild and intensely – romantically, I choose to think – political. He was a member of one of those youth groups attached to Colonel de la Roque's Croix de Feu movement. It's a tradition in our family, we were always Royalist, but I myself broke away and am a good Republican because the Republic for all its defects represents principles which I hold by. In my youth I even wrote for *L'Aurore* and knew Clemenceau when he edited the paper, not only knew him but revered him, as I still revere his memory. So you will understand that I find our present state to be shameful, though I have no doubt that the Marshal, poor man, is actuated, as he always has been, by noble motives and true patriotism. I trust I am not boring you?'

'Not at all,' Lannes said, and lit a cigarette. 'Pray continue.'

'Michel's an attractive boy, and intelligent, if also silly. You will know, I'm sure, superintendent, that intelligence and silliness are quite frequently found together. Unfortunately, as I say, I have no control over him, and I confess there have been times when I have all but shrugged my shoulders and told myself he must make his own way to perdition or redemption. Do you think that irresponsible of me?'

'There's a limit,' Lannes said, 'to what we can do for others, even for the young.'

'Nevertheless one has to try, but to my shame I have to admit that he has escaped me, for the time being anyway. My immediate concern is for his sister, my granddaughter Anne-Marie. She's only fourteen, an innocent child still, and I have a deep affection for her. I think she's fond of me, but she adores her brother, which is understandable. But he has got into bad company and I'm afraid for her.'

He took a handkerchief from his pocket and blew his nose loudly. A cloud passed over the sun and the room was darkened. Silence prolonged itself. Lannes wondered where this was leading, whether it could possibly concern him in any way. And yet he was concerned, aware of the old man's distress and perplexity, which awakened in him the same sense of pity that he now so often felt for Marguerite and was ashamed of feeling because it seemed that her unhappiness was a reflection of his own inadequacy, and because there is always something of condescension in pity.

'Excuse me a moment,' he said, and went out and asked Joseph to have the bar send up coffee for them. He smoked a cigarette. When he returned the professor had composed himself.

'To some extent,' he said, 'it's my fault, or rather, to be fair to myself, a consequence of my circumstances. My late wife had a brother, now also dead. His widow has always taken an interest in the children who have, as you will understand, lived with me for most of their lives, on account of their father's service overseas, in Algeria and Indo-China. I haven't encouraged this interest because, to speak frankly, I dislike her and disapprove of her. She's eaten up with pride of birth, and I should say that my late wife's family, who belonged to the "petite noblesse", suffered from the same affliction, as it is to my eyes. Moreover, since I consider her to be stupid, a woman of no intellectual interests and coarse sensibility, you will understand my reservations, even reluctance. However, she is the children's aunt, if only by marriage, and this, as you will agree, entitles her to take, as I say, an interest in them. I should perhaps add that Henri tells me you have yourself had dealings with her family, which is one of the factors that has emboldened me to trouble you with what must otherwise seem to be purely personal matters, no concern of yours as a policeman.'

'Perhaps you had better tell me who you are speaking of.'

'I don't wish to indulge in slander, but to my mind they're a disreputable family. The children's aunt, who is also of course my sister-in-law, is Madame Thibault de Polmont, and her father was the Comte de Grimaud who died recently.'

'Ah,' Lannes said. 'I understand your concern. It's a nest of vipers, that house.'

The professor smiled for the first time at this allusion to the title of a novel by Bordeaux's greatest man-of-letters, François Mauriac.

'I won't dispute your judgement,' he said.

There was a knock at the door and without waiting for a reply the boy from the bar came in with a pot of coffee and two cups. The professor stirred two lumps into his and continued, 'I wouldn't call my sister-in-law a viper. I might even, in a generous moment, say she was well-meaning, but her late father, yes indeed, a viper. Now, to come to the point, there are other members of the family who also merit that description. Have you, I wonder, encountered a young man who goes by the name of Sigi and who is some sort of disreputable connection, one of the old count's by-blows, I believe? Michel is dazzled by him. I don't think there is anything vicious in their relationship, but it is still an undesirable one. The whole family is pro-German – I should say that my late wife had German cousins, who were perfectly respectable, though I never found them sympathetic. Of course, in present circumstances, there's no danger in holding such views – quite the reverse indeed. Nevertheless, as one who doesn't despair of France – Henri tells me I may safely confess this to you – I can't believe that things will remain as they are. For which reason, if no other – and there are others – I find this association – the boy's hero-worship for this fellow – not only deplorable, but dangerous. He is quite capable of becoming deeply and foolishly engaged, and led into all sorts of folly. Do you know this man Sigi?'

'I know enough of him to be sure your fears for your grandson are justified.'

'I see. There's worse, I'm afraid. Do you know the present Comte de Grimaud?'

'I do.'

'Then you will also know that he has a certain reputation, in short that he's a degenerate. Michel has introduced his sister to him and . . . it's difficult to go on.'

'I understand.'

'I don't believe anything untoward has happened, but . . . he buys her little presents. She says he amuses her and is good fun. I've tried to warn her off but she just laughs and gives me a kiss and tells me not to be so silly.'

'Have you spoken to Jean-Christophe himself?'

The old man's hands trembled.

'He laughed at me. I didn't . . . couldn't go on. I suppose I'm a coward. But, as I say, I'm afraid, Anne-Marie's so innocent.'

She might not be, Lannes thought. He remembered what Miriam had said, about the perverse or corrupt desire of a young girl to be the plaything of an older man.

'And you would like me to intervene?'

'Is that too much to ask? Is it, as they say, "out of line"? It's not a police matter perhaps. Nevertheless I'm at my wits' end.'

'It will be a pleasure,' Lannes said. 'I've had words before with Jean-Christophe on other matters. He won't laugh at me.'

He may suppose, he thought, that he too is one of the 'Untouchables'. I'll show him how wrong he is.


## XII

Lannes sat smoking at his desk. It's like a maze, he said to himself. I go round and round in circles. I lay down markers for myself and pass them again and again. I don't know what lies at the centre, can't even be sure there is a centre. So, try to establish a chronology.

It begins with Pilar. I'm sure of that. Wish I had known her better. Wish I could be sure anyone really knew her. Gaston thought the Communists betrayed her to the Fascists who killed her. Why would they do that? When that would be collusion between enemies? If Gaston was right, why was he killed? What did his killers think he knew? Who were they protecting?

I'm no nearer to knowing the answer to these questions.

He took a sheet of paper and wrote.

1 Pilar murdered. That's an assumption. When? Why? By whom?

2 Sigi returns to Bordeaux? Winter 1939–40. Why?

3 Gaston murdered. February 1940. By Sigi and the Spaniard, Sombra – I've no doubt about that. But why was his body mutilated? To suggest a sex-crime? Or just for fun? He was tortured in an attempt to extract information and the apartment searched. Unsuccessfully (assumption).

4 The Comte de Grimaud asks me to investigate the authorship of anonymous letters. (His daughter – ghastly woman – says he wrote them himself.) Motive? To draw my attention to his house and family? But why? In any case Marthe says Jean-Christophe was their author.

5 The Catalan, Javier Cortazar, is tortured and dies of a heart attack. Murder in all but name. Perpetrators: almost certainly Sigi and Sombra. What information could he have had which connected him to Pilar? Did they find what they were looking for? Presumption negative.

6 The old count dies, falling downstairs. Marthe is sure that Sigi, his bastard son, pushed him. Impossible to prove. But, again, why?

7 Edmond de Grimaud warns me off; this following Rougerie's determination to have the investigation of Gaston's murder closed down. Later Edmond is happy his son Maurice should lodge with us (why?), until suddenly he summons him to Vichy.

8 Leaving the Hotel Splendide in company with Edmond, I am shot. Edmond pretends the bullet was intended for him. Improbable.

9 The shot was fired from a car belonging to a city employee, Jules Cortin, who reported it stolen. There were stubs of Virginian cigarttes in the car. Sigi smokes English cigarettes called Goldflake. We learn later that Cortin and Sigi were brought up together and that Cortin's father is Marthe's cousin.

10 It's made clear to me again – by Schnyder too – that the investigation can't be pursued. Untouchables.

11 Cortin is fished dead out of the Garonne. Strangled or garrotted. His wife admits he had gone to a meeting, pretends she knew nothing more. Lying probably.

12 The Mayor's office complains we are stalling on Cortin's case. When I tell Rougerie of its connections, he makes it clear he will turn the complaint aside. Running scared?

13 Professor (he picked up the card the old man had given him) Lazaire asks my help. His grandchildren (Michel and Anne-Marie) are in bad company: Sigi, to whom the boy has attached himself – hero-worship? – and Jean-Christophe who has a record of interfering with little girls. Anne-Marie is fourteen.

It all comes back to that house in the rue d'Aviau where German officers are now billeted.

(And what of the young lieutenant in his own building who had spoken to Cothilde and Alain, and whom Clothilde, he feared, found attractive?)

He read over his notes. What or whom had he left out?

Léon of course, who had been Gaston's boy-friend and who had seen Gaston afraid when Sigi came into the Café des Arts. Léon who had scarcely thought of himself as a Jew till the Occupation. Léon whom Lannes had been accused of protecting by an anonymous letter-writer who had called him 'a Jewish rent-boy'. Nasty, and who had written it?

That too was a question to be solved, but there wasn't going to be any mention of Léon in this memo which he would pass to Moncerre and young René for comment.

Was this reticence for the boy's sake or his own?

Any other questions?

He stubbed out his cigarette, lit another, and wrote: Why has there been no second attempt on my life?

Because Edmond has called them off? Which only moves the 'why?' one step back.

He added: Why did Jean-Christophe meet advocate Labiche chez Fernand? Is that significant? Is there any connection?

Sigi had issued that delicate hint of blackmail. He didn't record this either. Instead he wrote: In normal circumstances none of these 'whys' would matter. We have enough evidence to charge Sigi and probably the Spaniard. But neither the times nor the circumstances are normal. I want to know the answers all the same. I suspect Sigi is not a free agent – despite his rhetoric, but acts under orders. Whose? Edmond's surely. And precisely why have we been called off the case? It must turn on Pilar's activities and death. That's the starting-point of it all, with only one exception: the old count's summons and his murder, if it was murder.

He got up and looked out of the window. A pale sun made the damp branches of the planes trees glisten. What did Sigi want of the boy Michel? As, for me, he thought, I'm a hunter by trade, but I'm being stalked myself. The jungle and the village gates.

## XIII

Léon was dusting books which he was sure nobody would buy, handsome leather-bound editions of eighteenth-century sermons, when Alain came into the shop, and he liked the look of him at first sight. He replaced the volume he was holding, laid aside the duster, lit a cigarette, and, good bookshop assistant, said, 'Can I help you?'

'Well, you could give me a cigarette, if you can spare one, that is.'

'Willingly.'

'Are you sure?'

'Oh yes, even though they are coming to be in short supply. I'm fortunate because my aunt who now runs the tabac that used to belong to my grandfather sees that I don't run short. She thinks it helps to keep me out of mischief.'

'Thanks. Why should she think you would get into mischief?'

'Don't you find that the older generation are always afraid of that? Or perhaps yours are different?'

'Not that different,' Alain said. 'You're new here, aren't you? What happened to old Bloch?'

'You knew him, did you? He got away. North Africa, Algeria or Tunis, I don't know which.'

'Lucky man.'

'You think so?'

'Don't you?'

'I don't know. It's quite interesting being here just now.'

He smiled, to hold Alain's attention and knowing that he had said this to make himself appear interesting too.

'Was there anything in particular you were looking for?'

'Not really,' Alain said. 'I just like old bookshops, and anyway Monsieur Chambolley's a friend of the family, well of my father really.'

'Would you like some coffee? I could make some while you browse.'

'That would be nice. Are you sure? Can you be bothered?'

'I was just going to make some for myself.'

Léon went through to the back-room where there was a paraffin-stove, prepared the coffee-pot and set it on the flame. While he waited for the water to boil, he shot glances at Alain reading, and liked the way his hair lay on his neck.

'Here we are,' he said.

Before closing his book, Alain said, 'This is good, isn't it? "Moments of crisis produce a redoubling of life in man." Or don't you think so?'

'I don't know. I'd have to think about that.'

He handed Alain a cup.

'Henri still has real coffee,' he said.

'Good of you to share it then.'

'It's a pleasure. Who said that, anyway?'

'Said what? Oh, what I read. Chateaubriand in his memoirs. He'd reason to know after all. He lived through the Revolution and the Napoleonic wars. Do you think it's true of our situation now? We're certainly living through a crisis.'

'Which is redoubling our life? It hadn't occurred to me.'

'No?' Alain said. 'But don't you feel that, however circumscribed our daily life is now, we are nevertheless living more intensely, and will remember this time as such, assuming we survive it of course.'

'Assuming?' Léon said. 'I'm a Jew. Things being as they are, I think I should tell you that.'

Alain flushed.

'And you think I should care about that? It's almost an insult. No, in fact it really is an insult.'

'Drink your coffee,' Léon said, and handed him another cigarette. 'I didn't mean to insult you. It's just we've got off to such a good start that I thought I should tell you. If we're going to be friends, as I hope we may be. I'm glad you think it's an insult though.'

He removed a pile of books from the chair to the right of the desk and sat down on the other one, indicating to Alain that he should take the one he had cleared. Alain removed his jacket and hung it on the back of the chair before sitting.

'This must be one of the few warm rooms in Bordeaux,' he said, 'you're lucky. How did you get the job?'

'I just came in and asked if there was by any chance one going.'

He hesitated. Alain had rolled his sleeves up. Léon reached out and touched his bare arm just above the elbow.

'Actually, that's not quite true. It's what I would tell most people who asked, but the truth is I used to know Henri's brother Gaston.'

He looked Alain in the eye, with some apprehension lest he knew about Gaston and guessed what their relationship had been and was offended or disgusted. He read neither response there, and emboldened, even hopeful, added, 'I suppose I can say we were friends.'

'And then he was murdered.'

'Yes. It was horrible, I don't like to speak about it.'

'Nor does my father. Oh, I should tell you he's a policeman, a superintendent, and in charge of investigating the case. He never talks about his cases at home, my mother doesn't like him to, but I know he has specially hated this one because Gaston was a friend when they were young.'

Léon wondered how much he dared say.

'I've met your father, and not only because of Henri, but . . . because of being a friend of Gaston too. I think he's a good man.'

'Yes. Yes, he is. Despite being a policeman, you mean?'

Léon laughed for the first time.

'Exactly, despite him being a policeman, just as, if we are to be friends, it's despite me being a Jew.'

'As far as I'm concerned that's irrelevant, means nothing. I think these anti-Jewish laws are monstrous.'

'It won't surprise you to know that I agree with you.'

This time they both laughed. Then Alain, serious, said, 'It almost makes me ashamed of being French.'

'Only "almost"?'

'More than "almost".'

Léon took a newspaper cutting from the drawer of the desk and handed it to Alain.

'Did you see this?'

It was the account Lannes had shown him of the death sentence imposed on the Polish Jew, Israel Karp, and carried out the following morning.

'Yes, I read it. It's disgusting, utterly vile.'

'Your father gave it to me. As a warning.'

'Why did he think you needed a warning.'

'Because of something I'd said.'

'Oh, you feel like that too? Good. And not just because you're Jewish?'

'Certainly not just because I'm Jewish.'

'What can we do? There must be something.'

'There's nothing at the moment, nothing I can think of, but . . . '

'Some day, you mean.'

'I hope so.'

'My mother's afraid for me,' Alain said, frowning. 'She keeps saying I mustn't speak out of turn. "Out of turn" – silly expression, isn't it. What makes it worse, or more frightening, from her point of view, is that my elder brother's a prisoner of war somewhere in Germany.'

'I know. Henri told me. Or my aunt. I forget which.'

'Your aunt?'

'The one who keeps the tabac. She's a friend of your father too.'

'Do you ever think of getting out?' Alain said. 'Like old Bloch.'

'My aunt would like me to, but . . . '

'But what?'

'Why should I? I'm French. That's what she says herself. Besides, there's my mother. I can't leave her and she certainly won't go.'

'What about your father?'

'He's dead. He wasn't a Jew by the way. Actually it's only since the war started that I've thought of myself as a Jew. Silly time to choose, wouldn't you say? I mean, we're not religious. I wouldn't know what to do or how to behave in a synagogue. Did you know Gaston?'

'No, but I've another friend who did. Who was fond of him, I think. They used to talk literature together. Maurice thinks he's a writer, a poet, or wants to be. Maybe he will, I don't know. What about you? Was it the same with you? How did you meet? I'm sorry if I seem inquisitive.'

'That's all right. Have another cigarette.'

'Thanks. Do you know, there's a regulation coming in that says you have to hand over an empty packet in order to get a new one?'

'I can get round that,' Léon said, 'thanks to my aunt. I can arrange to keep you in supplies too if you like. As for Gaston we met in the bank where I used to work and got talking. But you're right in one way. He got me started reading good books, and not just crime stories. Balzac especially.'

'Oh Balzac.'

Two German officers came into the shop. Léon went to ask them if he could be of any assistance. There was a short conversation which Alain couldn't catch. Léon fetched a book from a shelf and handed it to one of them, who examined it, shook his head, and returned it.

'Too expensive. You won't sell anything if your prices are so high. Not to me anyway, young man.'

He laughed, and, turning to his companion, said something in German. Then they left.

'It's odd,' Léon said. 'That's the third time these two have been in. That one always asks for a different book in some rare edition and then says it's too expensive. Actually Henri tells me his prices are very reasonable. What do you make of it? He's always very polite, I have to say.'

'Maybe you're lucky they don't just walk off with the books without paying. That's the German way, isn't it? Grab what you want. First the Rhineland, then Austria, then Czechoslovakia, then Poland, and now France. Why stop at a mere book?'

'That's how you feel, is it?'

'Don't you?'

'Yes, certainly, but not everyone thinks like that.'

'That's true. It disgusts me,' Alain said. 'I've an uncle who works in the mayor's cabinet and says "we must engage in a sincere collaboration". He's furious that the English haven't surrendered, since, he says, they got us into the war and then let us down. In his view they're our enemy, not the Germans who are in his opinion our only defence against Bolshevism. Actually I'm ashamed to tell you, he speaks of Jewish Bolshevism. It makes me sick. It's all so complicated though. My friend Maurice has an English mother, but his father is a minister at Vichy and has summoned him there. To do what I don't know. I wish there was some action we could take.'

'Me too,' Léon said. 'What does your father think?'

'He says we must be patient, the war won't last forever. But I don't see how it's going to end. Nobody seems to be doing any fighting now. I just don't know what's best.'

He looked puzzled, unhappy and lost. That was what Léon read in his face. He longed, but didn't dare, to draw Alain to him and kiss him.

'Maybe your father's right,' he said. 'Patience.'

'You must think me stupid and pathetic,' Alain said. 'To go on like this when you have real things to fear. As a Jew, I mean.'

'I don't think that at all. You seem to me anything but stupid, and, as for pathetic, don't be silly.'

'Oh good. I think we are going to be friends.'

'What do you do on Sundays?'

'I play rugby usually.'

'Goodness!'

They talked of this and that, of their interests, the books and movies they liked, and of their families. Alain explained how his mother could think only of Dominique.

'I can't blame her, but it does get me down.'

About half an hour after Alain had left, the German officer who had asked for the book returned, this time alone.

'I have decided after all it is not too expensive,' he said. 'So I shall buy it.'

He produced money and put his hand on Léon's shoulder.

'You resent me perhaps, resent our presence in your beautiful city. I understand that, and am sorry. I should like however to be your friend. There is no need for a quarrel now between Germans and Frenchmen. I have always admired French culture. But it is often lonely for me here. I am not always at ease with my colleagues, you understand. We do not think the same about everything. Their sensibility is not mine. Perhaps you, as an intelligent and attractive young man, can appreciate that. Isn't it so?'

Léon said, 'I'll wrap your book for you.'

'That is kind. Now that I have concluded that your prices are not too high, I shall return. By myself, without my colleague. I should very much enjoy the opportunity to have a long conversation with you. My name by the way is Schussmann, Marcus Karl Schussmann. What is yours, may I ask?'

'Léon.'

'Léon? A charming name. It suits you very well. Auf wiedersehen, as we say in Germany.'


## XIV


The rain had stopped and Moncerre was on his way back from the bar where he had gone for a coffee laced with brandy when the tall figure of the Spaniard emerged from the house in the rue d'Aviau. He stood for a moment looking at the washed-out sky. Then he set off with long-striding walk in the direction from which Moncerre was approaching. René signalled to his colleague that this was their man. Moncerre stopped him and asked for his papers.

'My papers?' he said, as if the request was strange to him. 'What right have you to demand them?'

'We're police officers,' Moncerre said, 'police judiciaire, and if you're the man I think you are, we have questions to put to you. So hand them over, please.'

The Spaniard shrugged and slipped his hand into his breast-pocket.

'You will find this is all nonsense,' he said, and pointed a gun at Moncerre. 'Now, step back or . . . '

René slammed down hard on the Spaniard's wrist, the gun fell to the pavement, and Moncerre launched himself in a rugby tackle which sent the man crashing. René picked up the gun. Moncerre snapped handcuffs on the Spaniard before he could recover, and hauled him to his feet. He kneed him hard in the groin. The man collapsed again whimpering in pain.

'Go get the car, kid. Oh, give me the gun first. Not that this daisy's going to make trouble just yet. Up you get, darling, or you'll feel my boot and that'll put you out of action with your lady-friends for a month.'

He bundled the Spaniard into the back of the car and got in beside him.

'You're all the same,' he said. 'You think a gun in the hand makes you tough.'

'You'll regret this. You've made a mistake. I've got diplomatic immunity. But take these bangles off, stop the car and I'm ready to allow this to be forgotten.'

'Oh I don't think so. I really don't think so. I don't give a shit for your diplomatic immunity.'

'He's a daisy,' Moncerre said, 'a real daisy. Diplomatic immunity, that's what he claims. But before then he pulled a gun on me. The kid did well, knocked it out of his hand, and then we sorted him out. He's waiting in the lobby, holding on to his balls.'

'Fine,' Lannes said. 'We'll let him stew for a bit. Are you all right yourself?'

'Haven't been better in weeks.'

'Did you both get some lunch?'

'Yes, we took it in turns. He pulled the gun soon as I asked for his papers, imbecile that he is.'

'Have it sent upstairs to be tested.'

'Sure.'

'See if it matches the bullet that was taken out of me. I don't expect it will. Sigi's bright enough to have dumped that one.'

He settled the Spaniard in the chair opposite the desk. There were dark damp stains on his camel-coloured overcoat where he had hit the wet pavement, and a nice bruise coming up on his right cheekbone. Lannes held his gaze till the Spaniard lowered his eyes. His mouth was twitching and he licked his lower lip.

'Your men have made a mistake.'

'Is that so?'

Lannes crossed to the cupboard, took out the bottle of marc and a glass, poured himself a drink, and set it on the desk in front of him. He tapped a cigarette on his thumb-nail and lit it.

'Did you fire the shot or were you the driver?'

'I don't know what you're talking about. I told your officers that I have diplomatic immunity and must ask you to respect it.'

'You pulled a gun on them. That's a criminal offence.'

'They were in plain clothes. I didn't believe they were policemen. I have enemies, you see, political enemies.'

'I'm sure you have, Senor Sombra. A man like you can't go through life without making enemies. You've got one in front of you now. I think it was you tried to kill me. Fired the shot and bungled it. Sigi can't have been pleased. I don't think he'd have failed himself.'

'I don't know what you're talking about.'

'Really? Do you think, Moncerre, his memory would improve if we started to pull his fingernails out. Did that make Javier Cortazar speak? Did he tell you what you wanted to know?'

No response. Lannes picked up his glass but didn't drink. Sombra eyed it, gave another flick of his tongue across his lips.

'I don't think he did,' Lannes said. 'He was a hard man, harder than you, not the type who lives off women.'

'I don't know who you're talking about. This Cortazar. Never heard of him.'

'Haven't you now? When we've a witness saw you going up to his apartment the night he was killed. And Gaston Chambolley? You've never heard of him either, I suppose. Yet we've another witness saw you enter his apartment building the evening he was murdered. And Jules Cortin? Just a name to you, though it was from his car that you tried to kill me. And Pilar? What do you know about her?'

'Pilar? It's a common Spanish name. I know lots of girls called Pilar.'

'I suppose you do, the trade you're in. But this one's another death to be explained. Think of it, Senor Sombra.'

He drank his marc and lit another cigarette.

'You've a lot of explaining to do.'

'I repeat. I have diplomatic immunity.'

'Forget it. Tell me about Pilar.'

The Spaniard was sweating. He was probably hot in his overcoat, but he was also afraid. Lannes knew the smell of fear.

'I demand to see the Spanish consul.'

'Oh I don't think so. We've a lot of talking to do before we reach that point. I know a bit about you, Sombra. You're a small-time pimp and procurer, and you've done time for fraud, passing dud cheques, wasn't it, but now you're out of your league. You've gone over the top. I've got enough on you to send you to the guillotine. Think about that. The seven in the morning call, then they bind your hands, blindfold you, and then . . . '

He slammed his hand, sidedown, hard on the desk.

'You'll need time to think about it. Moncerre, take him downstairs and bang him up in a cell. We'll talk more later. Think of Chambolley and Cortazar and Cortin and Pilar. And the guillotine of course.'

As soon as he was alone, Lannes gave himself another drink. He felt dirty, also on edge. He didn't like this sort of thing, had never taken pleasure in playing the hard cop, accepted it only with reluctance as sometimes necessary. At school, aged eleven, he had befriended a snotty white-haired boy with whom he had nothing in common simply because the boy was bullied by their class-mates. Sombra was a rat, he had no doubt about that; nevertheless . . . He wondered how long he had, how far he dared push him. That boy, Alphonse, had tried to hang himself in the school latrines. Lannes had come upon him by chance and just in time.

Moncerre returned.

'How would it be if I rough him up a bit, chief?'

'No, let him stew. It's what's going on in his mind is our best hope. Give yourself a drink.'

'These witnesses. We don't have them, do we?'

'You know we don't. We're not going to be able to hold him overnight, you know, and, even if he talks, we'll be prevented from acting on anything he tells us. But I want him to talk. Make him think he's not one of the Untouchables. He's out of his league, you know. I got on to an old friend in Paris. He knew a bit about him, knew his record. Small-time stuff, as I said. Used to hang about the bars in Montparnasse in the late Twenties, before the Depression, when there were rich American women to prey on. Then turned to a bit of pimping, ran a couple of girls, did time, as I said, for passing dud cheques. I suspect it was in prison he met Sigi. My chum put me on to someone in the Deuxième Bureau. He wasn't very forthcoming.'

'Spooks never are.'

'But he did go so far as to say that when the Spanish war broke out, our friend got involved in affairs that brought him to their attention. Wouldn't go further than that. No trade secrets to be divulged. But this may be the tie-up with Pilar's death, and that death is the starting-point of this whole bloody business.'

Hours later they were still at it. Lannes knew he was getting nowhere, but wouldn't give up. It was dark outside. There was no traffic, the curfew already in force. Every half-hour he took a break, turning the interrogation over to Moncerre, who put the same questions, went over the same ground. But the Spaniard's resistance held. Now Lannes was ready for what might be his last throw. He was conscious of the deep silence of the building, deserted by all except the officer on the desk and themselves. It was a couple of hours since young René had reported that the gun didn't match the one fired at him. He had never expected it would.

Sombra was still in his overcoat with the handcuffs on his wrists. His face was grey with exhaustion, there were dark circles under his eyes, but he was holding his ground, denying everything, though it was a long time since he had last protested they were not entitled to question him and asked that the Spanish consul be summoned. It was as if he too accepted that they were caught up in a dance from which others were excluded.

This time Lannes, re-entering the office, said to Moncerre, 'Take the cuffs off him,' and then offered the Spaniard the cigarette he had been denied for hours. He took it, accepted a light and sat looking at Lannes with a suggestion of uncertainty, while he rubbed first one wrist, then the other. He was wary, in case this was a trick, and waited for Lannes either to explain this change in his circumstances or simply to tell him he was free to leave.

'Give him a drink,' Lannes said. 'You can drink marc, I suppose, or would you prefer beer?'

'Marc is fine.'

'This diplomatic status you claim. How did you come by it, given your record which you needn't trouble yourself now to deny.'

'Superintendent, we have gone over the same ground time and again, and you realize you have made a mistake, and I have nothing to tell you about these cases you are concerned with. I don't hold it against you, as another man might. Nor do I pretend that my life has always been that which I might wish. I've experienced misfortune. I've not always been respectable. I have known poverty and poverty loosens what I believe is called the moral fibre. See: I conceal nothing. You know I have been in prison and for this reason you have suspected me. But then war broke out in my country, and this offered me the chance to redeem myself. I could not serve in the army on account of a lung condition, but I was eager to work for the cause.'

'What cause was that, chummy?' Moncerre said from his seat by the window.

'The cause of Patriotism.'

'Patriotism, was it?' Moncerre said again, his sardonic tone mocking the audible capital letters in the Spaniard's words. 'It's a big word, and in your mouth an empty one. Carry on all the same.'

Sombra shot him a look in which Lannes read a rising anger.

'Patriotism,' he said again. 'See, gentlemen, my poor Spain was in the hands of gangsters, Anarchists, Reds, Communists, enemies of the Church and true religion. Your government here in France – the government of the so-called Popular Front – aided and abetted the Republican government in Spain, which, I assure you, was composed of men devoted to the interests of the Soviet Union, Jewish-Bolshevism and World Communism. Fortunately while the Jew Blum was ready to do the work of the Comintern, there were others here in France who thought differently. I acted as an intermediary between them and the Nationalists. I may say this safely now, though a year ago it would have been dangerous to admit it, but French patriots are now in a position to save France as General Franco has saved Spain from Jewish-Bolshevism.'

'You acted as an intermediary?' Lannes said. 'What did your work consist of?'

'Even now I cannot give you details. The secrets are not mine to reveal. But I can say that thanks to my efforts Bolshevik agents here in France were unmasked and their conspiracies against both Spain and France were thwarted. And for this service I have been decorated by the Generalissimo himself and have been granted that diplomatic passe-partout which is now among the papers in front of you.'

'And was it in the course of this work that you encountered Pilar?' Lannes said.

'Always this Pilar! I tell you again I know nothing of her. But if, as I surmise from your questioning she was an agent of the Comintern and is now dead, do not ask me to regret it. And now, if you have finished, would you please return me my papers and let me go?'

'In a moment,' Lannes said, removing the French passport from the sheaf of papers. 'With your diplomatic immunity, you no longer need this. I'm confiscating it. For the time being, that is. And one other thing: the day will come when you find your association with Sigi is in danger of bringing even closer than you are now to that seven o'clock in the morning knock on a cell door. You should get in touch with me then.'

'We could have kept him in the cells and had another go in the morning,' Moncerre said.

'No. That would have had to be recorded. As it is, he's never been here. I'm making no report. Not even an unofficial one to Schnyder. Even if he'd been less obdurate I doubt if we'd have been allowed to pin anything on him. But the night hasn't been wasted. He'll tell Sigi about it and boast that he gave nothing away and won this round. But there'll be a doubt in his mind, anxiety about the day when things change. As for Sigi, he'll know we haven't given up, that we're still on his track, still got our teeth in the case. All the same I don't see our next move. I'm not even sure one is immediately possible.'

'There's still that priest. I'd really like to haul him in, have a go. If he doesn't know something, then I've not been a cop these twenty years.'

The priest? Perhaps? But he would have to ask Alain to identify him, and that wasn't on.

'Decorated by fat-arse Franco,' he said. 'I bet Edmond had a hand in that.'

Edmond was in it up to his neck. He was sure of that. But, even more than Sigi, Edmond was an Untouchable. For now anyway.


## XV

Lannes woke with a foul taste in his mouth and a throbbing head. The marc certainly, for he and Moncerre had finished the bottle after letting the Spaniard go. It was something they hadn't done for a long time, not since the early days of the war when they were all anxiously waiting for action. He felt ashamed. Fortunately Marguerite had been asleep when he returned and had done no more that turn over in bed with a muttered 'what time is it?' and had gone back to sleep before he answered.

He went through to the kitchen and made himself a pot of coffee. It was still dark and the city was silent. Coffee was already rationed and much that was available was adulterated. Lucky that he and Alain were the only members of the family who drank it regularly. Dominique too, but who knew what sort of thin ersatz muck he might get in his camp, wherever it was? He cut himself a slice of cheese and nibbled it: good Cantal. How long would that be on the market?

Though he had tried to persuade Moncerre otherwise – himself too, if it came to that – he had failed with the Spaniard. That was the cause of his wretched state, every bit as much as the marc. There had never – he went over the interrogation in his mind –

been a moment when he had truly sensed they were on the point of a breakthrough. He was almost sorry he hadn't yielded to Moncerre and allowed him to give Sombra that 'going-over' he had suggested. Eagerly suggested, for Moncerre would have enjoyed roughing him up. But of course he had been right to say no. They might already be in trouble, in line for a reprimand at least. He couldn't doubt that Sigi would be complaining to Edmond in Vichy, just as soon as he had debriefed Sombra.

Pilar? What made sense? Assuming she had indeed been murdered by the Communists in Spain. Why should that agitate Edmond, lead him to loose his dogs? Because she had learned something of the activities of certain Frenchmen, Edmond among them, engaged in selling arms to Franco – which was illegal? And because they believed she had left a record of their activities, entrusting it, as they supposed, either to Gaston or Javier Cortazar? Something like this was the only plausible explanation for torturing them and searching their apartments? But why betray her to the Communists? Why not deal with her themselves? Or had they indeed done so, committed a crime on French soil, the victim a French citizen by reason of her marriage to Henri? There was another puzzle here. Why had they left Henri alone? Why were they so sure she hadn't confided her secret to him, her husband, rather than to Gaston or Cortazar? He could think of no answer to that question.

And why, he thought again, has there been no second attempt on my life? Here at least there was an answer: Vichy. He was no longer deemed dangerous because of Edmond's position in the new regime; he had been tamed, emasculated. It was possible, admittedly, that Sigi and the Spaniard had been acting on their own initiative then. Unlikely, however: Edmond was the only person who knew that he was going to be in the Hotel Splendide. He must have arranged the shooting.

He took a couple of aspirin, poured another cup of coffee and lit his first cigarette of the day. Always the best one. He drew smoke deep into his lungs, expelled it, and felt better. Perhaps he had been right when he told Moncerre that the interrogation of the Spaniard hadn't been a complete failure. Even if it had yielded nothing concrete, it served to let Sigi – and Edmond – know that he hadn't given up, was still on the case. Might this alarm Edmond, lead him to do something rash?

One thing was clear. Despite what he had said to Moncerre, it would be wise to report to Schnyder. He might not be able to get him on his side. Though he had formed a liking for him and believed this was reciprocated, it was clear that Schnyder was determined first of all to protect his own position; he wasn't going to stick his neck out for Lannes or for anyone else. But since it was likely that a complaint about Lannes' behaviour would descend from on high, it was better that he learned of it from Lannes himself.

'You don't give up, do you?' Schnyder said.

Lannes shrugged.

'We're policemen,' he said.

'Oh, my dear chap, don't suppose I've forgotten that. A case is never closed, till, like the fucking Canadian Mounties, we've got our man. Absolutely and very admirable. But, by your own account, Jean, you got nothing from this Spaniard that you didn't know already, and all you've done is stir up a hornet's nest. A fine night's work – I don't think! Moreover you are guilty of disobedience, insubordination. I could throw the book at you. Can you give me one reason – one good reason – why I shouldn't?'

'That depends,' Lannes said, 'on where you stand.'

'Where I stand? I'll tell you where I stand. This town's full of fucking Germans and I have to work with them. At the same time I take my orders from Vichy and I've no choice in the matter. Oh yes, I could resign of course, toss away my career for high-minded reasons, but, no matter what you think of me, I can tell you this: you would find my replacement worse and a damned sight less sympathetic. I don't like this mess we're in any more than you do, but at least I've got my eyes open and can see the mess for what it is. That's where I stand.'

Lannes took the newspaper cutting from his pocket and placed it on Schnyder's desk.

'That's our man,' he said, putting his finger on the photograph of the Spaniard. 'I don't suppose you were introduced to him at the races, were you?'

'What did he say to that?' Moncerre asked.

They were lunching chez Fernand, liver with onions and fried potatoes, and a bottle of Médoc.

'Very little. Had been introduced, hadn't caught his name, made no particular impression on him.'

'Eyes only for La Jauzion, I expect. So what do we do now, chief?'

Lannes took hold of the bottle and poured them each a glass. The curious thing was that, though Schnyder had blustered and reproved him for disobedience, he had stopped short of action. It was as if he had given Lannes a wink, as much as to say, 'Just keep me out of it, I don't want to know.'

'Cortin,' he said. 'Have you had any success, René, in tracing his movements the night he was killed?'

René blushed, as he always did when confessing failure.

'Right,' Lannes said. 'Let's get the sorrowing widow in again. Six o'clock. You'd better both go since she's insensible to your charms, little one. We'll show her the photograph of Sombra.'

'What good will it do?' Moncerre asked. 'Not that I mind wasting time, since as I've said, there's nothing else to do with it.'

'No good immediately, I agree with you there of course. But I want to build up a dossier, for the day when we can use it.'

The advocate Labiche was again lunching at the corner table across the room, again studying a brief. He raised his head, looked at Lannes, and, when Lannes out-stared him, returned to his papers.

'Meanwhile,' Lannes said, 'I'm going to have another word with Jean-Christophe.'

There wasn't in fact anything he hoped to discover from the Count whose involvement in the case was marginal. But Professor Lazaire was on his conscience. The old man had come to him seeking help and he had done nothing about it. So he now presented himself again at the house in the rue d'Aviau. Two German officers were leaving it as he approached. Was it his imagination that led him to think they scrutinized him closely?

Old Marthe admitted him less grudgingly than before.

'Oh it's you again. If it's Jean-Christophe you want, you're in luck. He's sober, or near sober, for once. If it's me, you should have come to the kitchen door. Not that I've anything more to tell you. You know it all anyway, don't you?'

'I wish I did,' Lannes thought, as he followed the old woman whose black laced boots rang on the polished floor.

'It's that policeman again. What have you been up to now?'

Jean-Christophe was sitting in his father's chair with the canaries twittering in the cage behind him. He was smartly dressed in a checked tweed suit – English tweed, Lannes thought – cream-coloured silk shirt and green yellow-spotted bow-tie. He made no move to rise or extend his hand.

'I thought I'd seen the end of you,' he said. 'What do you want? Edmond told me you'd had orders to leave me alone.'

'Did he now?'

This time Lannes didn't bother to remove his overcoat or sit down.

'What I have to say won't take long. You're quite right in saying your brother stepped in to protect you, and so I've no questions for you. But there are criminal acts which have nothing to do with the cases under investigation, and I intend to see that you don't commit them. I know your record, it's no secret, so don't trouble yourself to protest. Anne-Marie Lazaire. She's a minor, the age you like them. Leave her alone. That's an order. From me. If you disobey, if you lay a finger on her, I'll have you in prison, banged up in a cell with a couple of hard boys. That's a promise. You're not to see her again. I hope you understand. I've a daughter of my own, older than little Anne-Marie, and I don't like men of your sort. That's all I have to say. Just do as you're told and remember I have my eye on you.'

## XVI

As he turned into the public garden Lannes found himself dizzy. He sat down on a bench, his hands folded on his stick, to compose himself. The sharpness of his words to Jean-Christophe had taken him by surprise. Had he merely been venting his frustration on the man? Hitting at him because he couldn't strike Edmond, or Sigi, or even the Spaniard? Partly, he admitted to himself. But also, when he mentioned Clothilde, he had pictured the Count pawing at her, a few years back when she was still a little girl: disgusting.

It was a cold clear afternoon now, weather he liked, with the black branches of the trees glistening after the morning rain. Mothers pushed prams or walked the paths holding their little children by the hand. A small boy in a blue belted overcoat ran past rolling a hoop. Old gentlemen took their constitutional, some with a dog on a lead. All of them, except the youngest of the children, would have their worries, anxieties, fears, but for the moment in the afternoon sunshine it was as if there was no war, no occupation. Yet you couldn't put it out of mind, avoid thinking of it and what it portended; not for long, you couldn't. As Schnyder said, it was the central fact of their life. You had to face up to it and to its significance. For Lannes as a policeman it meant frustration; for him as a father, something worse than that: fear. Marguerite had been more alert to this reality than he had been. Alain was a boy of spirit. She was afraid he would do something rash. And he might! How, at eighteen, could you fail to find humiliation – national and personal humiliation – insupportable? He would have to do as she asked: speak to the boy, warn him he must accept what he surely found unacceptable. And Clothilde? When she spoke of that young German officer who was 'nice', she was torn, painfully and puzzled, between her natural inclination and her sense of what was correct behaviour. They were being cheated of their youth, just as surely as poor Dominique in his prison camp. For that was the truth – Bordeaux had become a prison. Damn these politicians!

Four o'clock. Two hours till he was due back at the office to question Madame Cortin again. Ghastly woman who would tell him another pack of lies! He would call on the old professor, who lived in a street adjoining the garden, let him know that he had spoken to Jean-Christophe, warned him off, done his good deed for the day. There was bitterness in that reflection.

A maid admitted him to the second-floor apartment, asked him to wait in the gloomy hallway with its mahogany side-table on which stood a brass dish once intended doubtless as a receptacle for visiting-cards, now empty. She returned and showed him into the professor's study, book-lined as it should be – everything, Lannes thought, was as it should be. The old man rose to greet him and, as he did so, the shawl draped round his shoulders slipped off. Lannes retrieved it from the Turkey carpet, apologized for calling unannounced, hoped it wasn't inconvenient – the usual meaningless words. The professor bade him sit down, offered tea, which Lannes declined, then said, 'Ever since I made so bold as to ask for your assistance, I've wondered if I might have been importunate.'

Lannes made a gesture of dissent.

'Not at all. By no means, but with things as they are. Well, you will understand that there are difficulties. Nevertheless you were quite right to approach me, and in fact I've come to tell you that I've had a word with the Comte de Grimaud. I hope an effective one. At any rate I've warned him off your granddaughter and I think I've frightened him sufficiently for him to take heed of what I said. He's a feeble fellow really.'

'Not much of a man,' the professor said, 'but for that very reason disturbing. I'm sure you find that many criminals fit that description.'

'Most of them. It's their very inadequacy makes them dangerous. I don't speak of the professional ones who belong to a different category and psychological type. But the sexual deviants are usually every bit as inadequate as their actions are wicked. It's a difficult moral question how far they are to be held responsible, which doesn't of course mean that they should be regarded as innocents. Jean-Christophe is, as you say, not much of a man. However, as to your grandson – Michel, isn't it? – I'm afraid that I can't see that I can do anything there. Any warning from me that he is frequenting bad company – well, I'm afraid he would pay no attention. Moreover, though the man of whom you spoke, that he has attached himself to, is, as I said, a criminal, he's not only protected, but his protector belongs to the side that is now in the ascendancy.'

'That protector? You speak of Edmond de Grimaud.'

The maid who had not waited for instructions now brought in a tray with a teapot, two cups, sugar, slices of lemon and a plate of almond biscuits. She poured them both a cup. Lannes, forgetting he had declined the professor's offer, took his from her.

'It's a bad time to be young,' he said. 'Whichever way the war goes, there are young people who are going to find they have taken the wrong path and will suffer accordingly.'

'Poor France! We're divided as we were at the time of Dreyfus, and those who were wrong then are now in a position to take their revenge. Indeed the divisions exposed by the Affair have never been closed, the wounds never healed. The poor Marshal! He declared recently that we are either with him or against him. He deludes himself. Many who are now with him will turn against him when the war itself turns, as I believe it will. When I say this to Michel, warning him, he flares up and calls me a traitor. Yet he's a good boy at heart. That's the tragedy of our time.'

Lannes experienced a desire to ask this old man if it was shameful of him to remain in the service of Vichy, compelled to collaborate with the Germans or at least not to oppose them. But he didn't put the question. There are things you have to resolve for yourself.

The sound of singing came from the hall, a boy's voice, a cheerful light tenor. The door was flung open and he came in.

He was tall – well, taller than Lannes who stood five foot eight inches – blond, good-looking though his mouth was large and loose-lipped and his nose had a suggestion of snub. His face was flushed, no doubt because of the cold outside. He was long-legged but moved awkwardly as he crossed the room to lean over his grandfather and kiss him on the cheek. He took no notice of Lannes but a black-and-white smooth-coated fox-terrier which had followed him into the room approached Lannes and pawed at his leg.

'How was your lecture?' the professor asked, addressing the boy in the second person singular.

'Inspiring. We were told we all have a duty to forward the National Revolution as members of the Aquitaine Legion of French Youth.'

'You've really joined that organization?'

'But of course, Grandpa. Monsieur Grimaud says it's essential that boys and young men of my privileged background are ready to take their part in creating the new order which will raise France from its ruinous condition and let her take her rightful place in the New Europe that is in the process of formation. It's really exciting. I know that you don't altogether approve, but, forgive me, Grandpa, that's because you don't understand how my generation feels.'

He stopped abruptly, as if aware for the first time of Lannes' presence, blushed and held out his hand.

'You must think me frightfully rude, sir,' he said. 'If I am, it's because I'm so excited. But I apologize.'

'Not at all,' Lannes said, taking the boy's hand which was warm and dry. 'I was young myself once. I understand how you feel.'

The ardour of youth, he thought, how attractive it is, how often misplaced.

'We all have to rally round the Marshal. That's what we're told. He needs our support. He is the symbol of renascent France, but needs the support of young people like us. It's wonderful.'

'I suppose he does, poor man,' the professor said. 'Now, Michel, I have business to finish with my guest. I shall see you at dinner and hear more about your meeting and the plans for your Legion.'

The boy blushed for a second time.

'I apologize,' he said again, and with the terrier at his heels, left the study. They heard him singing in the hall and then there was silence. The professor took a cigar from the box on the marble-topped little table by his side, offered one to Lannes who declined, then busied himself sniffing it, rolling it between his fingers, and then clipped the end. He struck a long match which he held for several seconds to the cigar before lighting it.

'You see why I'm worried,' he said.

'He's fond of you. That's evident, and he's an attractive lad.'

'Undoubtedly. But not very intelligent and easily led. And I don't like the direction he is being persuaded to follow. They'll feed him with all sorts of nonsense, pernicious nonsense, in this legion of his, and I'm very much afraid he'll lap it up.'

Lannes had no consolation to offer. The old man was so clearly right. They were all afraid for the young: the professor for Michel, Miriam for Léon, and he himself for Alain and Clothilde. Whichever side they took, they were in danger, if not immediately than in time, and the higher their spirit, the greater the danger.

'This "New Order",' the professor said, 'it's meaningless, mere rhetoric, and, as a man of letters, I have learned to distrust rhetoric. High-flown abstract language, it's the curse of France, an affliction. This man who calls himself Grimaud – who may for all I know, be entitled to do so – despite what you say, is it, I wonder, possible for you to intervene?'

'I wish I could say I could.'

It was already almost dark and a wind was rising as Lannes made his way back to the Place de la République. People leaving work hurried home with heads lowered as if to a refuge. Which was indeed, he thought again, what home had become; the one place where you could be as you were before war and occupation. A lorry full of German troops hurtled past. He smacked his blackthorn against a lamp-post. Damn them all! What nonsense, what vile wicked nonsense, would that gullible enthusiastic boy be led into? He wished he could speak to Sigi as forcibly as he had spoken to Jean-Christophe and as the old professor had all but implored him to do. But it was impossible. He would be met with insolence, talk of the 'Herren-Moral'.

Moreover, a policeman seeking to deter a boy from joining an organization sponsored by 'Les Amis du Maréchal' – shocking. There would be a black mark against his name – yet another black mark.

Madame Cortin was already waiting when he returned to the office. She was dressed in black, widow's weeds, that matched his mood. He gave himself a glass of Armagnac before calling her in.

## XVII

As he had feared it was futile. However hard he tried, varying his approach, he got nowhere. She sat, filling the chair, obdurate, sullen, refusing to admit to what he was sure she knew: that her husband's meeting had been with his foster-brother. Yet she must have realized that Sigi was responsible for his murder, even if he had not actually killed him himself.

'He would have told me in time who he had gone to meet, I'd have seen to that,' she said, over and over again, 'but since he never returned, I know nothing.'

The refrain infuriated him, all the more so when she repeated her certainty that Jules had been murdered by 'one of these criminal types, foreigners many of them, who are to be found in the vicinity of the Gare St-Jean'.

And he couldn't budge her.

Afterwards Moncerre said, 'We're not only getting nowhere, chief, we're never going to get anywhere. All we are doing is banging our heads against a brick wall.'

'In that case,' Lannes said, 'we must try to find the door in the wall that will let us through.'

Walking home through deserted streets, his hip aching, Lannes turned the question over and over in his mind, searching for that door and the key that would open it. Why had Gaston and Cortazar been tortured? Because they wouldn't reveal something that Sigi had to know. And what was that? Information he believed Pilar had entrusted to them. If so, it must be in the form of a document that would compromise Edmond. Had the search of their apartments been successful? Surely not; the shot fired at him outside the Splendide – and the murder of Cortin – suggested alarm, apprehension. So, assuming Gaston had had it – which was more probable than supposing it was in Cortazar's possession, since there was no evidence that he had actually known Pilar, then where had Gaston successfully hidden it?

His reflections were interrupted by two uniformed policemen, demanding to know why he was breaching the curfew and requiring him to produce his papers. Apologies followed. 'Only doing our duty, superintendent. Instructions are that anyone on the streets is to be regarded as a suspicious character. If it wasn't us, it would be the Boches.'

Marguerite and Clothilde had gone to bed. Alain was still up, reading, his legs slung over the arm of the chair, the black cat – Sylvestre, No Neck – lying contentedly pressed against his chest. Lannes went through to the kitchen, made a pot of coffee and brought two cups and a glass of marc for himself back into the salon.

'Part of our school is going to be requisitioned by the Boches,' Alain said. 'Maybe the whole building. Nobody knows for sure, or whether we are going to be transferred elsewhere, or simply told there's nowhere for us to study. Even the profs don't know, they're as confused as we are.'

He laid aside his book – one of Simenon's novels. Lannes glanced at it. If only it was as easy for me as it is for Maigret, he thought.

'They're bound to find somewhere for you,' he said. 'The education authorities will see to that.'

'But what's the point?' Alain said, not for the first time.

'Let's not go into that again.'

He handed Alain one of the cups.

'You look tired, Papa, and worried.'

'We're all worried. Your mother's afraid you may do something rash. It's because you're intelligent, she says. I see her point. The intelligent – intellectuals – are easily carried away by ideas, and then do something that's dangerous – and in the circumstances, stupid – as a result. You won't, will you?'

Alain made no immediate reply. He looked very serious. Then he smiled.

'But I'm pleased to learn that you think I'm intelligent. I met that German officer again today, the one who's been billeted on the Romiers upstairs. He's called Siegfried, which, he says, embarrasses him because, "I'm not at all Wagnerian, I don't even like opera. I prefer jazz, despite the Fuehrer's disapproval." He's a nice guy. I wouldn't want to shoot him even if I had a gun. So you don't need to worry. By the way who's the boy who's working in my honorary uncle's bookshop? I went there the other day and we talked about books and things. He's nice too. He said he knew you.'

'He was a friend of Henri's brother. The one who was murdered. That's how I came across him, why Henri gave him a job, I suppose.'

'Yes, he told me that.'

'He's a Jew.'

'He told me that too. Indeed he made a point of doing so. I said, "So what? It doesn't matter to me." '

Lannes put his cup down, picked up the glass of marc, and knocked it back.

'Good,' he said. 'It shouldn't. But it matters to other people, I'm afraid.'

'I know it does. It's disgusting. To people like Uncle Albert.'

'And to others who are more important.'

'Are you warning me off him, Papa?'

'Not exactly, no. I'd be ashamed to do that just as I'd be ashamed if you shared your Uncle Albert's prejudices. But be careful. That's all I'm saying. Be careful, Alain.'

What I really wanted to say, he thought, as he lay unable to sleep, was, 'Don't get too close to Léon, not because he's queer or thinks he is and I'm afraid he would corrupt you, because I don't believe that at all, but simply for your own safety because very soon it's going to be compromising, therefore dangerous, to have Jewish friends.' But I couldn't and not only because Alain would have despised me if I had said that. I would have despised myself. And yet it makes sense. What times we live in when good sense is despicable. I might have added, remembering that letter sent to Rougerie, and Sigi's hint of blackmail over Miriam, that I myself am already compromised in that direction. But we're all compromised, one way or another. There's the professor, with that long-legged, awkward, eager boy, an enthusiast whom he's anxious and powerless to save from his ignorant idealism. And from Sigi too. I wish Alain would find a girl to fall in love with and distract him. We're enmeshed in lies, he thought, then, towards three in the morning, drifted into a sleep disturbed by a dream in which Dominique came home, embraced him, and then stood arm-in-arm with the boy Michel singing a song in praise of the Marshal. Michel detached himself from Dominique and brought his face close to Lannes; his breath was sweet and sickly. Like death, Lannes found himself muttering, like death.

## XVIII

There was a chill in the air and murmuring of disaffection. A shot was fired at an off-duty German soldier taking his ease on a bench in the public garden. It was dusk, the light was poor, and the gunman, reported to be 'a youth' missed his target. The bullet was embedded in the wood and the youth escaped into the shadows. Lannes was happy not to be involved in the search which was carried out by the Gendarmerie in association with the German military police. Even Moncerre was indignant. 'It's pointless,' he said. 'Things are bad enough without some idiot making them worse by setting out to be a hero and trying to pick off an ordinary private who is doing no harm to anyone. If it served any purpose, then of course I'd approve, but as things are it's sheer foolishness. Crazy.'

'There'll be more of it,' Lannes said. 'We have to accept that it's inevitable that there are young hotheads who resent the Occupation sufficiently to act in this way. They're patriots, after all, in their fashion.'

'Patriots be damned. Play-actors, that's all, comedians, and a bloody nuisance.'

'Well, so long as we can keep out of it.'

But the incident alarmed him, chiming with the fear that came to him in the night as he lay unable to sleep.

In the afternoon – again, the cold, clear weather that pleased him – he made his way to the rue des Remparts. He was surprised to find Schussmann there in conversation with Léon.

'Ah,' the German said, 'so we have an interest in literature in common, superintendent, assuming that, as I hope, you are not here on official business. See, this clever young man has unearthed for me a first edition of *Les nourritures terrestres* which previously I know only in translation. It made a great impression on me when I read it first in my last year in the Gymnasium. "A paean to paganism" my master called it, and drew my attention to the echoes of Nietzsche. I am delighted to have it now in French, and, see, it is numbered 406 of an edition of only 500 copies. Remarkable that so small an edition should have had so great an influence. Or perhaps not so remarkable: great oaks grow from little acorns. I am very grateful for the discovery.'

He laid his hand lightly on Léon's shoulder as he said this, then, remarking that pleasure must give way to duty, took his leave, very formally, of Lannes.

The door closed behind him.

'Interesting,' Lannes said, and saw that Léon looked ill-at-ease.

'Henri's upstairs. Drinking, I'm afraid. Are you going up?'

'In a moment.'

'It's not my fault,' the boy said.

'I'm not suggesting it is. I take it he's been here several times.'

'Quite a few. He says he's a collector. He's nice actually, but I've no desire to get involved. On the other hand I can't tell him to bugger off, can I? Or should I just tell him I'm a Jew? Is that what you think?'

'I don't think anything. I came to see that you are all right.'

'Well, you've seen. Are you going to tell my aunt?'

'Tell her what?' Lannes said. 'There's nothing to tell her, is there? Some young fool took a pot-shot at a German soldier in the public garden yesterday. Fortunately he missed and even more fortunately he got away. But they have a description.'

'You don't think that was me?'

'As I just said, I don't think anything. I hope it wasn't. The description could fit you. On the other hand it could fit dozens of young men in Bordeaux.'

'Well, there you are. But, if you want to know, it wasn't. I don't have a gun for one thing, and, for another, I told you I'm being a good boy.'

He smiled, for the first time, mischievously.

'I'm glad to hear it. Stay that way. Don't let Schussmann get too close.'

'How do I stop him?'

Henri wasn't drunk, but he wasn't quite sober either, unsteady as he rose from his chair to embrace Lannes. His cheek was bristly, he hadn't shaved for a couple of days at least, and, when he turned away to fetch a bottle and a glass for Lannes, his trousers sagged behind even more than they had done a few weeks ago.

'There's no more Johnnie,' he said, pouring Lannes a brandy and squirting soda into it. 'There'll be no more Johnnie till we're liberated, if we live long enough to see that day. I'm glad to see you, Jean, even though I'm scarcely fit to be seen myself. I can't sleep and I can't eat. If you hadn't provided me with Léon, I really think I'd have to shut up shop. Any word from Dominique?'

'A card, simply to say he's alive and well. No word of him coming home.'

'Poor boy, to have his youth stolen from him. I'm sorry, Jean.'

'Léon's proving satisfactory then?'

'He's a nice child. I don't know what I'd do without him.'

For some time they sat drinking, in silence, Lannes hesitating to put the question that had brought him there. His old friend's condition distressed him. Police work shouldn't be mixed with personal relations. Not for the first time he thought that it might have been better if he had insisted that he wasn't the person to investigate Gaston's murder. If he had done so, it would have been filed away long since. Cortazar might even still be alive, for it was likely that it was his questioning of the Catalan that had drawn Sigi's attention to him. Cortin too, for there would have been no need to borrow his car and take a shot at him from it. Well, it was too late for these thoughts.

He said: 'I haven't given up on Gaston. But there's something I have to ask you. Did he ever entrust a paper to you, for safe-keeping, anything like that.'

'No, of course not. I'd have given it you if he had. There was only that letter which came so long after he was dead. Nothing else. I don't have much to remember him by, except memories themselves. And now the boy Léon. What sort of paper?'

'I don't know.'

He couldn't say: something Pilar wrote and handed to him, something that explains her death and was the cause of his, something that still compromises the man responsible. He couldn't. If Henri didn't have the paper it would be futile to go on, painful too.

Instead he said: 'There was a German officer in the shop when I came in, one I've had dealings with, a decent enough type. He was buying a copy of Gide's *Les nourritures terrestres*. Léon says he's become quite a regular customer. I told him to be careful. You understand?'

Downstairs again, he said to Léon, 'When you dust the books, would you open each one and see if any paper falls out. I'm looking for something Gaston hid. There must be books here that are never likely to be bought, and he might have thought that such a one would serve as a hiding-place. It's a very long shot and perhaps crazy, but . . . '

'But? It'll give me something to do. There are books of sermons and theological tracts that nobody in their right mind's ever going to buy. But it doesn't seem likely, does it? After all it's not impossible that somebody might take a fancy to whichever book he'd slipped it into and, then, where would he have been? Still I accept it's the sort of crazy notion he might have had, like something out of Balzac.'

'He wouldn't have expected it would have to stay there for long. He was here the afternoon of the day he was killed and he had made an appointment with the man I am sure was his murderer. He would have expected to retrieve the paper the next day, in all probability. Just a temporary hiding-place, he'd have thought.'

'You're sure there is such a paper?'

'Yes, I'm sure, though not of course that it is here. By the way, why haven't you mentioned meeting Alain?'

Léon lowered his eyes.

'I thought you might not approve.'

'Why shouldn't I? He liked you. All I ask is that the pair of you don't do anything "heroic". That would be stupid.'

As he left the bookshop he found himself face-to-face with the advocate Labiche.

'Visiting your little Jewish friend, superintendent?'

Lannes took hold of the velvet collar of the lawyer's coat. His left hand formed itself into a fist which he brought up against Labiche's face. He restrained the impulse to hit him – hit him hard – but kept his fist there, and said, 'I was under the impression that lawyers signed their letters, Monsieur Labiche.'

'I don't know what you're talking about.'

'You don't? That's amusing.'

He released his grip and said, 'And another thing. I've given your client, the Comte de Grimaud, a warning. If he so much as touches that little girl, I'll have him in a cell, and it will be a pleasure to put him there.'

'Again I have no idea what you are referring to, but it sounds like slander. You're on edge, superintendent. It's you who should watch your step.'

Back at the office, young René said, 'There's a message for you, chief, from Madame Robartet. You remember, the old lady across the landing from Gaston's apartment. She would like you to call on her, no reason given. Perhaps she's ill, I don't know.'

## XIX

Léon hadn't been wholly frank with Lannes. Schussmann had been calling at the shop frequently, almost every day, often scarcely pretending that he was looking for a particular book or even that had come to browse. He talked mostly about literature – mentioning for instance that early work of Gide's which Léon had happened on quite by chance, for it had been on the wrong shelf, perhaps replaced there by some customer. Actually this wasn't remarkable. Léon had already concluded that his predecessor

Bloch, perhaps Henri himself too, had been careless or haphazard in their arrangement of the books. Of course, he reflected, some customers probably liked antiquarian bookshops where the stock was not arrayed in regularly regimented ranks. Anyway he had come on *Les nourritures terrestres* a couple of days after Schussmann had spoken of it, and had been happy to present him with it this afternoon.

The German didn't however restrict his conversation to literature. He spoke of his love of France, of the beauties of his home in the Black Forest – 'How I should like to show them to you,' he said, 'perhaps when we are at peace again it will be possible' – of his taste in music, of his father, a Professor of Philology, and eventually of his marriage.

'It is over, you understand,' he said. 'We were not suited. I say nothing against her. It is simply that I should not have married her. I am not made for marriage, but I did not realize that at the time. Besides, in 1934 it seemed wiser to marry, even for me, perhaps especially for a man like me. But it was a mistake. I married her because her brother was a special friend of mine. You understand? I loved him dearly. We both did. And then he was killed in a motor accident. We were left desolate and so we married. But it was only by thinking of him that I was able – I'm sorry if this embarrasses you, but I should like you to understand me, Léon – that I was able to fulfil my duties as a husband. Do you see?'

Léon looked away. Part of him wanted to laugh. Part of him felt sorry for the German. And indeed Schussmann was right – he was indeed embarrassed. But he was also alarmed. The bookshop had come to seem a refuge, a den where he was safe, and now it was as if a ferret had been introduced to flush him out.

'Lieutenant Schussmann,' he said, 'please don't go on. You will regret speaking so frankly.'

'But why, Léon? Because of this stupid war, there must be no sincerity? Is that what you think? Please call me Karl. I am Marcus Karl but my close friends say Karl. Because you are French and I am German, does that mean we can't be friends?'

Oh yes, Léon thought, and if I tell you I'm a Jew? And then he thought: What would Alain think? – Oh Alain!

'Look at me, Léon. I am lonely here in your beautiful Bordeaux which is nevertheless a foreign unwelcoming city to me.'

He stretched out his hand and took hold of Léon's chin, turning the boy's head towards him.

'Yes,' he said, 'you have lovely eyes.' For the first time he had dropped into the second person singular, and now repeated the words in his own language. 'Du hast schonen Augen. I should so much like it if you would one night have dinner with me.'

'There's the curfew,' Léon said.

'But that can be easily arranged. I should so much like it.'

It was at that moment that the door opened, with the ring of the little bell which Henri had installed in case he or his assistant was in the back shop. Schussmann let his hand fall away and turned to see Lannes.

Léon thought over the conversation while Lannes was upstairs with Henri, and again went over it, word for word, once Lannes had left. The dinner, if it ever took place, would be only a preliminary. That was obvious. How did he feel? Uncertain, even afraid, but also warm. If Schussmann – Karl – hadn't been a German . . . it was nice to be desired, he couldn't help feeling that. That was after all why he had first gone with Gaston, though admittedly he had from the first liked Gaston, who made him laugh, more than he liked the German. On the other hand, having a German friend might be useful. He disliked that thought, but he couldn't put it away. And Alain, that was different, but, he feared, hopeless. Only another sort of friendship possible there. He was sure of that, sadly sure. Alain had offered no responsive flicker. He saw Léon as a mate – a 'copain' – nothing more. Well, there was no need to commit himself. Spin it out, he said. He looked in the mirror – at the 'lovely eyes' – and felt in his imagination Karl's fingers running along the line of his jaw.

Lannes also had evidently had no doubt as to Schussmann's intentions. That was another consideration to bear in mind.

He was still turning these thoughts over when the bell rang again and Alain himself came in.

'Coffee?'

'If you still have some and can spare it.'

'For you certainly.'

For you, anything, was what he wanted, but didn't dare, to say.

'How's school?'

'Tedious. It all seems pointless now.'

'And your rugby?'

'That's all right.'

'I should like to see you play.'

'Would you? Come along one day then.'

'I'd like that.'

He brought through the coffee and poured it.

'Cigarette?'

'Thanks.'

'You've just missed your father. He seems quite happy we're friends. We are, aren't we? I'm glad you told him we'd met.'

'Why shouldn't I?'

'Oh I don't know. He also told me that someone took a shot at a German soldier in the public garden yesterday . . . and that I fitted the description.'

'And did you?'

'Fit the description? He thought so.'

'No. I meant; were you the guy that shot?'

'Certainly not. I don't know one end of a gun from the other. That's to say, I've never fired one in my life.'

Alain wrinkled his brow.

'I envy him, you know,' he said. 'At least he's tried to do something.'

'But he missed.'

'Pity.'

'Do you really think so.'

'Do I? I don't know. To some extent.'

For a little then they talked of books, those they had read, those that still awaited them, and, as they talked, they smoked, and Léon admired Alain's ability to speak whole paragraphs without removing the cigarette which dangled from the right corner of his lips.

Then Alain said, 'Of course all this talk is escapism, to divert us from reality. I wonder who he was.'

'Who?'

'The boy whose description you fit, who took a pot at the Boche. I really admire him even if he was a rotten shot. Maybe it's more difficult than we think. I've never fired a pistol or revolver. Have you?'

'I told you I haven't. Actually I do know which end you point, but that's about all. I don't suppose it's as easy to hit your target as it is in the movies, especially Westerns.'

'Everyone's been ordered to hand their guns in, but I expect there are lots hidden. My father's got one of course, but it wouldn't be right to use his.'

'What do you mean?'

'Well, they can identify guns from the bullets, can't they?'

'But you wouldn't, would you, even if you had one?'

Alain looked up and smiled broadly. His eyes were alight with enthusiasm or, perhaps, mischief.

'Why not?'

Léon hesitated. He didn't want to appear backward or cowardly. All the same . . .

'All the same,' he said, 'what would killing a single German soldier accomplish? And would it even be right? Not to speak of the reprisals that would probably follow, he would probably turn out to be a poor conscript – like your brother – who didn't even want to be in the army, not at all a real Nazi. And remember, I've even more reason to hate them than you do – being a Jew, don't forget. But I wouldn't do it.'

'Fair enough.' Alain was still smiling. 'It's too soon anyway. But the day will come, I'm sure of it, when we have to choose our side, choose between collaborating like my miserable uncle, and resisting.'

'We could do nothing. There's the other choice, neither one thing nor the other.'

'Oh yes, we could be like sheep. But how would we feel afterwards when those who did resist are hailed as heroes? No, when the time comes, I shall choose to act. In any case, Léon – I don't know just how to put this – do you really think that, as a Jew, you'll be allowed to opt for doing nothing? Sorry, that's horrid. Forgive me. But it may be true. Do you listen to the BBC?'

'No, well, not often. It was at a friend's house I heard the replay of de Gaulle's first broadcast. I suppose there have been others, but I haven't heard them. So – to answer your question – I don't listen to the BBC, not really.'

'Nor do I, because it would alarm my mother. But I've also a friend who does, and he says, there's no doubt the English are going to fight on – even if, it seems to me, they're not doing much fighting just now. So . . . give me another cigarette, please.'

Léon tossed him the packet.

'Oh, is this your last?'

'That's all right. Take it. We'll go and see my aunt and get more. I think I can shut the shop now.'

Léon thought: What would Alain think if I told him about Schussmann? Would he be disgusted?

## XX

The concierge was surly as on his earlier visit.

'Ill, is she?' she said. 'Don't you believe it. That kind takes good care of herself. Do you know, she complained the other day she couldn't find cream for her cat? For her cat, I ask you, and cream which we haven't seen in Bordeaux since I don't know when. All goes to the Germans, I suppose, not that I've seen anything to complain of in their behaviour. They're being very correct, aren't they? No, I haven't seen her in a couple of days, but then I don't look out for her, do I? Anything but, in fact.'

Lannes let the words wash over him. He knew the type only too well. They made eager but unreliable witnesses, their perceptions invariably distorted by malice and by their desire to make themselves seem important.

He had to ring twice before Madame Robartet opened the door. She was neatly dressed as she had been on their earlier encounter, but she walked more slowly and uncertainly, even in the carpet slippers she was wearing, and he didn't recall her hands shaking as they did now.

'It's good of you to come,' she said, 'and so promptly. I've been worried. Is there any news of Monsieur Biron? Ah, I see from your face. He's dead, isn't he? I was afraid of that. He's never been away for so long.'

'I'm afraid he was already dead when we spoke before.'

'Yes,' she said. 'I see now he must have been. I knew it really when you sent these other policemen to examine his apartment. But I wouldn't admit it to myself. He was such a gentle and thoughtful man. And then the way this other man spoke. I suppose he was murdered. Is that right? Why didn't you tell me?'

She took a lace-fringed handkerchief from her sleeve and dabbed her eyes. The whiff of lavender it gave off reminded Lannes of his grandmother – his mother's mother – who had always placed lavender in little muslin bags in the drawers where she kept sheets, pillow-cases, handkerchiefs – he couldn't remember what else.

Why hadn't he told her? Because in other ways too she was like that grandmother who had always shrunk from anything she deemed unpleasant, nasty or improper? There was no answer he could give now which didn't seem insulting or patronizing, as if she was too old and frail to be faced with the truth. Which was nonsense, because the old who live close to death are less disturbed than the young by the deaths of others.

'You look very tired, superintendent,' she said.

She got to her feet, stiffly, and took a bottle of Crème de Cassis and two small glasses from a cupboard.

'You'll find this reviving,' she said. 'I usually take a glass myself about this time of day. My doctor approves. He says it stimulates the heart. Poor Monsieur Biron! That's how I think of him though I gather now it wasn't his real name. That man who called said horrible things about him. I didn't believe them of course. But why did he choose to use another name? It's puzzled me.'

The cat leaped on to Lannes' knees, almost causing him to spill his drink and lay there purring as he stroked its glossy fur.

'Which man was that?'

'The one I called you to speak about. I didn't care for him, you see. Nor did Abanazar. He likes you, I can see that. That's good, he's a very discerning cat. But he hissed and spat when the man stretched out his hand towards him.'

'When was this?'

'Just yesterday. I think it was yesterday, but it might have been the previous day. I don't always keep note of the passage of time. Abanazar lets me know when he needs to be fed, you see.'

She nodded her head, twice, and closed her eyes, drifting into the sudden sleep of the very old.

The cat now thrust its head against Lannes' face, purring the more intensely and flexing its claws on the thin jersey he wore under his jacket. He continued to stroke it, and waited patiently, held there, unable to move without dislodging the cat and having in any case no desire to do so. The old woman was right; he was indeed weary, tired to the bone. He took in the room: the cane-bottomed walnut chairs, the little tables with photographs in silver frames and knick-knacks, a couple of Dresden shepherdesses, small tortoiseshell and porcelain boxes, the prints of old-fashioned country scenes, a glass-fronted bookcase that he supposed had not been opened for years, a case of stuffed birds, a card table on which a game of patience had been laid out, only half-finished for there was still a stack of cards to be dealt.

The old woman opened her eyes.

'I really disliked him,' she said. 'He was impertinent. Ill-mannered. I'm sorry, I must have dropped off for a moment. How rude of me!'

'Not at all,' Lannes said. 'Who was this man you were speaking of?'

'I've no idea. He didn't have the manners to introduce himself. I would never have let him in if he hadn't said he was a friend of poor Monsieur Biron. Which, as I discovered, he certainly wasn't. The things he said!'

'But what did he want? Can you remember?'

'I'm not likely to forget. He wanted the letter.'

'Which letter was that?'

'The one Monsieur Biron entrusted to me. Which other letter could it be?'

'You didn't mention a letter when I was here before.'

The old lady took a sip from her drink, holding the glass in both hands, and then replacing it, very carefully, on the little marble-topped table by her side.

'But I didn't know then that Monsieur Biron was dead. So of course there was no call to mention the letter, since I expected him to reclaim it. He had only given it to me for safe-keeping, as he said.'

'Did you ask him why?'

'But of course not. It was no matter of my concern.'

'And did you give it to the man?'

'I told you Abanazar didn't care for him, though he seemed to take to the boy.'

'Which boy was that?'

'The one who came with him of course. A nice-looking boy and well-mannered. Perhaps he was one of Monsieur Biron's students. I don't know. But I told the man I didn't know what he was talking about and that I certainly had no letter. There are times, I think, when it's permissible to tell a lie. When it's in a good cause.'

'So you do have the letter.'

'But certainly. That's why I asked you to come here. To give it you.'


## XXI


Though she had spoken of it as a letter, the envelope she gave Lannes contained three pieces of paper stapled together: some notes made by Gaston himself, a letter in Spanish or Catalan signed by Cortazar, and a typed document recording Pilar's death. Lannes called in young René and asked him to make a translation of Cortazar's letter, then turned his attention to Gaston's own writing.

I have never been a brave man, and now I am afraid. Marcel proposes to call on me this evening. (I must make sure to send Maurice, dear boy, away before he arrives.) He has information, he says. Has been in touch with Edmond and can satisfy my demands, answer my requests. Why does this frighten me? First, because I have this letter from Cortazar, which seems to tell me much of what I wanted to know, and the information he has provided me with is compromising. I'm in deeper waters than I thought of entering. (I must conceal Cortazar's letter before Marcel arrives. But where? Dare I trust it to Madame Robartet? Surely that wouldn't put her in danger?) I'm confused as well as frightened, scarcely know what it is I'm writing.

What a fool Pilar was, a brave fool certainly, even a noble one, but still rash to the point of . . . I don't know what. I only wish I had her courage.

Let me note down what I know and what I guess. I must be quick and brief.

Edmond was engaged in procuring weapons for the Fascists in Spain. That's clear. It was of course illegal.

He met Pilar in Paris where she was working raising funds and making propaganda for the Republican cause, and seduced her. (Or did she – for political reasons – seduce him?) No matter. They became lovers or what passed as lovers. She learned what he was doing and then what? Threatened to expose him? This was in the year of the Popular Front. Exposure would certainly have been followed by a criminal trial. (Certainly? I don't know but the possibility alarmed him.) But then what happened to stop her from exposing him? I don't know. It's clear however that he arranged – but how? – for her to be denounced as a Fascist agent and when she returned to Spain – on a mission for the Anarchist group to which she belonged, she was immediately arrested by the Communists and shot as a traitor without a trial. It was murder by proxy.

Where does Marcel come in? What part did he play? And who indeed is he, apart from being Edmond's creature?

Finally, what is his purpose in proposing this meeting? Does he intend to feed me false information? Or is it something worse he has in mind?

The writing tailed away. Then, across the bottom of the page, Gaston had scribbled: 'How ignoble to be such a coward.'

Lannes lit a cigarette and sat fingering the sheet of paper.

But you weren't such a coward, my poor Gaston, since you withstood torture and went to your death without telling Sigi what he had been sent to find out.

'What I know and what I guess.'

How much was knowledge, how much guesswork?

He passed the paper to Moncerre who read it and said, 'The poor sod, the poor bloody sod. Was he on to something or is it fantasy?'

'Whatever it was it brought him to his death. You can't get away from that.'

René returned, saying, 'He uses some words that I don't know, but I think this is the gist of it.'

Lannes took the paper from him.

Monsieur, I have to say first that, though I myself knew nothing but good of your esteemed sister-in-law, I have since learned that she was, or became, an object of suspicion to many in the Republican movement and among its supporters in Paris, and it was perhaps for this reason that she met her unhappy fate. (I attach a copy of the official record of her execution. Please do not ask me how I came by it – I've no wish to follow the same path.) This was because she entered into a liaison in Paris with a notorious French Fascist. Some say she was acting on orders and that the intention was to introduce her in this manner as a spy acting on behalf of the Republic, but others regarded her as untrustworthy and a potential traitor, if not an actual one. It was also reported that she had dealings with the French authorities, that is, with the body responsible for counter-espionage. (I don't know its title.) So, when she returned to Spain, it was natural that questions should be asked, all the more so because she had also unsuitable family connections there – her father, I believe, among them, and also a cousin in the inner councils of the Falange. So she was arrested by the Communist militia, acting on high authority, interrogated and her baggage searched. A letter addressed to her cousin was discovered sewn into the lining of her case. Its contents have never been divulged, but it was regarded as sufficient evidence to justify her immediate execution.

All this must be painful to you and to your brother, her husband. But, alas, there is more grief to follow, for my informant insists that, far from being a traitor, she was a true patriot and servant of the Republican cause, and that the incriminating letter found in her luggage was a forgery, not in her hand, though it purported to be. Furthermore, the Communist militia who arrested her knew in advance when she would cross the Border into Spain, and you will see that there are two dates on the document recording her execution, that of the signatory who commanded it being dated a full three weeks before she crossed over into Spain, the other that of the officer in command of the firing party or execution squad being correctly dated the day of her death. So it is clear that all was prepared in advance, that she was betrayed and doomed even before she left Paris, and denied any trial at which she might protest her innocence and seek to clear her name.

'I'm afraid my translation's pretty clumsy,' René said.

'Not at all. It's admirable.'

'Why didn't Cortazar come out with any of this when we had him in?' Moncerre said.

'He didn't trust us. I'm ashamed to say he didn't trust us. A pity. I liked him.'

He passed the death notice to the others.

'This seems clear enough anyway. There can be no real doubt Pilar is indeed dead.'

That was so, but really nothing here was satisfactory. It was all speculation, without hard evidence. Even the disparity of dates proved nothing. For all Lannes knew, the Communist judges might have been in the habit of signing blank death warrants; it wasn't impossible, not even improbable. And what Gaston wrote about Pilar's affair with Edmond was no more than rumour – Cortazar didn't name the notorious French Fascist and Lannes had no idea whether Edmond was indeed a member of any of the various French Fascist parties. Weren't they a bit petit-bourgeois for him?

He said: 'What we have here might be motive for murder, might just be motive for Gaston's murder. It doesn't explain why he was tortured or why Cortazar was, and their apartments searched. So there must be something more. Some paper that actually incriminates Edmond.'

'Or Sigi?'

'No. It must be Edmond. For all Sigi's bravado he's a tool, only a tool. I'm sure of that.'

'What about the old lady, Madame Robartet?' René said. 'Is she safe? I mean, do you think Sigi – I'm assuming it was Sigi who called on her – believed her when she said she had no letter?'

'I've put a guard on her apartment. That's only temporary. I'm going to have a word with Sigi myself. René, would you please have copies made of these papers, several copies. I intend to give one to Sigi and to tell him we got it from the old lady.'

'And then?'

'Then I'm going to fix a trip to Vichy. It's time I spoke to Edmond himself.'


## XXII

'Did you see this?'

Alain passed a copy of the *Sud-Ouest* to Léon, pointing to a short paragraph which announced that a retired wine-broker, Pierre Mourgues, had been sentenced to death for an act of violence against members of the German Army, and had accordingly been shot.

'I asked Papa about him. He was sixty-nine. Think of that. So old and still able to care, to feel the dishonour of our condition. It's tremendous.'

'What had he done?'

'Well, it seems that a few days ago a couple of German plain-clothes policemen called at his apartment, Cours de la Somme, in search of a young woman who lodged there and who, they said – listen to this – had "contaminated" – their word exactly – contaminated some German officers.'

'Given them VD you mean. Good for her!'

'Then the old boy said he didn't know anything about the girl, but in any case it was impossible to contaminate swine. They went away then, only to return with two or three Boche soldiers and the old man went for them with an axe. He was soon overpowered of course, and, well, you know the rest. What do you think of it?'

'What does your father say?'

'He sighs deeply, and says it's all foolishness, horrible foolishness.'

'I suppose he's right,' Léon said. 'You can't help admiring the old man though. Such spirit.'

'Of course he's right,' Miriam said, bringing a tray with coffee and cups and a plate of biscuits into the back-room of the tabac. 'It horrifies me to hear you boys even dreaming of any form of resistance. You've your whole lives before you. It's madness to throw them away for an empty gesture which does no good to anyone.'

'But what sort of lives?' Léon said.

Miriam poured coffee and handed a cup to each boy. She had lost weight since the summer and her black dress hung loosely on her. Now she settled herself in her chair and crossed her legs, giving Alain a brief glimpse of thigh. It was the second time Léon had brought him to the tabac and he had decided to set himself a test: he would come on his own, one day soon, and then . . . Miriam had laughed when he bent over to kiss her hand, but happily, he thought, not in mockery; and then she had allowed him to hold it a moment longer than – he was sure – convention regarded as proper. He had asked Léon how old his aunt was, but got an unsatisfactory reply. 'Oh I don't know, forty maybe.' That was nonsense, surely; she certainly wasn't that old. His own mother was forty, and there was no comparison. Perhaps Miriam was thirty-two, he thought. But would she laugh at him if . . . When? It was unfortunate if she thought of him simply as Léon's friend, since she evidently regarded Léon as a child.

'What sort of lives?' Miriam repeated Léon's question. 'Lives that are too short and too precious to be cut off by a German bullet, that's what.'

'Yes,' Alain said, and frowned, to show he was to be taken seriously. 'My father says the time for resistance will come, but we have to be patient. Even to speak of it now is premature.'

'Your father's a sensible man.'

'Besides, I don't see the point of shooting a solitary German soldier, as that boy in the park attempted. What good can that do?

Or of going for a couple of them with an axe like that old man. Moreover, as we agreed, Léon, collectively the Boches are our enemies, but individually one of them may be a decent sort, not even a Nazi. Take that chap you sold the book to, for instance. He seems all right. Or again, there's a young lieutenant billeted on the family who live in the apartment above ours. I've talked to him. So has my sister. I don't think he even wants to be in the army, let alone occupying France. We'd quite a long conversation the other day, the three of us. He misses his home and his little sisters and his dogs, a couple of English spaniels, he showed me their photograph. In different circumstances – say, if we met each other at university or on holiday somewhere – we might even be friends. I couldn't shoot him, though it would be easy to do so, if I had a gun, since he evidently trusts me and takes no precautions. In any case I'm against killing for the sake of killing. It's an empty gesture and a cruel one. Theatrical really in my opinion. Indeed it's no better than murder when you come to think of it. But sabotage, that's a different thing altogether. There's some point in that, for it must hinder or disrupt the German war effort. So some day, when the time is ripe, as my father says.'

Miriam was smiling, not patronisingly, but it seemed in agreement, even approval. He thought he had impressed her. Here then was one answer to Léon's question, 'What sort of lives?' A life that had room for a woman like Miriam. He certainly wasn't going to throw away his before . . .

'It's almost curfew time,' she said. 'You'd better be off home, the pair of you. Léon, I've made a cheese tart for your mother. Wait till I fetch it.'

Alain turned up the collar of his overcoat. It made him look older, a bit raffish, a bit film-star. Miriam gave them each a couple of packets of cigarettes, kissed Léon and shook hands with Alain. He held hers for as long as he dared.

'It's been nice seeing you,' she said. 'I'm so glad you're friends. Léon needs a good friend. Give my regards to your father and follow his advice. He's a sensible man, as I say, perhaps the most sensible in Bordeaux. But don't tell him I said that. Now be off with you both. Go carefully, and come again when you feel like it, even if you're not out of cigarettes.'

'She really likes you, I can see that,' Léon said as the shop door closed behind them and the iron shutters came down again.

'Well, I like her too.'

They parted at the corner of the street.

'See you soon,' Alain said.

'I hope so.'

'Don't do anything I wouldn't do. Like shooting Germans.'

'Certainly not. I promise.'

Léon hesitated a moment, then darted forward and kissed Alain quickly and lightly on both cheeks.


## XXIII


A cold clear frosty morning, the sky deep-blue – 'pre-war blue', Lannes said to himself – and the rich odour of roasting chestnuts coming from a stove by the kiosk at the end of the avenue. Lannes waited, smoking; he had no fear that Sigi would not keep the appointment, made by way of old Marthe. His vanity would forbid him to do so. For a moment it crossed Lannes' mind that he made a good target sitting there in the open at a rendez-vous of his own choice – a better target than that German private had offered. But that was foolishness. There was no reason to kill him now that there hadn't been over the last months. In any case, it wouldn't occur to Sigi that Lannes had taken no precautions, hadn't alerted anyone, not even Moncerre, to where he would be. As for Schnyder, the less he knew at this stage the better. Meanwhile he was content to wait. It had been a bad morning at home, Marguerite in low spirits, finding fault with Alain and Clothilde over matters of no importance. He wished he could find comfort for her. Last night she had turned away from him in bed, and when he realized she was weeping and placed his hand on her shoulder, had brushed it off. Her wretched brother Albert had failed her, his promise to arrange Dominique's return as worthless as Lannes had known it to be. When he continued to counsel patience, she sobbed more deeply. He was useless; there was nothing he could do to alleviate her misery.

'Superintendent.'

He looked up from his reverie to see Sigi standing before him, the boy Michel by his side.

'Send the lad away,' he said.

Sigi smiled, took a wallet from his breast-pocket, gave Michel a banknote and told him to wait for him by the kiosk.

'Buy yourself an orangeade or something,' he said.

The boy shrugged his shoulders, treated Lannes to a broad – impertinent? – smile, turned away and strolled with careless shambling gait towards the kiosk.

'Why did you bring him?'

'Not as a bodyguard, you may be sure of that, or even as a witness. We're attending a meeting later, and he arrived early. He's brimful of enthusiasm, you see. I presume you are not going to arrest me and that we shall be able to keep our appointment.'

He settled himself on the bench beside Lannes and unbuttoned his trench-coat.

'No, I'm not going to arrest you.'

He passed the envelope to Sigi who, before opening it, said, 'This is very conspiratorial, superintendent, as if we were playing in a movie, don't you think?'

He read the papers, quickly.

'And this concerns me?' He said. 'You really think so?'

'You were on the right track. Gaston did indeed entrust these papers to Madame Robartet. She didn't give them to you because her cat took a dislike to you. In any case, they're not what you were looking for, are they?'

'I don't know what you mean.'

He made to pass them back to Lannes.

'Keep them. They're copies, as you must know.'

'Mere fancies, wild fancies, I should say.'

'As you like, but you'll understand that there is nothing to be gained by troubling the old lady again. It took you a long time to get round to her, didn't it?'

'You also, it seems.'

'So we are both still in search of the incriminating document,' Lannes said. 'Where do you try next? I imagine Edmond must be getting impatient. Worried too.'

'Again, I repeat, I don't know what you are talking about.'

'Don't be silly. You tortured Gaston and Cortazar and ransacked their apartments. It must be important. And you didn't find it because, if you had done so, there would have been no need to visit Madame Robartet.'

'This is foolishness, like your interrogation of my friend Jaime. You frightened him, you know, with your talk of the guillotine. Absurd, but I had some difficulty in putting his mind at rest. You frightened my poor uncle, Jean-Christophe, too. He was in a dreadful state after you left him.'

'Good.'

'Not that I hold that against you, superintendent. Indeed we are at one on that point. I don't care for perversion and degeneracy myself.'

'And the boy? The little girl's brother?'

Lannes gestured toward Michel who was watching them from the kiosk where he stood smoking and looking bored.

'No, superintendent, I am not interested in that sort of thing. You really mustn't insult me by making such a suggestion. The boy's an enthusiast for the cause, that's all.'

'And what cause would that be?'

'The cause of the New Europe, naturally. What else?'

'You expect me to believe that? That you believe in such non-sense?'

'But why not? It's the direction the prevailing wind is blowing in.'

'Winds shift.'

Sigi held up both hands, palms open, in mock-horror.

'That's rash talk, superintendent, almost seditious. You are fortunate I am not a malicious man, or . . . well, where would your career be? Superintendent, I have a certain respect for you – don't ask me why. So also does my Uncle Edmond. Therefore I say this to you: you are pursuing a dangerous path, not in your own interest. Moreover you have enemies – I don't, you understand, speak of myself. You know the advocate Labiche? Very well, let me warn you. He is preparing a denunciation, accusing you of consorting with Jews – one handsome Jewess and one pretty little Jew-boy of dubious moral reputation. I tell you frankly: I don't give a damn whether there is anything in what he affirms. But such accusations are damaging these days, damaging for anyone, but especially for a policeman. Let us make a bargain. I have the means to call advocate Labiche to heel, the means to silence him. So I do that and you forget all this . . . ' he patted the papers which Lannes had given him ' . . . all this nonsense. What do you say?'

'It's an interesting suggestion.'

'Not only interesting, but in your interest. In your interest, my friend. Listen to me. You know very well that, no matter what sort of a case you concoct against me – and remember, I admit nothing – it is impossible that you should ever see it come to court. It's as impossible as that the corpses for which, to my amusement, you hold me responsible, should come to life and walk the streets again. They are kaput, dead and buried, and the dead stay dead. Besides, they were worthless people, you can't deny that. Perhaps this girl, this Pilar' – he tapped the papers again – 'was not worthless. I don't know, can't say, having had no acquaintance with her, but she too is dead, and there is nothing to be gained from pursuing the matter, from trying to disentangle the web of circumstance. She engaged, it seems, in war, and war is unforgiving. She paid the price of her commitment. Let her rest in peace. It is vain to weep over spilt wine.'

'Blood,' Lannes said. 'Blood, not wine. And you are mistaken. Actions have consequences, blood will have blood, and the dead do not always lie easy. The murdered cry out for vengeance, even for justice.'

'Words, words, words, fine words doubtless, but mere sounds in the air. What do you say to my offer, my friend?'

'What do I say?' Lannes smiled. 'It's matter for thought. I wonder what has prompted you to make it?'

'My respect for you, superintendent, my respect. Only that.'

'Only that?'

Sigi got to his feet. He held out the papers to Lannes and, when Lannes made no move to take them, laughed and stuffed them carelessly into his pocket.

'Think about my offer,' he said. 'It would, I assure you, give me great pleasure to twist advocate Labiche's tail, very painfully. I give you a fortnight. I can hold him off that long. He's a rat, you know, and a rat's bite is sharp and poisonous. He really hates you, though I don't know why. Stupid of me to say that. We never need a reason to hate, do we?'

He made to turn away and waved to summon Michel.

Lannes said: 'One other thing. Let the boy go. Break whatever hold you have on him.'

'Why should I do that, my friend?'

'Because yours will not always be the winning side, and enthusiasts like that boy will suffer when the wind shifts.'

'You speak rashly again. I really do admire you, superintendent. But you are wrong. The war is to all intents and purposes over. Germany is invincible. Why don't you join us? I assure you, there will be no place for rats like advocate Labiche in the New Europe.'


## XXIV

Lannes had never been in Vichy before the war. It wasn't his sort of place. Truth to tell, if he had ever thought of the town, it would have been with a certain distaste, even scorn. It was a make-believe place, a spa that doctors recommended to rich patients, many of whose ailments were doubtless imaginary. His own mother, after thirty years of hard work, had died of some form of kidney-disease; she couldn't have afforded to come to Vichy though he supposed the idea had never crossed her mind. And would it have done her any good if she had?

And now this make-believe town with its array of hotels in all styles representing the architectural fancies, often incongruous, of the last hundred years, with its Turkish baths crowned with vaguely oriental domes, its kiosks, its casinos, its pretentious villas designed according to the whims of rich women, its long promenades, its parks each with a bandstand and gravelled walks, was, bizarrely, the capital of the French State, selected, as he would learn, on impulse, after the government on the move from Bordeaux had spent one night at Clermont-Ferrand. There were cities in the Unoccupied Zone which might have seemed more obvious choices: Lyon,

Toulouse, Marseille. All had been rejected, the first two because they were strongholds of the Left, Marseille because . . . well, because, with its pervasive criminal underworld, its brothels and reputation for catering for all forms of vice, it hardly seemed a fitting place from which to launch the National Revolution. He smiled at the thought.

The Marshal himself, he had learned, was established in the Hôtel du Parc, which was therefore the seat of government. For a sceptic like Lannes there was encouragement here. Hotels were for transients, they spoke of impermanence, their guests here today and gone tomorrow. Weren't any of them, he wondered, alert to the symbolism?

In other circumstances it might almost have been charming. Outside the hotel, he had already been told, schoolchildren would gather in their hundreds every Sunday, to sing the anthem, 'Maréchal, nous voilà!' Now, even as he stood there picturing the scene, the old man himself appeared from the hotel, walking-stick in hand, wearing a light overcoat, a Homburg on his head, to take what must be his regular afternoon constitutional. He had only one companion – his doctor perhaps? – and he strode out briskly, very erect, his skin glowing pink with health, and the famous moustache white as new snow. He might have been an elderly banker come to Vichy to take the waters in the days of peace. Lannes, mindful of Verdun, took off his hat as the Marshal passed him, and received a brief acknowledgement, two gloved fingers being lifted to touch the brim of the Homburg.

There was a air of repose to the town, even on a winter afternoon when a soft mist clothed the low hills that encircled it. The air was mild. Lannes settled himself at a pavement café. Most of the tables on the terrace were occupied by women in fur coats and men who had the appearance of being government functionaries. The waiter was in no hurry to take his order – perhaps no one hurried in Vichy. It didn't matter; Lannes was content to wait. He had a curious sense of being on holiday, perhaps because of the absence of the German soldiers inescapable in Bordeaux. It was as if he had been allowed time out from real life. And this doubtless was what many visitors had felt there in the days before the war.

It had not been easy to get permission to make the journey. Schnyder had been reluctant to approve. 'I can see you intend to stir things up,' he said. 'I don't like it.'

Eventually Lannes had gone his own way, telephoning Edmond de Grimaud to make an appointment and at the same time extracting an invitation from him. Obligingly Edmond had confirmed this by telegram, thus cutting the ground from under Schnyder's feet. 'But why should he be willing to see you? I don't understand it,' he said. Lannes was surprised himself. He had half-expected he would have to force himself on Edmond. But all he said to Schnyder was, 'That's how it is.'

He ordered a cognac and a small bottle of Vichy water, not because he wanted it, but because it seemed the right thing to do. The woman at the table to his right was staring fixedly at the cream cake the waiter had brought with her pot of tea, and for a moment Lannes was tempted. There had been no cream available in Bordeaux for months now – it all went to the Boches of course – and he thought how eagerly Clothilde would have fallen on such a cake. But to order one would be taking the holiday spirit too far. He lit a cigarette and smoked placidly.

In a little the Marshal and his companion came past again on their way back to the hotel, the old man striding out like someone twenty, even thirty, years his junior. There was a ripple of applause, and someone behind Lannes said, 'He's wonderful, isn't he, for his age, and you know they say he still has an eye for a pretty woman.' Glancing round the terrace, Lannes thought, there's no shortage of that commodity here either.

He had two hours to kill before his appointment with Edmond. No problem: killing time was what everyone did, or had done, in Vichy. It was a town built for that, with its five hundred or more hotels and an equivalent number of bars, cafés and restaurants. It was a place where you filled the days, idling, between the set hours at which your doctor had ordered you to take the waters.

Finishing his brandy and leaving the bottle of water untouched, he decided that he too should take an afternoon stroll, for this was, he saw, a scarcely escapable, indeed necessary, part of the Vichy day. So, at a leisurely pace – for you don't hurry in Vichy – he set off, leaning on his stick, along the Avenue Thermale – a name you are unlikely to encounter in any real city – and then down the Avenue Victoria and the rue G. Clemenceau to arrive back in the Parc des Sources by the Opera House, the building where the National Assembly had taken the vote that killed off the Third Republic and accorded the authority and power to re-order the State to the aged Marshal. A band was playing in the soft greyish-yellow light of the afternoon, and the music was Offenbach's, airy, joyous music that seemed to mock the idea of war and misery.

Edmond had appointed the Hotel des Ambassadeurs as their meeting-place. It was one of the two grandest in the town and Lannes would in any circumstances have felt awkward and uncomfortable there. Now, entering the foyer, it seemed as if he had stepped on to the set of a movie. Page-boys in pillbox hats scurried here and there. All the small marble-topped tables seemed to be occupied. Waiters with trays held aloft glided between them. There were palm trees in pots and other plants that he couldn't identify. A string quartet was playing sweet music to which few, probably, were listening. Nobody approached him and there was no sign of Edmond. That wasn't surprising; he had expected to be made to wait. He strolled through the crowd coming on a long ill-lit passage at the end of which four elderly people sat round a card-table. He watched them for a little as one stout baldhead dealt out a new game with painful slowness, holding each card in the air before placing it on the green baize. It was like a film scene shot in slow motion.

He turned into a bar and ordered a pastis because that was what he had been drinking at the Hotel Splendide where Edmond tried to force champagne on him, and he had resisted. The barman served him silently; he was scarcely more than a boy, probably an apprentice, assigned this quiet time in the late afternoon before the cocktail hour. Had he dodged the army or was he lucky enough to have been demobilised?

'My dear superintendent!'

Edmond's hand was pressed firmly on his shoulder, as if they were old friends come together for a long-anticipated reunion.

'And how do you find our Vichy?'

'Strange.'

'Sometimes, you know, I think it is like one of these imaginary islands you find in poetry or novels, or a sort of Atlantis perhaps that has escaped engulfment by the waves, but then in other moods, it seems to me simply remarkable. Rather wonderful in any case. Certainly it has a compelling charm. Then of course one reminds oneself there is work to be done, important work. In my case driving forward a total reform of teaching in our lycées, a reform designed to produce a more vigorous and healthy youth. But you have not travelled here to listen to me speaking about the importance of my work. Pierre, bring us a bottle of my usual champagne. Come, superintendent.'

Taking Lannes by the elbow, again in the style of an old comrade, he guided him to a table in the far corner of the room where the lighting was subdued and they would be out of earshot of anyone standing at the bar.

'Maurice will be sorry to have missed you,' he said, 'but you must know that I have secured him a position with one of the new Youth organizations and he is even now leading a party of young lads on an excursion into the mountains. He's thriving on it, you'll be pleased to hear. Even his asthma has relented. And do you have word of your own son – Dominique, is it? – The one who is a prisoner of war?'

'The occasional card. He's been put to work on a farm. Which could, I suppose, be worse.'

'We must see what we can do to secure his repatriation. Such things are possible, if you have the right contacts and know the line to take. Ah, thank you, Pierre, just pour both glasses. That'll do. Your health, superintendent, your good health.'

This time Lannes did not resist. He sipped the wine – Pol Roger – which was good, far better than he could ever afford himself.

'I truly am concerned for your health – and your well-being in general,' Edmond said. 'That's why it distresses me to learn that you are still pursuing inquiries which are pointless in themselves and likely to damage your reputation with those that count nowadays. You won't be surprised to learn that my nephew Sigi has kept me up to date with your activities, which is of course why I acceded to your request for a meeting. They won't do, you know. They really won't do.'

Lannes said: 'I was shot after our last meeting. You pretended it was intended for you, but naturally you know it wasn't.'

'How can you be sure?'

'I'm tired of these games,' Lannes said. 'Sigi was driving the car which he had borrowed from his foster-brother, who has since been murdered himself, and the shot was fired by his Spanish friend Sombra who, fortunately for me, made a bosh of it. You know this as well as I do.'

'It pleases you to think so.'

'I have enough evidence to justify asking the examining magistrate for a warrant for their arrest.'

'But you haven't done so. Precisely. Instead you come here. To question me, which would be vain, or to seek my help?'

'And you agreed to see me,' Lannes said. 'Indeed you made my journey possible.'

'Just so.'

The man's calm was infuriating. As at their last meeting Lannes knew himself to be at a disadvantage. He was a policeman, but outside the loop. The structure which should support him was rotten, worm-eaten. Murder was no longer an offence against society, against nature and the order of things, but had become a political act, a means to a justified end. It came to him that his journey to this make-believe Vichy and this meeting itself were attempts to deny that things were as they were. Yet he had to press on. He owed it to himself, to his idea of his office, to Gaston and Cortazar. To Pilar also, and therefore to Henri. At the very least he could confront Edmond with the reality of his knowledge.

'She was your mistress, wasn't she?' he said.

This time Edmond, perhaps also wearying of the game, didn't pretend not to understand.

'Mistress? Scarcely that. We went to bed a couple of times. She was charming, a delightful lover. She was also, as I realized from the start, my enemy, seeking to make use of me and to compromise me. And I couldn't have that.'

'So you had her betrayed and killed.'

'So you say. Killed by her own people, not by me.'

'But you arranged it.'

'Whoever was responsible, it was an act of war.'

'There's a document,' Lannes said, 'a paper. I don't know what it is, but I know it would do you damage, even now. Which is why it's important. Important to you. I've no doubt about that. Sigi and the Spaniard searched Gaston's apartment, looking for it and the Catalan's also. Both men were tortured in an attempt to get them to reveal where it was. Neither did so. It's still out there. Somewhere. And it worries you. It's because of that paper you agreed to this meeting.'

Edmond smiled and taking the bottle from the ice-bucket re-filled their glasses.

'It would be very easy,' he said, 'to have you arrested. One telephone call is all it would take. I wonder why I don't make that call.'

'I believe Sigi killed your father too. Doesn't that distress you.'

'He was a very old man, feeble in body, who fell downstairs. I told you before: you really mustn't believe old Marthe. She adored Sigi once, and then, well, she stopped adoring him. Should I make that call? Give me a reason why I shouldn't.'

Lannes was tired of it all. He picked up his glass, drained it, and lit a cigarette.

'And what would the charge be?'

'That scarcely matters, does it? Unreliability, disaffection, lack of commitment to the National Revolution, suspicion of treason . . . anything would do. Moreover I understand that you are already in danger of being denounced in Bordeaux also.'

'You refer to the advocate Labiche? It's not yet an offence to have Jewish friends.'

'Not an offence, certainly not a criminal offence – not yet, as you say. But it's what? Unwise at the very least for a policeman? It calls his judgement into question. His loyalty also and his willingness to uphold the law.'

'Even if the friend in question is your father's widow?'

'Even so. Come, superintendent, let us stop this play-acting.

You are, to put it vulgarly, in deep shit. But, luckily for you, I'm not your enemy. I propose a bargain. Abandon your tiresome investigation which – yes, I admit this much – might, if you bring it to a conclusion, do me some harm – abandon it, call your dogs off, and I'll bring Labiche to heel. He can do you great damage. You know that. It scarcely matters whether my stepmother is indeed your mistress, or her pretty nephew your catamite – neither of which allegations, I assure you, I credit – the mere accusation relayed to certain quarters would be enough to ruin you. That's undeniable. But I have, as I say, a certain regard for you. I admire your persistence. You're a man of integrity, the sort of man we need on our side if we are to restore order and virtue to our wretched France. I have no wish to see you destroyed. Quite the contrary. But you will be, unless I bring Labiche down. Which I can do, believe me. I shall be happy to supply you with a weapon to use against him. He shares my poor brother's weakness, but whereas Jean-Christophe is feeble and in my view to be pitied, Labiche is malignant, sadistic, repulsive. I can furnish you with proof. Furthermore, I can – and will – arrange to have your son repatriated. All you have to do is say "yes" to my proposal and give me his particulars. What do you say, superintendent? Shall we shake hands on it?'

'And the document?'

'Oh the famous document. Naturally if such exists and comes into your possession, you will hand it over to me. I trust you to act honourably.'

'Honourably?'

'Yes, indeed. I too am a man of honour. Is it a bargain?'

## XXV

'She really likes you, I can see that.' Léon's words came insistently back to Alain. But how did she like him? Simply as Léon's new friend? Well, he was that of course, and pleased to be it, without reservations or embarrassment, but he couldn't help remarking that though she obviously cared for Léon, she treated him as little more than a child, and an irresponsible one indeed. He turned over in bed, thinking of how she had crossed her legs and of the glimpse of skin she had revealed above her suspender. She needn't be more than thirty, he told himself again; she was too attractive to be more than that. It was time to lose his virginity, as half a dozen of his classmates already boasted of having done, but to lose it to a real woman, not a little shop-girl or prostitute. He pictured himself being permitted to place his hand on her breast, and then to watch her undress, or, better still, to do that for her, article by article, with kisses in between.

'I'm in love,' he said to himself. 'I really am, in love with a woman.'

The Alain of even a few days before would have been ashamed of the naivety of the words, for he had been at pains to cultivate a bored and superior manner whenever any of his mates talked of love. Romantic language was out-of-date, out-of-place anywhere but the cinema, and, even there, well, the standard love-scene was matter for laughter.

Would Miriam laugh at him if he said the words he was eager to speak? Would she say, 'How sweet, but really you're only a boy, I don't go in for cradle-snatching?'

Besides, I'm a brute to think of her as I do, to imagine myself undressing her. She's in danger as a Jewess. I ought to be thinking of how I can protect her. What's more, she's been recently widowed, even though Léon says she is well rid of her husband who was old enough to be her grandfather – how disgusting. Well, I don't know. I've got to put it to the test. There's no alternative. I can't think of anything else.

Léon's noticed it, he thought. Why else would he have said, 'My aunt seems to have made quite an impression on you?' I suppose I kept introducing her name into our conversation. I've read that that's a sign of being in love. Will he be jealous? I'm not a fool. I knew how he felt even before that evening he kissed me twice and then made off. It doesn't affect our friendship but I've put that sort of thing behind me. Last year for two months I was mad for Olivier in the year below, and now he's just an ordinary boy. I'm fond of Léon, but not like that. I enjoy his company, he's a good mate, one of the best . . .

He drifted into sleep. In the morning he was sure he had dreamed of Miriam, even though any dream had slipped away and was lost to him.

He left the house early and skipped school. Everything seemed strange to him, at once sharper and more distant than usual. It's another proof I'm in love, he thought. I'm seeing the world as a poet might.

He turned towards the river which, his father had often told him, had made Bordeaux what it was, not just a provincial French city, self-sufficient and self-satisfied, but one that looked out west to a wider world. 'All the same,' his father always added, ruefully, 'I have to admit that there can be few people as self-satisfied as us Bordelais, and, if there are any, I don't wish to know them.'

Now Alain walked along the quays, downstream. It was a bright cold morning with a sharp wind blowing in from the Atlantic. A German tank and two armoured cars were parked by the Monument to the Girondins. Their crews stood by the vehicles chatting and smoking. They looked to have not a care in the world. One of them laughed. It's as if they owned the place, he thought; as if they owned us; and, then, for the moment they do. But it'll change. Some day it must. We'll chase them out, back over the Rhine. Meanwhile we have to endure it, and them, filthy Boches.

He had hours to kill. It was impossible that he should present himself at the tabac before the afternoon, and then, well, we'll see, put it to the test. The words rang in his head: put it to the test. He stopped off in a little bar and called for a glass of rum. He had never drunk rum before and couldn't say why he had ordered it. But it was good, rich, mouth-filling, invigorating. He was tempted to have another, but no, self-control, that was the thing. All the same, no matter how things turned out, he knew he would always associate rum with this day, with either failure or triumph. He turned up the collar of his coat and stuck a cigarette in his mouth, examined himself in the mirror behind the bar, and thought: It's all right, I don't look bad, I look like a man of the world, not a boy, the kind of man who can order a glass of rum with assurance. He took the cigarette from his mouth, holding it between his thumb and first two fingers, and looked through the smoke at his reflection. Then, with a flick of his hand and a confident 'au 'voir' to the barman, who made no acknowledgement in return, he set off on his walk again.

He walked for hours, stopping only for a coffee and sandwich at lunchtime. Poor stuff, both of them; but it didn't matter, he was buoyed up by expectation. Then he settled himself on the terrace of a café in the Place Gambetta to wait and prepare himself. He ordered another rum and remained there till the winter light began to fade.

Miriam was behind the counter serving a squat toad-like man when Alain entered. She looked tired and unhappy, but when her customer left, without a word of thanks, and she looked up and saw Alain, she smiled and – he thought – was immediately young and beautiful again.

'There are some,' she said, 'as I'd rather not serve, and that fellow is one of them. He's pure poison. I know him well, better than I would wish, for he used to do business for my husband.'

'Who is he?'

'An advocate, name of Labiche, and a thoroughly nasty bit of work.'

'So that's who he is,' Alain said. 'I'm not surprised you don't care to serve him.'

'I shouldn't have thought he'd have come your way, and indeed I hope he hasn't.'

'I read a letter he had published in the *Sud-Ouest*. It was vile, horrible. He's a real Nazi, I think.'

'Which didn't prevent him from once . . . But never mind, it was years ago. Let's just say I've no time for him. How's your father?'

'He's gone to Vichy. I don't know why. He never talks about police business at home.'

'Go through to the back room,' she said. 'I'll be shutting in a few minutes, and there are things I want to talk to you about.'

It wasn't long before she joined him but it seemed long to him.

'I was grateful to you for speaking as you did the other day,' she said. 'I worry about Léon, he's so emotional. You're a good influence on him. He's fond of you and less bitter and angry since you met. He listens to you, I'm sure. You'll see to it he doesn't do anything stupid, won't you?'

'I'll do what I can. You can trust me. But it's only talk, I think.'

'Talk's dangerous. These days, talk's very dangerous.'

She couldn't settle. Sat down for a moment, then rose almost at once and went to make coffee. Yet, even in agitation, there was a grace to her walk. She was a big woman, but she scarcely seemed to touch the ground. It was as if she floated, and, more than ever, Alain ached to take hold of her.

'That Labiche,' she said.

'He's really disturbed you, hasn't he?'

'I'm ashamed to admit it. He's vicious and I have a dread of vice.'

'Let's forget him, put him out of our minds.'

'If only it was that easy,' she said, 'but I'm willing to try.'

Her smile came slowly at first, the blossomed with a rush, like an expression of her heart.

'I never asked you,' she said. 'Did you come for cigarettes?'

'No,' he said, then, as if to prove it, took out his packet and lit one, and found that his hands were trembling. She saw it too and stretched out to touch him.

'Give me one,' she said.

He passed over the cigarette he had already lit, and she put it between her lips, drew in smoke, expelled it, and gave the cigarette back to him. He took it as if it had been a kiss.

'I just had to see you,' he said. 'I can't stop thinking about you.'

'Oh dear,' she said, and her voice was scarcely more than a sigh.

'And when I saw you looking so unhappy . . . '

'My dear boy, I'm nearly forty. At my age . . . '

'That doesn't matter. It doesn't mean anything to me.'

She leaned forward, took the cigarette from him again, and kissed him on the lips.

'I shouldn't have done that,' she said.

'I'm not a child.'

Later, in darkness, she ran her fingers across his belly.

'You have lovely skin. And you're well-muscled.'

'That's rugby. I play rugby, you know. I'm so happy. I don't think I've ever been so happy. What about you? Are you happy?

Happy now? You looked so miserable when I came in.'

She didn't answer in words, but stroked his cheek.

'At least you shave,' she murmured. 'It was the first time for you, wasn't it?'

'Yes,' he said. Then, shyly, 'Does that mean I was no good, that you could tell?'

'You were perfect. And I've never been anyone's first before. It's rather wonderful.'

'You're crying. What's wrong?'

'Nothing's wrong. Everything's right for the moment. That's why I'm crying. And because it can't last.'

'Does that mean you won't . . . another time?'

'I didn't say that. I should but I didn't.'

'I love you. Don't you believe me?'

'Oh yes, my dear,' she said, and kissed him, softly, on the lips. 'You won't tell Léon, will you?'

'If you like,' he said, wanting to tell all the world, but knowing also that he must not indeed tell Léon. But wouldn't he guess?


## XXVI


Of course he was ashamed. He couldn't not be. He'd been bought off and it would be humiliating to have to admit this to Moncerre and young René. Moncerre, cynic as well as bull-terrier, would understand, would nevertheless surely despise him. As for René who felt a sort of hero-worship for him – something at once pleasing and embarrassing – well, he was going to be sadly disillusioned. Not in the long run such a bad thing perhaps; it would help the boy to grow up, to realize what the world was like, a place of shabby compromise with few heroes – among whom Lannes himself shouldn't be numbered. This reflection didn't make the prospect of explaining why he had consented to abandon their case any more agreeable. On the other hand, Schnyder would be happy. As indeed he was.

'Glad to see that you're finally looking reality in the face,' he said. 'There's other business, you know. A shopkeeper was bludgeoned to death in the rue Porte-Dijeaux, robbery gone wrong, it appears.

Straightforward matter, I should think. Anyway I put Moncerre on the case. It's his sort of thing, isn't it?'

Lannes nodded agreement. Truth to tell, he felt numb, unable to care. In the train on the way back from Vichy he had sat for hours, not reading as he usually liked to do on journeys, looking out of the window, seeing nothing. Edmond's promise sang in his mind: 'Sigi will furnish you with what you need to silence Labiche. You'll be able to check-mate him. That'll do, won't it? And I'll set wheels in motion to arrange your son's repatriation. That's a promise. You can trust me, superintendent.'

He couldn't have refused. To deny Marguerite Dominique's safe return – that was impossible. He couldn't have looked her in the face. Now she might even smile again. And what sort of father would he have been if he had condemned the boy to remain a prisoner of war, in order that he might satisfy his conscience by pursuing an investigation he would never be able to bring to a successful conclusion? So he had yielded, admitted defeat – and was to be rewarded. Rewarded with Labiche's head also! Well, that was a relief. He had been more worried than he had cared to admit, anxious for himself and his career, anxious, more honourably, for Miriam and the boy Léon. Moreover it would be a pleasure to pull the advocate down, even if, as Edmond had warned, the evidence with which he would be provided, would not be enough to bring him to justice. Labiche had too many friends in the administration to protect him. But at least Lannes would have the satisfaction of confronting him. He looked forward to that encounter.

Moncerre had cleared up the rue Porte-Dijeaux case without difficulty.

'Stupid bugger,' he said. 'An old customer of ours – name of Pierre Marchand – you'll remember him. Hasn't got the brains of a rabbit. Panicked and then left a trail of evidence. Routine stuff. If only everything was so easy.'

'If only . . . '

'So we're beaten on the big one then, are we?'

'Yes,' Lannes said. 'It's escaped us. We're beaten.'

'Never expected anything else, to tell the truth. What convinced you, chief?'

'Vichy,' Lannes said. 'It's a strange place. They feel so secure, planning for a new France, a new Europe, and yet it's a dream-world, utterly insubstantial. Nevertheless for the moment anyway we can't fight against it. Vichy and the Boches . . . between them we're caught in a vice.'

That was true, though far from the whole truth. He could see that Moncerre wasn't satisfied, knew there was more to it, suspected a deal had been done.

'The truth is they leaned on me, leaned very hard.'

He hesitated, then, 'Come outside,' he said, 'let's go for a walk.'

It was cold, no wind, the sky heavy with clouds the colour of German uniforms. They walked in silence, Lannes torn between the wish to unburden himself and a pride which restrained him.

Moncerre said: 'Saw that bloody Spaniard yesterday. He had the cheek to tip his hat to me. It was all I could do to stop myself from kicking him in the balls. Wish I had really.'

A week ago Lannes might have said, 'Don't worry, you'll get your chance some day.'

They came to the river and the water was grey as the sky. There was dampness in the air. Lannes leaned his elbows on the wet stone of the parapet. Gulls circled above them, shrieking.

'Storm at sea,' Moncerre said.

'There are two ways to break a man,' Lannes said. 'You bribe him or bully him, and sometimes you do both. Don't need to tell you that, old man, do I? We've both extracted confessions by these methods, haven't we?'

'Sure. Often. That what they did to you then?'

'More or less.'

'Want to talk about it?'

'No.'

'All right by me,' Moncerre said.

A tug passed below them, on its way to bring a ship up-river.

'All I can say now is that we have to hold on. I realized that I have to stay a policeman, come what may. If we allow them to get rid of men like us – and young René – what sort of bastards will take our place? At least while we remain in the Force we have the chance to do some good. Not much, but some. You agree?'

'Sure,' Moncerre said. 'Besides, if I resigned or allowed myself to be kicked out, I'd have to spend more time at home. I suppose our Alsatian's happy.'

'He's of the same mind.'

It began to rain, first single drops, then heavily. Lannes turned up the collar of his coat, and looked down at the grey water.